The Chokecherry Tree

The
Chokecherry
Tree

Frederick Manfred

Introduction by Delbert E. Wylder

A Zia Book

UNIVERSITY OF NEW MEXICO PRESS
Albuquerque

*The characters and the incidents in this book are entirely
the product of the author's imagination and have no rela-
tion to any person or event in real life.*

For Paul C. Hillestad

INTRODUCTION

This is a novel of a time and a place, and of a people who lived in that time and place. It is a novel told in a distinctive voice—the voice of one who understood the times, who felt the place, who knew the deeper instincts as well as the frustrating problems of the people. Finally, it is a novel of Elof Lofblom's successful attempt to find himself in a world of time, place, and people.

The time is the Great Depression of the 1930s, when men of all ages roamed the country looking for work. With hardship in the cities and in the countryside, there was little work to be found. Young men, looking for a place, looking for success, found no place to go, found that they were lucky just to survive. Bread was a nickel a loaf, but many a man didn't have a nickel. Studs Terkel's *Hard Times* paints a picture of the spirit of shame and defeat and hopelessness—the sense of failure—created in men by these times. Frederick Manfred's Elof Lofblom is a young man who has looked for a place in this world without finding one, and he has come back to the home place, come back not defeated but needing to lick his wounds and gain strength before returning to the struggle.

The home place he comes back to is that area where, on the map, the state lines of Iowa, South Dakota, and Minnesota divide the uninterrupted prairies, the beginnings of the American West. The prairie provides a horizon impossible to encompass. Here and there, it is spotted by the outlines of clumps of tall cottonwoods and the seemingly inconsequential chokecherries. The trees furnish windbreaks for the lonely farm buildings and, in the towns that are spread thinly throughout the region, offer shade and comfort. Sioux Falls and Sioux City are the only cities of any size in Frederick Manfred's Siouxland. The area was once the hunting grounds of the Sioux, before immigrants from northern Europe moved in. The white settlers were mostly Norsemen: Swedes, Icelanders, Norwegians, Danes. Some were German, Frisian, Dutch, or Polish. The progenitors of the characters in *The Chokecherry Tree* people the novels of Ole Rolvaag and Herbert Quick. Sinclair Lewis's Gopher Prairie is not very far north of this land, the action of *Main Street* just two decades in the past, and the people have changed little.

Chokecherry Corner is an even smaller town than Gopher Prairie. The people who live in Chokecherry Corner and the surrounding farms are simple in their wants. They are, of course, as complex as anyone else, have the same psychological drives and human needs that demand fulfillment. But they have settled on the land and are close to the land, and the land has settled in them. They have neither the craving for excitement found in the city people of a Dos Passos novel— the maniacal truck driver who brings Elof home is not from Chokecherry Corner—nor the sophistication. They find stimulation in youthful courtship, in softball games, an occasional traveling carnival, even in a game of checkers. The old-time Calvinist religion, with the ringing tones of the Bible, is still strong in the lives of the old people, though its effectiveness with the young is beginning to diminish. The land, or the farm, is the basis of the economy and fundamental to the way of life.

Frederick Manfred knew the times, the place, and the people. He was born of Frisian ancestry in the southeastern section of this Siouxland area—actually northwestern Iowa— on a farm near Doon, January 6, 1912. As the eldest son, he would, in the Netherlands, have been given the name of Feike Feikes Feikema VII. But this was America, and he was baptized Frederick Feikema. He went by the nickname of Feike Feikema and published his first seven novels under this name.

He learned to work on the farm, and still likes working out of doors. At the age of sixteen he was graduated from Western Academy in Hull, Iowa. Then he returned to the farm for two years. In 1929, his mother died; in 1930, he

entered Calvin College. He became an English major, published poetry in the school magazines and yearbook, and was
graduated in 1934. That was the year that, in Siouxland, the
drought was at its worst. There had been a drought in the
lower Mississippi Valley in 1930. Several dry years led to a
devastating drought in almost all the grain-producing states.
Manfred's novel *The Golden Bowl* records the drought with
strikingly effective realism. The recovery from drought and
depression was slow. Frederick Manfred, recent graduate of
Calvin College, hitchhiked both east and west, working at
odd jobs, seeing America and Americans in the worst of times.
He remembered much. When he first settled down in 1937,
it was as a sportswriter for the *Minneapolis Journal*. He
was active in union affairs, worked for the reelection of
Governor Elmer Benson, and started work on *The Golden
Bowl*. Overwork and chain-smoking resulted in tuberculosis,
and he entered the Glen Lake Sanatorium in Oak Terrace,
Minnesota. The battle was a long one, but the disease was
finally arrested, and he was released in March of 1942. In the
sanatorium, he had met his future wife, Maryanna Shorba,
another patient. After a short time with the scientific journal
Modern Medicine and some political work for Hubert
Humphrey, Manfred sensed that it was time to put all his
efforts into writing. The result was that *The Golden Bowl*
was published in 1944, by a St. Paul publisher. *Boy Almighty*
was published in 1945. Sinclair Lewis had heard of *The
Golden Bowl,* and he invited Manfred to Duluth for a week-
end at his home. Lewis was impressed with the manuscript of
This Is The Year, and recommended it to Doubleday, which
published it in 1947. *The Chokecherry Tree* followed in
1948; then came *The Primitive* (1949), *The Brother* (1950),
and *The Giant* (1951). McGraw-Hill published the first of
his Buckskin Man tales, *Lord Grizzly,* in 1954; this was also
the first book published under the name Frederick Manfred.
Lord Grizzly is generally recognized as one of the best of the
mountain man novels, *Riders of Judgment* (1957) as one of
the finest cow-country novels, and *Conquering Horse* (1959)
as one of the most sensitive Indian novels. Manfred's percep-

tive handling of the mythical implications of the American West brought him an honorary life membership in the Western Literature Association, and scholarly attention to the Buckskin Man novels and later works has stimulated an interest in the earlier novels published under the name of Feike Feikema. In the Boise State University Western Writers Series study of Manfred, Joseph M. Flora gives almost equal time to the early farmland novels. And this brings us to *The Chokecherry Tree,* one of the early novels of Frederick Manfred.

When Manfred moved to Blue Mound, just north of Luverne, Minnesota, he could sit at the top of an outcrop of rocks in front of his home and look out over the prairie into three states. That is almost exactly the perspective of one of the narrative voices of *The Chokecherry Tree,* the voice that broods over Elof, talking to itself, to Elof, and to the reader. It is an educated, cultured voice, hinting of an omniscience that comes from distance and the long view. The rhythms flow as smoothly as time. The second narrative voice, that of the narrator of the story of Elof Lofblom, is so close to Elof's mind and expression that we frequently find a merging of Elof and the narrator. It is the voice of the people of this area, and the rhythms are generally rough, masculine, hinting of old-country influences, but with as much flexibility as old Pa Hansen, who can improvise a prayer in the language of the King James Bible. It is a narrative voice in harmony with the minds and hearts of the characters in the novel.

The story itself is of the return of Elof Lofblom. He comes home, looking forward to seeing his mother again, equipped with a pair of worn shoes, a copy of *Peregrine Pickle,* and a plan for using his time at home for self-improvement. His shoes are ruined when he jumps from the truck, his mother is dead, and his tyrannical father is going to see to it that he keeps busy. Elof is small. He has small feet. Even worse, his second toe is longer than his big toe and, according to the folklore of the place, this means that his woman will dominate him. He is also sensitive about his undersize genitals.

Elof's mother had had faith that Elof would be a hero, and

an almost miraculous escape from death as a child has convinced him, too, that that will be his role. And, after all, this is America, where any boy can grow up to be president. Armed with his copy of *Peregrine Pickle* and the first few free lessons of a correspondence course in accounting, and even despite the fact that he must wear the used size 14 bluchers his father has grudgingly given him, our hero starts out to conquer women and the world. The trouble and the fun begin on Elof's heroic quest.

Elof, unlike Peregrine Pickle, is not destined for the life of a picaro. His feelings of inferiority and his moral background leave him helpless with women. His romantic escapades are failures. Nor will Elof ever become the American business hero, in the tradition of Horatio Alger. Opportunistically, he leaves for Sioux Falls to become a traveling salesman. Again it is his sensitivity and his moral background that keep him from success. He finds himself incapable of selling people things they neither need nor want. He returns home without illusions.

It isn't that Elof totally lacks heroic qualities. He is honest, and his battle with blood poisoning shows both endurance and determination. Elof is just not presidential timber. He finds this out for himself. In finding himself in his own time, and in his own place, he learns a great deal, even without finishing his accounting course or *Peregrine Pickle*. He may have limitations that keep him from becoming a Casanova or a Carnegie, or even a Coolidge, but he finds that he can survive, he can love, he can be himself, and, at home with himself, he can assert himself. He even discovers that his father, despite the gruff exterior, loves him. The discovery is expressed in an image typical of the novel, the unsentimental image of a pear-shaped tear suspended momentarily on Pa's nose, directly above a "pock-sized blackhead."

I think that William Dean Howells would have liked this book for many things. It would have proved his theory that the common man could be the subject for good literature. Mark Twain would have liked the humor in the way that Elof Lofblom, little man that he is, comes to terms with his conscience, recognizes his own limitations, and then learns to assert himself in his own way. In *Studies in Classic American Literature,* that marvelously wild assessment of America, Americans, and their literature, D. H. Lawrence screams that America is not a blood-home-land. But Elof and the narrators are sensitive to the past, to the gravestones that represent the lives that have gone back into the land. Manfred makes this part of America a blood-home-land. Lawrence, I think, also would have liked this novel. I think you will too.

Delbert E. Wylder
Southwest Minnesota State College
Marshall, Minnesota

CONTENTS

The Chokecherry Tree

But first I pray yow, of your curteisye,
That ye n'arette it nat my vileinye,
Thogh that I pleynly speke in this matere,
To tell yow hir wordes and hir chere;
Ne thogh I speke hir wordes properly.
For this ye knowen al-so wel as I,
Who-so shal telle a tale after a man,
He moot reherce, as ny as ever he can,
Everich a word, if it be in his charge,
Al speke he never so rudeliche and large;
Or elles he moot telle his tale untrewe,
Or feyne thing, or finde wordes newe.
He may nat spare, al-thogh he were his brother;
He moot as wel seye o word as another.
Crist spak him-self ful brode in holy writ,
And wel ye woot, no vileinye is it.
Eek Plato seith, who-so that can him rede,
The wordes mote be cosin to the dede.
Also I prey yow to foryeve it me,
Al have I nat set folk in hir degree
Here in this tale, as that they sholde stonde;
My wit is short, ye may well understonde.

—Chaucer

THE CANTERBURY TALES

*Embracing Gorky, Tolstoy said, "You are a real muzhik! You will
have a hard time among the writers, but fear nothing, and speak
always as you feel no matter if it comes out coarsely. Wise people
will understand."*

—E. J. Simmons

LEO TOLSTOY: The Later Years

CHAPTER I: Elof Comes Home

> . . . *Here from the brow of this Siouxland bluff,*
> *a stone my seat, I watch your troubled swervelings*
> *to and fro. The valley you live in is green and it is*
> *moving—its cells are proliferating and its people*
> *are working. I watch all this, and watch you, and*
> *this is what my laboring fingers write on the*
> *page . . .*

Stubby red-faced Elof Lofblom stood thumbing a ride on an Iowa highway corner.

Elof hadn't had any luck for an hour. Only two cars had gone by in all that time: one, a sleek sedan; the other, an old truck weighted down with junk. The first car whipped by before he could get his thumb raised; the second was obviously going only a short distance.

Then a big blue-gray truck came up and stopped. The driver got out and walked around the machine, looking for flats, and sniffed at the sweet morning air of early June, and got in, and began goosing the motor to start off again.

"Hey!" Elof shouted. "Hey, how about a ride?"

The driver gave him a derailed look. The driver's black greasy cap, pulled down too far on one side, hid an ear and an eye and gave the free eye the sinister hooded look of a mad dog. And the man's hands, fastened onto the steering wheel with a maniac's fierceness, were white over the grimy knuckles.

"Hey!" Elof shouted again. He wasn't used to this, pushing himself forward, but he had a desperate case. It was either yell or starve. "Hey, ain't you got a ride for me?"

"Get in," the driver grunted finally, roaring up the motor with a nervous toe on the foot-feed.

Elof clambered in. He threw his black imitation-leather suitcase up on the shelf behind the seat. He closed the door.

The gears ground. The motor snapped. Again the gears ground. Again. And then the truck was rolling.

The big cross-country truck sped down the Atlantic-Yellowstone-Pacific Highway, swerving, blatting, heading hard into the west. On jug-handle corners it teetered on two wheels; slowly righted itself.

Elof sat pinching his knees together. Every second Elof expected to see the snub-nosed truck roll into the ditch. The paved highway rushed toward them like a gray river raging.

"What's the all-fired hurry?" Elof asked at last, forcing a little spirit into his innocent blue eyes.

The driver said nothing.

Elof worried. He ran his freckled hand over his gray trousers. He buttoned up his suit jacket. He combed his gold hair with stubby fingers. "I'm going as far as Chokecherry Corner. To Siouxland," he said. He hoped the other would give him a hint on how far he was going. "It's about fifty-five miles west of here. Straight west as the crow flies."

The driver flicked his crazed eyes.

"Just how far you going?" Elof asked again, forcing himself to talk firmly, and loudly enough to be heard over the pounding motor.

Still no answer.

Elof sat straighter. He had the feeling something disastrous, even spectacular, was about to happen. Little sparkles of light exploded in his head. His fingers felt suddenly thick. A gut-ache turned in his belly.

He glanced at the speedometer. Sixty-five. A loaded twenty-ton truck roaring sixty-five miles an hour down the highway. Anything they would hit would fly a mile into the sky.

Elof's mind lashed around. No use to show fear, he counseled himself. If the man intended to kill both of them there wasn't much he could do about it. In that case they were just dead ducks. Best thing to do was to accept the worst and start from there.

Cautiously Elof said, "I'll let you know at Hello when we're close to Chokecherry Corner. That's two miles this side of it."

No answer.

Elof watched the telephone poles fly past. The country was table-flat and rushed past underneath them like canvas on a bindering platform. Every mile a farmyard surrounded by a wind-break of green maples or yellow ash flashed past like a hastily glanced-at picture.

So this was going home. Going home.

Six years before, Elof had left home to go to the Saint Comus Theological Seminary to study for the ministry. He had gone on the insistence of the local Hello preacher, Old Domeny Hillich. Elof, the Lofblom boy, and Bud, his own son, were chosen ones, the old preacher had said. The Lord had given the boys a special sign, a sign proclaiming them as destined for domenydom. The old preacher knew. He, too, had once heard the call to work in the Lord's vineyard. The Lord had a certain way of showing his intention, and once you heard it, or saw it, you never forgot it.

Of course rud-faced Ma Lofblom, enraptured that issue from her womb should become exalted, fervently assented. But Pa Lofblom glowered, and hemmed and hawed, and pinched his pennies, and made dire predictions.

From the first Elof hadn't liked the seminary. Its atmosphere was inhuman, almost false, he thought. And it didn't surprise him too much to find that its name, Saint Comus, didn't fit. In pioneer times, an emigrant domeny had tried to show off his knowledge of "good" literature. The domeny knew that Milton was a good Protestant and that a Comus had been celebrated by him in one of his poems. By the time it was discovered what Milton really meant by Comus, a god of festive joy and mirth become sorcerer and son of Circe and Bacchus, it was too late. The sainting and the naming had been written into the laws of the land and into the souls of the sect. Later, some of the sect's academes and exegetes had tried to rig up a religious antecedent. But though they didn't altogether convince themselves they at least

blurred enough of its pagan origin to quiet the misgivings of the
board of trustees.

Halfway through the seminary it became apparent that Elof
had waded in over his depth. He was flunking more than half
his classes. At about the same time, a distaste for the text-quoting
heroes-in-the-Lord yeasted up within him. And so, after many a
sleepless night and halfhearted prayers to His Maker, he abruptly
left the seminary.

Having half a notion that he might make a go of it in the
worldly atmosphere of State University, he tried that. He was
too proud to go home and admit defeat. He had a liking for ad-
venture, so majored in history, and had been exposed to lofty
ministerial phrasing, so minored in literature. And it wasn't until
he had enrolled in his classes and had spent Pa's money that he
wrote to tell his folks about the change. But before long, about
two years, it became evident that he had once more tried to pull
a stallion's load with a billy goat's back. So he left State.

Still reluctant to go home and admit failure, he roamed the
country looking for work, any kind of work. There was a depression on, but to Elof it wasn't so much the fault of society that he
couldn't find work as it was his own shortcomings. He just didn't
have it. The ant-swift disciples of business who stood ahead of
him a hundred deep in the unemployment lines all had a trade,
a specific training, a definite commodity to sell on the labor
market, while he had none. A few of them were even clever at
scheming, and that was something Elof had no notion of at all.

For two years he tried to break in somewhere. He took little
odd jobs. He bummed. He rode the rods. He tried to keep his
soul in tune by reading *Peregrine Pickle,* a book he somehow just
couldn't find time to finish. At last, hungry, a little stunned by it
all, he made up his mind there was only one thing left to do. Go
home. Make up his mind to face the silent jeering of the villagers.

Ma's condition had helped him decide. Pa had flatly written in
his last letter that Ma was failing, "she's been off her feed for a
month," and that if Elof knew what was good for him he would
get the hell home or he wouldn't see his ma alive no more in this
old hell-hole world. Pa hinted, too, that it was about time Elof
came to his senses and took the job the good Lord had intended

him for, hard work by the sweat of his brow. Though of course if he still wanted to try for the ministry again, they would think it over, specially since it might give Ma courage to go on living in this den of Beelzebub. Not that Pa ever thought much of the high monkey-monk idea, but it might make a good housewife and cook out of Ma again.

Elof snickered. Had Pa let up on the tyranny once in a while, Ma wouldn't've got run down in the first place.

Elof stirred on the hard leather seat of the racing truck. The smell of oil from the burning engine stung his nose. His bowels pinched with pain. He held himself tightly.

The madly careening truck roared through Hartley, through Passage, swerved and swung down the Atlantic-Yellowstone-Pacific Highway west, the AYP, on toward Siouxland. Already Elof began to recognize certain landmarks, certain farms where he had worked during summer vacations before going off to college.

He glanced at the speedometer again. The maniac had increased the speed to seventy miles an hour.

Elof had the feeling that his going home was more a hurried departure than a happy arrival. It was almost as if society, culture, civilization, was showing him the door, kicking him back into the sticks, telling him that there was where he should have stayed in the first place. It was as if Ma's dream of his becoming a hero someday was repugnant to society, that this was its way of showing its derision. Rushing him away. Spewing him from its presence.

Elof laughed nervously. It was probably true that he wasn't an especial favorite of the Lord's just now, but there was still a chance that the Lord might change His mind. And when the good Lord did, he, Elof Lofblom, would be back someday to show society, prove that it had made a mistake. He would do it —if only for Ma's sake. For her he just had to become a hero.

Just what kind of someday hero Elof couldn't say. But he would become one. It might not be in the ministry, but it would be somewhere. Some morning he would awake and there the big surprise would be.

First, though, there were some things to be done. He had to go home and get himself straightened out. He had to calm Ma. Talk sense to Pa. Then rest awhile from his travels. Take it easy. Maybe push ahead a little in *Peregrine Pickle*. Maybe reread some of the chapters describing Perry's madcap adventures. Especially the one in which Perry had humiliated his professor in school. Or the one in which Perry had pulled a wild prank on his foster father, Commodore Hawser Trunnion, in the garrison.

Yes, Elof thought, yes, that would make a fine program. Then, with Ma feeding him and Pa putting clothes on his back, he would maybe take an accounting course from the American School of Correspondence. Correspondence courses were bound to be less exacting than straight college courses. Maybe. Give himself a trade, a tool, and then tackle society again. Maybe accounting could give him the start he needed in a world controlled by financiers.

Yes. That was it. And once he got a job, a real job, he could pile up a big reserve and then look around and see what he really wanted from life. Yep.

But first, home.

Elof cringed when he looked at the clothes he was wearing. Pa would be sure to make some wisecrack about them. The soles of his shoes were so badly worn he couldn't walk on anything except fresh green grass. He didn't dare take a quick step, or make a sudden stop, for fear his foot would pop through the end. And he was down to two pair of socks, two pair of shorts, one badly worn shirt, a couple of ties, and a gray suit with a belt in back. And an overall, a work shirt, a sloppy straw hat. And two cents. He didn't even have a dress hat—thank God, he at least had a little gold hair growing out of his scalp.

Elof watched the green land flood by, looked uneasily at the flickering seventy-two on the speedometer, held himself for a curve in the highway, let go again when they were around it, began to count the miles to Chokecherry Corner.

The name Chokecherry Corner always gave him a chuckle. It was a place where a tiny, crooked chokecherry tree cowered beneath thirteen massive cottonwoods. The chokecherry hardly thrived, but the cottonwoods were tremendous creatures, with immane, corrugated, five-foot trunks holding up umbrellas of green glinting leaves more than a hundred feet high in the air. Naming the corner after the chokecherry tree instead of the cottonwoods was evidence of at least a little humor among the Siouxland folk.

It was also the corner where the north-south King's Trail Highway crossed the east-west AYP. There were three filling stations on it, one to a corner, and a bog, and, a little ways to the west, a depot and an elevator beside the Cannonball railroad. Since Hello, two miles east, siphoned off most of the trade in the area, only one general store flanked the tracks and the highway. That store was Pa's: Lofblom's Grocery.

The building of the Cannonball railway three miles west of Hello also reflected a human touch. The city fathers, in trying to plot the metropolis of Hello, had planned that both the Cannonball, which came down from Sioux Falls in the northwest, and the Thunderbolt, which paralleled the AYP, should cross at the edge of town—thereby insuring a mighty boom. But they had reckoned without the powers that be. The Thunderbolt people absolutely refused to let the Cannonball through Hello. And so the Cannonball grade, already headed toward Hello, had to double back west again to stay outside the law-stipulated three miles. The refusal crippled Hello's future and made a lonely hamlet out of Chokecherry Corner.

Elof wondered what the coming home would be like. If Ma was well she would right away get busy on the stove and feed him lemon pie with yellow shine and egg fluff. And Pa would growl and give him a pair of shoes. And then after a couple of days one or the other would smile and life would begin again, and all be happiness.

Oh, just so Ma was well, at least up and going, then all would still be right. Oh, just so Ma was well. Was well.

The truck zoomed up a little rise, held steady on the prairie land.

Five miles west, on the horizon, the trees of Hello hove up to view. The truck thundered on, hopping on three, on two, on three, sometimes on four wheels, toward it.

"My God, do you have to go so fast?" Elof demanded.

The truck roared louder.

Hello rushed up. In a moment the wooden water tower, the four steepling churches, the red brick building where he had gone to high school, the outlying dairy farms flashed by like panoramic shots in a whirling camera's eye.

"Say, better slow up," Elof stuttered. "It's only three miles to where I get off now."

Rooom-bah-rooom-bah-roarrr.

"You can see it there. The cottonwoods. And the three filling stations. And the store. Lofblom's Grocery."

Rooom-bah-rooom-bah-roarrr.

Elof grabbed the driver's arm. "Say, you crazy nut, goddammit, I want to get off here. Stop now!"

The trucker slapped Elof's hand away.

Desperate, his eyes tight, Elof daringly snapped off the ignition. There was a coughing from the motor, a silence, and the wind from the coasting speed sang and howled in the cab.

The trucker turned on Elof fiercely. "Keep them mitts off a my truck, see, or there'll be hell to pay, see."

"But I want to get off here."

"Oh, you want to get off here, huh."

"Yes. I live here. Please."

"Go t'hell!" the driver grated. "You kin get off at the next stop. I ain't got the time to stop for every little pile of horse biscuits we run into."

Again Elof reached down, snapped it off.

The driver lifted his arm, tried to ram his elbow deep into Elof's side. They fought for the keys.

The driver let go of the steering wheel, lifted his arm for another punch.

Elof held the arm, held the steering wheel. The truck lurched back and forth and weaved across the road.

The junction stop, the filling stations on the corner, the crooked chokecherry tree, the mighty cottonwoods, Pa's two-story grocery came up.

Elof pushed against the trucker and freed one arm and pulled back the hand brake. He and the driver wrestled.

Elof glanced at the speedometer. The truck had slowed to twenty-five. He could chance it now.

Suddenly he jerked himself free of the man and, grabbing his scabby suitcase in one hand and opening the door with the other, heaved himself out from the truck. He sailed through the air. He let go of the suitcase and held himself tightly for the fall. He hit, feet first in the grass, and rolled. When he stopped rolling he sat up.

The truck wavered; straightened; roared; then rolled on.

Elof glanced around for his suitcase, saw it spilled open beneath the fence.

He glanced at himself. He was surprised to find himself unhurt.

When he got to his feet he found his shoes shot to hell. The force of his body hitting the ground had popped the seams apart. The leather soles had been torn from the uppers.

He stepped around. The soles flapped in the grass.

He sat down and unlaced the shoes and tossed them into the weeds.

. . . Elof, were it not for these scratches which limn your passage here, forgot you should be by all, by none. Never a god to give your land a name, yet of enough mite consequence to be given a grave by it, solitary yet many, you bungle forth from the bloody womb, you stumble through a life, blinking, lifting an occasional short arm to the sky, and utterly pass away forever. Cells dead, bones moldered, dust speckles drifting north when South opens its hollow halls of wind, hoar flakes drifting south when North mounts its massive polar colds . . .

When Elof looked up, he saw Pa standing in the doorway of the two-story grocery. The white-frame, green-trimmed building loomed high over Elof. Pa was wearing a white shirt and a pair of black trousers and he was staring at him. Pa looked like an angered bullheaded duke—all horns and shoulders.

"Hi," Elof greeted cautiously.

"Unhh," Pa grunted, brushing his hand over his ruddy bald head. Like Elof's own, Pa's hands were blotched with freckles as big as pale brown pennies. The hands were the only place where the sun had fried the Lofblom pigment.

"I guess I had a little accident," Elof said.

"Unhh." Pa drew a pipe from his pants pocket, lighted it. It was a heavy black underslung stoker, and, seeing it, Elof suddenly remembered all his boy days before Pa turned mean.

Elof got up out of the ditch and went over to the fence and

collected his spilled effects and piled them into his suitcase and then walked slowly across toward Pa. The graveled drive-in cut his feet. His left second toe protruded from a hole in his sock. He walked past Pa's old pickup truck parked off to one side. He climbed the steps onto the cement front before the door.

Pa looked at Elof's feet.

Elof put out a hand. "Hello," he said again.

Pa ignored the proffer. Slowly Pa's eyes took in Elof's clothing.

"Yes," Elof said, dropping his hand, aware that his manner was hang-dog and his air apologetic, "yeh, that son of a gun. He didn't want to stop. So I had to jump."

"I see."

"Almost broke my neck."

"Maybe it's too bad you didn't."

"What?"

Pa puffed slowly, smoke almost hiding his eyes. A mean smile twisted Pa's lips.

It hurt Elof to see the old kindly pipe hanging from the bitter lips, and he looked off to one side. And for the first time noticed that something was wrong. He wicked his eyes and looked carefully. Yes. The drive-in. It wasn't the same. The stones hadn't been painted freshly white this spring; the bordering flower bed hadn't been seeded. It had always been a joy to him to come up the circling drive-in, low clouds of petal red and yellow, petunia and zinnia and poppy, gaily hailing him home.

"There ain't anything wrong, is there?" Elof asked. "Where's Ma?"

"Dead."

"Dead?"

"Yep. Dead. You finally got your way. Killed her off."

Elof leaned against the doorpost. He dropped the suitcase. "Oh," he soughed, "oh. So that's why the flowers ain't there."

"Yeh."

Elof closed his eyes. So Ma was gone. "When?" he asked.

"Last month. The first a May."

"Oh."

"Yeh."

"What'd she die of?"

"I told you. You killed her."

Elof ignored the damnation. "I wished I'd a known," he murmured.

Pa flared. He put his pipe away. "I warned you in the last letter. So don't give me that John-the-Baptist look."

"I know."

Pa noisily scratched his blond whiskers, abruptly said, "Well, get inside. No use givin' the neighbors an extry eyeful."

Elof said nothing. For the first time he became aware that a hundred yards east out of each filling station and its after-shanty people were staring, the Hinkes, the Coopers, the Solens. He picked up his suitcase and followed his broad-hipped father inside.

Elof smelled it the moment he came in. The family. Its foods, its rituals, its terrors and joys. Its intimacy: closet odors, sweat in clothes, ironed shirts, baking, Pa's secretive gases, and—no, the eau de cologne smell was gone. Gone.

The place reminded him of the other, too, especially the shadowy corners—that one horror time when Pa had got mad, when he had beat Ma.

Elof could see the beating: the slow build-up, the almost imperceptible changing from the jovial wide-grinned comrade to the narrow-eyed tyrant, then sudden snapping of something in Pa, his going crazy, his grabbing Ma by the neck and trying to choke her, his throttling her until she turned black in the face, his shaking her until her blond legs and arms and her ginghamed body shook like sacks of broken slats.

Elof righted himself. He looked quickly at Pa and asked, "You sure you didn't kill her?"

"What?"

"You didn't beat her again?"

Pa seemed to swell, to rise to his toes. With a terrible effort, with a roll of wild eyes, Pa controlled himself.

After a moment, shrinking to normal size again, Pa asked harshly, "How long you gonna stay?"

"I don't know. A couple of days or so."

"Uh-huh."

"I'd like to visit around a little. An' visit Ma's grave."

Pa said, shaking a fat stubby finger at him, "One thing I

wantcha to get through your woodhead, then. If you're gonna stay, you're gonna work for your keep. You ain't gonna loaf around here like yuh been a-doin' on the road. Trampin'. Bummin'. Hear me?"

Elof stiffened a little. "What do you think I am, a bloodsucker?"

"Unhh. Just so you understand." Pa's hard gray eyes bored into him. "You kin bunk up in the back room there. There's a single bed in the attic we kin bring down. Yer old bed. An' there's sheets an' quilts in the trunk in my bedroom. Behind the commode there."

"What's wrong with my old room upstairs?"

"Usin' it fer storage. It's plumb full a sacks a sugar."

"Oh."

"Remember. You're workin' for your board an' room. An' only your board an' room. This store earns just enough money to keep one man goin'. That one man is me. So there ain't any extra money around for wages."

Elof went to the back room. Egg crates were stacked neatly along one wall near the testing machine, reserve dry goods along another wall, white dusty sacks of flour along the third. The fourth, the north, was free. It was to be his.

Elof went to the window and looked out. Northward spread an immaculate cultivated prairie. It was flat and lush with corn and waving grain. It was speckled with clusters of farm buildings: red barns and white houses and green windbreaks. It spread till where green fields blurred off into a blue horizon.

Elof brought the bed down and set it up. He got the sheets and quilts.

He opened the suitcase. He laid out his overall and work shirt on the bed. He unpacked his extra socks and dress shirt and put them neatly on a shelf. He hid *Peregrine Pickle* beneath the pillow. He put out a supply of writing paper and filled his pen with ink. He took off his gray suit with the belt in back.

In his undershirt and patched shorts, he sat down on the edge of the bed and wriggled his toes. He noted the hole in his sock.

He pulled a sour face, looking at the pink toe peering out. Most men, when they wore out their socks, wore them out over the big toe. But not he. No. He had been blessed with a stubby big toe, almost a half inch shorter than the little piggie next to it. Which accounted for the odd place his socks always wore out. People said if your big toe was shorter than the second one you would never be boss in your family. But if it was longer, you would. Like Pa.

Huh, better get a wife first.

And get some shoes to cover up the toes. No use advertising a shortcoming. None of nobody's business. A pair of pointed oxfords would do the trick.

He put on the overall and shirt, rolling back the pant legs and shirt sleeves an extra roll to give his short limbs freedom.

He went out front. There were no customers in the store.

With a little show of courage he took a couple of steps toward Pa and said, "Pa, I might as well tell you right out." Elof looked down at his shoeless feet. "I tell you, Pa, if you don't mind, I'd like to stay awhile. Two months or so. I'm kind've mixed up and I'd like to—well, I ought to do some studying. Train my mind. And as soon as I'm done I'll high-tail it out of here and bother you none no more."

"More studyin'?"

"Yes."

"Godalmighty. Ain't it been beat in yer head yet that probably you ain't meant for that?"

"I guess not."

"Godalmighty. T'ud been better if you'd a gone off to a barber's school 'steada that Comus Seminary. Or that goddamn university school."

"Well, I guess it would've at that."

"Damn right it would a."

"That's why I'm thinking of taking something practical for once. Accounting. I can get me a month's trial course for free."

Pa swore. "An' I suppose you think you're gonna take up with the girlin' where you left off?"

"Might. Never can tell."

Pa swore once more.

"Besides, Pa, what's it to you? You were young yourself once."

"Yeh, but I never give no woman no false hopes. Never led her on an' then run out on her."

"You mean Gert?"

"Yeh. I mean Gert."

"Look, Pa." Elof almost snickered. "You don't know me at all when you think I'm a whiz around the women. I'm so damned scared of 'em I almost wet my pants every time I look at them. And as for Gert, why, I only had one date with her. A Sunday-night supper date. You can't even call that puppy love. Nope, in Gert I ain't the least bit int'rested."

"You sure about that?"

"Yes."

"She still ain't married, you know."

"I can't help that." Elof almost snickered again. "That's the way it goes in these damn little hick towns. Take out a girl once and you're practically married to her. Cripes."

"Huh."

"What makes you so all-fired int'rested in Gert?"

Pa ignored the question; instead went back to his best punch. "Goddammit, why couldn't y'u ha' made it at the seminary? An' ha' become a domeny like young Bud Hillich?"

Elof retreated a step. "Bud a minister now?" Elof's mind spun a picture cylinder. Of course. Three years in pre-seminary. Three in seminary. "But he must've just graduated."

"Sure. An' got himself a call."

"Where?"

"Right here. T'Hello."

"Here? My God in heaven." Elof backed another step. "What's happened to Old Domeny Hillich then?"

"He died too."

Elof swallowed. In six years . . . Yes, life went on, people birthing and dying. Both Ma Lofblom and Old Domeny Hillich. The two who had named him a chosen one. Meant for the ministry.

And Bud the Young Domeny Hillich. Elof could see him. Dressed in black, of moderate height, rosy-eared, hearty, social, his blue eyes cocksure, his blond-fuzz body strong and plump, his faith a rock of ages. The shepherd of a flock. A village druid.

"Yeh," Pa broke in. "Yeh, an' he's got himself a fambly too. A wife an' boy."

"Fer godsakes. I suppose he got them along with his diploma."

"Naw, naw. He got married his second year in the seminary. Our church t'Hello made a special 'sessment for him. Got a nice wife too. A first-class frau."

"Good for him."

They stood facing each other for a moment, silent, taut.

Elof said, "Well, I'm glad you told me all this. Remind me to keep out of Bud's way."

"Young Domeny Hillich, you mean."

Elof cleared his throat. It was time to get switched back to his own life. "By the way, you ain't got an old pack a cigarettes laying around somewhere, have you?"

Reluctantly Pa reached into the tobacco counter and tossed him a package of Bull Durham and a packet of rolling papers.

"And how about an old pair of shoes? I'll pay you when I get the money together."

Pa stared at Elof's feet again. After a moment Pa smiled to himself and went in back. He came out carrying a pair of huge bluchers.

Elof gawked at them.

"Here," Pa said, throwing the footwear at him.

"These?"

"Yeh."

Elof picked up one of the monsters. They were well scuffed. Their soles were shiny with wear. He glanced inside, read: *Men's 14.* "I can't wear these."

"Why not? That's all ye're gettin'. Think I kin afford to give you a week's profit for nothin'?"

"But I said I'd pay for new shoes."

"Huh. I know how you pay for things."

Elof dropped the bluchers to the floor.

"I'm tellin' yuh. That's all you get. I got 'em for nothin' an' you kin have 'em for nothin'."

"Where'd you get 'em?"

"A giant bum stayed here one night. When I went to wake him in the mornin' he was dead. The coroner give me his clothes."

Slowly Elof picked up the clodhoppers and went in back.

He rolled himself a cigarette. He smoked it. He put it out carefully.

After a while he went outdoors barefooted.

He walked out under the cottonwoods. The misshapen chokecherry tree, its white flowers hanging in racemes and its seedlings budding below, was still struggling for growth beneath them.

He glanced up at the soaring cottonwoods, up to where the green leaves chittered happily. He heard the high winds of the sky stirring in them and he remembered the old days of boyhood glory: nest hunting, soaring swings, picnics.

It was cool in the shadows. The grass tickled his feet.

CHAPTER III: Settling Down

> *. . . Elof boy, most times your kind never gets a glimpse of the hero's glory land, though ever among you it is whispered of and vaguely hoped for. Most times your kind never learns to know what it means to become a single individual, to be a soul apart with a separate pride . . .*

Breakfast. It was the only meal the storekeeping Lofbloms made a ritual of. The rest of the day the family was too broken up.

The first thing Elof noticed about the ritual was that he had almost forgotten how it went. It was only vaguely familiar to him any more.

Elof and Pa were in the neat-white kitchen on the second floor. Steam rose from cooked oatmeal and freshly made coffee.

Pa bowed his head and mumblingly asked a blessing:

"God Our Father in heaven. Come to Thee in this morning hour, refreshed by the night's long sleep, full of thanks that Thou has kept us through the dark hours, that Thou hast given us life and breath. Wilt Thou bless this food that we have harvested from Thy fields. Bless it unto our bodies. Give us strength thereby so that we may continue to labor fruitfully in Thy vineyards. O God . . ."

Elof followed the words along. It came to him for the first time that the prayer had been handed down to Pa from Grampa, and to Grampa from the family ancients, that the eloquence of the phrases were the result of centuries of polishing by the Lofblom ancestors, some of whom no doubt had been poets. No wonder praying meant so much to the old man. It tied him to eternity. To God. It gave his life a meaning, a meaning such as lovers of literature experienced. At least the Bible gave that much to grubbers—lyrics to offset manure piles.

Pa prayed on:

"We are prone to sin. We are all fallible. We are as dust in Thy eyes. We stumble toward the light, and it is only by Thy grace that we see it and live at all. O Lord, forgive us all our sins. We ask it in Thy name. Amen."

There was a moment of silence. The old brown pendulum clock of the Lofblom family kenick-tocked, kenick-tocked.

Elof sat with his eyes closed, still in the grip of the thought that he had just heard his eldfathers, all the way back to Adam, chanting at the table.

There was a clink of spoon on dish. "Will you pass the sugar?" Pa asked gruffly. "An' help yourself."

Elof opened his eyes. "Oh." He reached out a glass bowl of white grains. "Sure. Here."

"Thanks." Pa scattered two spoons of sugar over the warm oatmeal with a tapping forefinger, then poured on a splash of milk. The old man passed the sugar back to Elof and began eating.

Elof had his own way of preparing the oatmeal. He poured milk over it first, then sugared it. That way the sugar didn't wash to the bottom of the dish.

It was a shock to do the old things at the table; play-acting. It was as if a show had been rehearsed; then canceled for six years; then suddenly put on the boards again.

He felt his way along, knowing the ritual and not knowing it. He ate slowly, savoring the meal and the past.

Once there had been a time when the household habits had so possessed him that he was not aware of them. They were, and he was of them, a non-reflective participant.

But today he was a spectator, and they did not own him, and he was watching Pa hurry through the meal, and he was passing Pa the fried eggs, and eating an egg himself, and sipping his sweet creamed coffee, and watching how he himself must have done things before he had left home.

He noted the blue china on the wall shelf. He saw again the

green tablecloth beneath his plate, the dark mysterious corners in the cupboard, the improvised tools and dust rags and dishcloths stacked neatly away in the upper part of the nickel-shining range. Even the cistern pump dripped water into the white sink as of old. And all the while the old brown pendulum clock clicked on: *kenick-tock, kenick-tock.*

When Pa finished eating he reached under the table and handed Elof the old family Holy Bible.

Elof nodded. That too. Ah yes. Decent people couldn't eat a meal without hearing a verse or two from the Word of God. The Holy Bible was always read at the table. Elof remembered that when he was a little fellow and had become old enough to read Ma had given him the chore.

Elof paged through the old tome. He glanced at the *Family Register* pages where Ma had traced out the family tree. He noted the oily fingerprints along the edges.

It was six years ago when he had last read from the Good Book. It was his last day home and Ma had asked him to turn to Job 18: 10–21. The passage was to have some special message for him as he went out into the world, to college. He turned to it now and read aloud:

"The snare is laid for him in the ground, and a trap for him in the way.

"Terrors shall make him afraid on every side, and shall drive him to his feet.

"His strength shall be hungerbitten, and destruction shall be ready at his side.

"It shall devour the strength of his skin: even the firstborn of death shall devour his strength.

"His confidence shall be rooted out of his tabernacle; and it shall bring him to the king of terrors.

"It shall dwell in his tabernacle, because it is none of his: brimstone shall be scattered upon his habitation.

"His roots shall be dried up beneath, and above shall his branch be cut off.

"His remembrance shall perish from the earth, and he shall have no name in the street.

"He shall be driven from light into darkness, and chased out of the world.

"He shall neither have son nor nephew among his people, nor any remaining in his dwellings.

"They that come after him shall be astonied at his day, as they that went before were affrighted.

"Surely such are the dwellings of the wicked, and this is the place of him that knoweth not God."

When Elof finished, Pa grunted.

Then Pa folded his hands up to his red face, and closed his eyes submissively, and bowed his head a little, and offered a thanksgiving:

"God Our Father in heaven. Come to Thee again this morning hour to thank Thee for all Thy bountiful gifts. O God, give us this day strength to do our work. Give us courage to resist all temptation. Give us power to fight Satan and all his works, so that it may all redown to Thy honor and Thy glory. Bring light to the heathen who knows no better. Punish them that harden their hearts against Thee. Be with the chosen ones everywhere. Forgive us all our sins. In Jesus name we ask it. Amen."

Elof heard only the first words of the old chant; the rest came to him as a lullaby. His mind drifted off.

The day had begun.

Pa continued to be gruff, even brutal. And for a week Elof didn't know whether to stay or leave.

Then the first of the accounting lessons came in the mail and Elof vowed to overlook the old man's attitude. Hate with room and board was better than hate with no board and room at all.

Pa had put Elof on the late afternoon shift, from three to eleven. For the first time in a long while Elof found himself very tired and hungry after a day's work. He slept fourteen hours. It took him two weeks to get caught up, to get to where he could put in four hours a day on his lessons and in between times read a little in *Peregrine Pickle*.

The shoes, four sizes too large, were the worst. Elof felt depraved when he wore them, especially during working hours. Memorizing prices wasn't half as bad as keeping his big shoes hid from customers. All day long he was at his wit's end to invent excuses for not coming from behind the counter. The shoes were so big they slobbered on the ends of his legs, as if he had thrust his bare feet into loose rubbers.

Elof tried to do a little studying on the job too.

Until one day Pa caught him. Apparently the old man had come stealthily down the stairs, for all of a sudden there he stood, stopped short, his face thickening. "What the hell you think you're doin' there?"

"Nothin'," Elof said, shoving the lesson under the counter.

"Is that so!" Pa snarled. He bulked around the counter and reached under it.

Anticipating him, Elof grabbed the lesson and held it behind his back.

"Give it here."

Elof straightened as much as he dared. "No."

Pa stared; then waggled a fat finger in his face. "Look, you bum, when you work for me you work."

"But there wasn't no customers. So I thought I'd——"

Pa waved a freckled hand. "Clean up then." He pointed at the dry-goods counter across the aisle of the store. "See them bits a lint an' so? An' that dust up there on the shoe-box section?"

Elof nodded mutely.

"An' here." Pa pointed at the counter Elof was leaning on. "Look at that sticky stuff there. Vinegar. Dammit, clean up after ye're done. Hear?"

Elof nodded tiredly. He allowed his hand with the lesson to fall to his side.

Pa had been waiting for just such a lapse. He grabbed at the lesson again. This time he wrested it away from Elof. He thumbed through it. "Figures, huh? What the hell's this?"

"Like I told you. Accounting."

"Didn't they teach you this stuff in college?"

"Certainly not in that Saint Comus domeny factory."

"I mean in State?"

"No."

"Why not?"

"I just didn't happen to take that course."

"Just didn't happen . . . I suppose you thought it fun to waste the taxpayers' money—my money—learnin' nothin'. What kind of crap did you learn?"

"Oh—ideas."

"Ideas, hell. What good does them do yuh? Huh?"

"I don't know."

"That's just it. You educated bums ought to be shot at sunrise. Runnin' aroun' the country. Beggin'. So poor you ain't got the price of a peg to hang your hat on. So goddamn poor you got to use yer back fer a mattress an' yer belly fer a blanket. Out in the open."

Elof reached out a hand. "Can I please have that now?"

"Not until I get good an' ready to give it to yuh." Pa's eyes screwed up with suspicion. "You sure this stuff'll help you?"

Elof swallowed. "Will you please give me my lesson?"

"Arracch!" The old man flung the lesson in Elof's face. He thundered off. At the stair door he turned once more. "When you work for me you work, you hear?"

"Do I get a pair of decent shoes out of it then?" Elof asked. "And the right to use the pickup?" The two questions slipped out of his mouth before he was aware of it. The last one was the worst because Pa had always been tight with the car.

The door slammed.

CHAPTER IV: Thoughts in a Graveyard

. . . Yet you glimpsed the hero's heaven. Once the blessing hands were laid on you, you were a chosen one, and up you had to rise, driving up out of obscurity and mediocrity, your simple mind popping and crackling with the dream of becoming a great, a hero. Ah yes, the mystic druids of the village are always finding spiritual sons, are always placing hand-woven halos on heads of young bulls never destined to grow antlers . . .

For an hour Elof managed to keep from thinking. He cleaned up the vinegar marks. He arranged the candy jars: peppermints, root-beer barrels, strawberry cubes, chocolate drops, lemon drops, all-day suckers, licorice, peanut brittle—all of them—neatly along one end. He closed the cooky containers. He rearranged the raw vegetables—peas, carrots, beans, red beets—on the vegetable stand. He lined up the canned stuff in stiff rows on the shelves behind. He went upstairs and got armfuls of dry cereal—oats and corn and wheat—and piled them up on the top shelves with a wooden long-arm.

On the dry-goods side he pulled out exactly two inches of cloth from each bolt for display. He set the spool-thread disk in order. Then he swept up.

A customer came in: a hesitant farm woman beneath a wide sunbonnet. He recognized her. Mrs. Nelson. The mother of darling Hilda, his childhood sweetheart. His Hilda, she of the blue robin-egg eyes, she who had died in a truck that was picnic-bound. Mrs. Nelson's husband owned the half section across the corner to the southeast. Her other children were triplets, boys, and she had once been acclaimed the village heroine for having brought them into the world. She bought a box of cornflakes and a loaf of bread. She had gray eyes. She leaned a little. She reminded him of Ma. Like Ma, she had the air of a woman who got a regular Saturday-night beating from her old man. She stood a long time looking at a bolt of red silk at the far end of the store. After a while she scuffed off.

Elof knew he should have pressed for a sale, but he just didn't have the heart to rob the tired old mother of her last few nickels; at least not the mother of Hilda.

An hour later he could still see, in his mind's eye, the tired old woman looking longingly at the red silk. He could stand it no longer. He called upstairs. "Pa."

"Ya?"

"Come down here. I've got to get out of here."

There was a silence.

When Pa didn't come or say anything, Elof decided the old man was probably thinking he was leaving him for good again, so he said, "I'll be back in a couple of hours."

Then the old man's feet hit the floor above.

Elof left.

He strode past Pa's pickup standing out in front. One of its bicycle-thin tires was flat. He walked down the neglected drive-in, went east down the highway toward the filling stations.

Above him, to his left and on the north side of the highway, the cottonwoods towered, their leaves chiddering sociably, and their shades engulfing the single chokecherry and its foot-high seedlings growing at the edge of Pa's lawn. Elof threw an admiring glance at the cottonwoods, the biggest tree growing in Siouxland. He remembered the Sioux Indian legend that a cottonwood's shade possessed an intelligence which, if properly prayed to, gave one guidance in the coming year's wanderings. The shade of a shrub or a stubby tree like a chokecherry was of no account.

Elof stepped on, his big shoes clobbering noisily on the shattered gravel of the highway.

He ignored Loren Solen, who owned the station set in the northwest angle of Chokecherry Corner. The station stood under the shade of the last huge cottonwood just at the edge of Pa's property. Loren Solen was a coughing, complaining, greasy, nosy fellow who sold a sour motor-fouling gas at cut-rate prices and whose sign asked:

CUT-RATE GAS
CHEAP
WHY PAY MORE?

The biggest station, on the furtherest corner to the northeast, was run by porky Kaes Hinke. Kaes Hinke divided his and his wife's time between farming and selling gas. Today his station was closed. His big red-and-white sign advertising sweet gas, Arctic, high test and regular, was covered with a film of dust. Elof read it:

GET NEW PEP, NEW ZIP, NEW SPEED-UP
AND ALL-AROUND HUSTLE-BUSTLE BUZZ
FROM **ARCTIC** GAS
WITH **ARCTIC**
YOU CAN GO LIKE THE OLD HARRY

Elof walked over to Kaes Hinke's bitterest rival, Bill Cooper, who had a station on the southwest corner and who sold the only other kind of sweet gas to be found in the world. A huge tin sign, painted blue and white, anked in the wind. It read:

FILL'ER UP WITH
ANTARCTIC
AND YOU'LL FIND
YOUR MOTOR
GOING ON THE WORD **GO**

Elof stepped inside.

A skinny dark-faced man got to his feet. It was Bill Cooper, the bachelor who loved dogs as if they were his own children.

"Hi, Bill."

"Elof. I've been wonderin' when you'd drop over an' see yer old friend Bill. Thought maybe you'd gone high hat on me."

"No, no."

"Well, what can I do for you?"

"Well, Bill, I tell you. Did Pa bury Ma out to Old Settlers'?"

"I don't know. I didn't go to the fun'ral myself."

"Which way did the funeral go from here? North?"

"By gosh, I guess it did at that."

Elof nodded. "That's it then."

Bill Cooper's booze-red eyes looked slyly at Elof. "With all that money yer dad's makin', funny he didn't bury her out t'Home Beautiful t'Jerusalem. That's as fancy a bone orchard as you'd care to get into, boy. Tea gardens, singing frogs, piano-playin' canaries. Rest couches all over the place. Good spot to take yer girl fer nooky."

Elof fiddled with his fingers. A fat black-and-white rat terrier came out of the back room and sniffed at Elof's pant legs.

"But then," Bill Cooper continued, "but then, yer Pa's probably savin' that money fer his new squaw."

"What?"

"Sure. Ain't you heard?" The dog left off smelling Elof and padded up to Bill Cooper. The dog growled a little and Bill Cooper patted it. "Now, now, Hippy. He don't mean no harm. He's all right. Just a neighbor boy." Bill Cooper addressed Elof again. "Sure. He's been junin' Gert Hansen. Yer old gal friend."

"OhmyGod!" Ah. So that was why Pa had asked if he were going to girl the women again. The dirty old fool.

"Yeh. An' you better step fast if you still intend to double-tree up with her. 'Cause I hear she's about ready to take him on."

Elof said curtly, "Just rest your mind easy on that one. I ain't. I'm only staying a couple of weeks and then shoving on." Elof looked out of the oily filling-station window to the north. "Ma's only dead a couple of weeks and already that old fool's looking around."

Bill Cooper chuckled.

Elof was tempted to pick up a wrench and brain the nervy gossip. But with great effort he turned away and left.

Just as he stepped past the gas pumps, Hippy, the dog, sneaked out of the door and nipped at his pant leg. Elof kicked viciously, barely missing the dog's black nose. Hippy set up a roar of barking.

"Hey, hey!" Bill Cooper shouted, coming to the door. "Hey! What's goin' on out here? Hippy, you bastard, came back here. Come. Come."

Elof took the highway north, the King's Trail. The Old Settlers' Cemetery was on a country road two miles north and a mile east from Chokecherry Corner.

Elof walked rapidly despite his clumsy bluchers. The slick soles slid a little on the round rolling stones of the graveled road.

He crossed the east-west Thunderbolt railway.

The grass in the ditch was short but green. Purple pasques had already gone to seed. Buffalo beans were budding. A pair of red-wings were building a nest in a swale.

A train, the Cannonball, approaching from the north, came down rails that ran through a cornfield on Elof's left. Its long stripe of smoke smudged the sky. The smoke was darkest near the train; and then, as it lifted gently, easily, it became gray, became white. The train whistled. Soon it was close enough for him to see people looking out of the coaches. The train nosed south, going on swiftly, like a madly rushing chain of gray beetles, an occasional iron bone in its belly clanking. With a champing flash it went past, leaving all around the smell of steam and coal smoke. And finally, all that was left was the distant sound of a second screaming whistle as it bulged up its muscles for the stop at Chokecherry Corner.

Elof passed the first-mile corner. Sunlight began to slant across the countryside. Light green and dark green checkered the sward. Corn rustled, grew, rustled. Oat fields tossed; silver chased green and green chased silver; oat heads rattled together, making the faint sound of a surf on the shore of a sea.

He sweat. He wiped his brow. He clumsed on.

It was clean and clear in the country. He could see for miles. Wide and high and blue and far was the sky. Scents of summer breathed into his nose. Seeded bluegrass, wild white clover waved under the gray and weather-faded wooden fence posts.

He came to the second corner, turned east.

He came to a creek. He stood a moment on the cement culvert, looking down, wondering: where were the squirting minnows? and the water-dancing whirligigs? Did they still skip and wrinkle the water's surface like they did in the old days? He picked up a gravel stone, dropped it. *Flummp!* Instantly the cast stone spread concentric rippling rundles. And the whirligigs hiding in the weeds awoke and prinked the undulating gloss.

He looked around. He saw a low bluegrass pasture on his left, dotted with black-and-white Frisian-Holstein cattle. Elof counted forty head. They cropped at the short grass, working feverishly to get their fill before daylight vanished. Off to one side an impudent bull calf was trying to mount a bulling cow. She was willing, but he wasn't big enough.

A sudden bellow, and Elof was startled to see a huge hornless domino-speckled bull come charging through the herd, cleaving it, scattering the cows and calves. The snorting bull rushed the cocky little bull calf, knocked it over legs up. It bucked the young bull, bumped it with rib-cracking, sickening thumps. The bull calf scrambled to its feet, galloped away to the safety of a farmyard. And the old bull, grunting, challenging, pawing the pasture grass, surveyed the conquered field. Then, sure of himself, the bull sniffed the bulling cow, allowed himself to get into a fever about her, and calmly bestrode her and bred her.

Elof's sympathies went out to the young bull calf. Those damned old bullheaded dukes were always butting into a young male's life, he muttered to himself.

He clodhopped on.

And everywhere were farms. He stood on a toe and spun around, his reaching eye seeing farmyards to all corners of the horizon, red barns and white houses set in shielding windbreaks. And on each were boys and girls, some happy, some sad; on each were fathers and mothers, some kindly, some gruff.

At last, to his right, he saw the graveyard lying on a low knoll. It barely rose out of the outspread prairie.

He entered the rusty gate, walked slowly through the rustling grass.

As always, it lay neglected. Tall knee-high stalks of blue-joint grass hid most of the stones. Save for the graves delved therein, the little acre was the only virgin prairie around. He was walking on ground hallowed by thousands of years of free growth.

Short columbine and wild strawberries softened the fall of his heavy shoes. A smell of faraway ancient times arose.

There were only a few headstones. Some had slipped and fallen.

Off to his left grew a hedge of shrubbery thirty feet long. He stepped over to it. He noticed something white hidden in the bushes. Parting the branches, he found a row of headstones. Apparently there had been a community burying on the spot. One stone had broken.

He stooped over and fitted the white-yellow pieces together. Grass rust and brush stain had obscured the words. With lightly touching finger tips he traced out the letters. And read:

DAUGHTER

OF

LYMAN AND HESTER
HARKNESS

———

DIED

OCT. 19, 1879
ONE MONTH, ONE DAY

———

OUR DARLING ONE HAS GONE ON BEFORE
TO MEET US ON THE BLISSFUL SHORE.

He glanced at the other stones.

No! It couldn't be.

He looked again, parting the branches to either side.

Yes. Yes. It was true. All the little stones had the same date: *October 19, 1879.*

He read the names:

NETTIE, DAUGHTER, ONE WEEK
HETTIE, DAUGHTER, ONE YEAR, 23 DAYS
DAVID, SON, SIX MONTHS, ONE DAY
ALMOND, SON, TWO YEARS, FOUR DAYS
BETTS, DAUGHTER, THREE WEEKS, SIX DAYS
AVVIE, DAUGHTER, THREE YEARS, TWO DAYS

He glanced at the surnames:

MATTHOMAS
WAGNER
McSMITH
FREAR

What dire catastrophe had stroked here in days of another time? Tornado? Cholera? Indians? Rattlesnakes?

He savored the names. Yankees. Or newly arrived Britishers. Pioneers in an empty land. No people.

Or maybe Mormons, and here shot and persecuted.

But why children? No old people?

Think of all the heroes lost. Had they lived they would have been fifty-seven. One of them a second Lincoln. Another an Ole Edvart Rölvaag. Another a Sappho. Another an Eleanor Roosevelt. Chosen ones.

He stood up and slowly turned and saw the land as the sorrowing mothers had seen it.

Pitiful. The prairie wind blowing against the tendon-tight frames, against stringy limbs, showing the cleft of legs entering the thigh, revealing the low much-suckled breast, outlining the hipbone sharp. The prairie wind drying the crying face, the wrenched muscles around the eye socket ache-swollen, the long hate-hot glance burning the vast sweeps of the undulating loess.

The father reading from the Bible. Praying.

Psalms bleated into the blue ears of the zenith.

Alone. Far distances alone. No people at all. Cut off from the world. From clean pans and white-framed windows and fence-top gossip. Alone. No people at all. And crying apart from all mankind. The terrible pain the first people paid.

He stood in a trance, looking at all of it.

Dead children. Frosted seedlings. Dead.

Or, frosted failures. Potential malcontents luckily killed before all the trouble began.

Yes, perhaps. Saved from much grief, from immense heart pain. Saved from having to learn that one was striving for goals never meant for one.

Like himself. They had called him a chosen one. When he wasn't.

He remembered how it had happened, how Old Domeny Hillich had called him and Bud Hillich, his son, chosen ones. And why.

. . . It was the last Saturday in May, and a glorious day. The faces of flowers and children were lifted to the blue veneer of the Siouxland sky.

Old Domeny Hillich had at last agreed to a picnic for the first-year Sunday-school class. The words had wheezed through his gray spade beard, and he had looked like God announcing an extra Sunday to all mankind. The children had all behaved very well that spring, no fights, no flunks, had even exclaimed ecstatically at the old druid's stories from the Bible.

They were all standing and sitting inside the rack of a cattle truck and heading west, heading for Perk's Park, a farmer's pasture spreading below some towering bluffs along the Big Sioux River banks.

Elof, and Bud Hillich, the Old Domeny's son, and sweetheart Hilda pure who had thrown a buttered glance, and all the neighbors' children, some six years old, most seven, some nine, boys and girls, all were going to picnic heaven. They shouted. They waved at farmers resting horses at the end of the field. They exchanged seats, flirted, told a few odd stories—Oh, happy childhood! 'Tis then the flowers are always blooming, and the flesh is still unstained, and the guggling blood wants what it wants!—and longed hungrily for the wild hours just ahead. Cowlicks and stiff new pants, pigtails beribboned blue and braided, sturdy limbs and porcelain arms, boys and girls, sly eyes and doe eyes, jostling and cheering, all rushing on, following on where the truck driver led them.

Rushing on. And just as they were almost there, as they were going down the last steep grade, descending from the Sioux County prairie above to the Big Sioux River holms below, through a vast road cut in the bluffs, it happened. Quicker than eye saw, before the heart could double its beat in fright, it happened.

Perhaps there had been a fault in the bluff, a fault the highway engineers had overlooked. Perhaps the mighty cowcatcher of an old-time glacier front had piled the till and the blue clay too loosely, perhaps God had given the edge of the cut a stamp with His foot just then, perhaps the vibrations from the rumbling truck had jarred it loose—who knows?—but down it came, green-lacquered sod, tons of yellow-and-blue subsoil, vast purple Sioux quartzite boulders, massive weights of earth, down, and it engulfed the cattle truck on the highway below, crushing its eggshell thinness. Like drops of broken yolk and white welling from a basket of hoof-crushed eggs, blood instantly pinched out of the mashed little bodies.

And only Elof and Bud unhurt.

Like tail-stiff, eyes-wide mice surviving a house cave-in, they scampered free of the clouding dust and disaster and stood silent in a pasture across the fence.

Old Domeny Hillich, following after, barely braking his old jitney in time, his front wheels climbing the outer edge of clod and gash-opened clay, viewed it, judgment-stricken.

He got out; ponderously climbed the pile. He stared; and then raised his face and palms to God; and cried:

"Naked came I out of my mother's womb, and naked shall I return thither: the Lord gave, and the Lord hath taken away; blessed be the name of the Lord."

It was Elof who had called out then. "Here we are, Domeny."

Old Domeny Hillich whirled, his long black minister's coat and hard white collar holding him stiff and all in one piece. "What?"

"Here we are."

" 'The Lord be praised.' "

The boys scrambled through the fence; came up close.

Old Domeny Hillich put out a hand to either one, and looked up, and thanked God: "Wondrous are Thy ways, O Lord. Thy hand and Thy voice are everywhere. From amidst an awful calamity, one whole year's crop of baptized children gone, we hear Thy voice issuing forth unto us, saying, 'These are my chosen ones.' "

Old Domeny Hillich put an arm around them, still looking up

to God, and continued, "So be it. Henceforth, both my son Samuel and Sister Lofblom's son Elof shall be lent to Thee for as long as they live. Priests shall they become in Thy temple."

And so it came to pass. Old Domeny Hillich easily persuaded hysterical Ma Lofblom of God's intervention, of God's certain intention for Elof.

All Elof's days, through grade school, through high school, it was pressed upon him that the Lord had a special mission for him on earth. God had had some special reason for saving him. And what greater reason, what greater mission, than to save souls for the Kingdom of Christ? Elof was sent on to the Saint Comus Theological Seminary to become a domeny.

But even from the beginning all was not well. In addition to his mother's prayers, and money which a grumbling Pa gave out, certain questions accompanied him to college. And at about the time that he began to flunk his studies, the questions began to hound him like stubborn sins.

In the process of giving him a special message, why had God sacrificed so many Christian children? And why had He sacrificed dear sweet Hilda, she of the robin-egg eyes? And why wasn't Gert Hansen, who was Hilda's best friend and who had stayed home from the picnic with a bad chest cold, why wasn't she equally lucky? Equally a chosen one?

And, moreover, maybe, wasn't one of Ma's reasons for making a domeny out of him a way of getting even with Pa for that terrible beating he had given her? A domeny could punish a mad husband.

It wasn't long before Elof began his wandering. . . .

He stood a moment longer, looking at the little gravestones almost hidden in the shrubbery.

Then, snapping his eyes, he studied the grass on the burying acre, trying to see where the weepers at his mother's funeral had walked.

At last he saw where there had been a trampling, saw where it wound toward a fresh mound of yellow-and-black prairie till in the northwest corner of the cemetery.

He walked over to it.

A small marble stone . . .

THILDA LOFBLOM, NEE ALFREDSON
BORN FEB. 11, 1886
DIED MAY 4, 193–
SAFE IN THE ARMS OF JESUS

There was no sound from Elof's throat.

He stood looking down at her grave.

Thoughts flashed he couldn't suppress. Her soft blue eyes—gone? Her body—a rectangle of bones stretched out in the putrid air of a dark wood chamber? Her patient mouth—crawling with white-gray worms? Her careworn brow—a dirty white arch of bone in the ground? Her hollow skull where once love had kindled a warming fire—now? He could see the clay-cold white decay discarded on the molding satin.

Elof remembered the physical shells of two mothers.

One, when he was a boy, before the picnic catastrophe. She was smiling; she had a red flushed face that was almost too full with happiness. And she had a throaty laugh, a possessive glance for Pa.

The other, after Pa and scarlet fever had beaten her down, after the accident. She had lost all her hair, her teeth. And her youth. She had suddenly become a wrinkled pumpkin. Her eyes, once overflowing with lively humor, had become great blue questioning orbs of hurt. And though she tried to hide her baldness with a wig, she had still looked like a woman scalped and skinned by Indians. Those blue eyes so easily hurt. Little-girl eyes.

Elof remembered how she had loved oranges, in those days a luxury on the prairie; recalled how she had taken an orange seed and had planted it in a bay-window flower box; how she had nurtured the tiny plant; how she had exulted the day she had seen a fire color creeping over a green sphere. And though the fruit was sour, she still had thrilled to the glory of eating a home-grown orange in the midst of a bitter Siouxland snowstorm. Exotic tropical fruit in Siouxland.

It was that same quality, that same vague groping to grow petals everywhere, that had prompted her to line the circling drive-in with white-painted stones, to plant a bordering flower bed of rioting reds and yellows.

The vision of Ma and her oranges and flowered drive-in shattered, broke up, vanished—driven away by a feeling of shame, by a numbing dark.

The forward bank of an ink-black cloud-mood rushed toward him; engulfed him.

The next instant a great clear light burst like a skyrocket in his mind. Before him was a most vivid tableau, a tableau so humiliating that vomiting motions pulsed through his corse.

He swallowed, forcing the spasms down, swallowing the bitter acids burping up from his stomach.

But he couldn't get rid of the tableau.

. . . He was in the Hello high school, a senior, taking a shower after a pickup game of basketball. The boys often played such a game after school hours, and there was usually nothing out of the way in playing such a game.

But today something had happened. He and Bud Hillich, the other chosen one, had had a fight. In the heat of the contest, by dint of great effort, Elof had broken up a dribble of Bud's, had taken the ball from him, had scored a basket.

The few side-liners had whooped. And Bud, a star player, taller than Elof, handsome, had greened with injured pride and, a moment later, had tried to bust Elof in the nose with the ball. Elof had not only warded the blow but had actually busted Bud in the head instead.

And so now in the shower, knowing Bud was laying for him, Elof took care to be as unobtrusive as possible.

He usually managed to avoid attention quite well. In the post-game noise of bluster and brag, of studsy horseplay, of flying drops of sweat, of flung garments, of splashing water in the marble showers, he could easily hide himself, could easily slip in among the yelling, singing, skinned-shark bathers, get his shower from a spray bouncing off some behemoth's shoulder, get out again, and get into his clothes. And no one would be the wiser. No one would notice that at seventeen he still couldn't show too much manhood, that he had been short-armed all around. Three years before he had exulted in the growth of a triangular patch of pubic hair, had even made the wonderful handmade discovery of hot fainting. But hero size hadn't come to him. Just like his big toe, it was stubby.

Elof stood behind a giant of a basketeer, carefully washing his belly and back with spread palms and soap, slopping and rubbing and jumping in the gurgling water. At last he was finished, and with a quick look around to see where Bud might be, he darted out, reaching for his towel and obscurity.

But he didn't make it. Bud was standing by Elof's chair, and just as Elof touched his own towel, Bud jerked it away. And there Elof was, buck-naked.

Elof blushed. He could feel embarrassment bleeding out of his body. "Gimme my towel," he said, grabbing at it again. "Gimme it!"

Bud danced away, his bare limbs long and springy. And manly. Bud yelled, "Lookit. Lookit, fellas! Elof's been almost born without *it*."

Everybody dropped what they were doing. Everybody. And looked.

In the showers the spraying waters drenched down.

"An' lookit his big toe. I know who's gonna wear the pants when he gets married. Boy, oh boy, I sure pity Elof when his wife finds out about him."

Elof stood for a moment, darkness rushing at him from all sides, gulping him; then, leaping, he grabbed up his clothes and, still wet, splashed into the lavatory next door, barricading himself in.

His face contorted; his lips whitened. He keened; moaned low. When he looked out of himself, he found himself momentarily blinded.

"I could kill him," he cursed in misery. "I could kill him. I could choke him until he was dead. Grab him by the neck and choke him until he was dead."

He had a vision of how he would do it. As Pa had almost done to Ma once.

He went home.

He didn't tell Ma.

But Ma found out. A gossip told her.

And what followed was perhaps the only time Ma had ever

shown mother-fierceness. She took him upstairs, into the kitchen over the store, and closed the door, and set milk and cookies before him.

At last, when he had finished the snack, she said, "Elof, I'm going to tell you something. I was eighteen before I knew what it meant to be a woman. Other girls became women at twelve, thirteen. But me, I never bled until I was eighteen. So don't you worry. Maybe you inherited that slowness from me."

Maybe he had; maybe he hadn't.

Secretly he tried everything to encourage growth, from frog-wart sweat to prayers. But nothing helped. He remained a congenitally short-armed lad. . . .

Elof sank to his knees. He bowed over her grave. "Ma," he murmured, "Ma."

After a moment he caught hold of himself, and stood up, and walked out of the cemetery, and closed the gate.

The sun touched the horizon. The shadow of a gray fence post reached across the dusty road. Crickets, frogs chorused.

> . . . *Elof, there are at least three roads to choose from:*
>
> *One is death (accidental or premeditated).*
>
> *Another is conformity to the status quo (and that most likely will be a living death).*
>
> *Still another is "the search."*
>
> *The tragedy is that when you choose the last one, you've got to choose it over again every day . . . every day . . .*

A mustached Siouxland farmer, Billy Gothge, came into the store to buy some groceries. When he had bought what he wanted he stopped to talk a minute. He complained about tough luck. A brother living in the Red River Valley had died early in the morning and now he had to drive four hundred miles through the first hot dog days of July to attend a funeral. And that, too, just when threshing was about to begin.

"The worst is," he said to Pa, "the worst is, I ain't been able to find anybody who'll milk an' water my cows while I'm gone."

"Huh," Pa said, leaning his bulk over a counter. "That's funny. Right now the country's full a bums needin' work."

"That's just it. That's what makes it so crazy."

Elof, dressed in overall and work shirt, and sitting in the back room just out of sight but not out of earshot, his bare feet up on a box, put aside his accounting lesson and got up and went out front. Fixing his eyes on the mustached farmer, he asked, "How long you need a man?"

"At most, four days," Billy Gothge said, studying him.

"What're you paying?"

"Grub an' bed."

"No cash?"

"No cash."

"Huh, just like Pa here."

Elof thought a moment. Just milking, watering cattle, a man might have a lot of free time to do some studying. It was high time he finished his accounting lessons and got out of this dead-head country. Then, too, it would be a pleasure to get away from the old man for a while. Watching him meow after Gert was enough to sour anybody's stomach. "I'll take it," Elof said simply.

"Kin y'u milk?" Billy Gothge asked, glancing at his hands.

"Sure."

"He ought to," Pa sneered, "he's been milkin' me for board an' room, an' spendin' money, ever since he was born."

Mustached Billy Gothge glanced quickly from father to son, backed away a step.

"Well," Elof asked, his eyes hardening a little, "are you taking me or not?"

Billy Gothge coughed, and passed his hand over his brown mustache, and grumbled, and said at last, "Well, all right. C'mon. Before I drive off the yard I'll have you show me how you milk a cow. Just to make sure."

Elof went into the back room, put on the dead bum's bluchers, picked up his straw hat, wrapped up *Peregrine Pickle* and ten accounting lessons from the American School of Correspondence in a newspaper. He glanced around to see if he didn't need anything else and, finding nothing, stepped out front again.

"Ready?" Billy Gothge asked, his groceries up on a hip under his arm.

"Ready."

Elof went out to the old car with the farmer. Scatterings of seed corn lay over the cracked leather seat in back. A dusty buffalo robe lay on the floor. Elof put his package down behind the front seat and got in beside the farmer. He rolled and lighted a cigarette.

Billy Gothge turned the car off the graveled drive-in and headed west toward the Big Sioux River.

Every now and then Billy Gothge glanced at the burning end of Elof's cigarette. "I want y'u to be careful of them lung dusters on my place. It's been as dry as a bone this summer, an' them buildin's a mine'll go up like tinder."

"I will."

"Me, I chew snoose. Heifer dust. Never no fear a fire."

"Uh-huh."

Billy Gothge looked over the land as he drove along. "Boy, it sure ain't wet. Real weather for buzztails an' blood poison." He spat out of the window. "Noticed you walkin' around barefoot back there. Be careful a that on my place. It's dog days now an' ye're three miles from the nearest neighbor with a telephone. An' snakes move fast. An' so does blood poison."

"You got rattlers there?"

"Well, my wife's said she's seen some."

"Uh-huh."

They passed a farmyard. "That's the Mellonses. Last place before you get t'mine," Billy Gothge said, "an' if you should happen t'get into trouble, just call on Old Man Mellon. Lou Mellon. He'll he'p y'u. He's the one that tol' about my brother dyin'. Yep, mighty helpful neighbor."

Elof nodded. Now that he was away from the store he discovered that, instead of brightening, his mind was dulling. Billy Gothge seemed to have a more deadening effect on his spirit than Pa did. Thank God the fool would soon be on his way.

Elof hoped the man had a decent house with bright windows and furnishings. Brightness might cheer him up and help him study. Elof wiped sweat from his face and settled even deeper into the seat. He took a last puff from his cigarette and, remembering Billy Gothge's fear of fire, carefully pinched the lit end between his fingers. The callus on his thumb singed a little and the smell of burnt flesh was in the car for a moment.

At last the old car topped the drop-off hill and started down a hairpin road. Below lay the snaking Big Sioux River, wriggling east and west to go south, and catching up Billy Gothge's farm in one of its coils. Far to the west spread a vast plain, mile beyond mile, out to the world's end, to where glinting windmills flickered vaguely on the horizon, land of South Dakota.

As Billy Gothge juggled the rushing car down the road cut through the hill, Elof saw a big gap in the wall on his left and suddenly remembered that this was the place where tons upon tons of soil and stone had crashed down on a truckful of children picnic-bound, where Hilda had been killed, where all his misery had begun.

"This is the way to Perk's Park!" Elof exclaimed.

"Yep." Billy Gothge nodded. "It was."

"Was?"

"Yep. I bought it. An' now it's just a simple little ol' farm. An' it's gonna stay that way. Picnics are too hard on fences."

"Well, I'll be damned."

The car coasted to the corncrib. A dog came out and began to bark.

"Here we are," Billy Gothge said. "C'mon, I'll take you to the house an' let the old lady look you over an' then I guess we'll be goin'." Billy Gothge stepped out with the groceries, patted the collie's head, "Down, Rover, down," and hurried to the house.

Elof followed slowly, his big shoes clumsing on the dusty yard.

Billy Gothge held the door open for him.

Elof stepped inside. He was immediately pleased to find the inside of the two-story frame house neat. It was pin-clean. There was the good smell of soap and flowers about. A tall woman came toward him out of the dining room, and he blinked his eyes to get them accustomed to the inside of the house.

"Meet Elof Lofblom," Billy Gothge said. "Pa Lofblom's boy. You remember him, don't you, Millie?"

The tall woman nodded. "Yes." She had thin lips, cold eyes, a very white face. She studied him. There were tiny neat beads of sweat on her upper lip. Then she smiled. "Oh sure. You're the boy that's learnin' for the ministry, ain't you?"

Elof almost choked. Another woman raised on prunes and proverbs. "Well, once I was."

Mrs. Gothge chilled. "Ain't you keepin' up your studies?"

"Not for the ministry."

Elof noticed Billy Gothge trying to catch his eye, and he quickly added, "But I ain't through studying yet. And maybe, who knows, it'll be like you said after all." Elof was tempted to add that since he still didn't have a good job and that since he had flunked his try at orthodox ministry he might be forced to go into Holy Roller evangelical ministry, where marks and diplomas weren't a prerequisite. And where there was plenty of money to be had. Bushels of it.

Mrs. Gothge relaxed again and she patted his shoulder. "That's fine. I'm sure that the Lord will instruct you as He sees fit. My boy, never close your heart to the Lord. Heed His call and He'll bless your labors."

Elof swallowed.

"Well, Millie," Billy Gothge broke in, "ready?"

She sighed. "Yes, I guess we can go now." She turned tiredly to Elof. "Come, I'll show you where the food is." She started for the kitchen, stopped when she saw his package, asked, "Is that your Bible work you're carryin' with you?"

"Well, in a way, yes. My studies."

"Good boy. Yes, I'm sure the Lord will instruct you as He sees fit."

She showed him the kitchen, showed him his bed, showed him how to water the flowers. He was a little startled to find that she, too, like Ma, had an orange tree growing in a bay-window flower box.

Billy Gothge showed him how to do the chores.

And then they were gone.

With a shoulder-raising sigh, Elof settled into a rocker by a south window. It was almost noon out, and the heat from the ground streamed through the screen and open window. He gazed over the yard awhile, looking at the trees lining the distant Big Sioux banks to the west, looking at the brown bluffs to the east. It was hot in the valley. He took off his shoes and started studying.

An hour later he looked up, surprised to see how much he had done. It had been very quiet in the lonely house. A clock had ticked lightly. The brilliant sunlight had been silent. He was glad he had come.

He stood up, stretched, pulled his overall free of his sweat-sticky legs, stalked into the kitchen. He made a meal of fried eggs and bacon, bread, butter, jam, a glass of lemonade, and a big fat piece of shining lemon pie. He cleaned off the table neatly.

He remembered the noontime chores: pump water for the cattle, slop the hogs, fill chicken troughs with water. Elof laughed to himself and shrugged his shoulders when he recalled how easily mustached Billy Gothge had added a few extra jobs to the routine. It was an old Siouxland farmer trick: get you for one job and then, at the last minute, before you could work up an argument, load you down with others. "If you wanna," Billy Gothge had said, his sly eyes darting a blue look at Elof now and then, "if you wanna, you might slop the hogs at noon too. An' water the chickens. If you wanna." Elof laughed.

He slapped on his straw hat. He sat down on the front steps to put on his oversize shoes. He looked at them, decided they were too sticky and heavy for him this hot day. He got up and kicked them to one side. He would go barefoot. He would be free. A barefoot boy and free.

The dog Rover got up from under the porch where he had been snoozing and followed Elof across the rusty burnt lawn. Rover shook himself, gold-brown hair and dust floating up into the brittle sunlight. He came over and licked Elof's hand. Elof patted him and hurriedly stepped under a shady maple.

The water tank was empty when he got there and, looking up at the towering shiny steel windmill, he wondered if there was any wind stirring at all. He put it in gear. But it didn't turn, so he braked it again and started pumping.

There were no cows in sight and he wondered if they were down at the river drinking. He pumped awhile; then, for a change, swilled the hogs, watered the chickens. That done, he went back to pumping. Slowly, quarter inch by quarter inch, the water rose up the algae-green wall of the tank. Elof watched it edging past certain marks he set with his eye. He sweat. He tipped back his straw hat. The hot pump handle became slippery in his palms.

When the tank was full he saw Billy Gothge's red-and-white cows coming up the lane from the west. He noticed that a steer had jumped the fence and was in a cornfield, coming down the wrong side of the lane. He cursed. He studied a moment; then saw a lazy man's gate at the end of the lane near the barnyard. His eyes lighted. He would let the jumping critter go through that. He prayed the fence wasn't down somewhere. He hopped down off the gray wooden pumping platform. Rover, momentarily excited, got up from its shade and playfully leaped for Elof's hand.

The dog's sudden exuberance moved Elof and he skipped barefoot through the dust of the barnyard. He sprang across the dry crust of a manure pile, leaped over a little ditch, ran on toward the gate. The cattle coming down the lane stopped, eyed him, astounded. So did the steer across the fence. Elof bounded up a low mound, leaped, and, gliding over the earth in a long falling broad jump, landed on a patch of tough burnt grass. And fell. His left foot, always a little slow, had hooked in something. He heard his flesh rip. He fell hard on his face.

He scrambled to his feet. And saw it. A narrow, inch-long gash down the top of his stubby big toe, just below the first joint. It stung. He stood on one foot, looking at it, noticing that though it was deep, down past the tendon, it didn't bleed much. Red flesh welled out of it. He pinched it, trying to make the wound clean itself with a little flow. But it wouldn't.

He looked around in the patch of grass, wondering what could have tripped him. He knelt. A short hoop of barbed wire had lain hidden. Both ends had been buried securely in the ground by rain and erosion. His foot had landed squarely before the entrance of the prickly hoop, had caught the toe on the lift.

Sobered, he went up to the gate, opened it, chased the steer through, and closed it. He slopped the hogs; watered the chickens. Then he went back to the house.

He looked around for some antiseptic, a salve or so; and, not finding any, decided, what the heck, it would probably heal anyway.

The exertion had tired him a little and he succumbed to an impulse to take a nap before he went back to his studies. He lay on the rug floor of the living room—it was the coolest place in the house—and was soon asleep. He dreamed flies were running over his wound.

When he awoke there was a dull pain in his toe and instep. He stretched and sat up to look at the cut. It had swollen a little. It looked angry. A red at the opening hued off into a vague purple. He studied it, decided to soak it in warm water, even if the afternoon was dry-hell hot. He heated some on the kitchen kerosene burner.

The water in the basin felt good. In a little while his fears and his pains subsided.

He sat on the chair in the kitchen, his foot in a basin of water, working at his lesson. He sweat. The cistern pump on the sink sweat. The chill linoleum floor was damp too.

A quarter of an hour later his foot began to sting again. Looking at it, he was surprised to see that a tiny stripe of dull red had crept from the wound to the ankle. Blood poison. As Billy Gothge had warned.

He scoffed the idea from his mind. It just couldn't happen. He had too much studying to do. He had a perfect setup here for a couple of days to do a lot of work, to do a lot of thinking about his future, and he wasn't going to let anything spoil it.

He added some hot water.

By milking time the whole foot was involved. It was almost too painful to walk on. He didn't dare bend the toe. And for the first time, the left blucher was a perfect fit. He hobbled over the yard, feeding the hogs, horses, chickens, and milking the cows. He pumped water. He turned out the cows, carried the milk to the milkshed. He started up the milk separator, letting cream run into a long pail as Billy Gothge had told him to do, putting the foaming snow-white skim milk in the used pails. He caught some milk and cream for his own use. Finished, he rinsed the separator first with hot, then with cold, water, put the long pail of cream in the water cooler, fed the skim milk to the red-and-white calves in the barn, washed the pails, and hung them on the milk rack, all the while hobbling painfully about.

The upper horse-barn door was loose and he went over to hook it. He noticed a medicine cabinet stuck up on the wall between two hanging harnesses and, searching through it, found a bottle of horse liniment and a can of horse salve. He smelled the salve, found it powerful. He took both and, with the dog Rover following, stumbled back to the house. His shadow was long on the burnt grass. The sun began to turn dizzily on the west horizon, red, burning, dancing.

He took off his shoes, poured liniment over the sore. It was hot, but not as hot as he expected. That was bad. He touched his foot, noticed that where he put his finger it remained pitted. He applied some salve, gently, soothingly. It stunk.

And still he really did not worry. The toe and foot weren't black-and-blue yet, the real sign of blood poison. He was sure it would go down in the night and he could still get in a wonderful spell of studying so he could get out of this goddamn Siouxland country and get a job and look the world in the eye again. He was a young man who was going places and who would someday become a hero.

He went out on the back porch. There was a deep green cedar near the porch and he savored with great relish its fine woody smell. He sat studying. He looked up now and then. He worked on, bit his pencil as he added and subtracted figures, totaled columns of numbers, brought and carried over. He listened to the turtledoves churgling in the grove.

But his foot pained more. He got another chair and put his foot up on it. That eased it some.

At bedtime he examined it again. The foot seemed lumpy, almost an inch thicker than his right one. The stubby big toe was grotesquely swollen. The thin stripe had crept halfway up his calf. He worried. He pondered. He wondered if he should walk over to the Mellon farm before it was too late.

The problem hung balancing in his mind, falling neither to the one way nor the other. Then tiredness won, and he went to bed.

It was dark and hot when he popped up out of sleep, and it was his toe that had awakened him. He could count his pulse in it. *Throb. Throb. Throb.* It shook the bed a little. Leaning over, he lighted the kerosene night lamp on the bedstand. Slowly the room filled with light. The water bowl and the pitcher stood glinting white on the dresser.

He looked down. Lying on the clean white sheet, the toe and foot looked dirty, festering. Both were dull blue, and even more swollen than before. The stripe was an inch wide where it passed over his ankle, and had crept up past his knee. He wondered what time it was, wished he had been smart enough to take the alarm clock upstairs with him when he had gone to bed.

The night was silent. Even the crickets seemed to have had too much of the heat. The house didn't creak. The silence hurt his ears. He had an impulse to call the dog Rover. What if he should die here? Alone. With no one around at all and the big day not yet come to him.

How silent was the night. So very silent.

Strange that this should have happened to him. This spot on the Big Sioux was hoodoo for him. First the bluff cave-in and then this.

He lay staring in the wicking yellow light. He stroked his leg to ease the pain. Occasionally he stroked too hard and the skin turned a sickly white. Ever so slowly, pudging blood and life refilled the white blotches.

Silent night. He could hear the blood ticking through his toe.

He pondered the toe. Suppose he lost it because of blood poison? And chopped the other off accidentally on purpose? No one would ever know that he had been born too short.

He guessed it to be about three in the morning and finally, again tiring, dropped back into his wet pillow to wait for morning. Come dawn, he would go to neighbor Mellon for help. He blew out the lamp with an openmouthed breath.

About an hour later the pain became so intense he awoke again. He lay in the dark, thinking. He shifted around to find some way of reclining that would ease the stinging. He hit upon the idea of putting his foot up on the brass end of the bed. Once more he dozed off.

Glistering morning sunlight awoke him. Quickly, hopefully, he looked at his toe. But it was worse. It was thicker, blacker, and the stripe had now gone up into his groin. The whole foot looked like a very badly molded loaf of bread.

He lowered the leg from the brass end. It had fallen asleep. He swung his foot to the floor and sat on the edge of the bed. He tried to put a little pressure on the foot. The bones went down dully into the sodden lump. There was no doubt of it. He had blood poison. Experimentally he chewed his teeth to make sure he still didn't have lockjaw. He made up his mind to hobble somehow through the morning chores and then make his way over to neighbor Mellon and from there phone Pa or Dr. Mars at Hello.

He tried to cross the yard; fainted.

He came to after a moment and knew the chores were out. He got to his knees and thought of shouting to attract somebody's attention. A glance at the huge towering bluffs to the east told him they would throw his voice back across the Big Sioux into South Dakota. Somehow he would have to crawl up the bluff road to the top and then call. There was a light breeze out and, worse luck, it came from the east. He would have to shout against the wind.

He remembered that Old Lady Gothge had told him to water the flowers and he went painfully into the kitchen and carried a dipper of water to the window box of flowers. Ma would have liked it that he had been kind to the old lady's dwarf orange tree. The water bubbled as it settled into the dirt, little gold balls shooting over the surface. He thought the orange-red petals of the geranium were brighter when he finished.

After he had wrapped up *Peregrine Pickle* and the lessons, he slapped on his straw hat, drew on one shoe, stuffed the other under his arm, and started off.

Gasping, staring, his heart tight with fear, the blood beating in his neck, he worked his way up the steep climb. The first ways he hopped on one foot. When the muscles of his good leg gave out, he got down on hands and knees, scurrying along like a crippled crab, holding his sore leg and foot aloft.

He stopped to rest. He sweat.

He sent the dog Rover back home a dozen times.

Viciously he chewed weeds to distract attention from the pain. But the devilish throbbing grew louder in his ears. His heart wrestled to get out of his chest. His whole right side seemed to stiffen.

He passed the spot where Hilda had died in the picnic-truck cave-in. He thought: If it was in the cards to die young, what better place than this?

He made the top of the bluff at last. And thankfully discovered that the wind had switched to the west. His voice could ride on the wind. He halloed. "Hi-yooo!" He shouted until his voice was hoarse. "HI-YOOO!"

No one came.

He lay down across the road. Someone coming to see Billy Gothge would find him in the way.

After a half-hour he got up and shouted again. "Hi-yooo! HI-YOOO!"

Five minutes later a car roared up. It stopped just in front of him, braking hard. A rusty-faced man hopped out. "Hey, what the hell's the matter with you?"

"Blood poison."

The man looked at Elof's foot. "Holy socks! That looks bad, boy." He leaned over. He helped Elof to his feet. "I better hurry you over to Dr. Mars."

"Take me to Lofblom's Grocery first," Elof said, so happy he could hardly mumble the words.

The man nodded and guided Elof onto the front seat carefully. He got in and drove breakneck up the road toward Chokecherry Corner.

"You Lou Mellon?" Elof asked through waves of unreality.

"That's right."

"I was doing chores for Billy Gothge while he was away to his brother's funeral up in Minnesota."

"Oho. So that's why I ain't seen him in the field then."

"Yeh. And say, I couldn't do his chores this morning."

"Never you worry, boy. I'll do 'em when I get back. You just get yourself better first. That's your job now."

"Uh-huh. And I think a fence is down somewhere. The corn-field fence along the pasture."

Pa cursed when he saw Elof's foot. "Dammit, an' I suppose ye're expectin' me to pay the doctor bill, huh? Well, you got another think a-comin' on that one. That's one time you guessed wrong, boy."

Rusty-faced Mellon stood astounded. "My God, Lofblom, is that a way to talk to yer own son?"

"Son? Son? You call that good-fer-nothin' bum my son?"

The rusty man burned. He picked up Elof again and half shagged him out of the store. "Come, son. I'll take you into town. You've got to see a doctor quick."

At Hello, Dr. Brander Mars, a black-browed drunk who in

between drinks was a tiptop doctor, said, "Can you still move your teeth?"

"Yeh."

Dr. Mars punched a hand bell.

A nurse ninced in. She was so neat she looked as if she had just been packaged up at the cleaner's.

Dr. Mars snapped, "Get a table ready for this fellow. He's a candidate for Embalmer Bloodsworth if we don't hurry." He glowered at Elof. "You damned fool. It's a miracle you haven't got lockjaw yet."

They laid Elof on a table on his belly.

Elof said, "I can't pay the bill right away." He coughed. "Probably never the way I feel."

"Don't talk nonsense. I'll send the bill to your father."

"No. Don't. He and I don't get along too well."

"The hell you say."

"Yeh. We was just there and he washed his hands of any debts I'd make."

"That's right," Lou Mellon said. "That's what he did. The bastard."

Dr. Mars nodded. "Well, then I'll make them county-board bums pay it out of the Poor Fund."

Elof closed his eyes. He felt very sleepy.

Dr. Mars jammed a long needle under his skin up along his backbone.

Doc also lanced the wound in his big toe. Doc swore mildly when it wouldn't pus.

At last Doc asked, "Got a place to stay?"

"Sure. At Pa's store."

"Oh. He will let you stay there, huh?"

"Yeh."

"Uh-huh. All right. Good. You get back home and I'll call tomorrow. Meantime, lay still, drink water, eat light, keep this bandage on, and by all means keep your bowels blowing."

Elof nodded.

Two days, and the wound on the little big toe still wouldn't pus. And two huge swellings balled up, one in his crotch and the other under his left arm. The fiery red stripe had worked its way up over his belly.

Sometimes Pa came in, looked briefly, scowled, walked out.

Elof lay in the hot back room, sleeping most of the time, his leg up on the windowsill. The window faced north.

Elof hung suspended for three days. His body swelled. He was sure he was a goner.

On the fourth day Pa came in again and looked at the foot and then began to unwrap the bandages.

"Hey, cut it out!" Elof exclaimed.

"Shut up," Pa said grimly.

"Hey. Doc says I was to keep it covered."

"Achh, Dr. Mars, he don't know from nothin'," Pa growled. "Always drunk. Heathen. God wouldn't use a sinner to help a sick man."

"Just the same, I'll thank you to keep your mitts off my foot."

"An' I'll thank you to shut up. Think I'm going to sit around here an' see you kick the bucket on me? It costs money to bury people, boy."

The old man's eyes were so deeply set back in his head that Elof didn't dare say any more. Pa had looked that way once before—that time he had beat the hell out of Ma. Elof watched.

Pa finished the unwrapping, looked at the sore, humphed, and shagged upstairs to the kitchen. He was back shortly with two dried crusts of bread and a pan of hot milk.

"What's that for?" Elof asked.

"You'll see." With a fork Pa dipped the hard bread into the steaming, filming milk and then suddenly slapped it over the sore. "Now," Pa grimmed, wrapping a bandage over it, "now we'll see who's better, the doc or me." He finished the wrapping. "There's only one way to lick blood poison. That's t'poultice it. Suck out the crap."

Elof said nothing. The hot slab didn't burn him. He guessed his leg had gone dead.

Ten minutes later his leg began to itch. A little more and he couldn't stand it. "Pa!" he called.

The old man bungled his huge chunky body through the door. He breathed roughly into Elof's face, his blond whiskers as drizzled as a worn-down hairbrush. He ripped off the bandage. And instantly the wound popped open, and yellow and purple and bloody pus geysered out and ran over Elof's foot and slopped over onto the bed.

Pa nodded sagely. "There. See? Now me, I call that pusin'."

The tightness went out of Elof's body, and in a little while he fell asleep.

Pa went out to run the store.

. . . Individual man says: I comb and cap my golden curls only to learn it is all for naught. For I will die and that will end it for me.

Individual man says: I am a creature glimpsing an eternity I can never have. For I will die and that will end it for me.

Individual man sighs and says: Oh! would that I had left my locks to wind and rain, matted, and had never known at all.

But—

Mankind says: We are here, therefore we are.

Mankind says: We do; we beget.

Mankind says: We go on . . .

Elof got a letter.
Opening it, he read:

MR. ELOF LOFBLOM
Chokecherry Corner, Iowa

DEAR MR. LOFBLOM:

I am sorry to inform you that the county board of supervisors has rejected your claim for aid from the Poor Fund.

We are therefore sending the bill to you.

Very sincerely,
DR. BRANDER MARS

Bm/s

Enclosed was an itemized account, listing services for administering anti-lockjaw serum and for dressing the barb-wire wound:

a total of fourteen dollars. Reasonable enough. Except that Elof didn't have it. And he trembled to think what Pa might say should he see the bill.

And then, as if a god in the wild were watching over him, something happened.

Elof heard a bellow from the front of the store. "Elof!"

"Yeh." He got out of bed, pushed out his cigarette on an ash tray, brushed tobacco crumbs off his overall front. "Coming."

Stepping noiselessly in his socks, he entered the store. "What's up?"

"Want a job?" Pa was just hanging up the receiver of their wall telephone.

"Sure. Why not?"

Pa cleared his throat, took a chew, put the plug of tobacco back into the pocket of his white shirt. "Kaes Hinke just called. Said he's short a harvest hand. Want a go?"

Elof considered. Ah. A chance to pay the bill. Sure, it meant slaving in the sun, and a hot one, but it also meant a chance to save himself from a Pa explosion. "Sure. I'll take it."

"Good. Better hurry then. Or them pool-hall bums t'Hello'll hear of it an' beat yuh to it."

Elof hurried. Quickly he threw his possessions into his suitcase. He folded in his gray suit with its belt in back, a clean dress shirt, a pair of socks, some red handkerchiefs, the last couple of accounting lessons, and *Peregrine Pickle*. Then he put on his clodhoppers.

On the way out he lingered a moment. "Say, Pa, I can't work in these. They make me look like a clown. Give me some real work shoes."

"Where's the money?"

"I ain't earned it yet."

"Bring the money an' I'll bring the shoes."

"But really, I can't work in these clunks."

"They're better than nothin'," Pa said grimly, bulking up ruddy and square. "Beggars can't be choosers."

"I wouldn't mind them bein' shoes stole from a dead hobo if only they'd fit."

"Like I said, I can't afford to give you a new pair. I just can't give you a whole week's profit."

"Size fourteen and I wear tens," Elof grumbled. "What a picklement I've gotten myself into."

"I'm glad ye're catchin' on at last, m'boy."

Elof grunted, hitched up his suspenders, slapped an old straw hat to his gold head, and started off. "Well, if that's the way you feel about it, okay. Good-by."

"Good-by." The old man scratched his blond beard. "An' this time make sure you come home with some cash in your pocket. Because as sure as hell is hot I ain't gonna give you none. An' come back showin' me you still got some git an' gumption t'yuh besides all that fop readin' an' educatin' you're doin' to yerself."

Elof trundled down the road toward the east, along the AYP. He passed the filling stations, noticing that Kaes's station was once more closed.

Again Elof noted the two brand names: ARCTIC and ANT-ARCTIC.

The two names always gave him a laugh. There were just two sources of sweet gas in the world, one under the icecap on the North Pole, and the other under the icecap on the South Pole, with a skinflint by the name of Old Harry Ferguson owning the first and a corporation the second. And all the while that Old Harry and the corporation were spending billions of dollars advertising Freedom, encouraging young men to make their million, they were also effectively blocking all projects involving their ice-capped holdings. Freedom. What Freedom? And where?

Elof walked on, his clodhoppers flopping. The graveled road shimmered in the drying, blistering sunlight. To keep from tripping himself flat on his face, Elof threw out his toes a little. Another month of these bluchers, he reflected, and he would have the strut of a city pimp.

At last, a half mile down the road from the Corner, he reached the head of Kaes's Lane. Shifting his suitcase to his strong arm, he started up the yard.

A weathered red barn stood on his right, with a herd of Frisian-Holsteins in the yard under the shade trees, maple and ash. On the left rose a house, a white green-trimmed frame structure.

Kaes, a burly man, was sitting on the porch steps tying his shoes. A collie pup played at his feet.

Elof started toward him. In the path a flock of chickens were feasting on a dead gopher. They scattered before his going.

"Hi," Elof greeted.

"Hum," Kaes grunted. Kaes finished tying his shoes and stood up. He buttoned a side flap of his overall. He tipped back his straw hat. A curl of dark hair slipped from under it and fell across his low forehead. "Elof."

"Right."

"I suppose you came for the job?"

"Right again."

The pup began to tug at Elof's pant leg.

Kaes commanded, kicking at the dog, "Get down, Snip."

"Oh, he's all right," Elof said. "I like dogs."

"Get down."

Kaes's eyes searched Elof's sturdy body. "How are them college muscles?"

"Never had any."

Kaes took a small pack of chewing tobacco out of his shirt pocket, filled his mouth with a pinch of coffee-brown leaves, chewed, spat, said, "You mean you've worked lately?"

"A little."

Kaes snorted. He glanced at the thermometer hanging on a porch pole. "It's already a hundred in the shade an' you come out here in this heat with them puddin'-soft arms?"

Elof flushed. "Well, it's your idea. You told Pa to send me out, didn't you?"

Kaes stared at him awhile and then, shrugging, said, "Well, I needed the help. So I thought I'd have a look at you. Go ahead. But if you fall dead, it'll be your own doin', d'you hear?"

"Sure. I know."

"All right then. How much you want?"

"What're they paying?"

"Two bucks a day. Board an' room thrown in."

"That's okay by me."

"Good. You'll find the boys in the north eighty there. They're cuttin' already."

"Cor and Wilbur?" They were Gert's brothers and a few years older than Elof.

"Yeh."

"I'll be the only one shockin' then?"

"Backin' out already?"

"No. Just wanted to know."

"Oh." Kaes chewed. "Well, I tell you. I'll help you when I can. But the chores an' changin' the horses keeps me hoppin'. Ain't even got time to keep my station open." Kaes muttered a little. "Except that it bein' closed don't matter none, what with Tightwad Harry kickin' up the base rate an' Sour Gas Solen undersellin' six cents t'the gallon." Then Kaes clamped shut, as if he realized he shouldn't be talking personals with a stranger. He lumbered off the porch and started toward the barn, Snip, the pup, following after. "Tell Gretch to put up your suitcase," he called over his shoulder, "an' you kin start right in. An' say, if you get dizzy with the heat out there, help yourself to a bottle a whisky I got coolin' in the cattle tank there. It'll probably tide you over for the first day."

"Thanks."

Elof stepped toward the house and up the porch, his bluchers flapping. He knocked.

A tall, narrow-faced woman came to the screen door. She was pregnant and she moved slowly. She was wearing her hair in an overlong, frizzle-ended brown bob. He recognized her instantly as Gretch, Gert's older sister. He remembered that she had married Kaes a year before he had gone off to college. He recalled, too, that everybody had wondered whatever had gotten into her to marry herself off to a middle-aged bachelor. Elof humphed to himself. With Gert just now lifting her tail for Pa, a man could almost say that the Hansen girls were old-buck crazy.

"Hi, Gretch," Elof said. "I'm your new hired hand. Can I put this up somewhere?"

"Sure. Just set it inside here. I'll take it up to your room later." From nowhere blue patches came and settled in under her eyes.

Elof reached the suitcase through the open screen door and parked it against the wall.

A bright-cheeked little girl peeked from behind Gretch's skirts.

Elof looked at the child and then reached down and snapped the lock on the suitcase. That copy of *Peregrine Pickle* was probably the only one for hundreds of miles around.

Gretch pushed the child back. "Toots. Get out a the way. Toots."

Elof smiled. "It's all right now."

The little girl smiled back at him, coyly. She looked a little like dead Hilda. Robin-egg eyes.

Elof patted her head, stroked her cheek. Already the child had desirable pink flesh.

The child put her arms around Elof's leg and hugged it.

The friendly smile that had been ripening on Gretch's face now vanished. She pulled the child away roughly. "Now, now, Toots. Elof's got work to do. Here. Get out of the way."

Elof's smile drained away too. "Good-by, little girl. Toots."

"Goom-by."

Elof stepped off the porch into the hot sun again. He wondered what the furtive look in Gretch's eye had meant.

He hitched along through the grove, stepped through a lazy man's gate, and started across a golden stubble field. Far to the other side the arms of two reel wheels, white and thin, stroked the summer shimmer. He recognized them for the binders Cor and Wilbur were driving.

Elof followed a binder track around to the southeast corner of the field and started in. The bundles were about three feet long, with middles the size of a slim girl's, and tops bristling with glowing oat kernels. He rolled down his shirt sleeves to protect his arms and then grabbed two of the sheaves, set them up, thumping the butt end into the stubbles and slamming the heads together. The bundles stood. He picked up two more, slammed them together against the south side of the first two. He picked up two more, set them on the north side. A shock was up.

Slowly he swung into the work, remembering the old motions, the old harvesting habits. Two shocks up. Four. Eight. Sixteen. Many.

Sweat began to bubble on his skin. Soon his back began to ache. He knew he was in for a rough day. He wondered if his just-healed foot would hold out. Already it throbbed a little. In case the big toe swelled any it was probably a good thing to be wearing bluchers—at least on the left foot.

Oat awns began to work into his clothes. He itched with them.

An idea occurred to him. He stopped and unhooked his suspenders, spreading his legs to keep the overall from falling to his feet. He took off his shirt, pulled up the overall again, rehooked the suspenders over his bare shoulders, and then drew the shirt over the top of his overall. Clothes should shed beards, not collect them.

He worked along steadily, air billowing up under his flowing shirttail. He held himself down to a crawling pace on the theory that if he started easy he might be able to survive the day. Big-league baseball pitchers warmed up the same way for a big game. If they got by the first few innings they were sure to finish strong and winning.

Salty moisture dripped, dripped, from his chin, from the end of his nose. Crossing his eyes, looking down his nose, he could see the bubbles forming, flashing in the sun.

He finished a windrow. He stopped to catch his breath. He tipped back his straw hat to let the air kiss his hot forehead. He could feel blood throbbing in the veins over his temples.

To divert attention from his pains, he plucked a head of oats from a bundle and looked at it, rubbing it in his palms and studying its kernels. They were full and fat.

Pulling his hat down again, he started up another row, bending, bowing, scraping, slamming. The bundles rustled, stirred, whispered. Oat heads jiggled. Awns scratched his face.

Two bucks a day. What a salary that was. Elof laughed. Two years each in two colleges and two bucks a day. In an oat field. Beneath a hell-hot sun. That was America for you. Where every child was a someday President. Elof scratched himself, snapped sweat from the end of his nose.

But the worst was he had no friend.

He worked along, bending, puffing, sweating, tiring.

The thing to do was to get himself a friend.

He started up another windrow.

A friend. If his plan to take another running jump at the big-time life in the Big City was ever to come to pass, the first thing he would have to do would be to build connections, make friends. Despite his shyness. Get himself a buddy, a chum who did some reading and who went to symphonies and who met and talked with great men every day. Who would be in the swim of things. The absence of such a friend had been one of his biggest handicaps so far.

Elof worked down still another row.

Of course there was no use kidding oneself. Though a city friend might like an elastic mind, a city friend would not like an empty purse. Things cost in the city, and even if one were lucky enough to be housemating with St. Francis of Assisi, St. Francis of Assisi would eventually raise a fuss if one couldn't foot the utility bills once in a while.

A bundle had broken open and he stooped over and rebound it.

A friend. If, on the other hand, his plan to leave should go all to smash, and if he should be condemned to village life for the rest of his natural days, he would have to find himself a friend right on the spot. But who? College, bummingdom, some reading had placed a barrier between himself and the village folk.

One thing about country friends—they were not to be sneered at. When you got into any kind of trouble, they were full of a sudden heart-warming animal concern for you. They might not be able to understand a single sentence in *Peregrine Pickle,* but they could understand wounds. Like that Lou Mellon fellow.

Farmers you could depend on. They were direct, solid, honest, good. They ate well, they slept well, they filled their days with something done. Concrete. Compared to the solid things Kaes and his wife were doing, he, Elof the half-educated bindle stiff, out of a job, was contributing nothing to society.

Elof shocked on. Slowly his shirt and overall became soggy wet. Prickly heat rashed his body pimple-red.

He nodded. If he did settle in the country, if he did become a storekeeper, or a Siouxland farmer, his going off to school would then become a complete joke.

Another thing was a cinch. The taste of books had forever spoiled him. He could never become the satisfied farmer that Kaes was today. Never. He had eaten of the tree of the knowledge of good and evil, and it made him forever alone and misunderstood. Alone.

'Twould have been much better had he gotten himself married

soon after he had finished high school. Then he would never have known about the fleshpots of the devil.

Of course, if one wanted to be strictly logical about it all, 'twould have been better if in the beginning there had never been no picnic accident and no blessing by Old Domeny Hillich. Hilda would have been alive and he wouldn't have had to go straining after something he could never get.

But even with Hilda out of it, he could still have married Gert, he could still have had two children by this time, he could, yes, he could have had a farm of his own. And, Pa his friend instead of his enemy.

Elof stopped to catch his breath. He looked across the east end of the field, saw where the farm buildings of Gert's folks lay. Old Man Hansen, her father, an arthritic cripple, was sitting under a shading maple tree. He didn't see Gert around and he guessed she was busy in the house with Ma Hansen, out of sight.

In some ways, any thoughts about Gert were ridiculous. In the first place, Elof didn't feel too excited thinking about her. She was nice, and he liked her. But as for loving . . . hardly. In the second place, she was too blasted tall, almost six inches taller than he. Moreover, she had the square shoulders of a man, had the lanky legs of a man. Only three things made her a woman in his eyes: she had soft brown shoulder-length hair, she had full-sized brood-mare breasts, and she had clean and industrious house-keeping instincts. A comely worker.

A yellow-and-black bumblebee sussed around his straw hat. He stood stock-still, knowing that a trembling finger, like a fluttering leaf or flower, might catch the glossy, staring eye of the hap-hazardly flying insect. He stood like a statue, hoping that if he made no move the stinging creature would buzz on. A cold shiver brushed over his skin as he watched it. He noted the blue-black shine of its head in the glinting sunlight. He envied it its fancies. It was both beauty and threat.

He thought a moment about the two qualities: beauty, threat. Perhaps it was for the lack of them that he wasn't traveling over the far curves of the earth-ball like a conquering hero.

The bumblebee sizzed right up under his straw hat, directly in front of his eyes, hovering not an inch from the point of his sweaty nose, hovering, its huge insect eyes peering at him, so close he fancied he saw his reflection in the black globe peepers. The suddenness of the bumblebee's interest didn't give him time to scare. And by the time his nervous system had worked up appropriate horror, the bee was gone.

Cor and Wilbur came up then on their rattling binders and Elof blinked and opened his eyes and awoke. Elof stood still a moment more, then waved.

The two youths studied him from under their sun-faded straw hats and, at last recognizing him, waved back. Cor was in front and his habit was to lean forward in his seat, his dark eyes narrow and cynical. Wilbur came behind and he lay back in his seat, smiling, easygoing.

Elof made a motion showing he wanted a drink, holding an imaginary jug to his mouth. Wilbur smiled broadly, white teeth glowing, and he pointed to a crudely set-up shock. And, following Cor, he rattled on, not stopping.

Elof went over and got down on his knees, his overall pinching and oozing sweat in the squeeze of his squat. He rustled around under the shock, was pricked by a thorny wild rose, chased out a rabbit, at last found the jug. It was covered with a wet sack for insulation. The cob cork came off with a *p-fummb!* and he lifted the jug onto the crook of his elbow and tipped it up and guggled awhile, letting the bubbles flap through the corners of his mouth, in and out, *glug-gleg, glug-glig.* He finished and recorked the jug and set it under the bundles and wiped his mouth and sighed a great lung-emptying sigh.

He turned to the shocking again, feeling tired. His mind drooped. Flies buzzed around his head. He tried to think of how Hilda might have looked had she lived, but his imagination wouldn't turn over. He shocked on, monotonously bending and bowing and scraping, sometimes wiping sweat from his face, sometimes involuntarily breaking wind, sometimes moaning a little to himself.

The bluchers heavied on his feet, and he began to walk awkwardly. They chafed the sides of his foot, and when he put his mind to it he could feel one of the seams sandpapering the scab on the blood-poison wound. Blisters formed along the edge of his heels and after a while he had a vision of flames shooting out from the soles of his feet.

By three o'clock in the afternoon, lunch time, he had worked his way around to the northeast corner where the field was bound by the east-west Thunderbolt railroad tracks and where some chokecherry brush was growing. Cor and Wilbur, stopping near the house yard across the field, waved for him to come up. Elof waved back and, grabbing a handful of red black berries from the brush, started in. He ate and savored and spat as he went, and in a little while found himself thirstier than ever from the puckering action of the chokecherries.

Elof saw Kaes coming from the yard with a change of horses, and, behind him, striding easily with a basket and pail, like a limber long yearling heifer, came Gert wearing a wide straw hat. So. She wasn't home with Ma Hansen after all. Pregnant Gretch, he guessed, had called her over to help.

When Elof came up Gert was sitting in the stubbles busy setting out the lunch in the shade of the first binder.

"Hi," Elof said, his glands and tongue still a mite paralyzed from the chokecherry astringent.

She looked up, shaking back her long bob beneath her hat. For a moment she apparently didn't know whether to acknowledge his greeting or not. She set out another white porcelain cup and finally said flatly, "Hello."

Elof didn't know what to do with the flatness, so he sat down.

An oat prickle had caught between the toes of his left foot, working down into the tender wet flesh of the webbing. It itched so badly he decided to take off his blucher. His bare, sweaty, straw-speckled foot came out with a slurking sound. He brushed off the straw and the prickle and rubbed a finger over the tender itching spots. It was a good feeling. He puffed like a dog just in from a wild romp.

He looked at Kaes and Cor and Wilbur replacing smoking horses with fresh ones. He knew he should have offered to help them, but he felt too tired. He tipped back his straw hat.

Gert poured him a cup of cold tea and handed him a cheese sandwich.

"Thanks," he said. He settled back into the stubbles, careful to stay in the shade of the binder. He gulped thirstily, finishing the cup in one draught. The cork-dust taste of the chokecherries still lingered and so he reached for more.

She filled his cup again. "You must be dry."

"Ate some chokecherries."

"Oh."

He asked for still another cup.

"Say, you must've worked too."

He looked up, pleased to note a pinch of admiration in her tone. "I'll say. First man's work I've done in a coon's age."

"Like it?"

"Well, I dunno. I'm doing it." Then, as an afterthought, he added, "I know this much. I was a fool to leave this country in the first place."

She said nothing.

Before he could curb his tongue he added another comment, "But I'll survive it. We Lofbloms're tough."

Still she said nothing. Her gray eyes narrowed a little, then opened again.

Disgusted with his sudden loose tongue, he bit viciously into the cheese sandwich.

She busied herself with the lunch basket.

As he ate he noted her clothes: a white dress with a fine red stripe, a blue belt, and strap shoes. Her dress billowed out over her hips, making her waist seem slim, slimmer than he remembered it, and it gave her fat, slightly pendulant bosom a matronly fullness.

Her lips, though thin and determined, were moist and inviting, and he remembered the quick good-night kiss she had given him on that one Sunday-night date he had had with her and how it had lingered with him a long time afterward. He remembered the date with double-edged shame: he had gone out with her because he had vaguely hoped she could give him a glimpse of his old-time Hilda-ecstasy, Gert had been Hilda's best friend; and he had gone out with her in the hope that he could overcome his fear of women, he was fearfully self-conscious of his shortcoming. But Gert had remained Gert, and he had remained a slowbull, a mama's boy. Thinking about it all now, he choked over the cheese and bread.

Just who and what was Gert? he asked himself. Just who and what? First, she was a farm maid. Second, since there wasn't a corpuscle of poetry in her, she was obviously created by the heavenly sportsmen for the purpose of breeding and baking bread. Her world was a world of dickering at the market with clerks who made penny overcharges, of gossiping with neighborhood wives about mysterious women's troubles, of talking about babies and abortions, of complaining about rough-and-ready husbands.

Elof nodded his conclusions to himself. Sure. Let Pa have her. She fits him to a T. Two dull clods in the same furrow.

He held out his cup for still another refill.

"Really," she said, "you must be bottomless."

"I am. Like I said, I ate chokecherries."

"Well. A person'd almost wonder why God created them if they make people so thirsty."

"Jelly."

She became instantly attentive. "That's one thing I never had any luck with. Making chokecherry jelly."

"Huh. Well, it's probably all in the recipe. Ma had one that raised the flavor warts on my tongue."

"Really?"

"It was wunnerful. Best jelly ever made."

"Where did"—she hesitated a second; then went on—"where did she get it?"

"Gramma Alfredson gave it to her."

"Well," Gert said. She sat erect, like a person doing some very fast thinking.

Kaes came up, puffing, his big thick legs swinging out a little in clumsy walk. He squatted on his heels and threw a log-heavy arm around her hips. "Well, an' how's my big hired girl today?" He wrestled her a little, roughed up her bosom until she pushed him away. "Gert, believe you me, it's a good thing I married yer sister or, wife or no wife, I'd chase you down a pasture lane."

Coolly she shooed exploring flies off the lunch.

Cor came up and slid silently to a crouch on the ground. He

groaned and closed his bitter dark eyes when his sore seat lit on a half-decayed cornstalk. In a moment Wilbur joined them, too, sitting cockily on his heels, rocking, smiling, his rosy face alight with health. Both Cor and Wilbur took sandwiches and tea from Gert and began to eat wolfishly.

"Yep," Kaes said, taking his lunch from her, too, and munching and hinting heavily, "yep, Gert'd make a real wife for somebody all right."

"Oh, for catsake, shut up," Gert said.

"Yep. A real wife. Strong legs. Fire. Kickback. An' such wonderful big puddin' soft charms she can take 'em an' throw 'em over her shoulder." He gestured to show how it might be done.

Gert slapped him.

Kaes and Wilbur choked over their food in laughter. Cor's face barely cracked.

"Yep. She could a long been married. But, so it goes. Other things come along an' things change. Yep." Kaes opened his wide mouth and surrounded the rest of his sandwich.

Elof tried to laugh with Kaes, with the same heavy accents, tried to grunt in tune with him, but found his stomach turning a little.

There was a noise behind them and Kaes, looking across the field from the shadow of the binder where they sat, remarked a car coming onto his yard. "By golly, that's Screech."

Elof glanced up inquiringly.

Wilbur said, "Screech is Kaes's Arctic boss from Sioux City."

"Yeh, an' I know what that buzzard's come for too," Kaes muttered. "He's gonna eat my ear out for closin' up the station through harvest." Kaes reached for another sandwich. "Well, he can good an' well wait until I've et my lunch."

There was a silence. Teeth nicked together. Food sluggled in throats.

At last Kaes couldn't stand it any longer and he got to his feet and made as if to start for the yard. But by that time Screech had spotted him and had begun walking toward them, Snip the pup following. Kaes stopped after a few steps.

Screech came up, tall, cadaverous, with a hitch in his walk and a smirk on his lips. He was well dressed in a gray suit, flashed a gold Waldemar watch chain on his vest. He wore a white straw panama hat.

The two men stood talking. They were out of earshot, and Elof turned his attention to his aching feet and the half cup of tea he still had left. Idly he watched Gert as she began to repack the lunch basket. When Cor and Wilbur lay back in the stubbles and rolled and lighted cigarettes, he joined them, carefully holding the lighted end over his sweaty straw hat to keep from starting a fire in the field.

The voices of the two men rose and then Kaes stalked toward the binder, Screech following, protesting, pleading. "Listen, Hinke, you can't do that. You signed a contract with us and that contract says you agree to handle our stuff every day of the year outside acts of God. And that means every day."

"Come down on your base rate an' I'll open her for business. This way I can't afford to do it right in the middle of harvest."

"Hinke, listen, man, if you don't open up we'll bust you."

"The hell you say," Kaes pushed Snip to one side. "Down, you danged fool."

"We will. And we can."

"Screech, that station, I own it timber an' shingle, an' the acre it's sittin' on. What I say goes."

Screech threw up his hands as if he were dealing with a mad man. "But, Hinke, you signed a contract. Black on white."

"Well, that's just too bad. Get down, Snip."

The pup squatted on its hairy, rosy belly. It looked up, ready for more play.

"Hinke, if you don't open up we'll build a station on the fourth corner."

"Go ahead. It'll cost you a pretty penny to build on that bog."

"Is that so?"

"Yes. It won't hold butterflies wearin' snowshoes. It'll cost you ten times what it'd cost you to lower the base rate for me."

"Hinke, I'm going to recommend that we take that agency away from you."

"Huh, I'll get another line then."

"Which one? There are no others but Antarctic. And they're selling at the same base rate."

"I'll get me the cut rate then."

"That's sour gas. You don't want that. You'll find yourself in the same predicament Solen's got himself in. Just two jumps ahead of the poorhouse." Screech paused, scratched his nose. "No, Hinke, you don't want sour gas."

Kaes flung out an arm. "What the hell do I care, as long as it makes the car run. Right today the neighbors're goin' over to Solen because they can get juice six cents cheaper than what Bill Cooper and I have to sell the good gas at."

"Yes, and in two months take a look at their motors. You know what wrecks they'll be. Besides, Solen isn't getting the tourist trade. And on this corner, that's the big thing."

Kaes stood with legs apart. The dog was up again and mischievously worrying his pant leg. "Screech, I te' you what I'll do. I'll open up again, but I'll leave off the three cents that's suppose to be my profit. I'll sell her for the same price you sell to me."

"Now you are crazy. A minute ago you wouldn't open up in harvesttime with three cents' profit, and now you're opening up with no profit at all."

"I hate to lose the neighbor trade."

"Besides, your contract stipulates you've got to charge three cents more than the wholesale price."

Kaes stood swollen. He looked blackly at the ground. The pup growled. "I suppose Old Harry needed some quick pin money an' so he upped the price a little?"

"Now, now, Hinke, let's not get personal. In fact, I didn't hear you."

"Well, why did he raise the base rate?"

"I don't know. I don't ask such questions." Screech wiped his sweating face with a glaring white handkerchief. "Maybe the cost of getting the sweet gas out of the ice-locked ground is gone up. Maybe a Christmas tree broke, or they hit thief sand, or they hit a stretch with mustang liniment it it. You see, it costs money to get black gold out of frozen ground. And then there's the loss that goes with breathing. Change in temperature."

Kaes stood dumb. The technical jargon stopped him.

Screech went on. "We can't let you sell three cents below our advertised price, even if you do take the loss yourself. We'll have all our other stations around, like at Hello and Hicksville and Amen, jumping down our throats. Besides, you signed a contract and you've got to follow company policy whether you like it or not."

Elof felt suddenly sorry for Kaes, and bitter against the city-slicking Screech. Forgetting his tired limbs, stumping his cigarette out in the dust, he moved on the ground a little and broke in, "Say, Mr. Screech, I don't like to be a buttinsky, but did you say the base rate at Bill Cooper's Antarctic was the same as Arctic's?"

Screech stared coldly at him. "Yes."

"Are the two in cahoots then?"

Screech turned to Kaes. "Who's he?"

Kaes said shortly, his face twisting as if he were surprised to get support from Elof's quarter, "A friend a mine." He reached down to pet the pup.

"Oh."

Elof saw Cor and Wilbur perk up too. He went after Screech. That college course in economics, one of the few courses he managed to get a passing grade in, might pay off at last. "You haven't answered my question, Mr. Screech." Elof tipped his straw hat on the back of his head, his straight gold hair slipping over one temple.

Screech's cold eyes ran over Elof's clothes, his big shoes, his patched and sweaty overalls, his floppy straw hat. At last Screech said, with the air of a man cautiously trying to figure out if he were talking to a prince in pauper's clothes, "Like I said, unexpected expenses."

"And not monopoly practices?"

Screech bore down on him with a long finger. "I see you've read a book."

"Could be."

"And I suppose that book told you about the Sherman Anti-Trust Law?"

"What's that got to do with it?"

"Just that it's illegal for both Arctic and Antarctic to connive at rigging prices."

"Baloney."

"What's more, Old Harry don't even run Arctic any more.

Arctic's been busted into forty-eight companies, one for each state, and each one has its own boss."

Elof dug into his memory. "What about interlocking directorships?"

"What about 'em?"

"In this case, Old Harry sits on all the boards, and in his person represents the tie-up between 'em all."

Again Screech stopped to study Elof, examining his clothes, his manner. He started to laugh, stopped, asked of Kaes, "Where'd that jackass learn to bray?"

Elof saw Kaes smile, saw him take out a pack of chewing tobacco, saw him take a lusty bite. Impishly, though he had never chewed in his life, Elof reached for the pack and, before the astonished eyes of all, took a big pinch and dropped it brown and draggling into his mouth. He chewed and spat, handed back the pack.

"Kaes, just who is this bird?" Screech asked again.

"My hired hand."

"Huh."

Screech stepped back a little. He asked Elof, "What're you doin' here on the farm?"

"I like it here."

"You don't belong here."

"No?"

"You should go to the big city. Work for some big corporation. You've got a future."

"Huh. Thanks. You ain't the first to mention it."

"No, really, I mean it."

"Screech, maybe you don't know your farm boys very well. Maybe you're a little behind the times. Maybe farm boys are smart nowadays. Maybe they read once in a while. Study." Elof stood up, spat. He opened his shirt and hooked his thumbs under his suspenders and hoisted up his overall pompously. Cool air rushed up inside his pant legs and breezed over his bottom. "Yep, that's us. Smart. You city slickers had better go back to school and get caught up or we country hicks'll skin you down to bone and toenails."

Screech snapped his mouth to. He glanced at the ground a

moment and then, pointing a long warning finger at Kaes, said, "Hinke, I'll give you till tomorrow morning to have your filling station open, or by all that's mighty I'll bust that agency right from under you." Screech wheeled, stilted away. When Screech reached the yard he got into his car, slammed the door shut, and drove off, kicking up a spume of gray dust.

Elof smiled, and he looked at the others, sure that he had really made a hit with them for having put Mr. Wisemouth in his place.

They were smiling all right, but they were eying him too, carefully, with the same look they had given Screech.

Elof's blue eyes opened, then closed.

He remembered. In his own small way, like Screech, he had a knowledge that was out of their ken, and they were suspicious of it, even though for a moment he had turned it to their advantage.

Elof dropped his suspenders, pulled his straw hat forward over his eyes. Tiredly he went over and picked up his left shoe and put it on. He kicked the pup out of his way. He started for a new windrow. He spat out the cud of raw, stinging tobacco and with his tongue thoroughly cleaned his mouth, spitting, rubbing his lips on a wet shirt sleeve.

It was when he had set up a half-dozen shocks that he suddenly realized what he had done. He had kicked away the one good chance he had had for months to hook on with a big outfit. Screech might have been able to land him the job.

Kicked it. Kicked it. And all because he was a lonesome show-off.

CHAPTER VII: A Little Fun

> . . . What do the Elofs live for? Food and its
> voiding? Sex and its issuance? God the Love? Satan
> the Hate? Self? Neighbors?
>> Or is it they live "in hope?"
>> We ask the Elofs and they don't know.
>> We ask the wise men and they won't say . . .

Elof had a summer cold and wasn't feeling too good. It wasn't a bad cold, just the sniffles with a thick head, but it was enough to remind him that he was really in a bad way.

But worse than the cold were the bluchers. After paying up his bill at Dr. Mars, he still hadn't had enough left out of Kaes's check to buy new shoes.

The bluchers were getting to be a serious problem. Every day there was evidence that they were stunting his mind, cramping his style. Only last week he had missed a chance at something terrific.

A lazy-smiling blond had come into the store and Elof had clerked her. Elof liked her the minute he saw her. After a while he got her name: Marge Berg, schoolmarm from the Little Rock District. Right away his eyes began to shine. And hers did. But then, as luck would have it, she had asked him to get a dress belt from the dry-goods section. Desperately he had tried to distract her attention, get her to think of something else, something he could get from the side he was standing on. A little surprised, she had insisted. At last he had reluctantly stepped from behind the counter and of course she had immediately spotted his bluchers and the way his feet slobbered around in them. It had cooked his goose.

Such things were hard to take. Especially for a young buck blessed with a decent supply of pep and sperm.

It was evening, and the sun was sinking fast.

Cor and Wilbur drove up in a two-door Chevy sedan, windows rolled down. Cor was driving, leaning over the wheel and, as always, looking dark and secretive, a bitter turn on his lips, and Wilbur was sitting beside him holding a bottle of pop fizzing with alcohol spike. They stopped and honked.

Elof stepped outside. "Hi."

"How's tricks?" Wilbur greeted, smiling, blooming with his usual red-faced health.

"Oh, so-so. What's up?"

"Get yer Sunday duds on an' we'll drive down an' jazz the girls t'Amen."

"On Thursday night?"

Cor said, his face grayish despite a summer's sunning, "It's Young People's Night at one of the churches there."

"Oh."

Wilbur said, "C'mon. Amen's full of girls, two to a man, an' they're just achin' to go out an' have a little fun."

"Can't," Elof said after a moment.

"Why not?"

"Ain't got the duds."

"What's wrong with those you wore Satiddy night?"

"Well—and I ain't got a decent hat."

"Go bareheaded."

"And then too, I ain't got the shoes."

"Oh."

"That's the worst of it. Look." Elof lifted his foot, showing the bulking toes of the bluchers. "A man can maybe walk in these, but he can't june a woman in 'em."

Cor looked a moment, snickered. "Cripes, what a hoof."

Elof colored. "It's the shoes. They're too big."

"Well, if they wasn't, you'd be a monstrosity."

Elof colored still more.

"Aw, t'heck with the shoes. Let's go," Wilbur said, tipping the fizzing bottle into his mouth, guggling a few swallows. He wiped his lips and held it out to Elof. When Elof declined Cor took it and finished the bottle.

Wilbur said, "C'mon, get yer duds on. Let's raise Old Ned. Do you good. Besides, it'll be dark by the time the meetin' lets out."

Elof stood still a moment, thinking. Cor and Wilbur were good muleys to have come for him. He just couldn't turn down this proffer of friendship. Elof nodded. Yes, he really did need a little fun, did need a girl. He was in a rut. "Okay. I'll ask the old man if he won't step out of turn tonight an' tend the store."

Pa grumbled. "Couldn't resist it, huh? Gonna start girlin' again, huh?"

"Maybe."

"Where you goin'?"

"Nowhere. Just around." Elof smiled a little.

"Where?"

"Amen."

"Oh."

"If Gert hasn't moved to Amen during the night, you won't have to worry."

Pa brushed his red face and bald head with a freckled hand. He had the hard glare of a man looking for a dog to kick.

"You want to be a little more careful, Pa, about how you show your hand. Because that's one time you got your tail over the line."

Pa raised surprised brows.

And before Pa could collect himself, Elof went to the back room to dress up.

He put on a red tie, a white shirt with a collar carefully starched to hide worn edges, his gray suit with the swing-back jacket, and a pair of gray cotton socks. And the big brown bluchers. He clubbed past Pa and out onto the porch.

"Shake it up," Cor said.

"Wait," Wilbur said, "how about some more pop?"

Elof stood uncertainly. Should he pay for it out of his own pocket? Or should he just go in and take some?

"We got the mix," Wilbur said, "how's about you furnishin' the pop?"

Elof nodded and turned back into the store. This time Pa could foot the fun.

"Now what?" Pa asked, taking a chew of tobacco from the pocket of his white shirt.

"Need some pop. We're going drinking."

"What? An' you a Covenant child?"

"So what?"

"Ye're really hungerin' to go to hell, ain't you?"

"Could be." Elof trembled inside. He was continually surprising himself tonight. Some demon seemed to have taken possession of his soul and have given him courage.

"An' your ma just dead?"

"Yeh. And Ma just dead." Elof looked directly into Pa's eyes. "Ma just dead and Gert alive."

Pa shut up.

Elof picked up six bottles of mix and walked out.

Pa followed him to the door, standing bulky and hard-eyed in the doorway. "I'm lockin' the door at twelve sharp," he said.

"Okay," Elof said, shrugging. He pointed to a haystack in a nearby field. "I can curl up in that if I have to."

The old man shut up again.

Elof crawled past Wilbur sitting on the front seat and dropped himself onto the back seat. He rolled a cigarette and lighted it.

Cor snickered once more and then started up the car. He took off on two wheels and in a minute had the car roaring down toward Amen.

Cor drove hard. He took the corners on the inside, whether he had the right of way or not, skinned telephone poles, and, topping a high hill just east of Amen, threw out the gear and began coasting. In the falling evening sunlight the car streaked into town like a flying, shining mackerel. Cor braked hard and stopped in front of a pool hall.

"Coastin' like that is dangerous," Elof remarked, throwing the butt of his cigarette away.

"Aw, cut it," Cor said.

"What if you'd a met somebody and had to stop quick? You'd've got thrown turn-turtle into the ditch."

"Aw, cut it."

Wilbur laughed and said, getting his neat narrow buttocks niftily out of the car, "Let's coke up in here."

"But I just got us some back at Pa's," Elof said.

"We'll save that for later on. When we get way out in the country with our chickens."

"Okay. Just as you say."

They entered the pool hall. Wilbur led the way to a booth.

On the table in the booth stood a cluster of utensils: salt and pepper shakers, a catsup bottle, a jar of sugar, a menu, a folder of paper napkins.

A greasy-faced man with an involuntary wink came up. "What'll you have, boys?"

"The usual."

"Comin' up."

The man brought three bottles of coke and left.

With a smile Wilbur looked around and then drew a narrow bottle out of a hip pocket. He screwed off the cap.

Like Cor and Wilbur, Elof drank a swallow or two off the top of his pop—it was of an old-blood color—and then held it out for Wilbur to pour in three fingers of silver spike. Elof put his thumb over the opening and tipped up the bottle, looking around to see if he had been seen doing it. The bottle fizzed, drips running over his thumb.

"Well, here's t'you," Elof said, drinking.

"T'you," Cor echoed, and drank.

"Ah," Wilbur said, "this stuff gives a guy ideas."

"Puts a whistle in your pist'l," Cor said.

"Yep," Elof said, feeling himself warm up. Imitating the boys, he rolled and lighted a cigarette. It surprised him that these country boys should act so worldly-wise.

He looked around the pool hall, drawing himself up tall in the seat of the booth. In back three farm boys were fumbling cues around a lighted green table, and in front two dark-browed truckers were leaning over a tobacco counter. A sign

NO SPIKING ALLOWED
PROSECUTED BY LAW

hung over a picture of the President.

Elof nodded. "Yep, good for what ails you."

"Yep."

Elof said, "I tell you what, fellows. When Young People's lets out, we'll drive around, see, drive down Dater's Lane there, and when we see three gals traipsing along, you two hop out and ask 'em, see, and then that way they won't get a glim at my hoofs."

Wilbur nodded.

"Think that's a good idea?" Elof asked Cor, who was sitting beside Wilbur across the table.

"Sure."

Wilbur said, "Better still, why not let Elof drive? Then he's got an excuse for not comin' out a the car."

"I'm drivin'," Cor said.

"Aw, c'mon," Wilbur said, "you kin drive again after we pick up the gals."

"I'm drivin'."

"But Elof's hoofs'll chase the girls away."

Cor held stiff for a moment, then sagged. "All right." Cor swigged down the rest of his drink.

Elof and Wilbur finished too.

They all got up then and stepped outdoors, Elof following the boys, trying to act as if he were as well dressed as they. He picked at an imaginary piece of lint on the front of his coat.

It was dark out and Elof put on the headlights as he backed away from the curb. He drove slowly, getting the feel of the old Chevy, while Wilbur and Cor spiked and drank the pop Elof had taken along. Occasionally Cor, sitting beside him, gave him a quick swig.

After a while Elof said, jiggling the steering wheel a little, "How you fellows drive this car is beyond me."

"What's wrong with it?" Cor asked.

"Why, you ain't got no brake. And the clutch, it catches the minute you let it out a little."

"If you don't like it, get from behind the wheel."

Elof shut up.

After a silence and a few more drinks Wilbur asked, "You goin' after it t'night, Elof, if you get a good bim?"

"After what?" Elof asked, tightening.

"Oh, come now."

"I don't know what you're talking about."

Cor snickered.

"Look," Elof said, abruptly turning his sails and going with the wind, "I once saw a line-up of syphilitic whores and I've never forgotten it. It's made me careful."

"Where?" Cor asked, curiosity suddenly making his eyes friendly.

"At State. A housemate was a pre-medic, and the morning he started the course he heard a lecture about women. I went along with him. His prof started talking, said, 'Well, boys, we know you're going after it, so this is what may happen if you do.' And a door opened and in walked a half-dozen women and men, whores and pimps, so on, all covered with watery sores." Thinking of it again, Elof shivered.

Wilbur laughed. "Aw, heck, the stuff around here is clean."

Elof shook his head. "You never know. Rotten salesmen have been known to seduce dumb farm bunnies, you know."

Cor slipped into his fierce mood again. "Well, I don't know about you, but I kin spot a sour one a mile off."

"That's what you think."

Wilbur broke in, leaning forward and putting his elbows on the backs of their seats: "One thing about these gals around here though. You gotta give 'em a false name or they'll check up on you. Everybody's related in Siouxland, practically, an' they'll track you down through their relatives."

Cor said, "Well, my name's always John Johnson."

Wilbur said, "An' mine's always Pete Peterson. From Sioux City. It's that big city Sioux City part that gets 'em."

Elof said, driving along, "Huh. Those names sound pretty phony to me. Me, I'll take the name of Perry. Perry Pickle."

"Pickle?" Cor scoffed.

"Yeh. Some people wear the name of Bean or Peabody, or Zach Wheat or Alfalfa Bill. So on. Me, I'm Pickle."

"Where in God's name did you get a-hold of that handle?"

"Oh—just picked it out of thin air." To mention Tobias Smollett's book was to ruin the mite of comradeship grown up among them this night.

Wilbur asked, his eyes beady with alcohol, "About time the meetin' lets out, ain't it?"

"I guess so."

"Drive around an' see."

Elof wheeled the car over to the church. The big-windowed structure loomed up sepulchrally white, its shingled tower spearing toward the stars.

Just as Wilbur guessed, the meeting was over. Headlights were flashing all around, engines were coughing and clearing throats, and cars were jumping into the street. Young men were shouting and waving and whirling steering wheels of lurching machines. Young girls giggled, screamed, broke up in twos and threes and fours, and headed toward Dater's Lane, nincing along, fluttering kerchiefs, emanating perfumes, brandishing imitation-leather purses.

All tingles, Elof nearly rammed a balking Ford.

"Hey, watch where ye're goin'," Cor growled, leaning forward. "Cripes."

"Danged fool never looked."

"That's what you say. You almost hit him."

Elof bit a lip and wheeled through the maze.

He fell in behind another car jerking along. He slowed his motor down to where it was but a whisker away from killing itself.

"Got a good motor here," he said. "That guy up ahead there is in second while I'm still in high."

Cor said, "I told you I had a good car."

They chugged along. Dust billowed up from the graveled street, pinked by the red taillight of the car ahead.

Anxiously Elof peered left, watching for datable girls.

He drove the length of the lane, started back.

"Damn," Wilbur said, "they're all in twos and fours tonight. No threes. Maybe we'll have to bust a four."

"Yeh."

Elof drove up and down the lane four times; still no trio.

"Try a side street," Cor said. "Sometimes them little sage hens drift off that way."

Elof wheeled in and out the cross streets; still no luck.

It became late. The buzzing lane thinned out. The sidewalks were only half populated with eligibles.

Then Cor spotted a trio going down a dark alley. "There!" he exclaimed, pointing past Elof's cheek. Right under his nose, Elof couldn't help noticing the calluses and nicotine stains on Cor's finger.

Elof turned on two wheels and shot up the alley. The three girls shrieked and scattered like chickens. They were farm blonds. Elof braked. Wilbur and Cor hopped out.

Elof watched them. The girls, recovering from their scare, grouped up again, arm around hip, waiting, giggling. All evening there had been occasional puffs of wind out on the prairie, and just now one of them came along and lifted the silk dresses well above the round knobs of their knees, once even showing pink flesh above hose tops. The middle girl had a hat with a feather on it, and for a brief second the wind-puff was strong enough to twirl it like a windmill blurring. Cor and Wilbur pounced on them, put lusty circling arms over the shoulders of the two out-side girls. They jabbered. In the headlight shine Elof could see their mouths flabbing.

The girls seemed reluctant. Elof sweat. He roared up the motor a little, let it fall to an idle.

Cor and Wilbur jollied the girls some more, word and hand. But the girls were firm.

At last Wilbur left them and stepped up to the car.

Elof leaned out. "What's the matter?"

"They won't go until Effie's seen who she's to get. She's the one in the middle there with the wild feather."

"Well, tell Effie to come here."

"She won't come."

"Why not?"

"She says she ain't goin' if you don't ask her personal."

"Oh, baloney." Elof shut off the lights. "I suppose I'll have to hobble out then."

"Hey, don't shut them off!"

"Well, cripes, I don't want her to see my shoes."

"T'heck with yer hoofs. Put on them lights or the gals'll fly."

Elof turned the headlights on again.

"Dang fool," Wilbur growled. "What you wanna worry about is: have you got what it takes to hold a girl after you got her?"

"Never mind. I'll get along."

Elof got out; shuffled up to Effie. "Hi," he said.

She looked at him in the lights. She looked and Elof could see she liked him. She nodded, the feather whirring.

"Good girl," Wilbur said, his arm tight around his own girl.

They all got in, Elof and Wilbur in back, girl on lap, and Cor in front with his. Cor drove off with a whosh, and in a little while they were idling down a country road.

The spiked drinks made Elof forget about his feet. He even put his arm around Effie.

At first Effie resisted him. He kidded her awhile and pretty soon tried to kiss her. She resisted. He waited some more; tried again. Then Effie kissed him, full and good, and she snuggled on his lap. She had skinny legs, a little bony, but they had appeal because they were soft just below the buttock and just above the knee. Elof's red face flushed. Gold hair fell over his temple. He pulled her close. In his excitement he hardly noticed she had buck teeth, that every time she smacked him she cut his upper lip a little.

This was the life, Elof thought. Real life. Something like this once a week made a man out of a man. It settled one. Settled one's nerves. Helped one forget one was a flop in life. Drove revolution out of the veins.

After a while Cor stopped the car. Elof looked out. They were on a farmer's yard, parked behind a corncrib. In the moonlight the yard was faintly luminescent, and beyond, a cornfield shimmered, row upon row of gold-tipped black-green.

Effie said, "It's Susie's place."

"John Johnson's girl?" Elof asked, carefully remembering Cor's new name.

"Yeh. An' Pete's too. Susie an' Nellie's sisters."

"Why don't somebody tell me these things?" Elof laughingly complained. He was surprised his tongue was so loose around girls this night. There was no doubt of it—alcohol made a fine social lubricant.

Up front Cor broke free from his girl a moment and turned around. "Gosh, I need a drink. Got anything back there that looks like one?"

"Well," Wilbur said slowly, breaking from his mate too. "I

dunno. I think so. I thought I saw some pop around in back here somewheres."

Elof leaned away from Effie. "Yeh, I'm pretty sure there's some there on the floor."

"Wait'll I light up," Wilbur said.

The girls were silent. Their silk dresses and underclothes rustled intimately in the dark of the car.

Wilbur flashed a match. Flushed male faces and pale powdered female visages leered at each other in the light of the flickering orange flame. "Yeh. Here they are." Wilbur doused the light.

"Got an opener?"

"Yeh."

There was a sound of uncorking; then a sprinkling; then a pouring.

"Who all wants some?" Wilbur asked.

The girls said nothing.

"Come, come, gals. You want a drink, don't you?"

Effie said suddenly, her rump muscles balling up hard on Elof's stubby thighs, "You spiked it, didn't you?"

"Why, no," Wilbur said.

"You did too. I heard you."

Susie said, "Oh, heck, Effie. What's the dif? You're always so scared you're gonna lose something." Susie laughed thickly.

"Yeh," Nellie murmured.

"Maybe I have got something to lose," Effie said.

Elof coughed, asked, "Mind if I have some?"

"No. Go ahead."

Elof joined the others, Effie sitting like a harsh pair of boards on his lap.

When the drinks were down Cor led Susie out of the car. They disappeared behind a haystack. Then Wilbur clambered into the front seat with Nellie and began to neck her madly.

Effie said, "That pop was spiked, wasn't it?"

"No."

"It was."

"Why?"

"Your breath stinks."

"Naw, that's just your imagination." Elof thought she was

pretty dumb. If it was spike she was sensitive to, why hadn't she smelled his earlier drinks, the one he had gulped down in the pool hall?

"Peuu! You did too spike it."

"Come now."

"Then you must a got some sour pop."

"Aw," Elof said, trying to keep her tight in his arms, "you're probably only smellin' my cold."

Effie struggled.

"Oh, c'mon, I only got the sniffles. It's all right."

"I don't know," Effie said. "You sure stink."

"Well, if you'd taken some a that sour pop you wouldn't've noticed it."

"The heck I wouldn't've. That's one stink I can always smell. Even if it comes from my own mouth." She jerked her head imperiously. The feather whirred.

The hat with the wild feather began to irk Elof. Not only did the hat serve to increase Effie's slender height, but the feather turning in its socket made a noise like teeth knersing together.

Elof whispered, drawing back a little, "Your little windmill needs a greasing. Some three-in-one, I'd say."

"Don't you like it?"

"Sure I like it. Except that it makes you look like an old hen running with the wind up under her tail."

"Is that so," she hissed.

"Yeh. Take it off."

She said nothing.

"Take it off," Elof said.

"I'll take it off if you'll take the stink off your tongue."

Elof sat still for a moment; then chuckled. "Well, that makes us even."

"Huh," she said.

"Oh, c'mon, let's neck."

"Huh," she said.

"Aw, c'mon," Elof purred, "let's get together here. Time's a-wastin'. Just think, tomorrow we both have to work like hell again. Let's have fun while we can."

"I don't know," Effie said doubtfully.

Elof put his arm around her and begun to hug her again. By concentrating on the high side of her upper lip, he occasionally managed to get a kiss without cutting himself on her buck teeth.

Then Nellie up in the front seat said she had to go in. She was the youngest and she had promised her old man she would be in by twelve o'clock. Besides, she didn't feel very well. Wilbur held her down and said, "Aw, why don't you wait till Susie comes back?"

"What she does is her business."

Wilbur murmured.

Nellie got out. "I have to go."

"Okay. Wait up a minute," Wilbur said, fussing with his clothes and then following her. "At least I kin take you to the door."

As soon as they were gone Elof got ideas. But Effie knew what he wanted and she put up a strong defense.

She was still defending herself when Wilbur came back. "John-son show up yet?" he asked.

"No."

Wilbur got in and sat awhile. By his movements up front Elof could tell he was nervous about them necking in back. Finally Wilbur said, "Look. How's about me drivin' you and yer girl home?"

"Well, Effie?" Elof asked, stroking her cheek.

"It's all right by me. I got to work hard tomorrow."

Wilbur nodded and whirled the car off the yard and started down the road.

"Where do you live?" Wilbur asked.

"At Henry's. Right where the Big Rock River joins the Sioux."

Again Wilbur nodded and he drove on, stonily silent.

It was Elof's last chance to get anywhere and he began to wrestle her in earnest.

They rumbled around on the back seat, and all of a sudden Elof's big shoe became hooked under the front seat that Wilbur was sitting on. He tried to pull it free, but it wouldn't come.

"Quit it," Effie said.

"I ain't doin' nothin'," Elof said. "I'm only——" Again he tried to jerk his blucher free. It was stuck in such a way that he couldn't get Effie where he wanted her. It had him pinned flat on his back.

"Say, I said to quit it!" Effie said.

Elof almost laughed out loud. What she was thinking about wasn't remotely possible, his foot being where it was. He was a lassoed, tied-down stallion.

He jerked again. Again. But the big blucher wouldn't come free.

And up front Wilbur stiffened, acting as if he were trying hard not to notice anything was out of the way, driving the car carefully to avoid the bumps in the road. Elof struggled; then lay back, laughing. This was really funny. It was so funny he didn't have the heart to ask Wilbur to lift up from his seat a little, to disillusion him as to what was really going on. Let Wilbur think the worst for the moment—that he was being a man with a woman. It was a role not often imputed to him. It was a pleasant myth; a most pleasant myth.

At last Wilbur turned on a yard.

Effie, stiff with fury, high-heeled out and quickly scurried up the walk and vanished into the frame farmhouse.

Elof lay there, pinned down, watching her go.

Wilbur turned, letting the motor idle. "You should'n'a rushed her, man."

"Rushed her?"

"Yeh. You probably hurt her feelin's goin' so fast."

"Hurt her feelings, hell. I was only trying to get my foot loose." Elof tried to sit up. "I couldn't've reached her with a ten-foot pole if I'd a wanted to. Get off that front seat once."

CHAPTER VIII: Crazy Stubborn

. . . What is this momentum that drives us on?
This mighty urge that scuds us over the sudsing
maelstrom? From where comes it? When were its
first arisings? When and where will be its final
subsidings?

What is there in us that "goes on," and hence
makes us believe in "going on"?

It is there. In me. In you.

It's strong enough in me to impel me to plant
and grow a garden, and marry and have a family,
and plan and write books . . .

Then Kaes Hinke called again and this time wanted to know if Elof could help him with the threshing.

Elof said he would. He still needed money bad.

He put on his clothes and bluchers. He packed up his belongings: his Sunday clothes, his *Peregrine Pickle,* and a lesson.

At the end of the first day, a day of pitching oat bundles on and off a rack from dawn to dusk, he was quite surprised to find he wasn't tired. Only one thing irked: his blucher had chafed open the blood-poison scar on his stubby toe.

The second day he took in stride, too, except that later in the afternoon, around five o'clock, a sleepy feeling came out of his sore foot and spread throughout his body: veins, tissues, glands, everywhere.

After he had pitched off his last load at dark, had driven home to Kaes's yard from a neighbor's, had stalled and unharnessed and fed his team of horses in the barn, had eaten supper, Elof clumsed out onto the back porch and in the light coming through the open door took off his shoe. There it was. The toe and the whole foot inflamed again.

The pup Snip, already possessing a keen nose for open meat, came up out of the dark, tried to lick it. Elof chased him away.

Elof sat looking at it awhile, numbly realizing it was serious, maybe even dangerous; and at last, pushing through a stupor fog, got up and went into the kitchen where Gretch, dressed in red-trimmed gray and heavily pregnant, was washing dishes.

"Got some salve, Gretch?"

She glanced around questioningly, then glanced down at his bare foot. "Oh my." Quick sympathy suffused her narrow lean face. Blue patches under her eyes deepened. She shook her head in commiseration, ruffling up the uneven, frizzled ends of her over-long brown bob.

Kaes, playing with Toots in her nightgown on the other side of the table, glanced up too. "Hey, that looks bad, boy. Better dope it up with something with a real bite to it. Stronger than ordinary salve, anyway."

"Got anything?"

"Yeh. Just a minute." Kaes stood up. "Now, Toots, get to bed. It's way after your bedtime anyway."

Toots whimpered a little.

" 'Get,' I said." Kaes shoved her toward the bedroom; then awked to the outside door. "Be back in a jiff."

Elof sat down on a chair, keeping his bare foot well in the shadow.

Gretch murmured, "You should a told us sooner." She wiped her hands in her apron, just above the mound of baby.

"Yeh, I know. But I guess I just didn't think of it."

"It hurts?"

"Some. But then a man can't stop for a hurt."

"That's true. Still an' all though———"

"Never get anything done that way."

Kaes came stamping in. "Yep. Just as I thought. Got some left yet. Real salve. Stronger than red onions cured in brine. You know that gelding I'm drivin'? That black on the right side?"

"Yeh?"

"Well, she once had a shoulder sore big enough to feed a quart a worms. Wouldn't heal worth sour apples. Wouldn't even heal in winter. So finally I got this salve from the vet'nary." Kaes waved a big oily box of purple salve. "Heals everything from A to Izzard. Just put it on an' in the mornin' it'll be as good as new."

"Kaes!" Gretch protested. "Horse salve?"

"Sure. Why not? If it heals horses, it should heal men. A sore is a sore, whether it's on horse meat or man meat."

Gretch shook her head. "But, Kaes. Men are Christians."

"Then I pity God on Judgment Day."

Elof said, trying to smile, "It's all right. I've used something like it before."

"Gretch. Get me some bandages. An' some hot water an' soap," Kaes ordered officiously, squatting short and broad on his heels. He lifted the foot onto his knee. He pressed a thumb here and there. "Hurt? Hurt here? Hurt?"

"A little."

Gretch brought some hot water and a bar of tar soap.

It surprised Elof to see how gentle Kaes's hands could be. The firm stubby fingers of the man fondled his foot with soft slippery touches.

Gretch then brought a laundered flour sack and tore off a series of narrow strips, the edges unraveling and dragging lint.

Kaes rubbed the horse salve over the sore on the big toe and well up over the whole top of the foot. "There. Now wrap it up." Kaes grunted as he wound on the rags. "Got something to fasten it with, Gretch?"

Gretch unhooked a safety pin from her blouse. She kept a collection of them there even though Toots was years past the diapering stage and the new baby was still a couple of months away.

"Ah," Kaes said, standing up. "That'll do her up in great shape. Now, if I was you, I'd get to bed."

Elof settled his foot slowly to the floor. The bound foot felt snug. He stood up. "Thanks a lot. I don't know what I'd a done without you."

"Forget it. Get to bed. Tomorry you'll run like a brand-new top."

When Elof awoke in the morning he found his foot puffed out around the bandages.

He dropped back into his sweated pillow. He turned slowly, wondering why he bothered to go on living. Ahead lay a long torturous day. The many mounting morning hours, the long noon hour, the long sloping afternoon, the thousands upon thousands of bundles to be pitched, all on a sore and soggy foot, the poison from it slowly seeping into his system and slowly killing him off, the sleepy toxic feeling—what was the use? And the relentless regret that each moment spent slaving was lost forever, never to be used for dreaming and hoping and reading—what was the use?

Why live in pain? For what? For whom?

There was a stir downstairs, a clumping of feet, a clattering as of someone banging on the black-and-nickel range in the kitchen. A short silence, and then the stair door opened and Kaes's voice sounded. "Elof! Time to get up. Coffee's ready."

Elof sat up and mechanically twisted on his rump and swung his feet to the floor. The neat gray rag rug felt surprisingly cool to the sole of his good foot. He threw out an arm to a white chair and picked up his shirt. And the first thing he knew he was stumbling down the stairs.

"Well," Kaes greeted, looking up over his steaming cup of creamed coffee, his dark hair pillow-tousled, "well, how's the hoof this mornin'?"

Elof swallowed a sudden, silly impulse to cry. "Well, not much better, I guess."

"Let's have a look at it."

Elof sat down and lifted the foot over the knee of his good leg.

Kaes came over and squatted before Elof once more. He unwrapped the bandages slowly. He shook his head. "Not so good. Not so good."

The toe and foot were purple. They were huge. The skin around the whole foot shone like stretched silk.

Elof asked, "Well, what do you think?"

"Better see Doc."

"I suppose I better."

"If it was mine, I know I would."

"Yeh," Elof said, "yeh." He shook his head. "What a life. The more I work, the more I owe."

"Boy, you said it that time. That goes for me too."

"And, what's more, once Doc gets a look at that, I won't be helpin' you for a while."

"Oh, now, don't you worry yourself about that. I'll get along," Kaes said vaguely.

A moment of silence followed.

Then Elof said, "T'hell with it. I'm stayin'."

"Now, now. I'd be careful."

"T'hell with it. I'm going to lick this on my feet. Otherwise I just get deeper in debt."

"Well, I kin use your work, boy, but remember—it's your leg, not mine."

Elof nodded. "Bring on the horse salve."

He forced himself through the morning hours. Each step on the left foot was a hot pain. The foot felt like a misplaced ulcerated tooth. His head bulged with stunning hurt each time he limped.

The horses were kind to him. They followed the long windrows, pulling the red hayrack along. They paced themselves to his speed.

He worked at saving motion. He threw up a whole shock at a time, six bundles. He figured the corners close. He set each bundle carefully.

He toiled on. Sweat. Bundles dripped oat awns into his neck. He scratched. He filled the rack surely, safely. This was the one time in his life he couldn't afford waste motions. He drove the filled rack onto the yard, headed it beside the laughing thresher.

He pitched off, his mind fighting against pain, his mind worrying at saving energy.

He toiled. Ached.

He rested at the morning coffee time.

He pushed on, climbing the high steep forenoon.

Toward noon the threshers moved to Kaes's yard.

Elof was last to load up before dinner. When he came back onto the yard from the north field he found four racks loaded ahead of him. It meant he could eat dinner slowly and take a short nap afterward.

He watered his horses. With hitching straps he tied them up to the back of his full rack to let them munch on the protruding butts of oat bundles.

He trudged slowly across the yard to the house. A gang of men were washing themselves under the trees. They splashed in basins set on chairs. One of them, seeing Elof hobble past, said just loud enough for him to hear, "The kid's got kind of a bad leg there." Elof stiffened himself against an involuntary self-pitying sob. He spotted Cor and Wilbur among the men and he smiled at them. Instantly, with a warming of heart, he remembered the girling party he had shared with them at Amen. The memory of the gay night was so real he could almost taste Effie's toothy kisses again, could almost see the gray whir of her windmill feather.

He hopped slowly past them and climbed the back porch out of the sun.

He sat down and took off his shoe. The puffiness had crept up his leg to his knee.

He took off the bandage. It had cut deep rings into the smelly foot.

He heard little Toots at the screen door. He turned on the step. "Say, Tootsie, will you go get your momma a minute?"

Toots's blue eyes opened wide. She pittered away.

In a moment the door opened and steps came toward him.

He didn't look up. He said, "Well, Gretch, I guess I'm going to lose this leg after all."

"That's no way to talk."

He whirled. It was Gert. "Oh," he grunted. Once again Gert had come over to give Gretch a hand; this time with the big thresher dinner. "I didn't know you was here."

"What did you do to that?"

Elof thought of mentioning the big bluchers; desisted. He made a move to hide his foot from her.

"For catsake, man, you better go see Doc."

Elof shook his head. "No, it'll be all right. Just get me a pan of hot water. The hotter, the better. And if that don't work, I'll make me a hot-milk poultice."

To himself he added, "I'll make me a hot-milk poultice with twice the bite of Pa's." Then, the moment he thought of Pa, with Gert standing near, a soured horse-radish taste spread over his tongue. He spat into the weeds nearby.

She stood a second; then went into the house.

In a little while she came out with a basin of cold water and a kettle of hot steaming water.

He put his foot into the basin, thick toes doubling against the side, skin wrinkling over joints. The foot was numb.

"Pour it in," he said. "I'll tell you when I can't stand it any longer."

She poured, watching him, her eyes narrowed.

At last, when he felt a vague stinging above the ankle, he held up his hand. "That's it."

He watched the steam rise. The smell of melted salve and pus rose to his nostrils. Strangely, he found it pleasant.

Gert stood motionless beside him. There was a feeling about her as if she were on the point of doing something very tender for him but didn't quite dare.

He waited for her to begin talking again.

"I guess I better go in and help Gretch," she said at last.

"Yeh."

He soaked his leg a full hour, delighting in it.

Then wrapping it up again, he went inside and ate a light dinner and took a nap.

At two o'clock the bundle wagons ahead were almost empty and he hurried out to work again.

Once more it was dusk before he got his horses in the barn. He came wearily up the path to the house, his foot a dragging lump.

Again Kaes looked at it, shook his head.

"What shall I do?" Elof asked, trembling. "Pa put a bread-in-hot-milk poultice on it the other time."

"My God. Not that." Kaes swore. "No, if you're gonna poultice 'er, put on a piece a bacon."

"Okay. Let's try that then. Anything."

"Gretch, we've still got a strip a smoked bacon in the cellar, ain't we? One with no salt in?"

"Why—I think so. Sure."

"Good."

With Gert and Gretch watching, Kaes cut a hunk three inches by six from a jerk of bacon, sliced away a good share of the fat and sheet meat, and, with the hard smoke-browned hide up, placed it over Elof's foot, carefully centering the sore beneath. Finally, with some fresh bandages, Kaes tied down the half-inch-thick slab to the foot.

Kaes also found an old red four-buckle boot of his and cut out the end over the toe. "Now," he said, "tomorry, if you still wanna navigate, you wear this."

Elof hobbled off to bed.

Later Gretch came up to his lonely room with a dim night lamp and put a rubber sheet, once Toots's, under his leg to protect the white sheet and mattress beneath.

He lay waiting for sleep. It was strange to feel another creature's flesh warm upon his own.

The next morning, when Elof wanted to take off the bacon and have a look at the foot, Kaes said, "No, no. Let it work some more first."

"Okay, if you say so."

"Does it hurt?"

"Not this morning."

Kaes opened his eyes a little; then half closed them.

At noon Elof couldn't resist taking a peek. He sat on the back porch and pulled the foot out of the red boot. Untying the knot, he slipped off the bandages. The foot came free from the slab with a sucking sound. Both the bacon and the sore had a changed appearance: the one wizened and pale, the other puckered and sickly black. The odd aroma of both smoked and decayed flesh came to him.

Gert brought him a basin of warm water. When he had washed it clean, he found the foot still as swollen as ever.

Kaes came out on the porch. He chewed his wad of tobacco a moment, spat into the weeds, and said, "Well, if you still don't want to go see Doc, there's only one thing left."

"What's that?"

Kaes studied him. "After readin' all them books, ye've probably got too fussy to try it."

"Get it and we'll see."

Kaes lumbered off.

Moments later the squeal of an animal in anguish came from the barn; then the fall of a stroking instrument; then silence.

Elof sat waiting.

The pup Snip came up unawares and once again began licking the swollen purple-black foot. It reminded Elof of Lazarus. "Damn you, get away!" With his good foot he kicked the dog down the steps.

Snip howled.

"Yell, you bastard. Go ahead." Elof contemplated the howling pup with curling lips. "You lucky critter you. Only you don't know it. When you die, you just die. But me, when I die, I go to hell t'boot."

Kaes came up the path, puffing, carrying a large gunny sack filled with something weighty. The smell of linseed-oil meal came to Elof.

Gert and Gretch came out on the porch, holding their noses.

Gretch, pear-shaped from her pregnancy, exclaimed, "What in the name of heaven you got there?"

Kaes laughed. "Yeh, poke fun a me, will you? But this is the best goddamn-betcha poultice made. Good ol' oil meal. With the heart of a just-killed cat scattered through it. This'll be the freshest medicine ever put on."

"You must be crazy," Gretch said, catching up her filling breasts in her arms. "Killin' a cat for that."

"Maybe so, maybe so. But my old man always swore by it. Said a cat's heart never failed him. Nor his pa either."

"But a cat."

"What's a cat? We got thousands of 'em. A whole barnful. When milkin' time comes around, there's three cat's for every cow, yowlin' for a drip a milk. Too damn many."

Elof had misgivings too. "Are you sure that's safe?"

"Sure it's safe." With the flourish of an expert veterinarian Kaes soaked the oil meal and cat's heart with hot water to make it a yeasty mass, thrust Elof's foot into it, tied up the sack around his leg, slipped on the cut-out red boot. The warm clinging mass came halfway up Elof's calf.

Elof got to his feet. He walked around. Little bones in his foot nibbed against each other, came to rest on substance as soft as pond mud.

Gretch threw up her hands. "One thing I know. Ye're not comin' into the house with that foot. You can good an' well eat out here on the porch." She cleared her throat with a scathing hack. "Such men!"

Three in the afternoon, and the threshing ring was finished at Kaes's.

Elof drove off the yard and headed for the Hansen farm, next on the threshing ring's schedule.

The team of bays trotted easily along, kicking up little puffs of dust on the earthen road, their backs running with tiny rivulets of sweat. He held the lines loosely in one hand. With the other he leaned on a fork, its tines, worn to a gleaming silver by ceaseless forking, bending a little under his weight. He stood on one leg, holding the lump of the other above the vibrating, throbbing floor boards of the wooden rack.

He studied the monstrous lump at the end of his leg. Had he gone nuts completely? Other people would long ago have called it quits, have slid between the cool sheets of a bed, have called Dr. Mars, have cried out for pity and sympathy. But not he. He had to go on being crazy stubborn.

Crazy stubborn. That hit it exactly.

The horses joggled on. Dust rose. The rack jiggled.

The vague feeling that the beast in him—blood, lymph, nerve —was taking over the management of his life came to him. What little mind he possessed was leaving.

The horses came to the highway corner. Numbly, with a slow twist of wrist, Elof turned them northward toward the Hansen farm a quarter of a mile away. In the distance he could see the Hansen cows ringed around the water tank, see white chickens dotting the green pasture land, see a fuss of people under the shade trees by the house.

Questions, thoughts blew like vapors through his skull. Why

was he driving toward that cluster of life: trees, people, animals? Why? How did it happen he was here? And his foot a black and rotted stump?

Yes. There was only one explanation. Yes. The vague feeling he had had a moment ago, that he was no longer in control of his destiny, was true. He nodded to himself. Yes. He was no longer the emperor of the life within the envelope, his skin. Something else, an animal thing, had taken over. And it was crazy stubborn.

The horses trotted; the wheels crinched; the wagon rolled on.

He was so absorbed, so lost in himself, he didn't see the deep rut in the road. The jolting of the wagon threw him down on the whanging floor boards, jerking the lines out of his hands. He landed on his belly with his leg crumpled under him. And within the numbness of his leg a pain prickled suddenly.

"Whoa!" he shouted at the horses. "Whoa!"

The horses coasted slowly to a stop. The four-foot wheels beneath the boards anked on the gravel.

He rolled over and sat up. He straightened out his leg. There was a flood of warmth over his foot inside the red boot.

Strange, he thought, strange. The foot wasn't supposed to feel no more. His mind worked like a stung finger.

He took off the boot and the sack of gray-red oil meal. With the upper end of the sack he wiped the wound clean. And saw at once that the wound was pusing again. The sweet smell of rotted seed was about.

CHAPTER IX: Of Moan and Moonlight

. . . Perhaps this "going on" is related to that voice I hear occasionally. I say "occasionally" because I have only a mortal ear and its range is not quite great enough to pick up immortal notes.

But I hear it, a little. Straining, heart still, ears cocked, I hear it arising from the very center of the turbulent welter of chaos, a noncombative voice, a voice of hope, a voice as of a struggling God, which tells me I should not bow my head meekly to an "inevitable fate" (or bend my back to masters who seem always to be the favorites of such fate) . . .

Elof burst up through enveloping layers of white sleep, found himself sitting bolt upright in bed. He whirled his head around. His eyes clawed the black night for something to hold onto.

His heart beat agonized. He puffed. His belly hurt.

He reached for his foot and was astounded to find it whole. No longer was it wrapped in a sack swollen with warm oil meal. Earthquake?

And then his eye caught a vague rectangle of gray and he knew it for the window over the foot of his bed and he remembered that he was once more bunking in the back room of the Lofblom Grocery, that his foot had healed a week ago. With a great weary sigh he sank back onto his pillow.

And, thank God, it was still too early to get up. He guessed it to be about three or four o'clock in the morning, which meant he could still sleep a couple of hours before getting up to begin another dumbhead day of clerking.

He felt himself invaded by massive, black-tipped waves of gray. Nothing to look forward to but toil, toil, toil. Nothing ahead but drudgery. Nothing on the horizon but a hateful day weighted with hated slavery.

What a life.

He couldn't understand why he didn't rebel. Couldn't understand it.

Here he was, so full of black despair, so charged with abhorrence for the work he did, that an accidental touching of his conscience by the wandering ball of his dreaming mind had awakened him neck-stretched-up out of his pillow.

He was so charged with antipathy to life that the moment he fell asleep his honest body broke into a sweat. And yet when Pa or Kaes called him in the morning he got up like an obedient steer in a treadmill and went to work. From where did that sense of duty come? Where was that trigger of habit hidden?

He rolled on his pillow. The slip smelled of sweat, of hair oil. He ran his hand over his naked body, touching his jutting hip joints, touching his limp penis, touching his thigh. This body, what was this length of tissue, this skein of blood veins? To what part of this stretch of bone and skin did one point to identify the seat of the wavering I?

A cool gust of wind came through the window. He closed his eyes. The wind brushed the golden fuzz on his skin. It was a soothing touch and he thought of mare-breasted Gert and in a moment was sure that she had come, that she had snuck into his bedroom instead of Pa's, that she was stroking him. He could feel a stirring deep below the golden hair on his thigh and he wondered if she would dare. He slipped off into sleep.

There was a thundering crack and horror lightning rived his sleep and he found himself once more bolt upright in bed, dripping sweat, his fingers feeling as thick as logs. He listened, mouth open, panting, heart drumming under tongue.

A storm?

He remembered the window of the other awakening and stared hard at the rectangle of gray, hoping to see a dart of lightning cut wriggling gashes of yellow through the night sky.

But none came. Nor a second doom-pound.

What had happened then? The slam of a door? The fall of a chair? The noise had been so loud it was as if an ax had popped into his skull.

His mind whirled, seeking light. Just what was it that his Old Adam was trying to tell him?

Then an idea sparked and, like a blast of meteor light, knowledge of what had happened came to him. He had had a nightmare. He had dreamt he would never become a hero.

Never a hero. Never. He wasn't going to be anything after all. Chilling.

He sank back into his pillow. He nuzzled cool linen.

Slowly his mind quieted; gradually his fingers became thin again.

He brushed a stubby arched leg back and forth over the sheet of his bed, letting its coolness soothe his sweating skin.

Never a hero.

He looked at the words. Now that he had calmed, now that he had successfully emerged from black dreamland, he was a little startled to think that he had been frightened by so mild an idea.

Never a hero.

Certainly he wasn't the first to have come to that conclusion. Pa and Kaes, Cor and Wilbur, and hundreds and thousands and millions of people living the world over, or who had ever lived, had tried to climb the same ethereal ladder.

What had been so scary then about the words: *never a hero?* There must have been vast threatful reaches of meaning behind the words, a meaning which the protective, wakeful part of his mind had abhorred but which the dreaming part hadn't minded.

He laughed at himself. There was nothing wrong, really, with a man who couldn't become a hero. Nothing.

He brooded.

Yet, given the breaks . . . in another clime . . . away from the hellhole Lofblom Grocery . . . who knows?

He brushed sweat from his brow.

And after a while he composed himself for one more quick nap before Pa called. He closed his eyes; lay waiting.

But something kept prickling.

He threw out an amoebean limb to pull The Something up, but The Something kept slipping out of his watery fingers.

Sleep wouldn't quite come.

At last, knowing he couldn't fall asleep before dawn, he sat up, swung his feet to the floor. His skin was still sticky with sweat. Ignoring his underclothes and shirt, he slipped naked into his blue overall. On bare feet he padded softly out of the room, closing the door. He stepped out of the side door facing the west and walked around to the north side of the store on the clipped lawn.

Ahead the Farmers' Co-op Elevator loomed up black, like a monster dog sitting on its haunches. The depot beside it was a crouching mate. Far in the distance, up the railroad tracks, the switch signal glowed blue-green. A nearby cornfield rustled frond-like leaves.

A sinking moon hung low and red-orange on the west horizon. A section of the shiny used railroad tracks gleamed gold. The outdoor night brushed him. He let the wind stir in his hair a moment. Then he slowly stepped toward the thirteen towering cottonwoods lining the north side of the road between Pa's store and Loren Solen's station.

The grass tickled his toes.

He looked up. He heard the night moaning in the leaves above. Some of the leaves were tipped with moon's gold. A few cloud lumps far above were edged with yellow-silver.

If there were only a friend. Only. A friend would salve his bleeding fingers, would reassure his hoping mind. A friend would try to show him that suffering was not singular, that it helped build all lives—truths which he had trouble bringing himself to believe alone.

He walked slowly through the grass, in the deep hush of night on earth, alone, scuffing his toes, listening to the rising stirring leaves, to the receding stilling leaves, listening to the pulpy moon-dusk silence.

Elof stood still.

Friend or no friend, there was one fact he could never escape. He had been looking at it all the time.

He was the fool who had been taught to expect the world with a ring around it. He was the fool who had been told that he had a king's brain with which to reach to all horizons—when actually he could reach only as far as to the end of his finger tips.

A Siouxland store clerk.

Crung! Skull stinging.

Looking up, he found he had bumped head-on into the crooked chokecherry tree. He stumbled, gripped the tree's wrist-thick trunk, righted himself. He stared at the gray specks on the dark bark, barely discernible in the fading moonlight. Tiny branches, three of them, spread out vainly to either side, were ceaselessly reaching for the little light that splashed through the greedy arms of the monster cottonwoods above.

He noticed something. Little black dots spotted the brush of leaves here and there. Fruit. He reached in and caught a raceme of the last few dried-up black-red cherries. He popped a few into his mouth. For the first instant they were sweet; then suddenly astringent, tongue-shrinking.

The chokecherry and Elof Lofblom. A scrub tree and a stunted youth. And both a bitter fruit.

Yet he admired the lofty mammoths. They reached so far into the sky! They spread so much shade below! They climbed so far out of the lowly flat-spread prairie!

At last the moon set and was gone, leaving only a momentary scattering of golden ashes on the west Siouxland night horizon.

And the stars came out in their turn, and the sky was filled with them—so filled that it looked as if a giant painter in a moment of whimsey had sprettled the entire black tarpaulin of heaven with a mizzling spray of milk-white drops of light.

CHAPTER X: Hero; Lover

. . . Oh happy, oh a hundred times happy, is the man who can exult: "My whole life has been a miracle!" . . .

It was six o'clock in the evening and Elof had just finished supper. There were no customers in the store and he went out front to sit on the cement steps.

He had sat but a few minutes, picking his teeth, listening to the evening wind tinkling in the cottonwoods, hearing Pa wash dishes upstairs, musing on the slow growth of the crooked choke-cherry tree, when a car roared over the horizon from Hello way. In a moment he recognized it as the Hansen car with Cor and Wilbur in it. The Chevy hurtled past the filling stations on the Corner, came braking up the Lofblom drive-in with back wheels stiff. Elof drew back a little on the steps.

"Hi," Wilbur yelled, and leaped out. Both he and Cor were wearing green silk shirts and trousers trimmed in white.

"Hi."

"You busy?" Wilbur ran up to the steps.

"A little."

Still inside the car, Cor rolled and licked a cigarette. He said nothing.

"How busy?" Wilbur asked.

"What's it to you?"

"How'd you like to play ball with the Hello Homebrews to-night?"

"Ball?" Elof started.

"Yeh."

"Can't. Gotta tend store tonight. It's my shift." Elof threw his chewed-up toothpick away.

"Oh, come now."

"Nope."

Cor stirred in the car. "I told you, Wilbur, he wouldn't come. He's afraid of his pa."

Wilbur said, "God, Elof, we sure could use you. Hank Plotts got sick on us an' we need a left fielder bad."

Elof scuffed his bluchers on the top step, held his tongue.

Cor taunted, "I told you, Wilbur. He's never had any gimp of his own."

Elof asked, "Who you playing?"

"Amen. The Amen Night Owls," Wilbur said. "An' we're out to lick 'em. Lockman's pitchin' fer 'em an' we got to beat that bastard."

Elof thought of something. "Huh. I suppose Effie'll be there too."

"Might."

Cor said, "What's the dif? You got what you wanted from her."

Wilbur said, "C'mon, we got to beat that Lockman."

Elof puzzled. "Lockman. Lockman. Seems to me I've heard that name somewhere before."

"Sure you have. He used to pitch for us, the bastard, an' then got himself into a huff one day an' left us. The bastard."

"Say," Elof said, suddenly understanding that the green clothes both were wearing were softball uniforms, "say, you're talking about kittenball, ain't you?"

"That's right. Kittenball."

Elof cleared his throat, spat on the graveled drive-in. "Then I'm not playing for sure. I'm a hard-ball man myself. Baseball."

"Oh, fer godsakes."

"No, no kid's game for me."

"Kid's game? Listen, mister, it's a damn sight faster than baseball any day of the week. An' more fun because more people are able to play it."

"That's just it. It takes skill to play hard ball."

"Aw, nuts," Cor broke in sourly. "Wilbur, I told you he wouldn't come."

Wilbur stretched out his arms. "C'mon, Elof. We need a man bad."

"No," Elof said, shaking his head. "Besides, I'm a pitcher, not an outfielder."

"I know. But we saw you play the outfield once, saw you play it as if you owned it. Remember them high school tournaments?"

"Well . . ." Elof remembered the high school baseball games all right. But he also remembered his try at kittenball in the college intramural leagues. He had actually struck out forty-one times in a row. And had quit in a pet. There was something about a softball thrown underhand that baffled him. He always struck under it. Probably because it kept rising on the way from the pitcher's hand to the plate and as a hard-ball hitter he was used to having a ball come down in a slant. "I tell you, I ain't much of a hitter."

"What's the difference? Just so we got somebody there in left field we can trust."

"But the uniform?"

"You can play without."

"And what'll I use for shoes?"

"Christ," Cor said, "ain't you got new shoes yet?"

"No. Kaes ain't paid me for my last work there."

"Well, get after him. He's got the do-re-mi."

"Yeh, I know. But I don't like asking."

Wilbur said, "Comin' or not? We can't pay you, but you'll have a helluva lot of fun. People yellin'."

Cor said, "Give him some a that wild mare's milk we got in back there an' he won't know if he's got shoes on or not."

"What the hell's that?" Elof asked.

"Whisky."

"Say, that's an idea." Elof laughed.

"Comin'?"

"Well—if I can get Pa to take my place." Elof went inside. He hated the thought of making an ass of himself on the diamond in front of the villagers, but at the same time he was hungry for a little excitement again.

The sun was almost down. The game was about to begin.

The Hello Homebrews, all except Elof suited up in green silk

uniforms, were taking their last warm-up throws. Elof found himself catching long-hit balls, running to his left and to his right, in
and back, all the while surprised to notice that he could cover
quite a lot of territory despite the bluchers. To his left, in center
field, was Pete Kroll, a skinny and long-armed lad. In far right
field trotted a swarthy-faced fellow whose name Elof couldn't remember. In short field behind second base galloped Frank Kreuger, a cocky, smiling, fleet-footed fellow who, from his actions,
seemed to have just found out that he had marvelous and fas-
cinating masculine powers. The Nelson triplets patrolled first,
second, and shortstop. They were blond, sleek-haired animals
whose very similitude gave the Homebrews a professional look.
They were, as the village sages said, "fine, good, clean boys."
Someday they would make solid citizens: go to church on Sunday,
praise God-from-Whom-all blessings-flow by making strong profits, refrain from worldly affairs like politics—except of course
when some national fever caused politics to take on a religious
hue. Elof regarded the triplets with a painful sense of loss—they
were brothers of hallowed Hilda, pale freckled childhood-glorious
Hilda. Third base was covered by Jack Moss, a one-armed
player. Over bobbing corncob pipes the sages claimed that Moss
could, all in one motion, catch a ball, tuck his glove under his
armpit, throw, and do it quicker than any normal man with two
hands. Cor and Wilbur formed the battery. Sometimes Wilbur
pitched, sometimes Cor. Tonight Cor was on the mound and
Manager Wilbur caught. As was customary, only the catcher and
the first baseman, and the exception Moss, wore gloves. All others
played bare-handed.

The entire village had come out for the game. Storekeepers
had locked up and gone home and had piled wife and kids and
protesting grammas into cars and had driven out to the ball field
on the edge of town. Farmers for miles around had milked and
chored early and had grabbed a bone of cold ham and chawed
and, cursing happily, had piled their families in cars, too, and
had driven in. Everybody had come.

Constable Van Horn, as usual, was plate umpire; Young
Domeny Hillich, Elof's old classmate at the Saint Comus Theological Seminary and fellow chosen one, was base arbiter.

Children screamed along the V-shaped field, and played tag, and bothered fathers who wanted to talk store profits and crops and machines. In cars parked along both first and third base women sat tatting and gossiping, and brushing mosquitoes away, and suckling babies, and blowing the horn when somebody hit the ball in the air, pop fly or home run. Girls in the stands behind home plate screamed at the least stir on the diamond. When handsome short fielder Kreuger so much as lifted a finger to wipe sweat from his nose, they rent the evening with shrill screeches.

Along the outer edges of the field towered massive red cedar poles to which were fastened batteries of floodlights. The moment the sun went down, the lights would go on and the game continue into the night. A ball could be pretty well followed in the light except when it was hit so high it disappeared into the purple dark above. Then a fielder had to stand and wait until it reappeared.

Just after Elof had finished his practice fly-chasing he had a ticklish moment. All evening he had managed to avoid a face-to-face meeting with his old roommate Bud, Young Domeny Hillich. But it was when he went over to get himself a drink of water from a can furnished by the Hello town council, and was just finishing a dripping dipperful, that he felt the familiar hand on his shoulder.

"Elof. At last. I heard you were home. Why haven't you looked me up?" Young Domeny Hillich was out of his black cloth and was wearing exaggerated knock-around clothes: an old suit pants and a silk summer shirt. He was as tall as ever and stood over Elof.

"Oh—just busy, I guess." Elof hung the dipper on the side of the can, hiding his face by the maneuver.

"Man, what've I done? You've been home all summer, and you've never once called." Young Domeny Hillich's blue eyes were crinked in protest.

"I know."

"I half expected to see you in church once in a while."

"And hear you preach?" Elof faced him directly for a fleeting second. "No, thanks. I heard you plenty in Practice Preaching."

Young Domeny Hillich's Jesus-soft eyes almost closed in pain.
"But you could at least have paid me a visit. For old times' sake,
you know."

"Play ball!" Umpire and Constable Van Horn shouted behind
them.

Elof said hastily, fidgeting, "I have to go now. See you later."

"Hey, wait a minute. I——"

"Really, I've got to go. Sorry, but you know how it is."

Young Domeny Hillich reached out a hand, but Elof ducked it.
Elof ran to the Homebrew bench.

Young Domeny Hillich slowly went out and took his position
as base umpire.

"PLAY BALL!" Umpire Van Horn shouted again.

Cars honked horns. Children leaped. Girls lifted knees, bared
summer-naked buttocks. Men puffed pipes, made quick side bets.

Umpire Van Horn waved his hand for silence. Partly because
he was constable, the crowd quieted a little. "Batteries for tonight's game. For Hello: Wilbur an' Cor Hansen. For Amen:
Lockman an' Betz. May the best team win. PLAY BALL!"

The visiting Amen Night Owls, sinister in blue uniforms, were
first at bat.

Elof ran out to his position in left field.

A few pitches by Cor, and Elof knew they were in for a battle.
It was three up and three down, but each Amen man drove out
a well-hit ball: one to the swarthy right fielder, two to the roving
Kreuger. The Amen amateurs, like Hello's, had just enough slick-
looking players to put up a real fight.

Elof trotted to the bench, puffing a little. He sat down.

The Nelson triplets led off. They worked as a unit, and if one
of them got on base, one of the others was sure to bring him in.
They were followed by Manager Wilbur, a slugger; then cocky
Kreuger, also a long-ball hitter; then Cor; then the two out-
fielders; then Moss, the one-armed third baseman; and, last, Elof
himself.

Elof was relieved to find himself at the tail end of the batting
order. He would probably get to bat but twice, maybe three times
at most, and so would have that much less chance to make a fool
of himself as a hitter.

The Homebrews went down in order too: one, two, three.

So it went, inning after inning of scoreless play, with only a couple of men on either side getting on base.

It was during the sixth inning, after the brilliant floodlights had gone on, that Elof noticed a car parked by itself far along the left-field foul line. It stood close to where he played his position.

When the Amen Night Owls had gone down again, one, two, three, Elof purposely strolled down the foul line to have a look. The idea of the apartness appealed to him. He was sure he had seen a girl behind the steering wheel.

He came close and saw it was Marge Berg, the schoolteacher from the Little Rock District, the girl who had gone for him in the store until she had spotted his bluchers. He looked down and instantly felt clumsy again.

He remembered how tempting she had seemed that day: all the curves in the right places, queenly tall, her flesh a tone of cream that made the sparks fly in his skull, her eyes one moment purple, the next blue, her hair blond and done up in a flowing bob. He looked at her, and in the shadow of the car with the mauve light from the floodlights faintly touching her, he saw again that her flesh had a peculiarly babylike texture. It reminded him of Toots, Kaes's baby; of pure-hearted Hilda.

"Hi," Elof said.

"You're playing a good game."

"Oh—only had two balls out my way all evening. And they were easy chances."

"And so close. It's still nothing to nothing, isn't it?"

"Yeh." Daringly he put a foot up on the running board, leaned over the door opposite her. "Yeh, it is close at that. Cor's a great pitcher when he's on, I guess."

"I'll say. Even from where I sit I can tell he's got something on the ball. What does it do, twist down?"

"No. He's got a twisting side shoot. And a little rise."

"No wonder he's good."

"Yeh, and when you hit such a ball, it either pops up or drills down. It spins off your bat."

There was an inviting smile on her lips.

Right now, Elof thought, right now, if a guy was only out alone somewheres with her, right now a guy could go places with her because she's turned friendly again, forgot all about them big bluchers. She was in the mood for something.

She said, "You know a lot about it, don't you?"

"Well . . . yeh . . ." Elof said haltingly, all numbs and thingers. He would like to have explained that he didn't particularly care for softball, but found no words ready on his tongue when he opened his lips to speak.

"Why don't you get in? Sit down."

"Me?" Elof asked, his eyes opening.

Just then there was a flurry of noise on the diamond, a sudden shout, a crescendo of screams.

Elof whirled around. Moss, the one-armed boy, had hit a ball over the infield into right center and was racing around the bases. Elof ran forward a few steps ahead of the car to watch. Home run? Elof leaned over, tense. He watched the Amen right fielder stop short, saw him pick up the fat white ball, saw him hurl it back unerringly to the infield. Wilbur, coaching at third, threw up his hands palms open to signal the one-armed lad to hold up. Moss came crashing into the base, dust billowing up. "Safe!" shouted base umpire Young Domeny Hillich.

In the eyes of the crowd, the Lord God Himself couldn't have called out a more glorious judgment. The swarm exploded to its feet, cheering hoarsely. "See!" shouted the sages. "See! He done it again. Moss. Told you he was as good as any man with two arms!" And the village women felt a surge of love for the young domeny; he was so "common," "like the rest of us," "a real boy."

And Marge thumped the horn of her car. She opened her mouth and screamed like the rest of the girls.

Elof glanced back at her, surprised. In a way he was a little disappointed that she should have gotten so excited over so minor a thing as a softball game. At the same time he was also pleased: the more she screamed, the better it might be for him—could even be that she would let him date her up for the night, maybe take him for a ride in her car, go someplace with him where they could have a good time on a couple of nickels.

His name was shouted. It took Elof a moment to realize they were calling him. It was his turn at bat. "Excuse me," Elof called to her.

He ran up to Wilbur at third. "How many out?"

"Two."

"OhmyGod. And me the All-American Out."

Wilbur jerked up, glaring. He grabbed Elof fiercely by the shirt front. "Lissen, you bum, if you're ever going to do anything big in your life this is the time to do it." Wilbur's chin jutted into Elof's face. Elof was startled to find such fire in the usually easy-going lad.

"Well, I'll try my best." Elof trotted heavily toward the bench to get a bat. He chose a short stubby one.

Elof did some figuring. He knew that if he took his usual swing he wouldn't even get close enough to hit a loud foul. To hit at all, he would have to pull some sort of trick. He remembered that on his first time up Lockman had thrown the first ball right down the groove, hip-high, with a slightly turning rise. After that Lockman had given him nothing but bad balls to look at. Maybe, thought Elof, his mind squirreling around furiously in his head, maybe if a guy was to close his eyes and hit a little high, maybe a guy . . .

He felt all eyes on him. Without a cap, he felt a little naked before the villagers.

It became still. The floodlights cast a purple-white glare over the diamond. The base lines, white with ground chalk, the foot-square bases, the Night Owl players, in their blue silk uniforms and tense at their positions, stood out in sharp relief. And the dreaded pitcher Lockman, a broad-shouldered giant with darting black eyes, loomed up before him.

Then from among the contingent of Amen supporters rose a shrill woman's voice. It shrieked derisively. Elof recognized it. Effie's. Looking from under the hair that had fallen over his brow, he saw her, recognized her by her buck teeth. She was too far away for him to see if she were wearing her windmill hat. When she shrilled again he colored a little.

Angering, he picked up a handful of dust in the batter's box, rubbed his hands. He even rubbed some under his eyes to cut down the glare of the lights. He spit in his hands to get a better grip on the bat.

He approached the plate slowly, staring at Lockman, studying the renegade pitcher. Elof threw a quick glance at the one-armed runner at third ready to dash in on the least sign of a hit.

He thought of cheering Marge, and his heart swelled, thinking that if he did get a hit maybe Marge would go out with him and then . . .

Biting his teeth, once again swearing to hit a little higher than he was wont, he stepped into the batter's box. Only vaguely, far off to one side and way in the back of his head, flicked thoughts of Pa, of Gert, who would be there watching her brothers Cor and Wilbur, of the unfinished accounting course, of *Peregrine Pickle*.

Lockman glowered, wound up, swung around. His hand came down, past his knee, swept up in a long rising graceful gesture.

The ball darted toward Elof: rising, looming, swelling. It came straight for the plate, just above the knees.

Elof aimed high, closed his eyes, doubled the muscles of his stubby arms, swung frenziedly, lashing his body around in a tight fierce whirl.

And hit.

It was a good feeling; a solid feeling; a conquering sensation; an annihilation. He had struck chains from his self.

The ball streaked away from him. It weaved a little, as if it couldn't part the air fast enough in its furious ascent. It shrank in size almost instantly. Elof saw it soar out over second base; saw it rise, rise, rise; saw it dwindle; and go on and on and on; and then, to his amazement, soar out of the range of the floodlights and disappear into the purple tarpaulin of night far overhead. He saw the Amen center fielder turn, saw him run wildly, saw him follow the flight of the ball far beyond.

The crowd stilled with amazement, drew in a great breath. Then it shot off scattered volleys of exclamation; then drummed up a great pandemonium.

A voice crackled in Elof's ear. "Run, you son of a bitch. Run!"

Elof, still standing at the plate stunned, his bat dangling awkwardly off to one side, turned. It was Cor.

"Run, you devil you. Run!"

Elof ran. His bluchers clubbed toward first base. The coach at first waved him on. He clodded toward second, gaining speed, gaining momentum. He turned for third, saw Wilbur, monster-tall, waving him on home, shouting, "Go! Go!"

Joy welled, burst up, exploded in Elof. He had done it! He had hit a home run! A wonderful home run! And Marge had seen him do it. What a wonderful world it was. After all. He clattered happily, triumphantly, over the plate, his face burning. A home run!

He turned toward the bench. Hands reached for him. Silk-clad arms hugged him. Clothes were almost torn from him. Moss, the one-armed lad, kissed him.

And over everything there were screams, shrills, screeches. Hello was back on the map. For the moment life was eternal for everybody.

There was Cor's voice, oddly happy, half sobbing. "You crazy bastard, why didn't you run?"

"I dunno. I didn't know I'd hit it, I guess."

"You crazy bastard, why didn't you run?"

"I dunno. I was . . ."

"You crazy . . ." Then Cor set his jaw. His tearing eyes slitted. "Now we'll win. I'll hold 'em the first of the seventh."

Elof pushed his way through the press of green-clad players. He sat down on the bench. And almost before he could adjust himself to what was going on, the first of the Nelson triplets had flied out and it was Amen's turn at bat and he had to run out to his position in left field.

The first Amen batter sent up a high fly behind third base. Elof trotted in and caught it easily. He could feel Marge's eyes on his back and shoulders. And on his feet.

Cor got two strikes on the next man and then lost him when the batter fouled off a dozen pitches. A fourth ball and the man was on.

The next man doubled cleanly down the right-field line. Two on. Second and third.

Except for the Amen crowd, everybody quieted. Laughing face lines became grayed sad lines. Some mouths hung open in fear.

Would the great ecstasy of a moment ago become the great misery in the moment to come? Pink- and light-blue- and green-dressed women sat tense; blue-overalled men chewed.

Then Lockman, next up, got off the Amen bench and approached the plate. Lockman, when he did hit, like Elof, drove a long ball. The Amen supporters set up a clamor of encouragement.

Cor got a strike in. Then a ball. Another ball. Another ball. Three and one.

Elof backed up a step on each pitch. His mind flickered sparks. He tried to guess where Lockman would hit. This far? This far? Maybe a little to the left? But what if Lockman sliced at the ball a little late? Anyway, back a step. A man could run faster going to either side than he could backward.

To make sure the ball would stick in his bare hands, he spat into them, rubbing the wet over his palms.

Cor stood balancing on the pitching rubber. He glared at Lockman. Lockman glared back at him, waving his war club, swishing it. He looked like an enormous cat ominously waving a tail.

Cor whirled through his pitching dance, lashed out his arm. Involuntarily Elof backed another step.

The ball streaked toward the plate—a line of white in the mauve floodlight.

Lockman twisted violently. His bat came around, hit the ball. It speared out toward Elof. It rose.

Elof saw instantly it would go over him. He thought of turning and running, to try catching it over his shoulder. But no. He might stumble over his bluchers. And that would be the ball game.

Vaguely he heard the Amen rooters, and Effie, shout to the heavens.

The ball looped higher and higher. Elof ran backward as fast as he dared. His heels felt snug, and for once his foot semed to know where it was going. He knit his teeth. He even tried to speed up his back-pedaling feet.

The ball began to fall.

He clabbered backward desperately.

The ball settled, lower, lower, drifting.

Racing, clumsing, feeling all eyes on him, heart tribbling, he lunged back, leaped up, stuck out a short arm, his left, opened the hand, fingers wide, hoping.

The ball hit. And, miraculously, stuck to his wet palm.

Elof, floating at the top of his jump, lost his balance and fell backward when the ball hit. He smacked the earth hard with his elbows. But the ball stayed stuck.

He was up in an instant. He saw the runners hesitate on their bases, saw them start running, the man on third for home, the man on second for third. Drawing on his old-time pitching skill, on his stubby strong arm and its control, he fired the ball in a tight line straight for the one-armed man waiting on the second-base side of third base. The ball went drilling in. It hit one-armed Moss's glove. There was a whirl of arm and glove and ball, and the man sliding in was tagged. Double play. Three out. One run in. Final score: 2 to 1.

Heaven had come down to earth again.

The crowd stampeded the field.

In the riot Elof heard Marge's horn. He looked.

She was waving at him out of the side of the car, waving for him to come up.

He approached her sleek car.

She opened the door and swung her legs to get out, revealing flesh all the way back to the web of her crotch. She ran up to him and threw her arms around his neck and bluntly kissed him. Amazed, her swelling lips so thrilling him he felt stunned, Elof tried to say something.

"You hero you!" she shrilled. "And so modest."

Elof mumbled.

"Come on," she shouted gaily. Her eyes were aflame with a blue fire. Her blond bob flared wildly over her slim shoulders, caught in the buttons of her sleeveless yellow dress. "Come on, just for that I'll take you out. It'll all be on me."

Obediently, numbly, Elof got into the car.

With a honking horn, laughing, she started up. She shrilled again: "Oh, wasn't that a wonderful game? Wasn't that a wonderful game? Oh!" She drove off the ball field and onto the lane leading into Hello. Cars pitched onto the road ahead of them, behind them; boiled up the surface. In a moment the traffic became so thick, everyone had to go along in low gear, bumper to bumper.

Carefully Marge tooled down the dusty thoroughfare, part of the cheering parade. Headlights cleared; then obscured; then glared gray-red in the flying powdered earth.

Presently the short road became a street and they were in Hello, passing both old and newly built homes. Elof had seen Hello many times, but this night he saw it with new eyes. He saw how the old homes were invariably built close to the ground, with no basement showing, the bottom of the first-floor windows sometimes no more than two feet above dirt; how the new homes were set high up on cement-block basements, with windows wide and free to the sun. The old homes usually were painted in dull colors: gun grays, dead browns, sparkless greens. The new ones were bright with bean yellows and snow whites. There were a couple of brick homes—one of them Young Domeny Hillich's. The Hillich parsonage had a huge forbidding porch and blank wide bay windows. A walk ran around one side of the house, leading to a mighty church on the other side of the block. The church was of white-painted clapboard, with a belfry built into a sky-needling tower. Windows were partly colored and in design were in harmony with the steeple. Hello, a little town, and in it were representatives of the varied peoples of the earth: the lowly, the middle, the high. And he, not even among the humblest of them.

The worm of cars ahead began to break up, some heading for the country, some for homes in town, a few for downtown, where the cafés and drugstores were open for pop and beer and sandwich and ice-cream business.

The graveled street became paved, and then they were passing places of business: Etin's greenstone implement shop, Westra's Mercantile with ware-cluttered show windows, Guthere's Printing Company, Ynglinga's Meat Market, Dr. Mars's washed Hello Hospital, Myringa's greasy garage, and then Hello's well-lighted big corner—a series of cafés and eateries.

When Marge stopped in front of Jake's Eat, the biggest restaurant in town, she was still excited.

"Shall we go in?" Elof asked, remembering his bluchers and hoping she would decline.

"It'll be pretty crowded, won't it?" she said, shutting off the ignition. Elof noted the slim baby-white fingers. He longed to touch them, hold them; longed to have them stroke his face.

"Yeh." He glanced at the shouting crowd of cigarette-tough young bucks and arm-in-arm does and chawing old men and darting kids. All were crawling in and out of Jake's Eat like ants wibbling in and out of a hole in the earth. "I tell you. I'll go in," he said. "I'll go in and get us something. What would you like?"

"Oh—get me an ice-cream cone."

Elof lifted a blond eyebrow. "Ice-cream cone?" That he could afford.

She laughed at him. "I love 'em. Besides, anything else would be too much bother."

Elof flushed. "I can afford it."

"No, no. Cones it is."

"If you say so." Elof slipped out of the car and, to hide his feet from her, made off as if he couldn't step ahead between her car and another parked next. He walked back around out of her sight.

In a few moments he was back, flushing, this time because of the cheering he had got in Jake's Eat. He gave her the cone with the largest helping.

"Quite a hero, aren't you?" she said, smiling, licking the top of her cream-bulging cone with a slippery pink tongue. "Mmmm. This is good."

A drop of melting ice cream fell on Elof's overall. Quickly he licked off the next forming drop and then brushed off the spot on his clothes.

"Let's get out of here," she said, switching on the ignition again. The motor bumbled, trembled beneath their feet, and in a moment, meshing the gears smoothly, she drove out into the dark country, the car's headlights, long shafts of saffron, peering boldly ahead into the night.

Elof sat licking his cone. The cones melted so fast both he and Marge were kept too busy slupping to talk.

Finally Elof threw the empty point of his cone out of the open window of the car.

She did too.

Elof slid down on the leather seat a little, uneasily. Now what?

She smiled at him. "Well, where to now?" She handled the wheel expertly.

"Oh . . . I dunno."

She laughed richly. "I know a certain place."

Elof said nothing. Again he was all numbs and thingers.

She sped up. The wind from the racing car lifted her shoulder bob, streamlining it. A faint luminous glow came into it.

Elof thought of touching the bewitching strands of waving gold, even tried to make his hand move. But it wouldn't. He was stiff. He tried to make his tongue move, make his lips talk, utter. But nothing happened. He had dared touch Effie because she was beneath him and because the boys were around. But Marge? She was above him.

She hummed as she drove. She drove faster and faster. The motor's mumbling rose; at last pitched into a fine high shriek. The car piercing the night was a fleeting arrow with a flame in its tail.

She slowed. She turned up a country lane. She idled the motor. Twice she wigged her hips a little, as if suggesting she were sidling along the seat toward him.

Still Elof couldn't unthaw the freeze in his limbs.

She stopped the car. She pulled up the brakes. She turned off the lights.

Elof's mind milled desperately. Maybe if he took off the bluchers he might suddenly feel free.

But just as he reached down to untie the laces he remembered that he had been sweating. His feet were sure to stink.

She flicked her slim fingers impatiently. She rolled the steering wheel a little. She looked out into the mysterious and sex-suggestive night.

Crickets sounded around them. It was black out. No moonlight. Stars were steady white above. Corn leaves rustled like coarse silk in a nearby field. A flutter of wings told of a weaving, insect-eating bat.

"I . . . I . . ." began Elof. "I . . . What have you been reading lately?"

"Oh—nothing much. It's been too hot."

"I'm in the middle of *Peregrine Pickle*."

"You are? I remember that book. I wrote a report on it once in college. I remember going to the library and getting the gist of it from another book."

"Say, that's just what I did."

"How come you're reading it now then?"

"Why—later on I heard my favorite prof raving about it. About a young fellow named Perry who was always getting into messes. My prof said no man could claim he was well read until he'd read it. So one time I took out the two-volume work, started it, liked it, liked it so much I went out with my last few pennies and bought it. Two volumes bound in one."

"Is it really good?"

"Good? It's my Bible. If I had only half the crust Perry had, I'd get somewhere."

"Maybe."

"Sure I would," Elof said.

"Well, you probably know," she said.

Elof swallowed. "Yeh. *Peregrine Pickle's* great stuff. Real literature."

She sagged then.

"Great literature."

After a moment she yawned. "Yeh," she said, fluttering her slim fingers over her open, sweet-lipped mouth.

Agonizedly Elof thought of something to say. "What have you been doing to keep busy these days?"

"Swim."

"Swim?"

"Up at the Sioux Center sandpit."

He nodded. He knew where it was. A deep crater dug out of the prairie surface by a steam shovel. In it welled cold green water. It had wonderful white sand along its entire oblong shore. There were steep drop-offs after one entered.

"You go alone?"

"Sometimes," she said, reaching for the ignition. She yawned again.

He thought: OhmyGod, what a clumsy question. That's me for you. Of course she goes with some Sioux Center dude. Of course.

He sat for a few moments, fiercely trying to make himself do something to distract her from starting the car. He tried to force his mind to think down to his hands and finger tips, to make them move toward her soft arms and half-exposed knee. He tried to force his mind to think to his lips, to make them move with a lover's whisper and murmur.

But nothing happened and so at last he turned to her and said, almost mumbling the words, "Better take me home. I took off tonight and that means I've got to be in the store bright and early in the morning."

CHAPTER XI: Fire in the Bowels

. . . Elof, the only one capable of putting into writing the true pit of your self is you yourself. Yet, the moment you become capable of doing so, you are no longer Elof.

Will no one ever write it then?

No one.

Even at best (Tolstoy, Steinbeck, Hemingway, Twain) we get what we "think" is an Elof, a studied or a styled Elof. (It is much easier to record the lives of the literates. There is a flux of material to be found on them, tons and tons of it. Just listen to the chant of the choir rising from Psyche's couch.)

Of course, at the same time, there is no harm in trying the impossible. In fact, to write the approximate story of an Elof may do some good. It may make the gruff kind, the haughty humble, the rich benevolent. It may even give the brights some hope to live . . .

The next Saturday after supper Elof went upstairs to talk to Pa. He found him in the kitchen drinking a cup of coffee.

"Yeh?" Pa queried, looking up, the front of his bald head wrinkling in even lines.

"I'd like to use the pickup."

Pa set his cup down in the saucer. "What for?"

"I want to drive over to Kaes and get my check."

"Can't you walk?"

"No. Been on my feet all day and am all tired out."

Pa gulped a few swallows. "How long'll you be gone?"

"Just a few minutes." Elof added quickly, "I'll be back in time to help you with tonight's business."

"Well—mind that you do."

Elof couldn't resist thinking to himself that it wouldn't really hurt if he didn't come back right away. On Saturday nights the farmers and their families usually went to the big towns anyway to do their shopping, and so Pa alone in his country store wouldn't be too busy. Elof held out his hand. "You got the key?"

Pa set his cup down again and reluctantly fumbled in his pocket. "Here."

"Thanks. And when I come back I'm going to pick me out a pair of shoes."

Pa said nothing.

Elof went downstairs and out to the thin-tired truck. He set the spark lever, the gas, pulled back the brake, and cranked. The motor guggled twice and then popped up into a hopping rumble. The truck started to move a little, and, with a running leap, Elof lit on the running board and vaulted into the seat. He released the brake, pedaled, his short legs barely reaching them, backed up, and whirled off the graveled drive-in. He set the spark and gas for speed.

Elof sailed past the immense cottonwoods, past the Corner, made sure that Kaes wasn't in his gas station, and then blatted down the road east.

The wind swooped over the windshield and invaded the topless cab. It pressed against his face and chest and snapped his golden hair. Even the bib of his clean blue overall belled out. For a moment he felt joyous and free, and a-move in the big wide world. The green pollinating weeds and the brush and grass on the roadside rushed past like a hurrying moss-covered river.

Kaes's yard came up and he slowed for the lane. He turned, and turned too sharply, the front wheels locking. He bored into the ditch. Desperately he braked and stopped, the motor choking and dying, with the nose of the pickup into the wall of the ditch.

He cursed the pickup, recalling that this make had wheels that, when turned too far, had a habit of snapping over almost at right angles.

He set the spark and gas again and got out, rubbing his belly and arm. He walked around the vehicle, looking for damage. Finding none, he went in front to crank. The protruding fenders and bumper touching the wall of the ditch gave him just enough room to get in and spin the handle. He cranked and the car popped up readily enough. He vaulted into the seat again and backed up. This time he took the lane easily. He drove up to the front of the house.

Gourd-shaped Gretch was coming up from the barn carrying a pail of milk, Toots following her. Gretch managed a tiny muted smile over her burdens.

"Kaes home?"

"No. He helped the boys put up some alfalfy today."

"Over t'Hansens?"

"Yes."

"Good. I'll drive over there then."

"I can't help you?"

"No." He waved. "No, I'll just go over and see him there." He smiled at Toots and was off.

When he drove onto the Hansen yard he saw no one about and guessed they were eating supper late tonight. He parked the truck in front of the house and walked through the gate and went slowly up the cement sidewalk. The house yard had been fenced in, and there were occasional trees to either side. It faced the south; and on the north side it gave on to a grove of box elders and ash, thick enough to give the impression of impenetrability. Off to one side of the yard a huge maple spread out a magnificent canopy of cut-leaf foliage. A rope-and-board swing hung from one of its fat limbs. Just east of the living-room door a weeping willow tree trailed sad silver leaves.

The kitchen door faced south. Elof knocked on it.

"Come in," a voice called.

Elof recognized it as Wilbur's. He stepped in.

The family was gathered around the table. Savory vapors steamed up from it. The kitchen seemed momentarily dusk to

Elof, but after a moment he made out arthritic Pa Hansen sitting
in an armchair at the head of the table, and Cor and Wilbur next
to him on the left. Kaes sat on the old man's right, and beside
him was an empty chair. Across from Pa Hansen sat fat queenly
Ma Hansen. She was chewing on a slice of red sausage. Elof heard
a noise on the range behind him and, looking around, saw Gert.
She was getting more warm food—bleeding beets, flake-skinned
potatoes, muted-green beans—and Elof guessed the empty chair
by Kaes was hers. Once again, with both standing up, he saw that
she was taller than he.

"Hi," Kaes roared, his fork heavy with gravied potatoes, "sit
down an' take a load off yer feet."

Wilbur shoved up a chair.

Ma Hansen waved a meringue-soft elephant arm at Gert. "Set
out a plate for the boy."

"Nono, Mrs. Hansen," Elof said hastily, "no, I already had
supper."

"What? A young feller like you can't eat more? To, Gert, set
out a plate."

"Nono."

"I say yes," Ma Hansen commanded, again waving a tree-trunk
arm, her blue eyes sharp on Elof. "Give the boy some food."

"Please," Elof begged.

"Well, you'll have some tea then? An' a cooky?"

"Well . . ."

"Sure."

"All right then. But nothing else."

Gert, standing all the while at the stove, brought a pot of
tea and a cup and saucer and poured for him, her dark bob falling
around her face. She hardly glanced at him, but Elof could
see that she had sparked up at his coming. Her fingers were
trembling.

He took the chair and drew up to the table. Sipping his tea, he
couldn't help noticing how much the daughter resembled the
mother. A good close look and he could see in Gert's body what
Ma Hansen's body must have looked like in youth. Though
slimness somewhat became it at first and served to entrap the
mate, just let it bear a child or two, and it would house itself in a

voluminous insulating envelope like a fattened sow. The Master Architect had designed this particular type of skeleton for weight bearing.

"Well," Kaes said, "an' I'll bet you came for a check?"

"Yes and no. I don't want to——"

"Don't apologize. I should have paid you long ago, man. How much you got comin'? I'll pay you right tonight."

Elof sipped some tea. "About a week's work."

"Two bucks a day. That makes fourteen. Right?"

Elof nodded.

Kaes dug his pocketbook out of his overall and fumbled through it. "I guess I got the change all right. That'll save me makin' a check. Them damn banks are chargin' two cents a check fer handlin' now'days." He handed Elof a few bills. "That right?"

Elof counted. "Yep, that's it." He pocketed it.

Pa Hansen, lifting his brushy white brows and directing strong blue eyes at him, asked, "Well, an' how do you like the old home ground again?"

"Good," Elof said, "good."

Ma Hansen frowned.

Kaes winked at Cor and Wilbur. Cor's bitter gray eyes flicked.

Pa Hansen held his eyes on Elof a moment longer and then, finished chewing something, turned and pointed a knobby arthritis-thickened hand at a pile of bread. "Pass me a slice, please."

Gert, who had just sat down, quickly reached him the plate. The old man's disease-folded claw pinched off the top slice. Fumblingly he buttered it.

Elof continued to sip his tea, hot from the cup.

Kaes, however, poured his tea into the saucer and then slupped at it. Saucered tea was cool, Elof knew, and pleasant to the tongue. But for himself tea drunk that way was out.

He looked around, remembering the old things. The walls were papered tan, and above the modern blue-enameled stove and the freshly curtained windows, darker streaks reached to the ceiling. A magazine rack hung on the wall behind the old man. It was stuffed with farm and religious papers. Below it was a short shelf; there was just enough room on it for an alarm clock, a much-

fingered black leather spectacle case, and a pail of cut plug tobacco. A calendar from the Hello National Bank, proclaiming
good cheer and solid citizenry, hung above the sink. Water
dripped from the St. Bernard-nosed cistern pump.

At last the family finished eating, and Cor reached under the
table and pulled out the family Holy Bible. A few pages were loose
and the corners of the leather book covers were worn through.
Certain sections were well marked and oily from daily paging. Cor
handed it to the old man.

The old man took it. Groaning, he stretched out a disease-
crooked arm and drew from between the clock and the tobacco
pail his spectacle case. It opened with a snap and, with claw
fingers, he thumbed out a pair of fragile gold-rimmed bifocals. He
hooked on the earpieces one at a time and adjusted them. When
he looked out the dime-small glasses, his staring eyes suddenly
looked like flat robin eggs. And in a moment, because of the strain
put on them, they became watery.

The old man opened the Good Book and coughed.

The kitchen became instantly quiet. Only the alarm clock
ticked.

"And now we'll read a portion out of God's Word," the old
man said. He looked around at the circle; then at Elof sitting off
to one side. He said to Elof, "We are reading out of the book of
Leviticus. Chapter Eighteen."

Elof nodded.

The old man lifted a quavering, singing voice. It was so completely unlike his everyday voice that Elof's mind stumbled a little
trying to adjust it.

*"And the Lord spake unto Moses, saying, Speak unto the children
of Israel, and say unto them, I am the Lord your God . . ."*

Stinging, eye-moistening memories assailed Elof. He recalled
the time he had come to the Hansen home for Sunday supper with
Gert; and how afterward he had taken her in Pa's buggy to Young
People's Endeavor. The memory was as clear as a child story told
in large block-sized print, rich with the detail of grass and sky
and moving buggy and new clothes and shining well-washed faces.

That was the time he had searched Gert for some hint of the Hilda that might have been hidden in her.

He glanced around the table, wondering what the others were thinking, wondering if they were actually listening to the old Judean poetry or if their attention were wandering too. Ma Hansen was fanning her face with a handkerchief and blowing the sweat drops back up over her nose and face, her blue eyes empty and dreamless. Wilbur was paring his fingernails with a jackknife. Gert was sitting with bowed head, her work-red hands in her lap, her bosom neatly caught between strong biceps. Cor was staring at his plate. Kaes had put a hand over his face, and it was hard to tell if he were praying or sleeping.

The old man's voice lifted the chant:

"The nakedness of thy father's wife shalt thou not uncover: it is thy father's nakedness."

Elof nodded. Yes. It would be a terrible thing to see one's mother naked. And the idea of sleeping with her—blll!

"The nakedness of thy father's wife's daughter, begotten of thy father, she is thy sister, thou shalt not uncover her nakedness."

Elof was startled to see an odd look narrow Cor's eyes, to see him look down in his lap as if someone had mentioned aloud a secret of his.

Elof stiffened a little. Could Cor have touched Gert? It sometimes happened between brothers and sisters, especially in kid time: on Saturday night before or after the bathtub, or on Sunday morning when the rest of the family had gone to church and the kids were left home to take care of the cattle, or in the haymow hunting eggs, or in the pasture getting the cows, or in the oat field at lunch time, or in the cornfield, or maybe even swimming together flesh-naked.

He glanced quickly at Gert. She sat unmoved.

Again Elof glanced at Cor. But now Cor was still; so still, Elof wasn't sure he ever had seen uneasy expressions flickering over his face and lips.

"Thou shalt not uncover the nakedness of thy daughter in law: she is thy son's wife; thou shalt not uncover her nakedness."

That one, Elof thought, that one Pa Lofblom should hear. That would teach him not to reach down into the younger generation.

Elof had a vindictive thought: Wasn't the old man just about entering that age where he was supposed to be drying up, where, like a steer, he could try but it wouldn't do him any good? If so, what was he doing with a heifer as young as Gert, a young heifer who had every right to look forward to a ripe life of cohabitation with someone of her own age? So that they could rise and fall together?

"Neither shalt thou lie with any beast to defile thyself therewith: neither shall any woman stand before a beast to lie down thereto: it is confusion."

Of course. It was silly to think that a woman—Gert, or Ma Hansen, or Gretch, or Marge, or Ma (most certainly not her!)— would lay down to a . . . to a . . .

But men . . . ?

He had heard of young boys playing with calves. Even sows. And then, there were the sheepherders, they who said that if only an ewe could wash dishes they would marry it.

Again, involuntarily, he glanced at Cor. Once more he saw an uneasy stir on his face.

Elof's mind clicked. Aha! Maybe that was why Cor always looked so sour, so cheated; maybe that was why he always glimmered so secretively out of that gray rheumatic face of his.

The quavering patriarch's voice rose, almost whined:

"Defile not ye yourselves in any of these things: for in all these the nations are defiled which I cast out before you:

And the land is defiled: therefore I do visit the iniquity thereof upon it, and the land itself vomiteth out her inhabitants."

The aged voice ceased. The old man closed the sacred book. He took off his spectacles, closed them, and slid them into the case. The case closed with a loud pop. He glanced around at each of them. There were darknesses in his blue eyes, as if his white brows like clouds were casting shadows in them. Then, slowly closing his eyelids, like a dying man on his deathbed at last reclining, Pa Hansen murmured, "Let us give thanks."

The humble words rose like the lament of a choral:

"Our Father which art in Heaven. We come to Thee in this evening hour, at the end of the day and its wearisome labors, to render thanks unto Thee for all Thy bountiful blessings. Thou hast given us strength to do our work and health to enjoy life and grace through Christ Jesus to save ourselves from everlasting destruction. We thank Thee for the food set before us on our table. May it strengthen our body. We thank Thee for Thy Word, and It read to us. May it strengthen our soul. May we carry with us in our hearts in the hours yet remaining to us this day its true message. O Lord, we thank Thee we are not as the heathen . . ."

The old man's voice hesitated. An instant silence gripped the listeners in the kitchen. All were aware that Pa Hansen was about to improvise; all held breaths, wondering what was about to pop out. Elof was sure the old patriarch was about to make some oblique reference to his having come home (*Safe! We thank Thee O Lord!*), a wandering prodigal from the fleshpots of Sodom and Gomorrah.

". . . as the heathen who know nothing, who are an abomination before Thy sight, who are everywhere to be driven forth from Thy presence. Just as thou didst once cast out of the land of Canaan from before Thy chosen people all the sinners of Jericho and Ai and the kings of Lebanon, the Hittite, the Amorite, the Perizzite, the Hevite, and the Jebuzite, so didst Thou cast out of Siouxland from before Thy chosen people all the heathen of the Sioux tribes and their kings, Chief Yellow Smoke, Chief Sitting Bull, Chief Crazy Horse, and Chief Inkpadutah, the son of the devil himself. The land was defiled and Thou didst visit the iniquity thereof upon it. Pray that we may truly labor in this land Thou gavest us as Thy children, as Thy chosen people, so that the land will never vomit us forth."

Breaths were still held.

"We pray O Lord . . ."

The old man had made it. And in a moment he was back in the groove of his usual prayer. The listeners in the kitchen moved a little on their chairs and breathed easy once more.

"Forgive us this day all our sins. In His name we ask it."

The moment "Amen" was sounded, the family stirred, and each pushed back his chair and coughed. The boys, Cor and Wilbur, Elof with them, rolled cigarettes. Pa Hansen put away the Holy Bible, reached for his burnt-black pipe.

Kaes stood up. "Guess I better hustle home or my wife'll divorce me. Lettin' her do all the chores alone."

"Yeh," Ma Hansen said, "that I believe."

Kaes grinned. He said, putting a hand on Elof's shoulder, "Gonna do a little sparkin' tonight, huh, boy? All that cash?"

"Might if I had a car."

"What's a matter with that tin lizzie out there?"

"Huh. You know how tight Pa is."

There was an odd silence. Gert got to her feet and hurriedly brought the creamer and sugar and salt and pepper shakers into the pantry.

Kaes stood back on a leg. "Elof, you know what you ought to do?"

"What."

"Tell him to go t'hell. Take that pickup tonight an' get yerself a gal an' have yerself a helluva time."

"You don't know Pa."

"I know him well enough to know I could kick the stuffin's out a him any day of the week."

"Now, now," Ma Hansen put in, "not so rough with that tongue now, Kaes."

Pa Hansen looked up too. "That's pretty strong talk, ain't it, Kaes?"

Kaes looked back at him. "Pa, you know damn well everybody runs when I want something. Even you." Kaes shoved out his powerful chest. He swung his arms freely—they were pistons ready for the stroke of powerful punches.

Gert came out of the pantry, obviously thinking the conversation safe again.

Kaes spotted her. He swaggered to her side, put his arm around her. "Ain't it so, Gert?"

"What?" she said, pushing him aside, allowing herself a smile.

"Elof," Kaes announced jovially, "Elof, I tell you what. If you

don't spend some of that money I just give you on Gert tonight,
I'm gonna take it away from you again."

Elof drew deeply on his cigarette, parried, "But I first got to buy
me some shoes."

"Ain't that pinchpenny pa a yers give you a pair yet?"

Elof took another deep puff.

"Well, Elof, is it a deal?" Kaes asked, at the same time jollying
Gert some more with a stroking spade-wide palm. "Huh?"

"Leave me be," Gert said, pulling herself free.

"Well, I—don't know," Elof said slowly. He noticed that Cor
and Wilbur were gleeing together, that Pa and Ma Hansen were
alert for something to happen.

All of a sudden Kaes let out a cackle. He slapped his leg.
"Wouldn't that be the best joke ever!" He held himself in laughter. "Elof takin' out his pa's girl in his pa's pickup."

For something to do, Elof stood up.

"That'd be the best yet."

Elof swallowed, and before he could stop himself, his lips and
tongue were saying, "Well, Gert, how about it?"

"I don't know."

Kaes pushed her toward Elof. "Go to it, boy. She's sayin' 'no' so
she kin get ready to say 'yes.' "

Gert shot Elof an excited glance.

Elof, this time daring, asked, "Well?"

"Oh, but I ain't dressed."

"You kin change, can't you?"

"Oh, but I still got to help Ma wash dishes yet."

"That I can do. Go on, get your duds on. I'll help Ma while
you change. I used to help my ma, and I don't know of a reason
why I can't help yours."

Gert looked down. "Well . . . but . . . all right then, if you
say so." She bolted through a door and up the stairs.

The last bit Elof saw of her fleeing body was her solid buttocks.
They reminded him of a foal's rump—two firm outthrust tubers.
He liked them on her.

"Good boy," Kaes said.

The others, Ma and Pa Hansen and Wilbur, nodded. Cor
didn't show what he thought.

By the time Elof was ready to leave the Hansen yard with Gert, the boys, Cor and Wilbur, had already left for their Saturday night's fun in town, and Kaes had gone to take Gretch shopping.

"Where, where shall we go?" Elof asked.

"I don't know," Gert said, shifting uneasily beside him on the hard-leather, button-dented cushion, lifting first one leg, then the other, to smooth her dress over her fundament. "The boys sometimes go to Passage to see a movie."

"That where we go then?" Elof found himself admiring her. She was dressed in white rayon shantung, and for contrast had buckled on a red leather belt, had caught a red silk ribbon over her head behind her ears, had selected a red imitation-leather purse. "I'll have to tell you though," he added, "I'll have to tell you that maybe the old tin lizzie won't hold up on such a long trip."

"Well, there's Blow Out. That's only half as far."

"That city of sin? All that gambling and murdering? And wet-haired boys? Gertrude!"

She laughed. "Well, then we can go to Hicksville. For dumb-heads and decent people they show old-time cowboy movies. Free. The store there puts it on to draw the trade."

Elof laughed and slapped the steering wheel. "Not really?"

"Sure."

"I bet even the reel numbers come out on the screen."

Gert smiled. "They do."

"For godsakes. You know, I have half a notion to go there and see one. I've never yet gandered an old cowboy thriller. Okay?"

"Okay by me." Gert looked down at her work-red hands.

Elof wheeled off the yard and headed north, going past the thick grove, on past the patch of chokecherry brush, crossing the east-west Thunderbolt railroad tracks.

The sun was setting. Shadows were beginning to deepen through the golden stubbles. Mulatto-brown corn tassels trailed rains of pollen. Pastures, slowly crispening in the dry August weather, showed patches of yellow and luminous gray.

The dusty road led on, going north a few miles, then east a few. The dirt road top was surprisingly smooth. Sometimes the old pickup hardly rattled. It purred along like a brand-new job.

Elof pointed to a field of corn to the north. It spread wide and level like a troweled floor. "Look at that patch. I'll bet that's two hundred acres if it's a square foot. My God, that's beautiful. All gold." Sunlight slanted through the braidlike tasseled tops, and deep in the undergrowth night's purples were gathering. "And look at those ears. Them's the best I've seen this year."

Gert, too, looked with a speculative eye. "That corn should go good all right. Maybe fifty to the acre."

"At least. At least. They must've had a shower at the right time."

"Looks like it, don't it?"

"It sure does."

He drove on.

After a while Gert said, "Say, I smell something burning." She sniffed, looked around. "Yes. Burning."

Elof widened a nostril too. "By gosh, you're right. Something is burning."

"Smells like wood."

"Uh-huh. Kind of an oily wood."

"Well, stop then, you goony, an' see what's the matter. First thing you know, we'll blow sky high."

Elof pulled up, stopping on the shoulder of the country road. "Can't imagine . . ." He got out, looked around under the engine hood; couldn't find anything.

"It smells like maybe it's coming from under the seat here."

"Well, it's a cinch it ain't anywheres around near the motor." Elof went to her side of the pickup, peered under the seat a little, very aware of her thighs and bare legs nearby.

"Lift up your legs a minute, will you?"

She did.

He pried up a floor board; saw it. The bowel-like exhaust pipe was red hot, and where it passed close beneath the boards, within an inch, it had almost ignited the wood. A faint spiral of smoke rose from it. Charred areas indicated it had almost ignited before. "Huh. Another one of them cheap construction jobs. Letting the hot exhaust come that close. And, worse, within a whisker or two of the gas tank." He muttered to himself, low enough so he thought she wouldn't hear it, "Like the way the Good Lord planned the human body. Put a man's nuggets on the outside where they can get kicked. Instead a the inside where they'd be pertected."

"Elof!"

"What?"

"I heard you."

"Well—it's the truth just the same. Them designers. Big or little, it's always proved they don't know it all."

"That's enough now."

"Uh-huh."

She looked past her raised legs at the burnt board. "Is it dangerous? I can still smell it."

"Dangerous? No. Not at all. Not if you don't mind being blown straight into the lap of God. Short cut. Like you said."

"Well, for catsake, do something then."

"I am," he said, "and don't get your water hot." He picked up a handful of dust and smothered the few glowing sparks left. "There."

"You sure it's safe now?"

"Safe until the next time."

She was silent.

"Dumb bunnies," he muttered.

"You better have that fixed."

"I will. Don't worry." He put down the floor board and she resettled herself and he got in.

They drove on; a little slower than before.

The sun hit the horizon just as they turned north and headed toward Hicksville a mile away. Spread out before them was a gas station and a store and a produce depot, each on a corner.

The sun was half cut off by the horizon and the near fire forgotten when Elof made a slow U turn and headed back up the road, hunting for a place to park.

By the time Elof came to the end of a line of cars already parked in the roadside ditch, the sun was down. Dusk came on rapidly.

"Well, where's that mustang movie?"

"They show it over there behind the store." She smoothed her white dress over her knees. Her gray eyes laughed.

"Well, let's amble over and see what's up." Elof reached across her lap and opened the door. He brushed against her and was mildly pleased that the touch of her felt good.

She got out, Elof watching her leg reach for the ground. He liked its slimness, even the knotted muscles in the calf. It was odd, he thought, odd that so lean a leg went with so matronly a bosom.

They strolled slowly along the road. Dust boiled up as more and more cars loaded with women and children came up and parked.

Elof became conscious again of her height and he maneuvered her into walking along the edge of the road and he on it to make his eyes at least level with hers.

A floodlight had been strung over the road, and beneath it, in the swirling gold-brown dust, crowds of old-timers and kids and breast-feeding mothers milled together. Cars entering the cone of light slammed on brakes, rising a little on their front wheels, and blew horns, and turned to one side or another.

Elof said, "Let's go see if they sell ice cream in the store."

"Okay." She stepped up beside them.

The store, Elof saw right away, was like Pa's. It handled a little of everything. Also the ice cream he sought. He bought two cones from a harried farm-wife clerk and handed one to Gert; then he led the way through the press of farmyard-smelling people and outdoors.

A floodlight had also been hung in a cottonwood behind the store, giving its leaves a curious tinting of gold-green. There were rough seats beneath it, boards over barrels, and to the south end a huge screen had been set up.

It soon became pitch dark, and the crowd came milling around the side of the store. In a moment the benches were full of women in well-ironed cottons and men in new blue overalls and children in store-cute going-out clothes. Elof selected a seat for themselves far in the rear.

The floodlight went off, and all was plunged into an impenetrable black. Then something flicked on behind them, and a beam of bright yellow light in the shape of a phonograph horn shot out at the screen. Kids shrilled up around them.

The movie was an old one, silent, and it started and stopped, repeated and jerked, showed reel numbers just as Elof had guessed, went on, off, on. Flying bugs and mosquitoes, caught in the projector light, cast huge fearsome shadows on the screen, sometimes completely blotting out a face or the crest of a hill. The movie showed a saint with hair on his chest but without any bullhood chasing cattle rustlers through woods and over dizzy tops of mountains and across dusty plains. Occasionally the saint stopped to save a pretty woman. Every gunfight brought forth volleys of unconscious yelps from the kids. Handkerchief-waving old ladies sussed loud gasps. Old men bit hard on pipes.

Elof laughed. And turned to Gert. "You know, they act like they've never seen anything else but these galloping blinkies."

"They haven't."

"Wow. What hicks."

She wiped sweat from her brow with a clean white, red-monogrammed handkerchief and stirred uneasily on the board seat. Her dress caught on a splinter and Elof reached across her lap and helped her unhook herself. "Just the same," Gert said, "just the same, for people who ain't got money, it's a real treat."

Elof sobered. "Yeh, I guess it is at that." He brushed sweat from his face too. "Yeh, I guess if I'd a never seen the real thing I'd had a yen for oats opery myself."

She moved beside him, lifting her dress from her sweating knees a little.

"Had enough of it?"

"If you did."

"Lady, it's running out of my ears. Let's go."

They got up and walked out of the darkness and into the bug-whirling light in front of the store.

"I tell you what," Elof said. "Let's take a spin instead. We'll fill 'er up with gas and go."

"Okay by me."

He drove into the single filling station; braked; shut off the ignition. The station had two pumps. There were no large advertising signs about. Even the proprietor's name was absent.

A bowed little man, wrinkled, with wise wry eyes, came out. He peered at them from underneath his black-visored station attendant's cap. A close look and Elof could see the old boy's skin had once been fair blond and his hair fair gold. And, like Elof, he had short flipperlike arms—except that they were thin and stiff with age.

"Fill 'er up," Elof said. "Sweet gas."

"Okay." The little old fellow went slowly about his business, his soiled coverall rustling. "You'll have to get out, ma'am," he said to Gert. "The tank's under the seat."

"Oh. Oh, that's right," Elof said hastily. "We'll have to get out, Gert. Sorry." He opened the door on her side and helped her.

While Gert stood off to one side holding her purse and pride, Elof watched the man drop the steel nozzle of the hose into the tank. Elof strolled around a little, looking at things, noting the little gray-painted shack that passed for a station, glancing at the graying house in back, noting the huge maple that leaned over the greasing pit.

Then he saw something else. "Hey, you sell both, don't you? Arctic and Antarctic both?"

"Yeh."

"Both high-test sweet gases. Huh. And here I was thinking you was selling one outfit's two grades of sweet gas."

"Nope."

"Huh. You must get all the trade hereabouts then."

"Most."

Elof noted that the tanks stood quite close to each other. Elof stared awhile, then said, "If I didn't know better, I'd almost say those two pumps are tapping the same tank. Below there."

The man laughed softly. "They are."

"Holy cats. No!"

"Yeh."

"You mean, a guy drives up, and he gets one gas no matter what he asks for?"

The dried-up blond man nodded. He finished filling the tank and hung up the dripping nozzle. He recapped the gas tank; replaced the car seat. "That's right."

"Do the companies know it?"

"I don't know. They've never asked an' I ain't told."

"How come you told me then?"

"You asked. You're the first. An' I told because there ain't nothin' to lie about."

Elof laughed.

"Sure. If the public wants to be caught by a name, let it. I'm here to give 'em what they want. Just so's I make a livin'." The old man held out his hand. "See?"

Elof laughed again. "Well, I never——" Then he noticed the open palm of the man's hand. "Oh, yeh." He dug into his overall, came up with a bill.

The old man wrestled some dirty coins out of a pocket of his coverall, gave Elof his change. Then, smiling a little, sagging, with an oily rag hanging out of his back pocket, he went back into the gray station and pulled up an easy chair and sat down and put up his feet on an oil barrel.

Elof chuckled and helped Gert into the pickup and set the spark and gas levers and cranked and, hopping in, was off.

He drove aimlessly into the country, into the dark night.

"Funny mutt," he said.

"Yes."

"What's his name?"

"I don't know."

Elof tooled along, musing to himself. Servant of the public. Service. Compared to Pa, he was a wise man. He worked under no false pretenses. He knew what the score was.

Elof drove on, almost idling the motor.

The thought of Pa switched Elof off onto another subject.

He smiled to himself. It was really something all right. Really something. A son using his father's pickup to take out his father's girl. That was one for the book.

Presently Elof found himself studying Gert. In the vague saffron reflection from the pickup's headlights he could just make out her face and figure.

What a woman. She, too, was really something for the jaybirds to cackle about.

She didn't have any of Marge's gay airs, but she had certain other qualities to make up for it: she didn't fill a man's ears with a lot of claptrap gossip; she was becoming in her strong muscular country way; and she had whopping breasts and a big fine behind.

He noted something else. He didn't feel uncomfortable wearing clodhoppers in the presence of Gert. It meant that he was in control, not the woman.

The dull orange headlights of the pickup barely lighted up the road. Cornfields and barren stubble fields came alternately and casually along. Elof studied each gray wooden fence post as the pickup purred forward. The motor below smelled comfortably of warmed oil.

Then, before he knew it, they were at the chokecherry brush by the railroad tracks north of the Hansen house. It startled him to think that the happy lark of the night was almost over.

He pulled up on the brake and parked off to one side of the road just across the tracks. He turned off the lights. Instantly masses of black night closed over them. Frosty stars lustered like motionless fireflies. Crickets chirked; frogs bayed.

He turned to her, a wavering smile on his lips.

She sat stiff; looked straight ahead.

"Gert," he said.

She turned shyly, glancing at him in the starlight with quick eyes.

He put his arm clumsily over her shoulder.

She waited a moment; then gently shook it off.

Surprised, he put it back.

Again she shook it away; this time firmly.

"Hey, what's the matter?"

"I don't neck the first night," she said.

Elof swallowed, hurrying his mind along to keep up with what had happened. "But this ain't the first night for us."

"It might as well be. After six years, do you still think that first one counts?"

Elof tried to slide his arm over her shoulder again.

"Cut it out," she commanded.

Elof angered. "Well, if that's the way you feel about it, t'hell with it." He flicked on the ignition, set the gas and spark, and got out and cranked up the pickup again. It popped merrily on the first turn.

He was angry until he drove onto the Hansen yard and pulled up in front of the house-yard gate. Then as quickly as he had angered, he found himself relenting. It wasn't every day that a man found himself beside so fulsome a woman.

He shut off the ignition and the headlights. "I'll take you to the door," he said.

"I can find my own way," she said. "After all, I've lived here all my life." She got out and started up the walk.

"Now look here, Gert, I didn't mean——"

"To neck me?" she put in, stopping halfway up the walk. "The heck you didn't. An' you better get it through your wood head I ain't like them pretty wimmen you knew at college, a quick cheap neck." In the dark her gray eyes glowed like almost-hidden lights. "Or like them girls t'Amen."

So she had overheard her brothers, Cor and Wilbur. "But, Gert, I thought, old times' sake——"

"No," she said. "No." She turned to go again.

Elof hopped out of the car and caught up with her. He touched her arm. "Please," he said.

She hesitated.

Elof looked around desperately, both inside and outside his head. It was on the outside that he found something. On the house yard, in the dark, he could just make out the board seat of the swing he had seen earlier in the evening, its two ropes coming down from a huge branch in the maple above. "Aw, Gert, don't go off in a huff. I didn't mean—— Look, Gert, remember how on that one date we had I gave you those great big pushes on the swing? Way up? C'mon, let me push you once again."

She hesitated.

"C'mon." He took her arm firmly; led her toward the big maple.

"Just a couple then."

"Sure, sure."

Elof helped her up on the seat. In a moment he was backing up, holding the swing board and her just ahead. She smelled daintily of perfume. Gathering his muscles and shoving, he rushed forward with all his stubby might, sending her high up above his outstretched hands, sailing her high into the night. Momentum carried him forward a few steps.

He turned to watch her, suddenly puffing.

Her white dress fluttered in the hot dry air of the swart night. She swung wondrously: high, downward, low, upward, high—

high, downward, low, upward, high. And after a while, slowly, the
arcs of her flight became shorter and shorter.

"Want another push?"

"If you wanna."

Again he heaved her high into the maple's branches. Again she
flowed in long white swooping arcs.

An idea occurred to him, and when she had slowed a little he
hopped up onto the swing beside her, catching the ropes above
her and planting his clumsy bluchers on the outside edges of the
board.

"Hey!" she said.

"C'mon," he said, still puffing from the pushing run, "c'mon,
swing with me. Get up on your feet and let's swing like we used
to, each pumping his turn."

"Ochh. You."

But she got up and stood against him.

At the top of his side of the arc, hanging onto the ropes, he
pumped down hard on his heels and shoved. The swing drove
down, went up in a long stroke. On the way back, she pumped
down and shoved. They worked rhythmically until the swing
soared almost level with its anchorage on the limb.

They coasted; puffed.

Elof, still not satisfied, started pumping once again. She joined
him. This time they worked until they were swinging above the
anchorage, until the swing whipped loosely about, jerked dan-
gerously at each end of the arc.

"What if the ropes should break?" she gasped, out of breath,
softening against him.

"They won't," he said.

He stood straight beside her tallness, folding his arm around
the ropes, holding himself rigid. His thighs were tight against
hers. He could feel where her body ended and divided into two
legs just a little above his own. It was right over his groin. And
his groin felt hot; it was almost as eloquent as a literate finger.
He pressed against her slyly, to divide her even more. Again and
again, at the end of each coasting swing, his arm pressured into
her bosom.

She said nothing; did not move.

Swooning a little, his hand slipped. The rope burned his palm. Abruptly he came to and made a new grab to keep from falling. The motion jostled love out of his mind.

The next moment, clearly, he saw himself—saw what was happening.

Gert represented a way of life he had been trying to escape. And here he was, rushing to get back into it.

Quickly he reached down a foot and dragged it through the grass and stopped the swing.

He contained himself long enough to help her down, to walk her to the door. Then he hurried away.

"Good night," she called.

He ignored her; clumsed through the gate.

Vaguely he heard her exclaim, "Well, for catsake! What got into him so all of a sudden?"

He set the spark and gas and whirled the crank; drove off the yard.

Yes. Just what had gotten in him?

Only that he wished he weren't where he was. That he wished he were in a new land where he would be shed of hated work, where he would have time to read his book, where he could become the hero and be loved for it, where he could have forever the feeling that he was as good a king bull as any other male alive.

A change of place, a change of home, that's what he needed.

If only he hadn't lacked technical knowledge, if only his father had been kindly, if only the world had been rid of greedy graspers, then, ah, then he would have been happy in the heaven-land of what should have been.

He drove hard, drove so furiously that once more the floor of the pickup began to burn. There was the smell of singed wood. Through a crack in the floor board he could see the red hot exhaust pipe.

Stubborn, he drove on.

He was turning into the Lofblom drive-in when, looking down, he saw flames. Braking, mouth tight, he pulled up in front of the store and shut off the motor and jumped out.

Grabbing a handful of sand and gravel and dust, and getting

up on the running board, with the flames almost singeing his face, he let fly at the colon-thick exhaust pipe. There was a sizz, a smothered sound, a sudden dousing of light around, a stuffy smell. The fire was out.

He looked up. And there in the dark sat Pa, smoking, a black blur on gray cement steps.

Elof waited, expecting the worst.

"I see you had yourself some fun," Pa said.

"Yeh."

"Gert?"

"Well . . . yeh."

The old man puffed on his pipe. Momentarily the fire in the bowl lighted up. Two pink cheeks and two sharp eyes came out of the night like a Rembrandt face: suddenly illuminated flesh in surrounding brown-black.

Elof waited some more.

Still Pa sat unmoved, puffing.

"Was it awful busy tonight?" Elof asked.

"Some."

"Uh-huh." Elof put his blunt hands into his pockets. "Yeh. Well . . . By the way, I had a fire."

"So I saw."

"Better bend that exhaust down a little."

"Was that what was the matter?"

"Yeh."

"Well, then why don't you get at it the first thing in the mornin'?"

Elof stood a moment. "Okay. That's just what I'll do." Then quietly, not slinking, Elof stepped past him and went in back and to bed.

CHAPTER XII: T'Hell with It

. . . Who can foretell the exact moment when a catalyst begins the brewing?

Who can select the exact second when rambling atoms suddenly become orderly?

Who can pick the exact moment when a man makes up his mind?

And who knows why? . . .

It was after breakfast and Elof had the whole morning to himself.

The day was muggy out and the idea of studying accounting, or even reading *Peregrine Pickle,* just didn't appeal to him.

He walked out on the cement steps on the sunny side of the store and looked over the country. Just before him stood the pickup he had fixed a couple of days ago. Beyond, across the road and fence, was a field of corn, just now relaxing from its season's growth and letting hang hairy ears. Still farther beyond, near the green windbreak grove of a farmstead, a moldboard plow slowly blackened a stubble field. And far on the horizon, a dozen miles away, wavered the unsteady dots and tiny child blocks that he knew to be clumps of farmhouses and barns and silos and trees.

From habit his eyes swung southeast toward the Nelson home, there where Hilda had once hunted Easter eggs with him, where alone at night she had slept sweet in a child's clean bed—and was now no more. God grant that if he did not find her eyes among womankind again he would still never forget how blue they had been. Hilda.

Above and to his left, the cottonwoods fluttered aery green gills.

The chokecherry tree below turned each of its oval, abruptly pointed leaves to filtered light.

Elof saw some activity over at Kaes Hinke's gas station. Wondering what was up, he went down the steps and started toward it. He had on new shoes, a pair of gray suède oxfords, and he walked lightly and quickly down the graveled road.

He passed Loren Solen sitting apathetically in front of his cut-rate station on the northwest corner, saw Bill Cooper leering out of a window of his station on the southwest corner, and, walking all the while into the lazy morning sun, turned at last into Hinke's drive-in on the northeast corner.

There was something different about the place and, looking closely, he discovered that Kaes was no longer selling Arctic gas. Instead there was a huge sign declaring to all the world and its travelers that this was the only and exclusive station selling Antarctic products in the vicinity. Elof whirled around. Sure enough. Cooper was now selling Arctic. Screech had broken with Kaes after all.

Kaes was off to one side of the station fixing a flat for a skinny youth. The youth, wearing a dark blue suit, a white shirt and red tie, leaned with one hand against the black fender of a dusty old-model coupé. White cuffs protruded from the sleeves of the slim's blue suit, and deft gold links shone in the light.

Elof said, "Hi, Kaes."

"Hi," Kaes responded shortly, puffing, squatting, trying desperately to pry a casing over a drop rim.

"See you switched companies."

Kaes laughed. "Yeh. The minute Arctic pulled out, the Antarctic boys were right here waving a brand-new contract under my nose. Them big companies may be in cahoots, but if one of 'em slips the other is sure to catch up on him. Like a couple of bears huggin' an' holdin' hands—until one of 'em gets a paw loose. Then look out."

Elof smiled. "Well, maybe you'll be happier with this new outfit."

"I dunno. I hope so," Kaes said, at last getting the tire over the rim and nodding triumphantly at the lad. "I hope so. But runnin' both the farm an' this joint, I'm still busier'n a one-armed monkey with the seven-year itch."

"You better bounce the tire," the young man said quietly, pointing. "Make sure the tube is even all through there." The young man puffed a little, as if he had trouble getting his wind.

"Sure thing."

The young man stood up and coughed lightly, softly. "Got any coke in there?"

"Yeh. To yer right as you go in."

"No hamburgers?"

"No. But that's in the works. It's coming. That little shanty you see off to the side there is gonna be made over. Gonna hire me a man or a woman an' sell chow along with the gas. Gotta do something to keep the trade from goin' across the road along with Arctic gas."

Elof watched the coughing slim smiling to himself. He noticed the gray-edged, almost powdered purple pallor of his face, the mauve humped fingernails.

Feeling thirsty for a coke himself, Elof stepped inside too. Together he and the stranger each dug out a bottle from the cooler.

The slim uncapped his and, tipping it up, said, "Here's t'you."

"T'you."

The young man guggled a moment and then, wiping his lips, set down his bottle on the top of the cooler. He pulled out a pack of cigarettes, offered Elof one, took one himself, put the pack back, lighted up for both Elof and himself. He coughed and blew out a broken smoke ring.

"Come far?" Elof asked.

The slim combed thin black hair away from a high forehead. "Yeh. From Anxious." The slim's gray eyes surveyed Elof leisurely.

"Heading for Sioux City?"

"No. Sioux Falls."

Elof looked down, vaguely seeing his own shoes. "Maybe this is kind a nosy, but I'm curious to know what kind of work you're in."

"Why," the other said softly, "why, I sell."

"Sell?"

"Yeh."

"Make a living at it?"

"Sure."

"Good one?"

"Sure."

"How good?"

"Just got through makin' a hundred bucks."

"What's your line?"

"Kingsfood Grocery. Direct from the factory to you. No middleman."

Elof leaned a hand against a greasy oil drum. "Well, uh—but, uh—I mean, how do you go about it?"

The slim swigged from his bottle, drew on his cigarette, waved a lanky elbow-jutting arm. "You interested in sellin'?"

"I don't know." Then, "I do know, though, I don't like where I am."

"And what's that?"

"Clerking a store." Elof pointed at his father's store down the road.

"Why, then you're sellin' too." The coughing man brightened. "I tell you. I'm what they call an advance salesman. Open up new territory. Get new customers. Take orders for groceries. Get a dollar for every order I place, big or small. Tea, coffee, oatmeal, so on. Send in the orders to the branch office. Sioux Falls." The slim drew on his cigarette again. His short sentences fit exactly between puffing breaths. "They give the orders to a follow-up man. He delivers it. Talks the housewife into taking a second order. Next thing the housewife knows, she's a regular customer. And part of a new route."

"Is it tough going?"

"I just told you. Made a hundred last week. Near Anxious. You know, where the Lord's dished out six tornadoes an' they're anxious about when the seventh's comin'?"

Elof finished his bottle, set it aside. The laconic slim revived memories of old-time hiking days: of lonely daisy-bright road corners, of waiting, of wondrous new hills and valleys.

One thing bothered Elof. If the young man was such a hot-shot, why wasn't he driving a better car? "This hundred bucks, how often can you pull it off?"

"Whenever I feel like it." The slim coughed. "Trouble is, I don't feel like it every week."

"Could a guy sell as fast as he wanted to? Every week?"

"Sure."

"Oh." Four hundred a month—a king's income!

"Sure. It's a wrap-up."

"Think a guy like me could do it too?"

The slim's eyes narrowed. "If you'd stick your chin out a little and grow a smile on it, yeh."

Elof pondered. "This company, what's it again?"

"Kingsfood Grocery."

"They couldn't use another man, could they?"

"I think so. The company's a new one an' they're lookin' for new blood."

"They are, huh."

"Yeh." The slim puffed on his cigarette. "When can you start?"

"Well, right now if I wanted to."

"You sure?"

"Sure I'm sure. Change clothes and pack a few duds, and I'd be ready." Elof cast around in his mind for any obstructions in the way. He found one. "Only one thing. I ain't got a car."

"Well, you could travel with me. At least for a while. Best anyway to have two men hit a new territory. Save money. Gas. Room. An' it gives you four eyes to see things with. T'catch onto the tricks of the country."

"Could I—could I really go along with you?"

"Sure." The slim puffed. "I tell you. They're holdin' a sales convention in Sioux Falls this afternoon. That's where I'm headin' for right now. I can introduce you to my super an' see what he says."

"Today?"

"Today."

Elof gave it a last thought; then exclaimed, "T'hell with it. I'm gonna do it. Give it a try." He stuck out his right hand. "It's a deal. Maybe I can get going before I finish my accounting. My name's Elof Lofblom."

The slim closed a lean claw over Elof's blunt hand. "Good. Mine's Morton Pott. They call me Fats for short."

"Fats?"

Fats said, "I was a big man once."

"Oh."

"Well, get your duds changed. I'm waitin'."

At noon they topped a long wide hill. And there below in a valley lay Sioux Falls. A sinuous river cut through the downtown district. Faint gray mists of smoke hung over the pink-purple prairie city.

Fats turned off on a side street. "I stay with my brother Larry and his wife Liz down here. He works in the stockyards. I got a room there I pop inta whenever I come in. Guess you kin stay there with me. We'll ask Liz."

They entered the worker section of town. Kitten children stalked the lawns, scattering blocks and broken toys and bottles and dirt everywhere. Hedges were not too well tended, and most of the housewives had baby wash hung out on the clotheslines in back.

Fats turned into a driveway and parked on the east side of a two-story frame house. Once-white paint was peeling from the structure. The porch needed repairs. The windows on the inside, however, had freshly starched white curtains.

"Here we are," Fats said, puffing lightly.

They got out and, stiff from the long ride on the hard seat of the old black coupé, walked slowly around up the porch, carrying their suitcases.

The door opened and a plump woman, about five months pregnant, blond hair done up in curlers, greeted them. "Hi, Fats. Hi."

"Hi," Fats said. "Picked me up a friend." Fats was winded from the short climb up the porch steps. "Gonna sell with me." He introduced them, "Elof Lofblom, meet my sis-in-law Liz."

"How'd you do."

"You do."

All three stood uncertainly a moment.

Liz said, "Won't you come in?"

"Why, sure. If it's all right," Elof said.

"Sure it's all right," Fats growled. "Lead the way."

Elof stepped into the parlor, Fats and Liz following.

Liz said to Fats, "I had an idea you was comin' in, so I made dinner for you. Read about the convention in the paper."

"Good." Fats put his suitcase to one side and sat down on the couch, sighing deeply. "Good. Got a little extra for him?"

"I think so."

"Put it on."

Elof stood hesitating.

"Sit down," Fats commanded.

Liz gave Elof a cool smile and she shoved up a parlor chair. "Make yourself t'home, won't you?"

"Okay," Elof said, putting his suitcase to one side, too, and settling down into the chair. He drew the trouser legs of his gray suit loose up over his knees. His short legs barely touched the blue carpet on the floor.

"Liz, I thought I told you to put on the grub."

Liz laughed a little. "You must be hungry."

"I am. About ready to turn cannibal."

Liz left for the kitchen.

Elof perked up an eye at the way Fats bossed Liz around and guessed that the Pott men dominated their women, dominated them to a point where even a brother-in-law could lay down the law.

Elof looked around the place. The design on the parlor wall looked like a mob of frogs in wild flight. The woodwork was of a dull mahogany color. Over the burgundy plush davenport on which Fats sat hung a huge family picture, a bearded father and a fat woman and two young boys standing between three older girls.

"Our family," Fats said. "That little shaver there is me. The other's Larry. The rest are my sisters. And the folks. Sisters're out to Hollywood tryin' out swimming pools." Fats took out a cigarette, offered Elof one. "Say, Larry's workin', ain't he?" he yelled into the kitchen.

Liz's muffled voice came back. "Yes. He'll be home tonight."

"Uh-huh."

Presently the food was on and the two lads fell to.

Liz watched the table nervously.

Elof wasn't sure, but he had the feeling she wasn't too anxious to have him around; as if she were afraid he might become a burden to them. Fats, the brother, was one thing. But Fats and a friend—that was another. The furnishings in the house told Elof Larry and Liz weren't too well off.

After dinner Fats drove downtown and parked near the City Auditorium. The side streets were jammed with parked cars. Fats locked up the old coupé and strolled slowly toward the building.

Fats recognized a few faces out front; introduced Elof.

Elof, his mind a whirl, mumbled vague responses.

They entered the lobby.

Fats said, looking at some doors off to one side, "My boss'll probably be in one a these." He drew in a fluttery breath. "Yeh."

Fats opened a door and a mass of acrid cigar smoke blew over them. Quick-eyed, slick-dressed men ringed a desk. An even quicker-eyed, more sleekly dressed man sat in the armchair at the desk. He was bald, and his face had the look of baby skin bronzed by golf-course sun.

"Van Dam," Fats said quietly, "hello."

"Hello." The very sleek one jumped up. "Why, it's Fats! Glad to see you again, you old buzzard." He turned to the others. "Man, fellows, here's the damn best salesman this side of Capone's Chicago. You should a seen what he did around Anxious last week. Crimpity cripes crap. The only thing he missed was the dead housewives in the graveyard."

The ring of mink-eyed men coughed forced laughter.

Fats said, clearing his throat, smiling as if inwardly he held the whole caboodle in contempt, "Say, what I dropped in for was— I'd like to have you meet one of our new salesmen. Elof Lofblom."

Van Dam's brown eyes wicked at Elof, held him, drilled him, sought out his soul. The other minks surveyed him too. From their actions Elof guessed he didn't look like too good a prospect. Elof sniffed and brushed back his gold hair and tried to make his gray-clad short body even shorter.

Van Dam tapped his desk slowly. "So you wanna sell, huh?" Van Dam brushed the fly of his trousers, brushed the curve of it lovingly, as if, all other things of life being vanity that unto vanity-hell must go, he at least had that, the power of procreation. "So you wanna sell, huh?"

Elof knew it was now or never, so he put on a bold front and desperately forced his mind to a point just ahead and said, "No, not sell, but bring service to the people. Give people their money's worth."

Van Dam's caution instantly vanished. He rose to his toes, leaned over the desk, wrung Elof's hand, pumped it again, shouted, waved a cigar at the others. "D'hear that, you doorbell punchers? There. That's what I call talk. That's the way I want all you houseworkers to talk. Get me?" He strode around his desk. He embraced Elof. Elof was short, but Van Dam was every bit as short. "My boy," Van Dam exclaimed, "my boy, you're gonna be a success. First off when I saw you, you didn't look so hot to me. But now I see I made a mistake. Anybody talking like you did now is bound to make a killing."

Fats said, "It's a wrap-up."

Elof blushed. He was dumfounded to have heard philistinery come out of his mouth.

He heard Van Dam ask Fats, "Where'd you pick him up?"

"In a fillin' station. Chokecherry Corner. Tendin' a store there. Knew right away he had it."

"Good boy." Van Dam slammed a fist on Elof's shoulder. "Young man, we're puttin' our men through their sellin' techniques to tear the ass out of 'em. Why don't you hang around this afternoon and keep your ears open, take it all in, and then tomorrow you can go out and sell? I mean, 'bring service to the people,' 'give people their money's worth.' "

Elof nodded soberly.

Elof sat with Fats and a few hundred salesmen near the front of the auditorium. Spirals of cigarette smoke rose from them, lifting into an indefinite gray-purple cloud through which ceiling lights drove saffron streams.

Men wore blue and brown and gray suits, mostly conservative in style. There was a shrillness in the voices, a quality of gritty rasp filings in the laughter.

Elof listened to the men go through their routines. Some were bold, some suave, some halting. One of them, a stooped-over man, stumbled pathetically and Van Dam, sitting in the front row, hopped up and ran to the platform and sailed into him. The salesman carried a mixing bowl as a leader, started his come-on talk with it. The bowl was to be given away, provided the prospect bought a considerable amount of groceries, preferably over a period of months. By the time the housewife could call the free gift her own, she was a steady customer, caught in the invisible but nevertheless powerful toils of habit and obligation. It was the stupe's handling of the giveaway that Van Dam pounced on.

And then Elof was called up front.

He stumbled as he got out of his seat. The clumsiness surprised him. Hadn't his feet gotten used to the new shoes yet?

He climbed the short stairs, stood in front of Van Dam. Van Dam had taken a chair on the stage and was acting the part of the housewife on whom Elof was to call.

"Before you go out on the road for us, kid, I want to see how you'll do. Give." Van Dam stroked his crotch. "Give. C'mon. I'm the lady of the house with a mouse in her blouse and you come along and knock. Go ahead. Knock."

For a second Elof found himself speechless. Words were like chokecherry stones—they clung to the tongue; they wouldn't come out.

"Give," Van Dam commanded, his bold black eyes fixing on Elof.

The authority in the other's voice broke open the door to Elof's word-hoard. "I'm not so good in front of a crowd."

"Best way to learn. If you can do it here, you're sure to do it on the road. Right, Fats?"

"It'll be a wrap-up," Fats burped up from the crowd.

"Sure. Give."

Elof imitated knocking on a door, answered Van Dam's simulated woman's voice, and, remembering how the others had begun their soft-song, mumbled, "Ma'am, ain't this just about the nicest thing you've ever set your eyes on?"

Someone in the crowd laughed.

Elof blushed.

"Never mind," Van Dam snapped.

Elof bore on, still mumbling.

When he finished, Van Dam said, "Not so good. You'll have to do better. Right now I'd say you couldn't sell ice water in a drought." Van Dam scratched his chin. "One thing I will say for you, though. You've got the right spirit. Right spirit. And you look like a nice momma's boy. So the wimmen'll probably open the door to you. But it's what you do after that counts." Van Dam paused. "There isn't much I can do for you right now except jack up your confidence a little." Van Dam ran an eloquent hand over his bald head. "I think the best thing is for you to go out on the road for a couple of weeks and learn the hard way. And then come back and we'll iron out the wrinkles up in my office. Meantime, all I can say is: hit it hard an' get behind it."

Elof thanked him softly.

Van Dam stood up. "All right, fellows. Let's break off for lunch. We're servin' some of our own wonderful coffee an' doughnuts in back there. Kingsfood coffee. Yum-yum." He waved his hand to silence a few gibes. "But before we do, let's sing"—he picked up a yellow booklet from the table on the platform—"let's sing from the *Kingsfood Singer,* page 21, 'The Jolly Kingsfood Man.' You sing it to the tune of 'The Star-Spangled Banner.' " Van Dam pointed to a piano at the edge of the orchestra pit. "Russ. Russ Benton. Get over there onto that stomp-box there and rattle them elephant's teeth."

A skinny man with a narrow and very high forehead got up and went over and reluctantly sat down before the instrument and began to tinkle the keys.

Van Dam waited for the prelude to finish and then, lifting himself to his toes and waving an arm, began to conduct the mink-eyes through the song:

> *"O say! can you see by the dawn's early light*
> *The ol' pickup all packed and the gas tank all streaming,*
> *The mixing bowl shining and the sale slip carbonned,*
> *A smile on his lips and service in his heart well-meaning,*
> *As the jolly Kingsfood man his day he prepares*
> *And heads down the highway to distribute his wares?"*

At the break in the seller's anthem Van Dam lifted high his hand, his gray gabardine trousers arching high above his oxfords, and shouted, "Hit that chorus, boys! Hit it hard!"

The mink-eyes leaned on it:

"O say, has that jolly young man yet called on yoouu,
The jolly young Kingsfood man with the eyes so bluue?"

Van Dam dropped his hand. "All right, now for the Kingsfood coffee an' doughnuts. Hop to it." And with a skip he was off the stage and gone into the crowd.

The mink-eyes, the fat, the slim, the sallow, all the hard-eyed, got up and broke into male talk and pushed up the aisles toward the back.

Later Elof got himself a cup of coffee and a doughnut and crawled off by himself in a corner.

Fats saw him. And disengaged himself from a group of guffawing storytellers. "What's up?"

"Nothing."

Fats puffed, took a bite, puffed. "You ain't backin' out?"

"No. But I don't feel right."

"What's the matter."

"All that hup-de-do and talk. Singing. I dunno, there's something false about it."

Fats looked at him with steady wolf-gray eyes. "Look, mister. I noticed you didn't join in with the boys singin'. Let me tell you something. One way to queer yourself in this game is to get your tail over the line at the start."

Elof said nothing. He took another bite of doughnut and swilled it down with a swallow of Kingsfood coffee.

. . . Maybe we wisenoses work ourselves into a lather over nothing. Maybe we read into Elof our own frets and worries when we consider the problem of: "Why am I here?"

Maybe Elof doesn't worry about it at all. Maybe he just lives. Exists.

Actually, we cannot be absolutely, categorically, finally, and at last sure that animals do not enjoy their lives. Just try once grappling barehanded with weasels, minks, skunks, bobcats, tigers, lions, with intent to kill. Even sheep will surprise you . . .

Bright and early the next day Elof and Fats dressed and shaved—Fats trying to hide the turgid flush on his face with a couple of pats of baby-buttock powder—and broke fast and roosted wholesomely on the can and packed their clothes and then were ready to go.

They drove downtown and parked and went up to Van Dam's office to get their assignment.

Fats knocked on the door of the sixth-floor Kingsfood office.

"C'mon in."

Fats entered, cleared his throat, a smile on his masklike face, Elof following after.

"Well, well." Van Dam hopped up from his armchair and held out a box of huge cigars. "Well, well. How are my soft-singers today?"

Both declined the proffer of long smokes.

Fats took a chair and caught his breath. "Don't want to take your time, boss, but where do we go?"

Van Dam waved Elof to a seat. "Sit down, sit down."

Elof found himself a chair near the door.

The mood of the room almost shushed what little enthusiasm Elof had awakened with that morning. The plastered walls were painted a cloudy-day gray, the ceiling a muted gray. The floor was covered with a tufted white-gray carpet. The office equipment was scant: two visitors' chairs, a huge map with red and white and blue pins, an armchair, and a gray steel desk. Outside of an ink pad and ash tray, the top of the desk was as empty as a twister-swept prairie. Elof had the distinct impression he had suddenly and willfully stepped into an iron jail; had gone into see a bald-headed miser living in a steel vault. Elof moved his chair still closer to the door.

Fats repeated his question. "Where do we go?"

Van Dam sucked on his big cigar, chewed it, squinted his glinting black-brown eyes at Fats, and then waved a hand. "Well, let's take a look at the map." He strode to the wall, planted his feet well apart before it. The map was a huge one, six by eight feet, and it spread out the geography of Siouxland and its neighboring territory: the southeast corner of North Dakota, the eastern half of South Dakota, the upper northwest section of Nebraska, the northwest corner of Iowa, and the southwest region of Minnesota. "Well, boys, this is our territory. Lots of it still virgin as far as Kingsfood is concerned. Now what I'd like to do is to send you two into fresh territory——"

"Good," Fats put in from his chair.

"—so you—— Huh?" The oversize cigar almost fell from Van Dam's mouth. He looked queerly at Fats a moment, brushed a hand over the fly of his pants, recovered, laughed, said, "Fats, no wonder you're a hot-shot salesman. You—well, never mind." Van Dam walked around in a circle, as if the idea he was nurturing were almost too big for the three of them to consider. "I tell you. There's an area here"—he waved his hand at the belly of what was to be seen of South Dakota—"an area right through here which always beats down the tail of my best men. Beats 'em down to a frazzle. Whips 'em. It's as tough to crack as a petrified nut. Can't seem to make inroads a-tall. And I thought maybe, since you did such a hot-shot job over at Passage, a tough territory too, full of them tight suspicious Hollanders——"

"What's the biggest town there?" Fats asked, pointing at South Dakota.

"Huh? Town? Heh, heh. Now, Fats, you know there ain't no towns out there. Just names for gopher holes."

"Well, what's the name then?"

"Iota."

Fats nodded.

Again Van Dam buzzed around in a circle. "Yessir, Iota, South Dakota. Hardest nut to crack in the Union."

Elof got up from his chair and studied the map while they talked. It occurred to him that the recent droughts, especially the blasting heat of August just gone, might have cleaned it out. "Maybe they ain't got no money, Van Dam."

"Hoch. Poch. Don't tell me that."

"They've had some pretty bad days in that part of the country. Some's been burnt and dusted out."

"Aw, don't tell me. Farmers are always complainin'. Always. And all along they've got a sockful of dough hidden on the place somewhere. Or buried in some old pisspot someplace. Or up the old lady's garter. Plenty a money."

Fats said, "Iota, is it?"

"Yeh."

"Let's get goin' then, Elof." Fats got up with an effort and stepped to the door. He offered Elof and himself a cigarette, and lit them, and said, "So long, boss," and stepped out into the hall with Elof.

"Huh? What?" Van Dam exclaimed. "Wait."

The door closed after them slowly, leaving Van Dam standing alone and flabbergasted in the middle of his empty office.

Fats went down the hall to the elevator door, pushed the *Down* button.

After a moment Fats said, "Trouble with Van Dam is that he smokes too many big cigars. Gives him a blown-up notion about himself. Gives him the bighead. Gives him the diarrhea of the jawbone."

Elof nodded. They went down the elevator and out into the street and a bright September sun. Fats got into his parked coupé.

Fats said, "Well, let's get goin'."

"Wait," Elof said, holding back. "One thing before we go. I'm down to two bucks. How soon before I get my first check?"

"Forget it."

"No, c'mon now, I——"

"Forget it."

"But——"

"Skip it. The car runs jut as cheap with two in it as one. A room with a double bed don't cost much more than one with a single. An' if we get real hungry, we'll dip into some of the sample groceries we got along with us. If we have to."

"But——"

"Forget it. I'll carry you till you get on your feet."

"Well—okay. But remember. I'm gonna pay you back."

"You goddamn right you are. Now shut up an' get into the car."

They were out on the road, riding west, going into the desolate country, following the narrow white ribbon of Highway 16 sliding past enormous rectangular farms and ranches. They saw corduroy-ribbed fields of green and yellow-drying corn, saw purple plowed stubble fields, saw gray sun-dried pastures. And every mile they went west, the land became drier, the air more burning and rasping, the country more lonely and empty. But it was wonderful land, Elof thought, wonderful. It fit what he felt in his heart.

They drove on; sometimes Fats driving the old black coupé, sometimes Elof.

A figment of an argument Elof had had with Fats earlier in the morning came back to him. He had been packing his account-ing-course lessons and *Peregrine Pickle* into his suitcase when Fats had interrupted with a sarcastic remark. "Guys readin' books're wastin' their time. An' wastin' the time of others."

Elof turned to Fats at the wheel. "That wisecrack you made this morning about reading books—how can a smart fellow like you make a statement like that? You know well enough that most ideas come from books. If it wasn't for books you wouldn't be driving this car right now today."

"Crap," Fats said, "crap. Books, goin' to college, all that guff, it's a big waste a time. Take me, f'rinstance. I've been sellin' six years and I'm makin' more money today than any guy in my high school class that went on to college."

"Sour grapes."

Fats turned slowly from his driving and drilled Elof with a cold gray eye. "You and Van Dam. You blab too much."

"I was only suggesting."

"Uh-huh."

But Elof couldn't resist bucking the other's belligerence. "Still and all, I think college, reading, education, ideas, books, they do something for you."

"What?"

"Well, they open up your mind. It's like flying like a butterfly instead of grubbing like a grubworm. Like living by a hundred-watt bulb instead of a ten. More light."

"Light for what?" Fats asked, coughing a little. "I take it you went to college?"

"Some. Yeh."

"Well, boy, I'll bet my light will lead me faster to more money than your light any day of the week. Includin' Sundays."

"But there's more to life than money."

"What?"

"Sure there is. I tell——"

"Look, bo. There's one thing I've learned from my short life. That's this. You see, I was born and raised on a farm, then went to high school, later worked in a packin' plant—and from that I learned one thing. That life's a fight. That the first law is to fill that belly. No matter what. If somebody gets in the way, you get rid of 'im. In such a way, of course, so that you don't land in jail. Because if your belly don't get filled reg'lar, your body dies. And if your body dies, where's your ideas then?"

Elof said nothing. Fats was right.

And, Fats was wrong. There was more to it than that. Just what, Elof couldn't say. He felt he should say something about the value of dreams and hopes, of being a hero, but against Fats's brilliant mink logic he had no matching argument.

They got to Iota about noon.

As Van Dam had suggested, it was little more than a gopher hole. The little village lay north of a railroad track: a depot, an elevator, a grocery store, a filling station, a town hall, a couple dozen scattered homes. And the sun was so bright in it, so white with heat, that the reflection from the cement sidewalks and streets had given the inhabitants all a sunburn under the chin.

The country around was as dry and as dusty as a street. And as barren of live growth. It was grazing country, and on the vast rolling terrain within the circle of the entire horizon only a half-dozen ranches could be seen.

Fats parked in front of an eat shop. "Well, no use hurrying out right away. Best time to hit is between two-thirty and five, just in between naptime and supper-making time. Babies are all awake by then, and hard-boiled hubbies still ain't home from work. So we might as well lunch. An' take a nap ourselves."

At two-thirty the boys drove down a short residential street. Clapboard frame houses predominated: some gray, some brown, some white. Only a banker and a preacher had been able to afford brick homes—just like in Hello.

"It won't take us long to work these," Elof said.

"I'll say not. That's what Van Dam meant when he said Iota. The son of a bitch."

Fats parked at the end of the street. With foxy eyes he studied the houses on both sides and at last said, "Well, those on the right look the easiest. I'll let you learn on them."

"Now, none of that. I can——"

"Take 'em. An' I mean take 'em."

They got out. Elof's bared gold hair tingled in the stinging heat of the sun.

Fats opened up the back of the old black coupé, broke into a box, and handed a giveaway mixing bowl to Elof. "Well, bo, here's your leader, the little item that's bound to put the bead in the little old lady's eye."

Elof took it gingerly.

"Well, bo, good luck. Hit it hard an' get behind it."

Elof nodded, swallowed, tried to quiet his leapfrogging heart.

He started up the street, carrying the bowl under his stubby arm. A sales pad jugged up and down inside the jacket pocket of his gray suit. Out of the corner of his eye he watched Fats approach a house, saw him knock nonchalantly.

"T'hell with it," Elof muttered to himself. "If he can, I can."

Whistling bravely, he went up a sidewalk. He sized up the house carefully, just as he had seen Fats size up the block.

The trees in front of the house were as bare of leaves as a dog-licked bone. The grass was brown and as brittle as flakes of ashes. Orts and shards littered the yard. The paint on the house had weathered off. The shades were all drawn. A dust dune behind the house rose to half the height of the first-story windows. Two black-eyed children played on a wind-ribbed side of it.

Elof knocked on the door.

After a moment he noticed a window shade moving. A face peered out onto the yard; saw him. The shade flapped to. There was a moment of silence. Then the door gave a little.

A life-weathered housewife looked at him. She was taller than he.

"Good afternoon, ma'am," Elof rattled hastily, "good afternoon. I've got something here that I'm sure you'll like." He held up the shining yellow mixing bowl. "Did you ever see anything like this?"

The woman stared. Her hands picked up her gray apron and slowly began to wring it and then wiped the sweat from her brow with it.

"No? Well, ma'am, it's all yours. Yes, yours. All you got to do is . . ." Elof singsonged off a series of phrases. Vaguely he realized it was an aping of Van Dam's demonstrators.

In the background, across the street, he could hear the murmur of Fats's voice and a customer's warm response.

Elof went on, tried to hit it hard. "Ma'am, this mixing bowl's put out by one of the finest kiln manufacturers in America. And I'm here to tell you . . ."

The woman still stared.

Elof caught himself scowling—instantly forced a happy grimace to his lips.

The woman loosened a little.

"Sure," Elof said. "And now I want to tell you something. This swell mixing bowl can be used for——"

"Step inside," the woman said, interrupting, "you're lettin' the heat in."

"—used for—— Huh?"

"Step in. You're lettin' the heat in."

"Oh." Elof popped inside.

She closed the door.

She said, "I keep the doors and windows closed and the shades down. I got a theory it keeps the house cool that way. It does." She pointed to a chair. "Take a seat."

For a moment the house seemed dark, but, forcing his eyes, Elof managed to make out the form of a chair by a window. He sat down.

"Now, what was it you said again?" the woman asked.

"Well—I've got a free mixing bowl here for you that——"

"No hooks or crooks to it?" The woman asked sharply.

"No. You just——"

Abruptly the brightening look of a cunning and a hungry shopper came into her eye. "I've crazed for one a them fer years. Let me see it."

The woman took it and loved it fumblingly in her calloused red-veined hands. She smiled to herself in the artificial dusk. "It's nice. Real nice."

Elof's heart melted. Her sudden longing was so pathetic, so endearing, that he had half a notion to give it to her with no strings attached. Had there been no mink-eyed, cocksure Fats to face later on, he would have. He looked away from her, looked at the shades casting buff twilight in the parlor, smelled the nose-clogging odor of summer house-sweat, and remembered his mother, remembered how she, too, had craved the best that a master potter's wheel might offer.

"What do I do to get it?" the woman asked.

"Well—give me an order for Kingsfood groceries, sign a receipt for it, and a bowl like this—not this one but one like it—is yours. Our follow-up man will give it to you when he delivers your order two days from now. And then, after you've bought about forty dollars' worth altogether, it's yours for good."

"You mean, I can't have this right away?"

"No, not this particular one. But one like it."

"When did you say I was to get it then?"

Poor people, Elof thought, poor people. Surprises were so rare in their songless lives that their minds had lost all one-time child elasticity. He started over. "You give me an order for groceries. You sign for it. I turn it in. Two days later a truck delivers it. And delivers you a shining yellow bowl."

"Oh."

"Sure." Elof sighed massively. He handed her an illustrated booklet.

She took it. "These the groceries?"

"That's right." Elof got out his pad and pencil, waited.

She paged through the book, looking at the colored pictures in what little light the shade-drawn windows allowed her. "Sure's nice groceries, all right. Sure would like to have some."

"Well, you know how to get 'em. All you got to do is to give me an order."

"We ain't got the money."

"You've got some kind of income though, haven't you?"

"Some. Relief checks. An' what my old man kin steal from the railroad."

Elof started. "But you get groceries somewhere, don't you?"

"Sure. What our one store will allow us on our relief checks." She looked at the booklet again. "Pretty high, ain't they?"

"But look at the quality you're getting."

The woman paused. She turned herself so that more of the dim light from the windows could fall on the glossy page. She looked off to one side, considering. A sly look came into her eyes; and vanished. "Well, I'll take some oatmeal. An' a bottle a vanilla. An' some flour. Five pounds."

"And the money?"

"I tell you. We got a little cash comin' in beside the relief check."

Elof scribbled. "Anything else?"

"I guess that's all."

"Now, will you sign right here?"

"Sign?"

"Yeh." Elof smiled at her, leaned off the edge of his chair toward her. "Right here." He held out the pencil.

She shook her head. "I don't sign things. Can't. My old man'd kill me."

"Well, now . . ."

"Nope. Don't like to sign things. Scared of it."

Elof swallowed, considered, retreated a little. "Well, I suppose—— I tell you what. I don't see why your word ain't as good as your signature. Mine is." He got to his feet. "I'll send this in, and in two days at the most you can expect our Kingsfood follow-up man here to deliver your order. And your mixing bowl."

"Fine." She stood up too.

"Good-by, Mrs. . . . ? Mrs. . . . ?" Elof hinted.

"Good-by."

Elof opened the door. Again he tried to get it out of her. "By the way, who shall I say this order is to be delivered to? Mrs. . . . ?"

"Mrs. Aasland."

"Mrs. Aasland? Henry Aasland?"

"No. Anders Aasland."

"Good. Well, Mrs. Aasland, I hope you like the mixing bowl."

"I hope so too." She shut the door.

Elof stumbled out into the sun. He was soaked with sweat. He pulled his shirt gingerly from his wet body, fluffed his suit jacket open like a bird preparing to take wing.

Fats was coming down the steps of the second house, saw him, stepped slowly across toward him, puffing. They met in the middle of the dusty street. The sun owled down on them.

"Well, did you get her?" Fats asked.

"Yeh."

Fats's eyes opened. "You did?"

"Yeh. It was as easy as eating lemon pie à la mode. All I had to do was smile."

Fats nodded. He eyed Elof. "Yeh, I think maybe you'll make a salesman after all. But one thing. Don't let them visit with you. Cut 'em short. Smile, but cut 'em short. Drive it home an' get. Because, you see, while you were doing one, I did two."

"But a man's got to be polite."

"Drive it in an' cut it short."

Elof shook his head. It didn't sound very civilized.

"Well, go get number two."

"Yeh."

Elof worked the street, going up each walk, knocking, talking, blushing, smiling desperately, watching himself learning the mechanical patter, inwardly noting that the faces he met began to blur into each other—also inwardly noting that he wasn't warming up to the game very much.

At five o'clock Fats called a halt. "No use buttin' in on their meals. Especially not when it's time for your own."

Elof let out a huge sigh. And discovered that his shoulders and back had been hunched up from the tension. He rolled his short arms and shrugged his shoulders to get rid of it.

"Well, bo, how many?"

"Seven," Elof said. He spoke uncertainly, not sure that unsigned orders counted.

"No!" Fats was stirred into giving him a white-toothed grin. "Huh. And I only got six myself."

Elof said nothing.

"Well, bo, you're on your way. You just earned yourself seven bucks in a little less than three hours. Easy work, ain't it?"

"Yeh," Elof said sourly.

They had reached the black coupé at the end of the block, and Elof opened the trunk and put away the bowl in its box.

Fats took him by the arm. "You act like you lost seven bucks."

"I lost more than that."

"What?"

Elof let it slip out. "My self-respect."

"Crap," Fats puffed, his light blue face turning purple.

"I did. There's something wrong with a guy who likes sellin'. It's too pushy."

"Got to fill that belly."

"There should be a better way of doing it." Elof waited until Fats had put away his sample mixing bowl, too, and then closed the trunk door. He got into the car. He rolled down a window and began fanning himself with a handkerchief.

Fats got in on the other side.

Elof said, "It's all so false, false. Babbittry. You go up to a door, and you smile, and you say, 'Ah, hello there, Mrs. Grizzle, how are you this fine bright sunny day? Ah, come now, give me a fine nice smile, Mrs. Grizzle, because in about ten minutes, after a nice heart-to-heart talk as old bosom friends, you're going to give me a hundred dollars for twenty dollars' worth of goods—the other eighty representing fast and friggy talk.' "

"You're gettin' your tail over the line again, bo."

"And, by God, she falls for it. She falls for it so hard she even puckers up for you."

Fats took a cigarette and offered Elof one.

"Thanks," Elof said shortly, "but not this time. I've been sponging off you too much as it is."

Fats lighted up for himself. He smoked quietly for a while.

At last Fats asked, "Got any more to say?"

"No."

"Good, now let me get in my two bits' worth," he drawled slowly. "Bo, what you need is a little success."

"Huh."

"Grow yourself a pair a horns."

Elof said nothing. He looked out of the window and with a fingernail picked at the gray striped cloth on the door.

Fats started up the old coupé and drove slowly down the street. "Well, bo, you'll get used to it."

"If I do, I'll never look myself in the face again."

"You'll get used to it. You got the makin's. An' in the meantime, what you need is a little fun."

"What do you mean, 'fun'?"

Fats pointed. "See that sign?"

Elof looked. A crude placard hung in the show window of an empty false-front store. It read:

Big Dance And Jamboree
FREE
Bud Rudd's Orchestra
TOWN HALL
BIG RALLY
Auspices The People's Party
(Silver Collection)

"There's your fun," Fats said. "Come to think of it, I'm in the need of fun myself. Look, we'll get ourselves a quart a gin, load up, an' walk in. An' you just follow me around. Because, bo, me, I'm a politician of the puss."

Night came on, and the majestic bow of the heavens, the Milky Way, shimmered. From out of the wide outspread reaches of the short-grass or great plains country, came dozens of cars full of young people primed for the dance. The number amazed both Elof and Fats.

Elof said, "Van Dam was right. They do live in gopher holes. There just ain't that many houses around."

Fats said, "Just look at 'em. Every one means a buck. Bo, you an' I are goin' to spend the rest of the week rootin' 'em out a their holes."

Elof made a move to get out of the coupé.

Fats held him up. "Wait. Let's kill the bottle first, an' then go in. I want you all likkered up. Put out some a that light a yours. Cut your wolf loose. Because tonight your hoot owl's goin' to hoot."

Elof laughed. A whole evening ahead, and no selling until to-morrow. He swigged heartily.

Fats swigged.

They smoked awhile.

They swigged again.

"Funny," Elof said, "I don't feel nothing."

"Take some more."

Elof did.

"Now how do you feel?"

"All right. Don't feel nothing yet."

"Christ, you must put it away in your big toe. Don't you feel no yen to politic a puss yet?"

Elof listened to himself, shook his head. "No."

"For such a sawed-off runt, you sure got resistance to alky."

Elof grinned.

"Cripes, I could take on two right now myself."

Elof moved uneasily.

Fats said suddenly, a lusty wise gleam in his eyes, "Say, don't tell me you ain't had a woman yet."

Elof pawed for time. "Well . . . I . . ."

"Cripes, so that's it. Bo, there's two legs life stands on. One is fill that belly. The other is pussin'."

"Think so?"

"I know so. Now look, bo. Tonight I want you to pick yourself out a woman and then we'll take a long ride in the country and you do it, see? That'll make a man out a yuh. Give you horns. Give you such zip that tomorrow you'll sell Kingsfood in Iota like St. Peter workin' hell with popsicles."

"I hope so."

Fats handed him the bottle again.

Elof drank.

"Finish it."

Elof did.

"All right. Now you're primed. Get'n a woman'll be a wrap-up for you. Let's go." Solicitously, smiling a little, Fats opened the door and shoved Elof out. They started up the sidewalk toward the light of the unpainted hall.

Elof said, "I still don't feel nothing."

"Not a thing?"

"Nope."

"You're too high strung. But it'll hit you pretty soon."

Elof said, "Women. How do you find out when they want it?"

Fats laughed. He coughed, puffed shortly. "You'll learn that fast enough once you've had it. I was once green too. But then I had a couple an' now"—he snapped his thick-ended fingers—"now I kin spot 'em a mile off. Like once in Jerusalem last week. You know, that Hollander town near Anxious? Saw a girl walkin' along slow. It was sundown. After supper. I saw she was a christian, an' I was afraid she'd turn out to be a prune if I popped her the question the first night. I looked at her again, closer, an' then saw that she was moonin' to herself. You know. So I went around the block an' drove past her again. Stopped casual-like. Asked her if she wanted to go out in the country for a ride. Well, she acted like she didn't wanna. But she got in. So I drove around. Easy. Gassin' a little about this an' that. Then I sort a accidentally parked by a pasture." Fats stopped talking, puffed a moment, held still until a young couple had passed out of earshot. "Necked her awhile, an' then climbed her through a fence an' led her into the pasture a piece. On a blanket."

"She must a been a praying whore."

Fats coughed a laugh. "Naw. She was a virgin. I know. I can tell. But she was old enough an' her body was ready. An' I just happened to be the right guy around at just the exact right moment. Well, then I took her home. Got by the door. All of a sudden she wanted to again. Made me take her out to the pasture again."

"Really?"

Fats chuckled, coughed softly, stroked his lantern jaw. "Yeh." His eyes half closed in memory.

Elof said, excited, "That won't be my luck, though."

"You'll see," Fats said.

They approached the single light. The sound of a noisy but very rhythmic band came out of the hall. Squeals. Talk. And the sussing of scuffling feet.

Fats stepped inside, held open for Elof.

Both dropped dimes into a collection plate on a wooden table in the hall. Guarding the plate were three old roosters, chukking happily, chewing cigars, rolling eyes, leching after girls, rattling red wattles.

Elof and Fats stepped through another door.

And before them, on a poorly lighted waxed oak floor, swirled dozens of couples. The floor was almost clogged with them. Along the sides were two rows of folding chairs. The hall was of paneled pine knots, weathered. It had far too few windows. Dull gray shades hung down to the sill. Overhead leaped rusty-brown rafters. A chimney came down from the ceiling in the northwest corner, and beneath it, taken down for the summer, stood a tin-covered wood-burning stove.

On the far end, on the stage, gesticulated the band. A glaring conical spotlight held them pinned to their chairs. The maestro, Bud Rudd, dressed in white slacks and blue shirt, waved a baton. In contrast, the band members were dressed in blue pants and white shirts. Rudd, a chubby fellow, beat out a steady, clear-cut drum. Though Elof hadn't danced much, didn't have much sense of rhythm in his toes, he could feel this beat. Music pulsed up his legs.

Ten years ago, Elof thought, ten years ago there would have been kerosene lamps, accordions, fiddles, jugs. And ballads. But now there are the new fads: furtive hip flasks, pocketbook condoms, douches, and mad rides in fragile autos. And brittle music.

He listened a moment:

> *Who's afraid of the big bad wolf,*
> *the big bad wolf,*
> *the big bad wolf,*
> *Who's afraid of the big bad wolf,*
> *tra la la la la.*

Fats smiled to himself and, nodding to Elof, winking, picked himself a couple and tapped the man's shoulder, and gracefully, lightly, very slim, eased himself into the arms of the man's girl. Instantly Fats hobbled her fast tempo, led her into a slow one. He was masterful.

Elof envied him.

Elof studied the girls sitting around on the wall benches, saw none that appealed to him. Many had lined faces. All were as dark as walnuts from the burning sun. The country was hard on its people.

Young men stood around talking in clusters, laughing, stinking of strong raw alcohol spike, brown faces flushed almost black.

A tall, very plump young woman got up from a seat and approached a farmer standing alone. Her face was wreathed in smiles, as if she were a perpetually happy woman. She was wearing a wine-red dress, modestly long enough to hide her knees. She had a huge bosom, a strong and well-arched back. Her legs were huge, too, but they had the tapering of a vase and suggested form. She had the shape, all right, Elof saw, but she was just plain big.

In a moment she jogged past him in the arms of the farmer.

Elof studied her some more. And decided that, despite her size, she was the most likely candidate on the floor. A big plump jolly woman was his only chance.

When she came around again and the number had ended, Elof stepped out on the floor and touched her partner's shoulder.

The farmer stepped back, almost as if relieved he had been cut in on, and bowed, and nodded, and walked away.

"Can I have this dance?" Elof asked, remembering to smile.

"Why, I don't think I'd mind," she said. "Surely."

The band began to slam-bang into a new number:

Brother, can you spare a dime?

Elof took her free hand and arched it up. The judgment that she was big was confirmed the moment he put his arm around her. She not only stood almost a foot taller than he, but his finger tips just barely reached her deeply embedded spine. A big mare of a woman. Elof wondered what it was in him that impelled him into the bosoms of tall women. Ma; then Gert; and now this one. Even Marge Berg.

He closed his eyes to catch the strong beat, got it, and miraculously found himself in step with it. He drew the woman close to get her into it too.

At first she was with him. And Elof congratulated himself.

He turned her slowly around the side of the hall. The crowd jostled them, but she was too solid to be bumped out of rhythm.

After a few turns he became aware that she had horrible armpit odor. He sniffed a little to make sure it was she and not the sawdust on the floor. To help in the identification, he opened his eyes a little as he did so. Yes, it was she and not the floor. Then, remembering that he should be considerate, he closed his eyes. They circled the floor.

The number was over. They stepped back out of each other's embrace.

Fats was standing near. He winked at Elof.

The plump woman said to Elof, "You're a stranger around here, aren't you?"

Elof fumbled for a word. "How'd you guess?"

"I go to all the dances. And I never saw you around here before."

"Well, I guess you're right at that."

"What do you do?"

Elof remembered what Fats had once replied in answer to that question. "Why," Elof said softly, "why, I sell."

"Oh."

"And what do you do?"

"I?" She waggled her big mare's head. "Oh, I teach."

"Country school?"

"That's right."

"Uh-huh."

"Not very romantic, is it?"

"Oh, I wouldn't say that."

She laughed and winked broadly at him.

The band started up again; feet scuffled up around them.

Elof took her in his arms once more.

This time the number was a fast one, and, to his dismay, his partner started to hop. She didn't seem to make sense, she wasn't hopping in tune as far as he could see, so he took a firm grip on her and held her down and forced her to keep step with him and then fitted them both in the beat of the music.

> *You push the middle valve down*
> *and the music goes round and round—*
> *Oh-oh-oh, oh-oh-oh,*
> *And it comes out here.*

Dancing was wonderful, Elof thought. Wonderful. A great invention. Happily, cozily, he pressed his rosy cheeks between her breasts.

> *You push another valve down*
> *and the music goes round and round—*
> *Oh-oh-oh, oh-oh-oh,*
> *And it comes out here.*

But it wasn't long before she started hopping again, like a dancing mare in heat. And the next thing Elof knew she had galloped them both into a wild, jangling, banging run. A crashing of body against body.

Elof lifted his face a little to catch her eye. He glared at her. But she was galloping with her eyes closed, a beatific smile on her fleshy lips, her arms tight about him, irresistibly taking him with her, taking the lead.

Elof glanced around wildly, saw brown faces flying past, saw the room spinning.

The mare schoolteacher hurtled him round and round. She rammed his narrow hard buttocks crashing into the stage on which the band was playing, rammed her own broad beam into it, whirled off, rammed him into the tin-covered wood stove, thundering, rammed herself into it, buckling clanging tin, skipped on, heaving him around, knocking down couples, bursting couples apart, skimming, high-jumping, tromping.

"My God!" Elof muttered under his breath, "she's like a clock that's lost its balance wheel. Cripity, she's gonna kill me and her both!"

Then the number ended. Out of sheer momentum she gyrated on for a few moments, vulsed once or twice more, slowly came to a stop.

Her eyes opened. "Awh," she breathed, "that was wonderful."

Breathing hard, Elof grunted, "Yeh."

"Well," she said, "let's sit the next one out. I always sweat so."

They walked to a wall bench and sat down.

After a while, his breath caught, Elof turned to her and asked, "Did you say you was a schoolteacher?"

"Yes. Marthea Dix of District Six."

"Oh."

"And your name?" she asked brightly.

"Perry Pickle."

"Glad to meet you," she said gaily, curtsying a little, fluttering her eyelids.

Elof lowered his eyes. No wonder she was interested in strangers. They were the only ones she could get. "Where's this school of yours?"

"Fifteen miles north of here."

Elof whistled. "You drive in?"

"Caught a bus."

"Bus? You staying overnight?"

"Oh no. I've got to get back by morning. Teach. But I usually catch a ride." She trilled a knowing laugh.

Elof heard himself saying, and it told him the gin was working on him at last, "Why, then maybe I can see you home."

Marthea beamed. "See?" she said. "I always manage to get that ride home." She chittered. "Oh, that'll be just wonderful. Just wonderful."

Fats came up, smirking. He led a slim brunette. She had a simpering, bean-narrow mouth. "Like to have you meet a friend a mine, Teena," he said to her. "Elof Lofblom. Teena Metchouck. An' visa versa."

Elof got to his feet. "Glad t'meetcha."

"Meetcha."

Getting to her feet, too, Marthea gasped, "And I thought you just told me you were Perry Pickle?"

"I am. The other's my traveling name." Elof was astounded to hear the words ease out of his mouth.

Marthea's eyes cleared. She laughed and nudged him with a wise look. "You men. You know, I thought Pickle was an odd name."

"Oh, but Pickle is a real name. There's even a book by that name."

"Oh?"

Fats butted in, puffing, "How about tradin' wives?"

"Well . . ." Elof was reluctant. He found himself liking his woman despite her scenty armpits and her bulky domination on the dance floor.

"An' introducin' us?"

"Oh, excuse me," Elof said. "This is Marthea Dix. Morton Pott. Fats. And . . . ?"

"Teena Metchouck."

"Pleased to meetcha."

"Meetcha."

"Meetcha."

"Well, what about it?" Fats pressed.

"Well—all right."

The band struck up again, drumming it out:

Dancing cheek to cheek . . .

And then Elof found himself suddenly in the arms of the most willing and elastic body he had ever touched. For the first minute, because his sense of timing had been thrown out of gear by Marthea's hopping, he had trouble finding the step. But simpering Teena helped him. She nestled against him, her head coming even with his eyes—an odd sensation for him—and she soothed him, and gently suggested where the step was, and in a moment, to Elof's delighted surprise, they were undulating smoothly down the floor, in and out, up four steps, back two, and two to one side, on and on.

When the number was over, Fats came up, rasping for breath, wiping his face, and looking at Elof with a desperate eye.

Marthea was happily flushed.

Elof grinned.

Fats said, "You girls mind"—gasp—"if we step outside a minute?"

"Oh no."

"Go right ahead."

"Thanks," Fats said dryly.

The moment they were out in the cool night, Fats gripped Elof by the arm. "God! Where did you pick up that pickle?"

"Cucumber, you mean. I'm Pickle."

Fats chuckled, coughed, panted. "Cucumber is right. By God, not only is she bigger than a hippopotamus, but she's got more agitation to her than a trotter with a cocklebur under her tail. Why, she goes down the pike like a wild hog-headed boxcar."

Elof spilled guttering laughter; held his sides. He said, between bursts, "Anyway, she'll wear well."

Fats said, "Cripity. Such a critter."

"Yeh. And I'm stuck with her too. For the rest of the night."

"What?"

"Yeh. Like a damn fool with a loose Adam's apple I made a date with her."

Fats stared.

"Yeh, and she lives fifteen miles out."

"Which way?"

"District Six."

"Where the hell's that?"

"I dunno. But I'm stuck with her."

Fats said, "You better ditch her. An' quick."

Elof sobered. "Well, that wouldn't be fair. I asked her and now I've got to go through with it."

"You don't owe her nothin'. When they come that big, etiquette is out."

"Well—but when I give my word I mean it. She's my gal tonight."

Fats stood a moment, puffing. "Well, maybe at that it's all right. Maybe at that the good Lord picked her for the job of makin' a man of you. Yeh." Fats coughed. "Yeh. She looks a little hard up an' she'll probably go out of her way to help you."

They were parked on the yard of a rancher where Teena worked for two bucks a week and room and board. All four had crowded onto the single seat of the coupé. Fats was holding Teena on his lap under the steering wheel; Elof was submerged beneath Marthea on the passenger side.

From the noisy wet sound of mingling fleshes, it was apparent that Fats was going to town with his girl. But Elof himself was having a devil of a time surviving a tondrous crushing. Marthea had enveloped him like some huge amoeba gone cellulation crazy. Her big legs and rump literally folded halfway around him.

After a little he heard Fats whispering, heard him get out with Teena.

Wanting to see what Fats might be up to, Elof, with a terrific effort, pushed Marthea up. But by the time he had managed to get her perched up forward on his stubby knee points, Fats had already disappeared (into the barn?) with Teena. Elof saw nothing but moonlight glittering on a dusty yellow land.

Elof suggested that Marthea sit on the seat beside him.

"Aw gee," she trilled, "and I was having so much fun up here."

A half-hour later Fats appeared again, his breath short, licking his lips.

He coughed as he came near the car. "You folks about ready to go home?"

"Sure," Elof said. "Where's Teena?"

"She's gone in. T'bed."

Fats came around and got in.

Marthea moved over to make room. She sat between the two of them.

"Which way?" Fats asked her.

Marthea sighed. She pointed north.

Fats drove, following the country road, the headlights weaving through the moonglow. The moon was a full round burning orange.

At last Fats found her home. It was another ranch, this time tucked in between a fold of low hills like a clustering of child blocks caught in the hollow of a pillow. Fats parked in front of the weathered ranch house.

Marthea sighed again.

Fats licked his upper lip. "What's the matter, honey, ain't you been taken care of?"

She sighed once more.

The unusual charm and tenderness in Fats's voice made Elof cock up an ear. So that was how it was done.

Fats murmured, "Well, honey, maybe we better take care a that then, huh?"

The next thing Elof knew Fats had an arm around her. Elof followed suit.

Presently Fats had a hand over one of her muskmelon breasts. Again Elof copycatted. Fingers pinched and pressed and played.

Marthea giggled. She snuggled between them.

When they were driving back to Iota, skimming over the moon-silvered plains, Fats turned to Elof and grinned and said, "Kind a on the big side, wasn't she?"

"Well, judging from the area assigned to me, I'd say so."

CHAPTER XIV: Payday

> . . . *We who are enlightened, we who occasionally presume to some wisdom, just what can we tell Elof about the problem of: "What is life?"*
>
> *To the larger and musical problem of eternal life—well, uh, uh, here we're afraid we have no answer at all for him.*
>
> *To the immediate problem of earth life—well, uh, here we have some evidence that blood is guggling in the veins of brothers and sisters. Which is to say that in the long run, just as it has in the past, blood, live blood, may see mankind through almost any earthly catastrophe—at least keep it going as a species.*
>
> *Small comfort, that last, if you've been raised a christian. Though if you've been raised to believe that you were born in a universe without purpose, if you believe in the other aspect of eternity, nothing, then it is of great comfort. Because then you have more than "nothing." You have life . . .*

Elof and Fats cleaned up in Iota and then houseworked Round-up and Singletree and Broken Tug. Elof had a total of ninety-seven advance sales, Fats eighty-eight. At a dollar apiece it looked like pretty good pay for two weeks' work.

A couple of days later, a little past the middle of September,

Fats judged it time to report back to the main office in Sioux Falls. And time to pick up the biweekly pay check.

Elof was in a fever about the pay check. It would be the first in his life. After paying back what he owed Fats, and laying aside a sum for the next trip, he planned to give himself at least one good snorting binge.

On the twentieth of the month, he and Fats found themselves in Van Dam's office.

Van Dam greeted Fats effusively; Elof cagily.

"How'd you make out, Fats?"

"What does the check say?"

Van Dam chuckled, puffed on a cucumber-big cigar, fingered his fly, smirked, handed Fats a pink slip.

Fats looked at it, glimmered, coughed softly, folded the check into a vest pocket.

Jumpy, Elof forced himself to ask, "And me?"

Van Dam stilled. His oiled, golf-tanned face became impassive. "Well, Lofblom, frankly speaking, I'm disappointed in you."

"I see."

"I know you have a tough row to hoe with that one-cylinder personality of yours, but I had hopes that in time you'd know how to take advantage of that momma's boy face of yours. But— well, all I can say is, try again. Maybe you can still make it."

Elof reached out a hand. "Let me see it."

Van Dam picked up another pink piece of paper from his gray barren desk. He toyed with it, put it down again.

"Well, let me see it," Elof said, angering.

Van Dam reluctantly handed it over.

Elof looked. Eight dollars. "Eight dollars!" he choked. He looked around wildly, combed his gold hair with trembling stubby fingers. "There must be a mistake somewhere. Why, I sent in ninety-seven orders!"

Van Dam threw up his hands, shrugged. "Eight's all that came in. Our follow-up man said your orders didn't deliver. Your customers weren't sold. Just weren't sold. Some of them hadn't even heard of Kingsfood."

"That's a lie. I talked to every one I put down."

"Well, all I know is what the follow-up man told me. And those eight you got credit for, they really weren't sold either, you know. But since he got them to reconsider the original order with only a little urging, he gave you the credit anyway."

Elof jumped up. "Somebody's lying."

Van Dam said softly, "Careful. Careful."

"But, my God, man, I did talk to all those people and did take their orders. How else could I have gotten their names?"

"I dunno. All I know is that the follow-up man had to resell 'em. And when he has to work that hard, he gets credit for them."

Elof sank into a hard chair. He stared at the map, at the empty belly of South Dakota.

Van Dam oozed kindness. "Another thing we noticed. On not one of your sales slips was there a signature. Not one. Man, you've got to get those people to sign. So they can't say 'no' when they see their signature. Back out. Lofblom, you're too easy on prospective customers."

Elof mumbled, "Sorry."

Slowly Elof pocketed the check. To tell Van Dam and Fats that he hadn't had the heart to trick those poor, starving, justly suspicious people into signing their names would only give them a good laugh. He stood up. "Through, Fats?"

"For today I am. Yeh."

"Good. Let's get out a here."

Van Dam jumped up; blocked the door. His sleek green gabardine suit shone in the sunlit room. "Now wait a minute. Don't go away mad, young feller."

"I'm not mad. I'm just through."

"No more selling?"

"No."

Van Dam dropped his hands. He lipped his big cigar, glanced at Fats, blinked his eyes as if nodding to himself, then stepped aside. "Well, I'm sorry you see it that way."

Elof said nothing; brushed past the sales captain.

They were out on the street again, walking past show windows full of chalk-faced dummies clothed in fall garments.

Elof turned to Fats, asked, "Fats, why did Van Dam send us into that tough country?"

"To break me."

"Break you?"

"Sure." Fats chuckled, coughed. "Sure. I was gettin' too cocky for him. So he sent me to Iota to put me in my place."

"And what about me? Was I to be the innocent lamb sacrificed on the side?"

"Well, not exactly."

"What else, Fats? If you was to be broke out there, what else but a real breaking for me?"

"Well, of course, Van Dam didn't figure you'd outsell me. But he did figure that if you came back all in one piece you'd make a salesman."

Elof stopped. He saw outlines develop where they hadn't been before. Underneath the covering of Fats's and Van Dam's badinage flailed a bitter, knife-in-the-back struggle to the death. Fats was out to climb over Van Dam's corse, and Van Dam was fighting to prevent it. "Van Dam really didn't intend to hurt me?"

"That's right." Fats smiled. "But me he did. And, in intendin' so, he stubbed his toe. Stubbed it hard. I'm originally from the farm an' I can't be licked. A farm boy's always got the jump on the city slicker. Always. Because he's seen it where it's really rough. Claw on the throat."

Elof narrowed his eyes.

"Yeh," Fats coughed softly. "Yeh. Even with my dose a t.b., I'm a better man than that hot-shot city slicker any day of the week."

Elof started slowly down the street again. "What I can't get over is that nobody worried about me."

Fats said nothing, a smile pinking the powder-flecked purple of his face.

Elof said, more to himself than to the other, "Well, that cooks my goose. I wonder what I'm gonna do now."

*. . . Cuts and bruises, stings and pains, heartaches,
yes, even executions—and still the Elofs go on. Why
are they always "going on"?*

*Perhaps it is because consciousness, mind, light,
once you have it, turns out to be a possession worth
having—at least until something better comes along.
Just see how few people commit suicide. Just one
in millions . . .*

The following week, after Fats had left him to go selling in
The Bench country, the southeast point of South Dakota, Elof
hustled around to find himself another job.

Each evening he went through the Men Wanted section of the
Sioux Falls *Free Thought*, found a few promising opportunities,
and the next morning called on them. He first hit for solid jobs, for
sweat pay. But by the time he arrived to apply, he invariably
found the street in front of the shop, or factory, or store, or whatever it was that had advertised, full of job hunters. Gradually it broke over him that Sioux Falls swarmed with unem-
ployed.

Once Elof was the first man there. The job was to scatter horse
manure over a rich man's lawn. He was about ready to start
work when another applicant arrived. Elof heard the other tell
of his need, that he had a large family, four children and wife,
that he hadn't had steady work in five years, that two of his children had rickets, that almost all of the family's teeth had cavities.
The story smote Elof in the quick, hit him where he lived. Word-

lessly he handed over the fork and wheel barrow. Six mouths out-
voted one.

At last, reluctantly, he probed the idea of selling once more.
An advertisement read:

> WANTED: Aggressive young man. Splendid oppor-
> tunity limited only by your ability. Commission and
> expenses. Room 406. Redstone Hotel.

Elof went down to the Redstone, met two beady-eyed young
blades. They were throwing money and clothes around the room
with saturnalian abandon. One was on the phone murmuring
honeyed words into the earpiece, the other was ordering up drinks.
At last they found time for him. When they explained that they
were selling glossy national magazine subscriptions, singly or in
clubs, using candy as a come-on, Elof recognized old surroundings
—he was back in the vague queasy world of Kingsfood again. But
he decided to give it a try, and the next day he was on the road
with the boys. Grub, South Dakota, was the first town on the
itinerary. And once again Elof tried to be a combination brow-
beater and lover, this time to get three-month trial subscriptions.
What astounded Elof most was to see the boys list subscriptions on
one pad, seductions (with details and phone number) on another.
They were not selling to make a living; they were selling to make
bivulve conquests. After three days of it Elof quit. He had sold
only two subscriptions. But the wandering stallions, meanwhile,
had made a killing. Such a killing, in fact, that upon arriving at
the Redstone they began to whoop with joy, and showered, and
heaved soiled laundry and sale slips all over the place; and, naked,
laid plans for another frontal attack upon Dakota virginity.

It was after breakfast and Elof was sitting on the burgundy
plush davenport in Sis's parlor. Through the bay window Elof
could see the neighbor children playing in the street. Though his
eyes followed their movements, his mind was busy with his
troubles.

Sis, who had been rustling in the kitchen, came out and asked,
"Will you be home for noon lunch?"

Elof sat up and reddened a little. Another charged meal? And pregnant, flustered Sis even more worried that she wouldn't make ends meet? "No. No, I'm going downtown in a minute. Got an appointment."

Sis looked at him a second; dropped her eyes. She drew her pink housecoat over her swollen belly. "You'll be home for supper then?"

"I don't know. Depends. This new job may take me out of town. Like the other one. I'll let you know."

"All right then." Clumsily turning, she re-entered the kitchen.

Elof picked up last night's paper, desperately paged through the Want Ads again. He looked for honest jobs under Men Wanted; found none. He looked under Grand Opportunity; saw dozens listed.

He found the magazine-selling ad again; hurriedly jumped to the next paragraph.

He ran his finger down until he came to a promise set in heavy type:

Make $100 a week selling reliable line. Need enterprising, alert young man to bring real service to community. Room 709 Cody Building.

Elof stared at the advertisement for a while, at last decided to give it a try. And if this one didn't work—he would head for home.

The new opportunity to make millions involved selling Whingding cleaners. It was a blue-white aluminum all-purpose tank cleaner complete with attachments. The main section was made up of a one-foot-by-two cylinder with a long hose. To it the housewife attached various appliances, ranging all the way from suction lips to a round screened funnel. A housewife could clean rugs, floors, furniture, shades, walls, ceilings; could demoth clothes, blankets, plush chairs; could spray paint. The housewife paid down twenty-five dollars (the salesman's commission) (twenty-five dollars! sell two a week and be on easy street!); paid the rest on time. The production cost of the machine was fifteen dollars; the selling price, ninety-eight dollars. The whole thing fit into a little black satchel, so little a child could carry it.

Elof saw there was no point calling on the poor with such a remarkable invention. Only the rich would have the dough to buy it.

Carrying a sample unit, Elof hunted up the Park Avenue of Sioux Falls. Finding it, he selected a mansion suggesting fatty opulence. He adjusted his quiet green tie, combed back his gold hair with stubby fingers, brushed off his gray suède shoes, and stepped boldly up to the front door. He rang. The name on the bronze doorplate was *Phineas Flattard*.

A maid, wearing blue with white trim, came to the door. A fringed hood cowled her face. "Yes?"

"Could I speak to the lady of the house?"

"Well—what is it you want?"

Since the maid was elaborately formal, Elof fell in with the mood. "I have a matter of grave importance to discuss with her."

The maid looked at Elof's satchel, frisked his clothes with suspicious eyes, at last decided he was all right. She left.

After a moment a middle-aged lady, wearing her hair in a gray pompadour, and dressed in striped blue silk, came to the door. She leaned forward from her hips. "Yes?"

"Could I interest you in a matter of health?"

"Why . . . Yes, of course. Come in, won't you?"

Elof stepped in.

"Have a chair," she said, pointing to a blue lounging chair before an empty fireplace. A matching ottoman stood nearby.

Elof sat down.

Unbuttoning his suit jacket, he glanced around the room before beginning his song.

The place unsettled him. He had never seen such magnificence. This, without a doubt, was the home of a hero. Deep wine-red drapes hung from ceiling to floor. Walls were of oak paneling. Cathedralic arches soared across the ceiling. The blue rug underfoot was an inch deep—the kind which, when walked on, generated electricity in body and reaching hand. Two huge sofas and a collection of incidental chairs were tastefully scattered around. Before one davenport stood a yellow coffee table, Chinese, with a glass top.

Elof looked at the huge window again. Its panes were so clean, so clear, so free of smelting defects, it was as if the outdoors and the indoors were of the same heaven light.

"Yes?" Mrs. Flattard had perched herself on the edge of a couch.

Elof collected himself. "Oh yes. Well, Mrs. Flattard, I'm Elof Lofblom. What I have here has been mildly described at one time or another as a revolution in the housewife's life."

"Oh yes?"

Elof opened up his little black satchel, lifted out the cleaner. "A revolution, yes. Now this, this is the Whingding cleaner. It cleans everything from soup to"—Elof caught himself, quickly righted—"from curtains to floors to sofas." He saw Mrs. Flattard's face first wrinkle with surprise, then tighten with anger. Elof hurried to keep her from interrupting him. "And it does it more thoroughly, more efficiently, more economically, with less fuss and dust, with less disturbed, and therefore with cleaner air, than any machine on the market today. Here. I'll show you. Your maid's cleaned here today, I presume?"

"Why—I think so."

"Sure. Now watch." Elof opened up the cylinder. "Empty, see?" Closing the cylinder, he fastened the swivel rug nozzle neatly onto the hose of the cylinder, then plugged the cord into a wall socket behind a chair. There was a soft melodious hum. "Now." He ran the nozzle over an apparently clean place on the rug. He ran it back and forth twice; then shut off the machine. Again he opened the cylinder and held it up for her to see. A mound of dust and debris two inches high lay piled on its bottom. Mrs. Flattard, who had been about to get up, now slowed.

Elof, quite surprised himself, lifted a handful and declared, "That's what we call cleaning, Mrs. Flattard. Not that your maid doesn't clean good. But that she doesn't use the right kind of machine."

"Yes, I know. But——"

"Now, now, Mrs. Flattard"—Elof saw he was losing her, so leaped to the attack—"now, Mrs. Flattard, you see these extra attachments?" He pointed to a pile of bright aluminum.

"That's all very well, but——"

"That's what makes this a special machine. This thing"—and

he put the machine together again and fitted on another snout—
"this thing cleans your curtains and shades." He walked over to
the big window and, holding up the long rubber hose, expertly
ran the snout over the fixtures. "See?"

"But you see, young man——"

Next, Elof fitted on an anteater nozzle and pounced again.
"And this you use to clean out the furniture. Like so." He shoved
the nozzle into a corner of the couch she was sitting on. There
was a buzzing; some puffs of dust. "See? Did you know there was
dirt there?"

"No, but you see——"

"I tell you, Mrs. Flattard, there isn't a thing this machine can't
do."

Mrs. Flattard began to look ill.

Seeing her face, disgust at what he was doing suddenly over-
whelmed Elof like an October fog smothering a bush. His voice
trailed off. "You see, a woman . . . any woman . . ."

How foolish. How foolish and insane this was. He didn't care
a snap for the lady, had really no sympathy for the rich, yet here
he was, trying desperately to sell her something she didn't want
and which he himself wasn't sold on—except that he needed the
twenty-five-dollar commission.

The pause in his harangue was fatal. Popping up from her seat
as if chains had fallen from her limbs, Mrs. Flattard said crisply,
"No, really, young man, the cleaner we are using will suffice for
the present. Thank you just the same." Mrs. Flattard hurried to
the door, held it open for him.

Elof picked up the parts of his machine, packed them into the
little black satchel. As he walked out he said, "Thank you, Mrs.
Flattard. Thank you. You've been most kind to have listened at
all."

"Oh, that's all right." The door closed firmly behind him.

His blocky shoulders slumped.

CHAPTER XVI: A Desperate Measure

. . . Yes, "going on."

Some time ago, on a Sunday, this "going on" momentum was so strong in me

It was early Saturday morning and Elof was in his second-story room when he heard the front door downstairs open and then slam shut. There was a mumbling and then, quite clearly, Elof heard Fats's laconic voice.

"Elof still here?"

"Yes," Sis said.

"Where?"

"Up in his room. I think he's packin' up to go home."

"What's he doin' that for?"

"I dunno. Still ain't got a job, you know."

"What's he wanna go home for? He'll make it. He's a good bo."

"You think so?"

"Christ, yes." Fats coughed. "Guess I better go up an' put a little starch in his backbone again."

There were slow footsteps on the stairs and in a moment, puffing, face colored, Fats pushed wide the door. The instant he came in, the sad little room with its blue calcimined walls and its one little window facing north became a human abode.

"What's this"—gasp—"I'm hearin' about you?"

Elof quickly hid his eyes. He was sitting on the edge of the blue-flowered spread of the bed with an open suitcase at his feet. "Me?"

"Yeh, you. About your goin' home." Fats flopped on the bed beside Elof.

"What about it?"

"What're you goin' for?"

"Because I'm running up a big fat board bill here with no sign of an income to meet it, that's why. Sis and Larry can't afford to give charity."

"Crap."

"Just the same, I ain't leaning on no poor people."

"Look, bo. They won't go broke keepin' you for a couple a weeks more."

Elof dared an eye-to-eye look. "Besides, I've got a conscience."

"Never heard of it."

"Besides, I know when I'm licked."

"Never heard of that either."

"Well, I have."

Fats put a lean claw on Elof's shoulder. "Bo, don't give up yet. You're bound to find something. It's just about to turn for you."

"But what about Sis and Larry? Every day they look funnier and funnier at me."

"T'hell with 'em. Look. Larry owes me something. The way he used to kick me around when the old man was off the place, he owes me something, the son of a bitch. That's an older brother for you. So he's payin' me now, see? Keepin' you till you get on your feet."

Elof shook his head. "No, I can't. I've got a conscience."

Fats leaned back on the bed. He offered Elof a cigarette, was refused, lit one for himself. He gushed huge puffs of blue oily smoke toward the ceiling. "Take it easy, bo. Let's not get our water hot."

" 'Our water hot,' cripe." Elof started to pack again.

Fats lay quietly smoking for a time. When Elof was almost finished Fats said, "Look, bo, I want to make a proposition."

"Talk on. But it won't do you any good."

"Okay. Look. I wasn't due in from The Bench till next Tuesday. But I finished up fast an' came on in because I wanted a little extra cash. A little extra cash for a little extra-special fun. That's where you come in."

"Go on."

"Well, there's a three-day carnival goin' on right now t'No Place, South Dakota. A carnival I ain't missed for years. It's in its third day an' it should really be wild by now. A whorin' hell of a time. Gamblin', car races, horse races, baseball tournaments, wild wimmen, circus, drinkin', fightin', bettin'—a hell of a whorin' time." Fats cleared his throat. " 'By God,' I says to myself down on The Bench there, 'by God, Fats ol' boy, there ain't no good reason why you should skip the carnival this year, is there?' "

Elof said nothing.

"You follow me, bo?"

"Go on."

"Well, that's where you an' me are goin'. I've got my check from Van Dam, an' we're ready to go."

"Huh. But where's my check?"

"You don't need it. I'm poppin' for it. It's all on me."

"Oh no, you're not."

"Oh yes, I am."

"You've popped for it too often for me."

"Look, bo, this is something I do every year. It's part a my blood. I was born near there. On the other side of No Place, between Avon and Dante, out Bon Homme way. So it's part a my life. An' invitin' you down there is like invitin' you home for supper. An', bo, you ain't aimin' to turn down a supper invite, are you?"

"Well . . ."

"C'mon, get your hair combed an' let's move." Fats got up and kicked Elof's suitcase under the bed. "Let's move. We've got a long ways to go before we get there."

Reluctantly Elof got up too. He asked, to get from where he was to where he could feel somewhat at ease accepting still another gift from Fats, "Where's this No Place of yours?"

"As the crow goes, about seventy miles southwest a here."

Elof stepped up to the mirror on the dresser, began combing his gold thatch. He pulled out yet another question to cover the awkward space. "Was selling down on The Bench easier'n out to Iota?"

"Some."

"By the way, how was the schoolteachers out that way, just as big?"

Fats chuckled. "I dunno. I didn't need any educatin' the past week."

Elof juggled his tie up tight, adjusted his white collar. "Now me, me, I needed some."

"Boy, you opened your mouth an' really said it." Fats goosed him sharply, and Elof jumped. "Now maybe we can promote you out of the kindergarten class."

As they were going down the stairs Elof said, putting on the belt-in-back gray jacket of his suit, "Now remember, Fats, I'm making this up to you someday."

"Forget it."

They drove out on Highway 16, Fats at the wheel, once again going west out of Sioux Falls, going on, with the rising sun still low in the east, and the shimmering prairie land stretching far to every side. The day was a bit muggy out and the distant hollows were dense with luminous purple mists. A glance directly at the sun told Elof that humidity was blurring the edges of the coal-red ball.

They drove past clusters of farms, past solitary white school-houses and single white churches on knolls, going on, occasionally dipping through dry coulees, and rising, every ten miles, to the crest of a land swell.

Fats said, pointing south, "See there? Them buildin's?"

Looking across an immense expanse, Elof barely saw them. "Yeh."

"Talk about funny names for towns, there's one. It's called Tea. Pioneers didn't know what to name it. Had a hell of a fight about it. The wimmen were for Bethlehem an' Rose, the men for Sittin' Bull an' Clark. Then one day a freight train came through an' dropped off a consignment a tea. Well sir, nobody came to claim that tea for weeks an' weeks, an' it lay along the tracks there, out in the sun. Finally one old duffer says, 'Since nobody's claimin' it, an' there ain't no name on it ner no company mark on it savin' where it come from, I'm takin' it as a sign. Yup, a sign. Who knows—maybe God dropped it from heaven as a way of tellin' us what to name this place. Yup, I say, let's call this place Tea.' So Tea it was."

They rode on, bumping evenly and rhythmically over the tar strips on the pavement, *ta-thrump, ta-thrump, ta-thrump,* on and on. They flipped through Wall Lake—a country store and an auto clinic and a pond; and Pumpkin Center—a country store and an auto clinic and a round stone.

At Stanley Corners, Fats left Highway 16, turned south on an oiled way, Highway 81. The country became flatter. The horizons rose a little all around and the center sank.

The motor sang; brommed happily. Fats whistled.

Idly Elof noted the passing flood of man's leavings on earth. Across a ditch in a field lay the blown-up carcass of a gas truck. Black fire marks were on the ground around it. A careening gouge led from the road to it—the path of the exploding vehicle. Where was the driver? In heaven? Hell? Farther on, a dead cow, red, balloon-tight, lay on the shoulder of the road, its four legs and four fat tits pointing to the skies. Two men were busily skinning it; another was sharpening a cleaver and a knife on a hone. Poor creature. But a moment ago chewing its cud and well content and its tail free, and now suddenly the victim of a speeding auto and its own stupidity. And tomorrow a rotting meal in some man's gut.

Elof's reverie was abruptly broken into. The motor beneath his feet began to miss, to spit and to sputter.

"Damned wire is loose again," Fats muttered. "Guess I'll have to fix it."

Fats pulled up on the side of the road, shut off the ignition. Fats got out. "Ohhh," he groaned, pleasantly stretching, "ohhh."

Elof got out and stretched too. The sudden silence seemed unnatural. The motor continued to hum a little in his ears.

Fats raised the hood of the old coupé's motor. "Crap. Broke off this time. Well, guess I'll have to put on a new one. Good thing I got some spare wiring with me."

Elof noticed that they had stopped near a deserted graveyard. Curious, he stepped across the road to have a look at it while Fats fixed the car.

"Where you goin', bo?"

"Just for a look at this."

"Okay. But don't wander off."

Elof climbed down the roadside through tall bluestem, stepped across the ditch, and slipped between the strands of a barbwire fence.

The graveyard was about an acre in size and, like the Old Settlers' Graveyard back home, was lost out on an open country with no village or town nearby. Elof noted the old stones, noted the age of the matted grass over the mounded graves.

There were also some new stones, markers of polished marble, intrusions on the old acre:

TSCHETTER

MOTHER	FATHER
Sarah	Lorenz
Geb.	*Geb.*
2, Sept. 1857	*31, Aug. 1857*
Gest.	*Gest.*
4, Jan. 1928	*11, Okt. 1922*

Denn Christus ist mein leben
Und sterben ist mein gewinn

Another read, a thin tall shaft:

MARIA
Dec. 16, 1849
Dec. 16, 1927
JOSEPH
Jan. 20, 1849
Apr. 16, 193–
TSCHETTER
Blessed are the pure in heart
for they shall see God

A flat stone at his feet said:

KLEINSASSER

MARIA	JOHN E.
1882–193–	*1883–1920*

Standing on one foot, Elof brooded. Two of the three women had outlived the men. Siouxland wasn't always tough on the womenfolk then. And the one man who had outlived them all, Joseph, had anyone known at his birth that he was to outlive his generation by a couple of decades?

Elof studied the names. In what strange Old Country village had they been born?

Pioneers. Pioneers. Where was the sweat now? Where were the eyes and the muscles that had made a home in this Wild? Where was the trail they had trudged? Where were the settings they had crushed in the grass, eating and dunging and mating?

Man. A handful of troubled soil. Arising there and standing here and weathering there.

Ma? Where are you? I, Elof, I'm here.

"Elof."

What?

"Elof. Hey you there, bo. What's goin' on there, dreamin'?" It was Fats. He was standing on the edge of the road, hands on hips, looking down at Elof.

"Yeh."

"C'mon, bo. I got 'er fixed. Let's get movin'."

"Okay."

Reluctantly Elof started for the fence again, kicking through the virgin sod of bluestem and wild rose and pink buffalo-bean petal. The musk of last year's dust and leaf came to him—it was the smell of molting time. And with it rose the new flesh smell of this year's growth. Elof savored it. This was the way the Wild had smelled before mechanical man came along.

He climbed through the fence, climbed the side of the road.

Fats said, looking at him oddly as he came up to him, "Gettin' your tail over the line again, bo?"

"No."

Fats looked at him for a widening moment, lit a cigarette, and then climbed into the coupé. Elof followed.

They brommed on, skimming across the outspread. Going on. Going on.

Two birds flew high overhead, just below the sun's nooning summit, going southwest too, with wings white above and gray below, the undersides dark in each bird's shadow. The winged ones were two flitting sunlit black-and-whites spearing ahead.

At ten o'clock Fats said, "Dammit, I'm thirsty. How about you?"

Elof was thirsty but, with an empty pocketbook, didn't feel he could agree. "No, I'm all right."

Fats gave him a gray glare.

"Go ahead if you want to," Elof said.

Fats laughed shortly. "You bastard. You christian."

"What's the matter?"

"I know you."

Elof moved uneasily on the seat.

Fats drove on silently for a moment; then pointed ahead. "There's Free Men comin' up. Let's unravel ourselves an' get vinegared there."

The flat land distorted their notion of distance and, like a row-boat approaching a ship anchored out at sea, it took a little longer to get there than they expected.

But at last the little city came up and Fats slowed at the out-skirts and turned in past an Antarctic gas station.

Free Men surprised Elof. It boasted two parochial schools; a junior college. Its business center, though still somewhat in the grip of old frontier styles, had an air of vigorous enterprise. The streets were immaculate, the houses pridefully tailored in paint and putty, the lawns a deep green—everything proclaiming doughty people, a people solemnly and serenely going about the business of living, easily shrugging off dust bowls and depressions.

Elof said, "Looks like we landed in another world."

"We did. These're Mennonites. Russians." Fats coughed. "Well, really not Russians. First they was Germans. But they got persecuted there for their crackpot ideas. So they migrated to Russia. Got the deep goose there too. So came on here an' built up this town a Free Men."

"I never knew people like this were living in Siouxland. Never."

Fats purred the car down the main street. "Yeh, there's a whole colony of 'em through here. Bridgewater, west a Emery, all up an' down the Jim River, all the way to Olivet an' Menno." Fats parked the car in front of a café.

"Never knew about it."

"There's lots to see here, bo. Just keep your eyes peeled." Fats surveyed the street. "F'rinstance, just take a look at them two old mutts across the corner there."

Elof leaned forward to look past Fats. Two bearded sages, sitting on a green bench in the middle of a neat and vacant lot, were nodding and waving hands in delicious argument, every now and then popping something into their mouths and spitting it out again.

Fats grinned. "Yeh. Sunflower snussers."

"Sunflower seeds?"

"Nothin' but."

Elof watched them awhile; and envied them their content.

Fats said, "Yeh, bo, this is quite a town. Quite a town. Every-body in it is related. Full a Hofers and Kleinsassers and Tschet-ters." Fats cleared his nose with a guggling sniff. "Yeh, an' when the Hofers get t'huffin', an' the Kleinsassers t'sassin', an' the Tschetters t'spittin' seeds, you got somethin'." Fats allowed him-self a chuckle at his own wit.

But Elof said nothing. People had laughed at his name too. Elof scowled. How could one laugh after having seen the lonely stones of the Tschetters and Kleinsassers in the country graveyard?

"Well, bo, let's guzzle," Fats said. He got out and led the way into the café and took a booth in back.

The booth was built of maple wood, and on the table stood a salt and pepper shaker, a sugar bowl, and a jar of paper napkins.

A girl waitress came up, bringing each a glass of water. She was dressed in quiet gray, and her face, though rich and full with dimpled flesh, was subdued.

Fats said, "Hi, queenie. What you got today?"

She handed him a menu.

"No smiles today?"

The corners of her unrouged, light pink lips quirked.

"That all?"

"That's all."

Fats ran his quick gray eyes up and down the list. "No smiles on here either. Oh well, wasn't too hungry anyway. Guess all I want is an egg sandwich with the yolk standin' up. An' a bottle a coke."

She turned to Elof. "You?"

"Well . . ."

Fats said, handing her the menu, "Just double my order, lady, just two it."

"But I——" Elof began.

Fats put a lean claw on the waitress's plump arm. "Just two it." He winked. "The kid always has such a hard time makin' up his mind, I've got to do it for him."

"If you say so." She walked away.

Elof felt sick. "I don't like this," he said, taking a paper napkin and tearing it into little bits.

"Shut up." Fats played with the salt shaker, spilling a little in the palm of a hand, and licking it up with a white cheesy-flecked tongue.

There were no other customers about, and with Elof subsiding into an embarrassed silence, the air in the strange place became spooky. An Old Country clock, its face brown and its pendulum a shining brass, tocked loudly. The café was empty of the usual crass and shouting placards.

The waitress brought the order after a moment, each a steaming egg sandwich, cut diagonally across the square of bread, and each a bottle of coke.

"Will there be anything else?"

"Two more cokes. To take out."

She brought them.

"That all?"

"Right."

She took a sales pad from her apron and, frowning, her blond hair falling forward, laboriously worked out the bill. She laid the bill upside down on the table; started to leave.

Fats took her firm arm. "What's the rush?"

She tightened a little, carefully tugging to release herself.

"What's the hurry?"

"Please," she said.

"There's no other customers."

"Please," she said. "We don't do that here."

"Don't do what?"

She colored.

Fats said, "I'm pretty sure I'm not gonna like my sandwich now. Don't look too good to me."

She stood quietly resisting.

"Looks like that egg there is burnt."

She stood still then.

"Ah, that's better." Fats released her arm. "You see, I'm not so mean. It was only that I was a little lonesome. An' I thought maybe you might be able to do something about it. Give me a little smile or so."

She stood uncertainly, another quirking near smile tugging at the edges of her full pink lips.

"Nothin' wrong with smilin' at a man, is there?"

"No."

"Well, give then."

At last she smiled widely and, slowly retreating, went out back.

Elof twisted on his side of the booth, feeling sorry for her. At the same time, however, he also admired the way Fats could impose himself on a woman without getting slapped.

At the sight of the food Elof forgot his momentary sickness. He pitched in, gulping warm welling yellow yolk and firm white and fresh bread and savory butter, washing all down with swilling gurgles of red-brown coke.

Fats observed, "You wasn't hungry, huh?"

"Well . . ."

"Bet you didn't eat breakfast?"

"No, I didn't."

"Damned fool. You know Sis would a fed you if you'd a let her."

Elof clammed up.

"Well," Fats said, "well—time's shovin' on. Don't want to miss too much of the fun."

They were going out, Fats had just paid the bill by cashing in a ten-dollar bill, when Elof found himself being bumped from behind by a stumbling Fats. Fats grabbed him to keep from falling.

"Damned waxed floors," Fats growled. "They got things too clean in here." Fats glared at the waitress.

Elof held the door open for Fats. "Take it easy."

"Should wear skates in a place like this."

They stepped out on the street. There were a few loiterers about.

Fats stretched and then, just as he was about to step toward the coupé, straightened and knicked his head at something across the street. "Take a look there."

Elof glanced over, and for a moment or two couldn't understand it.

A modern two-ton truck had just pulled up to the curb. It was a blue-green vehicle and on its sides was written in square-headed lettering:

And all that believed were together, and all had things common;
And sold their possessions and goods, and parted them to all men,
as every man had need. Acts 2: 44-45.

In the truck's rack sat a collection of the most oddly dressed people Elof had ever seen in his life. They reminded him instantly of a picture he had seen of fifteenth-century peasants of Middle Europe. The men were all dressed in black: black felt hat, black shirt, black pants, black shoes, black socks. Some even wore beards, and since most were black, even their faces seemed funereally garbed. The women wore grays and blacks: long skirts, long sleeves, and full and tight babushkas cowling the head. Only the hands and full-moon visages were free to the stranger eye.

"Those prisoners?"

Fats coughed. "Depends. We might think so. But then they think we are."

"Who are they?"

"Hutterites. They're just like the Mennonites, except they practice their religion communistic. Live down along the Jim River bottoms. Out a sight. Come to town like this once in a great moon."

"Crimpity sakes."

Fats offered Elof a cigarette, took one himself, lit both. He blew out a plume of smoke. "Yeh. Now watch what happens. They won't get off that truck until the field boss lets 'em."

As Fats predicted, they sat meekly on their hams until a similarly clothed but much older Hutterite, a man, got out of the truck's cab up front. He came around and let down the endgate. Then the quiet crows got to their feet and slid out. As they stepped down, the field boss handed them each a quarter.

Fats said, "Just like a daddy with a batch a kids in town on Saturday night. Gives 'em each a little spendin' money."

Elof had forgotten he had a lit cigarette in his hand and it burned him. With a mild curse he hurled it into the cement gutter. He soothed his fingers with his pink tongue.

Fats said, "You know, there's where you belong. With them

Hutterites. Never have to worry about a thing. All you do is work your share in the colony, an' share the food an' clothes an' sleepin' with everybody. A treasurer does all yer buyin'. Yeh, bo, that sect was tailor-made for you. All christians. A reg'lar heaven on earth. Nobody gets ahead. But nobody gets behind either. Durin' the depressions an' the droughts these birds never needed relief. Even their cattle was prime durin' them times. Sundays they pray God an' listen to what their preacher finds in the Bible. Preacher has to work in the field too. Don't have movin' pictures. No papers. No magazines. Nothin'. Young bucks're raised in dormitories till they marry. Then they quit shavin', wear beards."

"Are they happy?"

"I dunno. They think they are."

"All of them?"

"All except the young bucks. They sometimes break out."

"I don't blame them."

"What?"

"Nothing."

"Well, bo, guess it's time to be goin' on. Sure you don't want to join up?"

Elof stepped once more on the cigarette in the gutter—it was still smoldering—and said, "Don't be nuts."

They were out eight miles, having just turned onto the Atlantic-Yellowstone-Pacific Highway which came out of the east at this point, when Fats said, "Bo, open up them cokes an' spike 'em. Got to get primed for fun."

"You can have some, but I ain't."

Fats chuckled. "Bo, you do belong to them communists."

Elof shut up. He opened up both bottles and, taking a bottle of alcohol spike from the glove compartment, made the mix.

They swigged and drove and smoked.

After a bit Elof began to warm up to the idea that fun was just ahead and, remembering they might date some girls, decided to get out his pocketknife to pare his nails. In hunting around on his person for it, he found a dollar bill.

He stared at it a little while; then realized where it had come from.

He turned angrily on Fats. "You son of a seacook! Now why did you have to do that?"

Fats said nothing; drove on; swigged; drove on.

"You son of a gun. I knew there was something odd about the way you stumbled against me back there."

Fats wheeled on.

"Look. I'm not going to take it." Elof tried to shove it into one of Fats's pockets.

Fats jabbed him with an elbow; then, freeing a hand from his driving, stuffed the bill into Elof's clothes again. "Bo, you're gettin' your tail over the line again."

"But why? Don't you understand people might not want to be given things?"

"I like the way you part your hair."

"Oh hell."

They swooped through the palm-up valley of Menno.

Another five miles, and Fats said, slowing the coupé, "Bo, I got high water. How about you?"

"Man, you hit it. My teeth are floating."

Fats stopped the car, and they got out on the same side and stood looking a moment at the open country, with the nearest farm home a mile away. Then turned away from each other, and stood buttock cheek to buttock cheek.

Elof trickled quietly. Weed pollen tickled his nose and he sneezed. He heard the faint brittle champing of insect claws in the undergrowth. In the striding forenoon sunlight, the shadows in the roots of the ironweeds were green-black.

An uneasy thought stung him: It ain't how big you are, it's what you do with yourself.

Behind him Fats hawked; spat.

Across the ditch spread a stubble field. Through it wriggled wheel tracks where hay racks had gone laden with grain. The wriggles reminded him of worm trails under long-lain boards.

Two pheasants, a multicolored male and a gray female, whooshed out of the stubbles across the fence, wing-wapping powerfully into the air, the male *uck-uck-ucking* angrily. They rose to a height of about ten feet, then stiffened their wings and became streaking monoplanes. In a moment they vanished beyond a knoll.

Elof jerked at the explosion of their flushing, and the usual gesture with which he finished his watering, a careful retreat into his trousers, was foregone this time. "Damned pheasants scared the hell out a me," he exclaimed.

"By God, me too," Fats said, turning around and, like Elof, buttoning up. "In fact, I think I wet my pants a little." Fats coughed. "Oh well, it'll be dry by the time we get there."

Elof laughed and got into the coupé.

Fats, puffing, got into the other side.

In a moment they were rolling again, tooling on, and sipping spiked coke.

On they went west. They cruised slowly through Olivet, through Tripp, and on.

They followed a dirt road.

Presently the road became heavy with traffic, mostly family cars filled with cheering children.

They came to a deep, tree-lined, dry-creek draw. They coasted into it in second gear; climbed out of it in low. Dust from the passing of previous cars hung high in the coulee.

Then the country began to change. It was bleaker. Except around the pastures, there were no fences. It was open to wind and man. There were scatterings of stones, of boulders, sometimes on the knolls, sometimes in the meadows.

The country rolled a little, rocking, just enough to break up the monotony of tableland, and on the tops of each swell, the horizons extended so far away into the haze of the muggy day that the earth and sky seemed continuous.

There were sudden tufted valleys, unseeable until Elof and Fats were upon them—the vacated beds of vanished and departed rivers.

"Where the heck is this No Place?" Elof asked finally, coughing in the dust stiving up behind the car ahead. "All we see is traffic, but no town."

"Bo, it's just a mile away."

Elof sat up. "That close? I don't see no steeples. No water towers."

"You won't either."

They rose on a prairie boss, and there, ahead and a little below, on a flat plain, where dust was rising to the sun, were herds of cars, and clusters of brown tents—some two stories high, one almost as big as a red butte—and two race tracks, and a diamond with a baseball game going on, and a joy-ride airplane warming up in a nearby grazestead.

"Is that the town?"

"Yeh." Fats laughed. "Yeh. Like I said, no steeples, no buildin's. An', no city fathers to bullox up the works with rules an' regulations. No curfew, no constables. Everything wide open."

"God."

"Yeh, bo. There's no stoppin' the human bein' when he wants fun. So every year they set up this town for three days, tents an' pasture streets, have their fun, an' then, flewt! it's all gone, an' everybody goes back home to work an' pray again."

"I'll be darned."

They stepped out, stretching stiff legs, putting away bottles, straightening clothes and ties, and looked around.

All about was merry sound. Children—naughty-eyed boys in overalls and proud slips of girls in pigtails and cotton prints— were whisking around cars, and licking ice-cream cones, and nibbling crackerjack. Farm and small-town wives were standing in bunches, and pulling corsets over burly buttocks, and sighing, and shrilling occasional laughter with breast pressed to breast in gossip, and waving autumn flies away with scented handkerchiefs. Older men, a philosophic foot to one side, calmly, some chewing tobacco and some snuss, heads down, eyes peering at eyes from underneath sunburnt brows, were talking bulls and boars and next year's mighty crops.

"Looks like an oversized threshers' picnic," Elof said.

"Yeh."

"But where are the frills you talked about? And the hot-shots juning them?"

"You'll see 'em," Fats said shortly, combing his sparse hair, wiping sweat from his flushed face with a snow-white kerchief. "You'll see 'em. They're down by the Midway tents there."

Elof and Fats picked their way through the mass of cars. Some of the cars were old and some new, some were black and some green, some were rain-rusted and some wax-shiny.

They walked at last into an open space filled with gangs of young folk heading for fun. Some of the gangs had stopped in to watch a baseball game: the All Nations nine—Sioux Indian and Negro and Chinee and Caucasian—against the Tennessee Rats— soft-spoken losers of syllables. Some had dropped in on an auto race: small streaking beetles brattling noisily on a smoking oval track.

Elof and Fats at last came to the entrance to the temporary Midway. They paid a dollar (Elof using the one Fats had thrust on him in Free Men) and strolled inside.

And then Elof saw the gay ones, girls exactly like the chickens he and Cor and Wilbur had chased in Amen, and youths like himself. Light tripping bird-talk tweeted all around, and sometimes a girl shrilled protest and flounced a dress. Color rioted in the agitated swarm: cherry red and orange dawn, and sunburnt brown and reindeer brown and water blue.

Fats said, nudging Elof, "Pretty nice, huh?"

" 'S wunnerful."

They legged it slowly down a fifty-foot-wide improvised street. To either side concession boys had set up stands, and barkers and hawkers were singing and howling and waving the people in to see the human freaks, and to spend pennies in the arcades, and to gallop on the mounts in the merry-go-rounds, and to take the airplane spins, and to try their luck in the shooting galleries, and to spike their mixes in the drinking lean-tos—everything to excite the human blood.

They passed a funhouse. Two girls in blue voile and shoulder-length bobs, twins, with thick lips stretched in violent screaming joy, came flying out of an exit. Air holes beneath their feet had blown up fierce blusts under their dresses; had prettily exposed naked thigh and tufted pubic triangle.

Elof and Fats saw two couples lightly loving in an open space.

Fats stopped. "Look at the bums them gals got. I'm of half a mind to bust it up an' give them gals a break."

Elof studied a moment. "The gals are nice, but I'm afraid them bums got a little too much muscle."

Fats continued to stare and to growl disapprovingly. "Bums!" He shook his head. "Them poor gals."

They ambled on.

Dust swirled, hanging lazily in the air, glinting.

Fats puffed; mopped his face. Elof took off his coat; hung it over an arm.

Fats drew Elof over to a beer-and-burger stand. Fats said, "Two both ways."

Elof demurred a little again.

Fats said, "Shut up."

A flushed hand-over-fist proprietor shouted at a cook in white who was over a sizzling open-air stove, "Two beer burgs!"

They ate, wolfing noisily, gulping. They looked; listened.

As they stepped away, Fats paying, Elof saw something glint in the trampled grass. He reached down, brushed away a broken tuft half covering it, thinking the glint but a tinfoil cigar band. It was a dime.

"Hey, look," Elof said. "Look what I found."

Fats stopped. "Huh. Bo, that's a sign. This is gonna be yer lucky day." He handed Elof a cigarette, took one himself, lighted up both.

"Could be." Elof stared at the shining silver in the palm of his square hand; then reached it out to Fats. "Here's part payment for that beer and burg I just had."

"Don't be a dumb bastard."

"What do you want me to do then, save it for a rainy day?"

"You're still talkin' dumb."

"Well, suppose you was in my boots, what would you do with it?"

"I'd take a chance on it. Gamble it."

"Where?"

Fats's eyes half closed. "Bo, I just got me an idea. Follow me."

Fats led him to a lot fronted by a huge sign:

THE TEMPLE OF POWER!
TEST YOUR STRENGTH!!
BING THE BINGER!!!
A DIME WILL GET YOU A DOLLAR!!!!

Behind the sign, the lot was filled with big-armed young bucks, with admiring ladies-for-the-day on their arms, all milling about a contraption that looked like an oversized scale. It was a bell binger.

"Here," Fats said. "Here, let's try this."

They pushed into the crowd, got to the front line. Some protested the sudden shoving.

Fats said, "An' watch close. There's a reason why they lose a dime. Or make a dollar."

Elof gave the machine a quick frisking look. It stood about fourteen feet tall. At its top was a nickel bell. Below, at its base, was a platform, a two-by-two affair, which, if hit with a sledge hammer, kicked a metal object up a groove. If the platform was hit exactly right, the metal went high enough to bing the bell. A dime gave you three tries at the bell. One hit returned you the dime, two gave you a quarter, and three brought you a full round silver dollar. What particularly caught Elof's eye were the names printed along the groove, each marking a level of attainment. At the bottom was Morgan, next came du Pont, then Ford, then Capone and, going up, near the top, where the goods were more good than bad, were Sinclair Lewis, Thomas Benton, Gershwin, and Henry Wallace, with Einstein at the very top. But the bell itself had no grade marked on it.

Elof asked—there was a lull for the moment in the business— "What's it when you hit the bell?"

The snuss-chewing harkee-proprietor leaned a long sly look into Elof. "Brother, then you're in a world by yourself."

Guffaws burbled up around in the crowd. One silly tittered.

The harkee said, "You want to give it a try?"

"No."

The harkee said, "Oh, a wise guy, huh? Well, back up there then. An' let another man try it. Back. Back."

Elof let himself be pushed a little.

But Fats held against the shoving. "Just a minute, bo," Fats whispered in Elof's ear. "When the next bo steps up, watch how he does it. There's a trick to it."

Presently a buffalo-heavy farmer decided to give it a try. He spat in his hands. Self-conscious, blushing a bit, he swung with a great sweat-flying effort. But it was no go. He failed to raise the binger more than a foot or two from its resting place.

Fats said, jolting Elof with an elbow, "See how it's done now?"

"No."

"Look, bo, give a good look. See how low that platform's built? See? When a guy hits it, he hits it with the edge of the sledge, not with its flat. Like so." Illustrating, Fats pounded a fist into the flat of his hand.

Elof said, "If you know so much about it, why don't you risk your dime?"

Fats hardened. "Bo, bo, who's needin' the money?"

"Well, yeh."

"Get on it then, bo."

Elof watched the buffalo swing again, saw instantly that Fats might be right. The man's power was too high off the ground.

"Get on it, bo. Get on it."

Elof held for a moment; then let go. "Okay. What the hell. It's only ten cents." He paged through his pockets; found the dime.

Elof stepped forward. "Here. I'll give it a try."

The man's chewing jaw stopped; his hard blue gimlet eyes flickered. He glanced at Elof's strong stubby body. He took the dime.

Elof tried a half-dozen sledges for weight; found one he liked; stepped up.

"Ready?"

"Ready."

Elof planted his feet far apart. He lifted the sledge slowly above his head, to a full long stretch. Then, with muscle-gathering power, he came down with a crouching stroke. The sledge landed with a flat solid smack. And miraculously, the binger shot to the top. *Bing!*

The clustering crowd cheered.

The harkee shouted, waving an arm, "There's his dime!"

Again Elof swung. Again the miracle. *Bing!*

"There's his two bits!"

Once more. Whish. *Bing!*

This time the harkee was a little sick. But he made a quick recovery. "You see, ladies an' gents? See how it's done? Three bings an' you get a big round silver dollar. Even the little squirts can do it."

Elof took the dollar.

Fats chuckled. "Bo, this is your lucky day all right." He patted Elof. "Now try it again."

"Oh no, he don't," the harkee said, "oh no, he don't. Only one chance for everybody."

They left, with a dozen blowing buffaloes wrestling for the next chance at the bell binger.

Outside the Temple of Power, Elof reached out the dollar to Fats.

"Keep it."

"But no. I owe it you."

"Let's first see if it'll double itself. Then you can pay me an' still be ahead."

They idled down the Midway, Fats grading the fillies, Elof fingering his riches.

They came upon a small zoo. A man was shouting. They stopped to listen.

"Everybody this way. Evvv-rybody. Come see the zebra with thirteen stripes around his belly and one around his—— Peter hand me down that rope."

Roars of coarse mirth boomed up around them.

Then they came upon another golden opportunity.

A sign bugled:

THE TEMPLE OF CHANCE
WHERE DIMES MAKE DOLLARS
WHERE DOLLARS MAKE TENNERS
WHERE TENNERS MAKE MILLIONS

"Ah," Fats said, "ah, here we are."

Elof held back. "Don't you think we've pressed our luck far enough?"

"Bo, I got a hunch. An', bo, when I get hunches, money comes in bunches."

They stepped inside a huge brown tent with a trampled grass floor. There was merriment, and the sound of jerking levers, and the sound of clicking wheels, and, occasionally, the sound of rattling coin.

"Slot machines," Elof said.

"Sure. One-armed bandits."

"Robbery."

"Sure. But sometimes in your favor."

"Nah," Elof said.

"Yeh," Fats said.

They watched a man punching half dollars into a machine, watched him trip the lever, watched him bite a mustached lip, watched him lose.

"Nah," Elof said.

"Yeh," Fats said.

"Well, which one then?"

"Wait. Let's size around a little first."

They mingled with the sweat-smelling crowd: farmers, small-town bankers, small-town barbers, and hard-line women. To give it all a happy-go-lucky air, the machines had been given names: Kentucky Derby, World Series, Luck-in-Love, Pot-o'-Gold, At-the-Foot-of-the-Rainbow, Fox-and-Geese. Some had dime, some had half-dollar, some had dollar slots.

Then Fats's hand was firm on Elof's arm. "Look, bo," Fats whispered, "look. I've been watchin' that Marriage Machine there an' I figure its about time——"

Elof put in, "My God, what a name for it."

"Yeh, I know. Look, I been watchin' that Marriage Machine there, an' I counted forty bucks goin' in, an' only five comin' out. Bo, that machine is about ripe to poop a jackpot. Get on it with your buck."

"A buck? A whole dollar?"

"Yeh."

"No. I'd rather pay back what I owe you."

"Get on it."

Reluctantly Elof let Fats push him up behind a man playing it.

The man dropped a silver dollar into a slot, shoved it in, jerked a crank. Three narrow drums, a section of their edges appearing in a gaudily colored panel, started whirling side by side. On the drums, at regular intervals, were pictures of fruit: a cherry, a peach, a date, a prune, a lemon, a crab apple. Three cherries brought fifty bucks, three peaches twenty-five, three dates ten. Any combination of the three brought sums all the way down to two dollars. However, any combination in which a prune or a lemon or a crab apple appeared automatically lost the player his dollar.

At last the man, a pool-hall shark, gave up. "Christ Almighty anyway. Stuck seven unlucky devils in there an' didn't raise a twitch."

An attendant, dressed in gray, shook his head in pretended commiseration.

Fats shoved Elof into position.

"Wait," Elof protested, "not so fast. Let me see what I'm gettin' into first."

"Just a lot of luck. Just a lot of luck. That's all."

"You hope."

"Bo, I got that hunch."

"If you say so, okay."

Elof shoved in his dollar; jerked the crank; stepped back; watched the drums.

At first the drums whirled so fast the fruits were all blurred together. Then the one on the left clicked and stopped and showed a date.

"Ah," Fats grunted.

The middle one clicked and showed a date.

"Ah," Fats coughed.

The third one clicked and showed a date.

"Ah hah," Fats chortled. "Three times an' out. Out she comes."

There was a whirl, a sliding of metal on metal, a click, a jangling, and then a little door at the bottom of the Marriage Machine opened up and ejaculated a handful of big round silver dollars. A rattling jackpot.

Dumfounded, Elof picked them up, counted ten.

"Lucky bastard," the man who had just lost seven in it muttered, "an' now I suppose you'll walk away without playin' more."

"Mister," Fats said, "there ain't no point in pushin' luck, is there?"

"But I play these things for fun," the man said, "not to make a lucky stab an' run."

"I suppose you think it ain't fun to pick up ten bucks. C'mon, Elof, let's vamoose."

Stepping out in the hot sticky sun again, with people pressing around, Elof reached out one of the ten silver dollars to Fats. "Here, darn you, this time you've got to take it."

"Keep it."

Elof grabbed Fats roughly and dropped it into Fats's pocket. Fats made a protesting move.

"No, no," Elof growled, "don't you dare give it back. Or for once I'll slug you."

Fats said, "Oh, I want that buck back from you all right. But I was thinkin' it might earn you another ten."

Elof retreated rapidly. "Now, now," he said, "I've played my luck far enough now."

"Bo, I'm still gettin' them messages. Hunches. Better play 'em." Fats in turn dropped the dollar into Elof's pocket.

"Please."

"Nope. Don't want it."

"Please."

Fats smiled a little and, taking Elof in tow again, stalked down the milling Midway.

They came upon a long tent. A banner read:

LOVE PALACE
DANCING AND DRINKS
BEAUTIFUL GIRLS
MUSIC AND ROMANCE

Elof said, "I suppose you want me to try that?"

"Nope. No money in it. But lots of grief. I wouldn't give you a plugged nickel for your chance a gettin' out a there without catchin' a dose."

Finally they were at the end of the wide Midway and were directly in front of a huge temporary gate. High over the entrance, like an arch of triumph, soared five-foot block lettering:

THE TEMPLE OF SPEED

Below it, a black etching against the bronze-blue sky, was the metal silhouette of a magnificent horse caught at the top of a gallop.

"Ah," Fats said, "a hoss strip. Playin' the ponies should really give you beginner's luck."

"Nah."

"Yeh."

"Nah."

"Big money in it, bo."

"Big sorrow in it too."

"Not if you know how. Look, bo, you kin play the ponies two ways. If you got lots a cash, play the sure-fires. If you got only a little, play the long shots."

"Fats, really, I don't think I——"

Fats placed sudden lean claws on Elof's arm. "Bo, just got another message. A hot hunch. Money in a bunch. Bo, walk in an' grab yourself a hundred."

"What? Again?" Elof wailed.

"Bo, walk in."

Bowing, Elof meekly went in under the arch of hoss triumph.

A temporary grandstand had been built at the stretch end of the bull-ring track. The track was a mile-and-a-quarter run.

Elof sensed instantly that here he was among a different kind of people. There were fewer farmers, more small-town men. And sprinkled among them, like pepper in white batter, were professional racing addicts: jockeys and stablemen and trainers and clockers, tip-slingers and dopesters, blind stabbers and track owls, railbirds, slip snatchers, horse lice, and fixers—all the mink-eyed worshipers of sudden fortune.

Fats led the way through the dust millers; got a racing form; studied it, frowning. Elof stood wondering at it all.

A man wearing tan clothes and dung-spattered boots came along.

Fats hailed him. "Got a minute, buddy?"

"Yeh." The man halted. He carried a whip which he cracked playfully against his legs. "What can I do you for?"

Fats held out the racing form. "What race're they in now?"

"They've just finished the tenth."

"Ah. Then the next is the big race of the day."

"Right."

"Who's the favorite?"

"Hamlet will lead the field down the stretch."

"What about Arabia Deserta? Heard a guy say he's a real monarch."

"Naw. That's a Doughty hoss. An' Doughty hosses ain't proved theirsel's yet. Naw, Arabia Deserta's an outside long shot."

"What about Anonymous?"

"A filly. A sprinter. Makes a fast start an' a slow finish."

"Does, huh?"

"Yeh."

"Well, thanks for the tip."

"That's okay."

The man passed on.

Fats studied some more, still frowning.

A little weasel of a man, wearing a burnt-out cigar in the corner of his brown-rimmed mouth, came up, winking, wagging. He held his narrow face to one side, as if the pose helped him get a better look at life. "Who you bettin' on in the eleventh, boys?"

Fats drew back his ear. "Heard Canterb'ry Tales had plenty of run in him."

"Naw."

"What about Tom Jones?"

"Naw. Doesn't quite have it."

Fats glanced at his form. "Faerie Queen?"

"Dead meat."

"Who, then?"

The burnt-out cigar jiggled between the weasel's brown lips. "Moby Dick. That's the hot hide. That's the well-sugared nose. Bet on him, boys. I got it right from the hoss's mouth hisself."

"Thanks."

"Uh-huh."

The little blinker passed on.

The feverish eyes in the crowd began to work on Elof. He reached for the racing form. "Give me a look."

"Just let me handle this, bo."

"But I——"

"Bo, just got another message. It's Beowulf. Pays ten to one. Bet your ten an' you can go home with a C-note. One hundred fish."

"Or no fish at all."

"Bo, that message was strong. Beowulf, the imported stallion, is a cinch. Post position lucky seven. Man, you can't miss. Give, an' I'll dump your wad at the mute window where it'll do the most good."

Anguished, yet unable to stop himself, Elof lifted the ten silver dollars out of his pockets and dropped them into Fats's lean claws. "Ah, now you're in the bucks."

Together they shoved through the thousand-elbowed crowd milling in front of the pari-mutuel window. Fats put the ten across through the wicket.

"Now let's get down to the saddlin' barn an' have a look at him. We got a minute or two before they begin."

Arriving in the tent barn, they were directed to Beowulf's stall by a blond stableboy. Elof and Fats stepped up close. Before them, on straw bedding, pranced a bridled and saddled black stallion, sleek, coat shining, alert, with 7 as its marking.

Fats nodded. "Hmmm. Just look at that. A sight for sore eyes. A winner if I ever saw one."

Elof blinked; tried to see what Fats was seeing.

A groom came up. He was a softhearted lank. "Like him?"

Fats coughed. "Like him? Hell, he's just gonna make us rich, is all."

The groom nodded. "He's been a little restless, though. I just came down now to walk him a little."

"What's wrong with him?"

The groom said nothing.

The groom went into the stall cautiously. "Whoa, boy, whoa. Easy, boy, easy. There." The groom took Beowulf by the bridle and led him out. The stallion whinnied.

"Whoa, boy."

Elof and Fats backed up. Other horses, also being saddled and readied for the next race, raised a little stir.

"Whoa, boy."

The groom led Beowulf down a wide clean alley. Just as they passed a filly, also being readied in a stall, with 11 as its marking,

Beowulf rumbled out a low whinny. The groom cursed softly and led Beowulf the other way.

"What filly is that?" Fats asked sharply.

"Anonymous." The groom flicked his deer-brown eyes at her bitterly.

"Cripes."

Elof asked, "Now what?"

"Don't you see? We've just bet on a horse that's fallen in love. He just got one whiff of that filly an' he dropped his rod. He ain't got his mind on runnin'."

"That's right," the groom agreed.

"Will he be scratched?" Fats asked.

"No."

"Will the filly?"

"No." The groom looked down sadly. "No, the concession boys need the money."

"Don't they know she's in heat?"

"The concession boys need the money."

"My God in heaven! There goes Elof's little fish."

The groom looked down.

"Cripes." Fats kicked at a mound of wet horse droppings, scattering them into brown bits.

The groom said, "You might have a chance if the jock'll get him started ahead of her. Beowulf here is seven an'll be closer to the rail."

"Has the jock been told?"

"Yes. I told him."

"Good. Because otherwise, once Beowulf gets his nose at her rump, she'll beat him by a length no matter what the other beetles do."

"Yeh."

Then the jockey came to get Beowulf for the parade to the post, and Fats and Elof left.

On the way across the grounds Fats rented a pair of field glasses.

They had taken but a half-dozen steps toward the track when a loud-speaker awakened and an ear-brasting voice announced, "THE HORSES ARE AT THE POST!"

Shouts, roars, whistles went up. Swarms of legs and arms thickened at the rail ahead.

By dint of vigorous wriggling, Elof opening up a hole and Fats following and widening it, they got to the rail. Elof climbed up on the bottom board, raised himself to see.

The horses, fifteen of them, entered in a fairly orderly manner. Only Beowulf moved uneasily. All were mounted by rump-in-the-air jockeys. Red and white and blue, silks and rayons—the array was a colorful mass of pulsing hair and bone.

The crowd hushed. All eyes became tense.

A bell rang. Gates opened.

"THERE THEY GO!" the loud-speaker cheered.

There was a pound of hoofs on soft earth, and sudden rising clouds of dust, and horse legs streaking past, and glossy necks stretching, and jockeys hopping high, and then a tower of dust blurred them and they were gone.

"AROUND THE CLUBHOUSE TURN. IT'S BEOWULF IN FRONT BY A LENGTH. ANONYMOUS IS SECOND. ARABIA DESERTA IS THIRD BY A NECK. DAWN IN BRITAIN IS FOURTH BY HALF A LENGTH."

"Wow!" Elof shouted.

"AT THE QUARTER. BEOWULF BY A LENGTH AND A HALF. ANONYMOUS IS SECOND. ARABIA DESERTA THIRD. THEN IT'S DAWN IN BRITAIN. CANTERB'RY TALES. HAMLET. LEAVES O' GRASS. TOM JONES. KING LEAR. MOBY DICK. FAERIE QUEEN."

"Wow!" Elof yelled.

Fats, looking through the glasses, frowned. "Wish that damned filly would drop back a little." He handed the glasses to Elof. "Here, you take a look."

"AT THE HALFWAY MARK. BEOWULF IS IN FRONT BY ONE LENGTH. ANONYMOUS MOVING UP ON THE OUTSIDE. ARABIA DESERTA THIRD. DAWN IN BRITAIN FOURTH."

"Still leading!" Elof shouted, waving his speckled hand wildly, his eyes googling into the glasses, his hair a throw of gold. "Good old Beowulf!"

Fats growled, "She'll bullox it up. Just so that jock keeps Beowulf's nose ahead of her."

Suddenly there was a commotion in the crowd. Exclamations of surprise. Elof, too, gulked. "My God!" Elof gasped.

"What? What?" Fats demanded, grabbing Elof's arm.

"Something screwy . . . I dunno . . . Beowulf, he——"

"Here, let me look," Fats said, grabbing the glasses from Elof.

Fats adjusted the glasses, glared through them. "Holy smokes!" Fats exclaimed. "That goddamned Beowulf's turned around an's swung in behind the filly." Fats gave the adjusting screw on the glasses another slight turn. "Yessir. That's just what he did. An' now he's got his nose stuck up her behind like a hand in a glove."

"AT THE THIRD-QUARTER MARK. ANONYMOUS BY A LENGTH. BEOWULF SECOND. ARABIA DESERTA AND DAWN IN BRITAIN NECK AND NECK AND MOVING UP. HAMLET. CANTERB'RY TALES. LEAVES O' GRASS. KING LEAR. MOBY DICK. FAERIE QUEEN. TOM JONES."

"That goddamned Beowulf."

"Oh," Elof said.

"That goddamned Beowulf." Fats spat over the rail onto the track. "That filly better not make a sudden stop or he'll have the honor a bein' the first beetle to start a race a cinch winner an' wind up a foal."

"THERE THEY COME INTO THE STRETCH. ARABIA DESERTA AND DAWN IN BRITAIN NOSING AHEAD AND STILL NECK AND NECK. CANTERB'RY TALES. HAMLET. LEAVES O' GRASS. ANONYMOUS. BEOWULF. KING LEAR. TOM JONES. MOBY DICK. FAERIE QUEEN."

Sadly Elof watched the thoroughbreds come in. The leaders could be distinctly seen, neck out, ears flicking, eyes bugging. The rest were partially obscured by a rolling mass of bursting dust. But not obscured enough to hide the strange antics of Anonymous and Beowulf. With his nose still tucked up under her tail, they came rolling along in a paired gallop, eight hoofs hitting the turf in unison.

Fats glared at the ground, chewing his teeth.

Screams, screeches, shrills, shouts rilled out above the roar mounting from the massing crowd.

"IT'S DAWN IN BRITAIN BY A NOSE! THEN ARABIA DESERTA! THEN CANTERB'RY TALES! AND HERE COMES HAMLET! AND LEAVES O' GRASS! WITH FAERIE QUEEN MOVING UP STRONG FOR THE NEXT SPOT! KING LEAR! TOM JONES! MOBY DICK! ANONYMOUS! BEOWULF!"

Then all was swallowed up by the brulling sounds of victory. An unknown had won. And another unknown had taken second. Long shots. Doughty stablemates. Monarchs.

Elof and Fats were having a bite to eat at the beer-and-burger stand.

Between munches Fats muttered, "It's always a mistake to run fillies in with stallions. Whether they're in heat or not." Fats cleared his throat. "Unless you want colts."

Elof said nothing.

"Damned stallion. Those concession boys were absolutely nuts."

Elof took another bite.

"An' what a slowpoke that filly was. Even with Beowulf's nose shoved up her seat, she still couldn't do better than come in second t'last." Fats bit viciously into his burger; swigged some beer. "Her jock sure come in with a lapful a horse that time."

Elof still made no comment.

"Played wink with him all the way."

Elof burrowed silently into his burger.

Fats wiped his pallor-and-purple face with a white kerchief. "That damned Beowulf. That damned hay-burner. That oats-grinder. That bangtail. Playin' last-couple-out with a filly."

Elof cleared his throat, said, "Oh, shut up."

Fats did.

The happy lark was over.

CHAPTER XVII: The Prodigal Son

. . . Elof boy, what was it that helped you escape
the crafty males, the scarred toms, the killer bulls?
The first time you left home, was it a voice that un-
thawed within you and sent you back to the warm
safety of your mother's house where you might heal
your ripped blond hide? And when you found
your ma dead and your pa brulling with lowered
horns, was it a voice again that saved you? And
when you ran away once more, what was it that led
you back again? And who was it that at last told
you that dreams were a luxury never meant for the
hornless, that finders are not keepers . . .

It was Sunday afternoon and still hot and sticky when Elof
started hiking for home. The humid air suggested rain.

He stood atop a bluff east of Sioux Falls, on the south side of
the highway, thumbing every passing motorist for a ride east.
His body broke sweat; his gray woolen suit itched.

In between cars he gazed at the endless unfolding of earth to
the north; traced out the rising and swelling until brown soil
blended off into hazy blue.

In a cornfield across the road, tassels were beginning to fall
out of the tops. Leaves were drying and yellowing. Corn ears,
many of them nubbins, hung limply. Behind him spread a dry
yellow-gray pasture. The land thirsted for rain.

A sparkling black car moaned toward him from the city way.
It slowed a little, and he looked closely to size it up for a potential

ride. But when he saw it was full with five people in it, he dropped his thumb. It came closer, softly murmuring, and then he saw that all five were old withered women, that all five wore black hats, each with a single gray-striped hen-pheasant feather cocked to the right, that all five faces and ten blank eyes were directed straight at him. Just as they were even with him, the lips of one in the back seat moved—he could see the lips were making a damning remark—and then all five feathered heads nodded vigorously. He knew it was about himself, that they were calling him a no-good bum—"Why doesn't he get himself a job and go to work?"; "Such lazy bums are the ruination of the country"; "Living off the taxpayers' money"; "Reliefers"; "Yes, we're living in the last days all right"; "Pastor Thorwald says we can expect Judgment Day any day now."

Elof's first impulse was to shrink. But a vision of what Fats might do in this spot came to him, and he stiffened his stubby back and raked his mind for some snarling retort. But all he could muster was, "Laugh, you dried-up sin-twisters, laugh, will you?" and a thumbing of the nose at them.

The car with the five old weathered feathers rolled on.

He stood alone again.

Time spent awhile ticking off ten minutes.

He fidgeted.

He was about to give up getting a ride when a car began to slow for him the moment it came over the brow of the hill. The car somehow seemed familiar to him. He tried to fix it in the past; couldn't. He set himself to snare the ride no matter who it might be, friend or stranger. He forced a happy smile to his lips, leaned on his toes, stretched far over his suitcase, and waved a stumpy freckled thumb with a forward motion.

The car stopped, its tires humming on the cement paving with a falling sound. And then, too late, Elof saw that it was Young Domeny Hillich of Hello, the other chosen one. And the only person outside of Pa who knew about his being short-armed all around. It was like facing one's conscience in the living flesh.

Young Domeny Hillich opened the door. "Well, Elof, I didn't expect to see you today. Get in."

"Hi, Bud," Elof said. He picked up his suitcase and put it in back, climbed in, closed the door. The seat was commodious and yielding. The instrument board sparkled.

"You're going home?" Domeny Hillich's blue eyes were warm with the old-time comradery.

"Yeh."

"Good." Young Domeny Hillich started up the car easily, drove on without clashing the gears. "I'm on my way back from The Dells. It was my preaching turn. Our one church there is just now without a shepherd."

Young Domeny Hillich drew two cigars from the lapel pocket of his black suit. "Smoke?"

"No, thanks. I don't care much for cigars."

Young Domeny Hillich put one of the cigars back in his pocket, fired the other with the dashboard lighter. "You smoke cigarettes?"

"When I got the makin's."

"I see. Sorry I haven't any tailor-mades with me."

"Oh, that's all right."

Young Domeny Hillich stepped on the foot feed. The car began to glide down the road with a rising whine. The white paving rushed toward them; slid beneath them.

The town of Squaw Tit appeared on the left—filling station, church, elevator, depot, store, saloon, a few homes—then was gone. Young Domeny Hillich hardly slowed for it.

Once again Elof found himself resenting his old roommate's well-being. Young Domeny Hillich and the good things of life had always got on well together. Elof remembered how in Saint Comus Theological College and Seminary he had envied Bud his slim well-proportioned body, his pink enduring health. He remembered how jealous he had been of Bud's A's in Greek and Hebrew and Beginning Exegetics. And of Bud's continual happy whistling.

Elof wondered if Young Domeny Hillich would make some comment about the sin of his having hiked a ride on Sunday, a desecration of the Lord's day, such as:

Remember the sabbath day, to keep it holy.
Six days shalt thou labour, and do all thy work:
But the seventh day is the sabbath of the Lord thy God . . .

If Young Domeny Hillich did, he would slam him with one from the lips of Christ Himself:

What man shall there be among you, that shall have one sheep, and if it fall into a pit on the sabbath day, will he not lay hold on it, and lift it out?

The sabbath was made for man, and not man for the sabbath.

Elof was a little pleased to find that his memory had not blurred on him. The biblical texts came up out of the haze like lettering over a movie entrance. The two years at the seminary were paying off at last.

Young Domeny Hillich drove on.

Ahead the village of Sometimes pricked its church spires and grain elevators into the horizon. Soon the village was in full view. It approached on the right; it revolved a little; it vanished behind them.

They crossed the state line, passing from South Dakota into Minnesota.

Elof looked out of the car window, noted that a cloud bank had begun to obscure the sun in the west. He craned his neck to examine it more closely but, because of the murk, couldn't make out its forward edge.

Young Domeny Hillich wheeled on silently, his fresh cigar glowing red in the car's wind.

The city of Whitebone came up and Young Domeny Hillich slowed down. The car entered it. Clean, white-painted frame houses floated by on either side of the street. A few purple stone and red brick homes appeared as the car neared the center and older portion of the city.

A sign announcing a highway junction, *King's Trail,* came up. Young Domeny Hillich pulled up for the stop sign, shifted gears, turned south.

Wordlessly they rolled between rows of houses. Few people were on the hot street.

In a few minutes they were out of the city again.

Then Elof saw it. Far off to the west, across immane plains, came the dark forehead of an approaching storm. It shadowed the entire west horizon; it was an oncoming looming planet.

They rolled on.

Elof began to fret. Why didn't the other say something? Anything at all!

Elof couldn't understand the silence. Maybe his old roommate was using a bit of psychology on him; was going to make him talk first.

Maybe the young domeny was concentrating on the question of his having left church and home the second time: "Yes, the first time, yes, that was perhaps a good thing. The intention was good. The ministry. But this second running away—no, Brother Lofblom, I'm sure that the Lord disapproves of it." So the young domeny could couch his reproaches. And go on to observe that the fleshpots of Egypt, the temptations of the "world," the whores of the devil, all these could never outweigh in the balances the idyllic safety of the christian village of Hello.

Elof set himself for the platitudes, hunted around on the landscape of his mind for retorts.

Or maybe the young domeny was merely brooding over the deplorable condition of the present-day world, thinking that if Christ were alive today, man, the people, would not recognize Him; in fact, might crucify Him all over again.

In that case, Elof was ready for him too.

Elof could just hear him. Just hear him.

And he could hear himself in rebuttal.

. . . Young Domeny Hillich: "Why, if Christ Jesus were alive today, and walking on the land, the people wouldn't recognize Him. No. They would crucify Him all over again."

Elof: "You said a mouthful, Bud."

"You agree with me?"

"Of course. I've been wandering through the land for many years now, ever since that picnic accident. Actually, you know, you were the only one saved that day. I—or rather, Elof Lofblom died, and I, Christ Jesus, a spirit, entered Elof's body and, entering, was able to scramble out of the mess with you and announce myself safe to your father, Old Domeny Hillich. And I went to high school with you, suffering that horrible indignity by you inspired in the shower room. And I went on to college with you, suffering that horrible gibberish by professors given in a course called 'The Christ Preached.' And I went on to State, to see if maybe the secular schools had true salvation in them. And I saw the 'world.' "

"Elof!"

"Yes, oddly enough, during all that time, no one recognized me. Saw who I truly was. Christ Jesus. Once more walking upon the face of the earth."

"Elof, in the name of all that's holy. Please!"

"Christ Jesus. Yes. And the reason I took over the body of little Elof, the little Elof who had been a bit shortchanged on everything, the reason I took him over was to see if the strong were treating the humble and the meek with human love."

"O God, forgive him, for he knoweth not what he doeth!"

"For verily, verily I say unto you, unless ye have not love and compassion in your heart for the least of these, then ye are wanting in the larger also."

"Elof."

"Yea, verily, and I say unto you that from where I have been sitting, on my Father's south porch just off Judgment Hall, it has been apparent that the earth and most of its inhabitants smell to high heaven."

"Oh, Elof."

"And verily, verily I say unto you that if this sump stink isn't gotten rid of pronto, I'm going to recommend to Father that We destroy you and all the land you live on."

"Elof. Now look. Are you really telling me that you are Christ Jesus Himself?"

"Of course, of course."

"But you can't be Christ! You just can't be! It would destroy everything we've built up so far. Churches. Governments. Even the Sacred Book!"

"Of course." Then, as if conversing with himself, Elof said, "Oh ye of little faith . . ."

So they would talk.
Elof chuckled to himself.

He watched the storm coming toward them. Its front came on low, a tattered, twisting threat. Miles away blue-white lightning pierced the earth. Thunder droned.

Young Domeny Hillich hurried through Rock Falls, hardly slowing for the city speed limits. He sped south.

Elof shifted around on the plush seat. The smell of the other's cigar at last awoke a desire in him for nicotine too. He took out his puff-light papers and powdery tobacco and rolled himself a cigarette. His stumpy fingers rolled it deftly.

Young Domeny Hillich began to race with the storm, apparently thinking he could slip south of it, out of its spread. He swooped through the Big Rock River Valley; then through the Little Rock.

The paved highway ended, became a rough gravel road. The car riggled over the washboard surface.

Elof listened to the noise of the jouncing tires, smoked, continued to mull to himself.

The gravel road was typical of the place. Typical. And all because the Sioux County farmers were tight. So tight that they had refused to co-operate with state and federal road commissions when the big highways were being spanned across the country. They were insular. Narrow-minded. They were eating their cake and having it too. They were having their heaven on earth and Old Europe too. Individuals like the young domeny weren't helping it any. Imagine living in a community where a man couldn't buy a gallon of gas on Sunday. Where the young folks had to drive miles to go to a movie. And, that secretly, guiltily, too. Remember the Sabbath day, to keep it holy. Such a bunch of backward hicks.

The oncoming crusher-front of the storm still came on. Young Domeny Hillich sped the car through yet another valley.

At last the very south edge of the gray mizzling mass was within a hundred feet of them. A row of cottonwoods suddenly threshed violently. Leaves and branches sleeted across the highway.

"Hey," Young Domeny Hillich finally exclaimed, "this is going to be a wild one."

And then they were lost in a raging welter of gray splashing water. The windshield wiper stuck.

Young Domeny Hillich pulled over to the side of the road; braked hard. The car stopped.

Young Domeny Hillich rolled up the window on his side; looked around to see if the back windows were up.

Elof noted the other's calm; wished he felt as easy.

A dart of lightning enveloped the car. Thunder exploded at the same time. There was a great shriek somewhere ahead in the storm.

Elof's knuckles went white on his knee. "What'n God's name was that?"

"Probably just a cottonwood losing a branch. Or falling to earth."

Again lightning licked; thunder brommed.

"I always worry until they're over."

Young Domeny Hillich smiled at him questioningly. "You do? They never bother me."

"With me it's probably some childhood fear."

"Perhaps. With me it's that I feel safe in the Lord."

"Huh."

Young Domeny Hillich puffed on the stub of his cigar. He watched the storm outside the car. Every once in a while his shiny black toe on the foot feed goosed the motor to keep it running.

Elof finished his cigarette; rolled another with jumpy fingers. He puffed, flicked ashes into the pull-out tray in the dashboard.

They sat quietly.

Rain swilled over the car.

Young Domeny Hillich mused, "Wonder if the little woman's worried about me."

"Who?"

"Esther. My wife." Young Domeny Hillich sighed. "Well, it can't be helped. I tried my best."

Elof said nothing.

"Yes," Young Domeny Hillich said, "it's pretty nice to have a wife worrying about one. It makes life worth while." He paused. "Yes, and it's even nicer to have a child. A boy. You know, Elof, back there in college, I used to have all kinds of romantic notions about married life."

"We all did."

Young Domeny Hillich chuckled to himself, his untroubled blue eyes twinkling. He flicked the ash end of his stub into the tray. "Yes, romantic notions. But the real thing—man, it was beyond my wildest dreams."

Elof twitched uneasily.

"My dreams'd told me that love, sheer love, would become more intense. Passionate. Well, as it turned out, love cooled down. And something else came in its place. Something solid, quiet, and yet more compelling than passions. Now what that something is, I'll be frank to say I don't know. I think the main thing is having a child." Young Domeny Hillich tipped his head to one side, considered, tipped it to the other, reconsidered. "Yes, I'm sure that's it. Having Bobby did it. Wonderful. Made it different, but more wonderful."

Lightning and thunder passed on.

Elof wondered what the other was driving at; waited for the catch.

"You know, Elof, having a child and watching it grow up tells you what your father went through, tells you how you yourself started out, gives you a notion of your complete self. That little mind each day lifting itself out of ignorance, it's an experience to observe, let me tell you. Like—some words Bobby can say, but others he can't. Because he hasn't said any words like it yet. But then one day he says one akin to it, and then, pop! a whole new flock of words are added to his vocabulary. Like— Bobby had trouble saying a word starting off with two consonants, especially when the second letter was *r,* like 'broke,' or 'breakfast,' or 'friend,' or 'free,' so on. Well, one day he was playing with a neighbor boy, in the other boy's coaster wagon. And they got going down a steep hill in town there and the other boy ordered Bobby to put on the brake. Anyway, that night Bobby came home telling me all about how a 'brake' works. He didn't say it clearly, but he was close. Sort of a combination 'bwake' and 'brake.' Then soon he began to say 'breakfast'—why, even my expression, 'brethren in Christ.' " Again Young Domeny Hillich chortled to himself.

Elof sucked deeply on his cigarette; kept his peace.

The rain began to let up.

"Yes, sometimes Esther complains I got too much drag with the boy. She thinks I favor him. Spoil him. Funny part is, I'm the one who spanks him once in a while. Not Esther. She tries to protect him even. But, still, he comes to me." Young Domeny Hillich crushed out the last of his wet cigar. "I think what really happens is this. Every time we get company, the women make too much of a to-do over him. They get inside the door and the first thing they do is to swoop down on him like hawks. And pet him and call him 'pretty boy.' But the men let him alone, sit back, treat him like a grownup. I think that's the real reason I'm his buddy."

Elof crushed out his smoke too.

Young Domeny Hillich shifted gears, goosed the motor, started up slowly again. The wiper began to work smoothly. "Yes, Elof, sometimes I wonder why you don't marry and settle down. It's good for what ails you."

Elof turned his face away. Aha, the young domeny had at last got around to it. But instead of going on, Young Domeny Hillich sighed. "Well, so it goes. Each man to his own taste."

The car began to rush through light rain.

Elof looked through the little half circle the wiper kept clean and saw, far to the west, along the entire horizon, a clearing sky. The thirsty land wasn't going to get a soaker after all. It was only a flashing line-storm.

When Domeny Hillich stopped the car at Chokecherry Corner in front of Lofblom's Grocery, the skies were already clear above them, a vast soaring blue, and the rustling, ripened corn across the road was glistening with myriads of dancing raindrop lights, and the plowed land farther to the south was gleaming a purple-black.

"Well, Elof, here we are. Safe and sound."

Elof nodded. He slid out; reached in back for his suitcase. "Thanks a lot for the ride, Bud. Thanks." Elof hesitated. "Or maybe I should say, 'Thanks, Domeny.' "

A frown wrinkled Young Domeny Hillich's pink forehead. "Elof, remember, I'm always Bud to you."

"Well—all right. Anyway, thanks a lot for the ride," Elof said lamely.

"Don't mention it."

Elof closed the door.

Young Domeny waved and then was off, his car rolling easily. Elof watched him go. "When they put it to you that way," he muttered to himself, "when they put it to you that way you just can't get mad. You can't bite a soothing hand." Elof shifted his suitcase from one hand to the other. "And this time he was smart enough not to invite me over. Got to hand it to him."

Out of the corner of his eye he caught a flash of yellow spurting from the chokecherry tree. Looking quickly, watching it go through and above the cottonwoods, he saw the flaming orange passage of an oriole against the blue-deep clouds of the departing storm.

He was stepping into the drive-in, slowly, when his eye caught it: the change that had come over the old homestead. The drive-in had been cleaned up. It had been regraveled and the trim stones repainted white as of old. Even the flower beds had been worked—the weeds cut down, the encroaching green grass of the lawn cut back, and the surface manured—ready for next year's clouds of red-and-white petals. It was almost like the old days. When Ma was alive.

What was up? Pa really courting Gert in earnest again, thinking that his boy, drifted off, was never coming back?

Elof climbed the wet cement steps. The door was locked, as it always was on Sunday. He paged through his pockets for a ring of keys. Finding it, selecting the right key, he opened, entered, closed the door after himself.

The same old smells: dry sweet cereal, dried dye in cloth, paste in boxes, peppermints, oil compound on the floors, mice dung, dank cellar smell, and, faintly, the odor of fried eggs. And this time, not only no Ma, but no Pa.

Idly he wondered where Pa might have gone, guessed that after church was over the Hansens had invited him out for supper. For Gert's sake.

Elof stepped through the neat store and went in back to his room. Entering, he was glad to see that his old bed was still set up, that it was made. He threw his suitcase up on the spread of it, snapped open the lock. He took out his dirty laundry, his *Peregrine Pickle,* still a long way from being finished, and his accounting lessons. Putting all neatly away, he noticed on the end of the shelf a stack of letters and fat brown envelopes from the American School of Correspondence, and guessed that his course mentor was probably wondering what was up with a lad by the name of Elof Lofblom.

He had put away his suit, was in his shorts and jersey, barefooted, when he thought he heard a rustling noise in the building. It seemed to come from upstairs.

Aha. Then Pa was home. And not over to Gert's. And probably napping and just now waking up.

Quickly Elof stepped into a clean shirt and a pair of overalls and, still barefoot, left the room and climbed the stairs to the second story.

He opened the door at the head of the stairs and stepped into the family parlor. He didn't see anyone around and set his lips to call out when he saw Pa on the couch immediately below on his right. Room shadow partially hid Pa, but his face, caught in a yellow stroke of falling evening sunlight, was as sharply defined as a photo taken in sunlight.

And Elof saw instantly that though Pa's eyes were closed he was not asleep. Pa had the look of a person who had just awakened but who was not yet ready to meet anyone, who needed a moment or two to compose his front, and to compose it had put on the pretense of still being asleep.

And Elof saw, trembling, as transparent as a dewdrop, a tiny pear-shaped tear coursing down the side of Pa's nose, saw it stop directly over a pock-sized blackhead.

Elof drew back and quietly closed the door and went downstairs and stood alone in the store.

Looking out through the show windows and seeing the white stones, he reflected that Ma's endless fussing to keep up the place hadn't gone to waste after all.

CHAPTER XVIII: The Magic Moment

. . . We know that way down, way back, deep in your fleshes (is it your Old Adam?), something is stirring within you. No, not a spectacular truth, or a colossal discovery affecting mankind—no, nothing so dramatic. Only the discovery of a place where you may live mostly happy, fifty-one to forty-nine, for better than for worse, happily, safely, happily within the cupped hand, your home. Slowly, indistinctly, like a room being lit up by a dim light coming from an opening door far down the hall, your mind is waking to a knowledge . . .

The next day, Monday, right after noon-hour lunch, Kaes asked Elof to come over to paint his house. Kaes said he was too busy putting up hay to think of doing it himself. And since Pa still wouldn't give Elof a salary for work, though he would board and room, Elof once more trudged over to Kaes's farm.

Armed with an old overall, a brush, a ladder, a pail of white paint, and a straw broom to clean off the dust and old scaly paint, Elof tackled the rectangular house.

He worked hard all day. At first he had trouble getting the paint on evenly. It had a way of patching. But at last he discovered how to flow it on, and how to connect the flows together, to make the house look as if it had been spray-gunned.

He found, too, that standing on the rungs of the ladder was hard on the balls of his feet. But the worst was the ache that set in below his right shoulder.

The day was a bright one out, with a late-September balm

mellowly breathing over the limp leaves of the trees and the burnt grass. Sometimes a light northwest breeze came around the corner of the house. The lead smell in the paint soured his taste for the afternoon lunch; spoiled the rich molting smell of autumn. And he heaved a sigh of relief when Kaes at five o'clock asked him to help with the chores: milking the black-and-white cows, swilling the hogs, feeding the chickens, getting the eggs. Work around animals cleaned the senses, rinsed them, enabled them to recover from partial knockout.

Chores done, he stepped into the house with Kaes. And noticed what he had observed at lunch, that because of pregnant Gretch, now pretty far gone, there was a mood of gloom in the house, a gloom with somewhere in it, like a spark in a cloud of smoke, a hint of joy. Gretch had only to bring forth the baby, and the gloom would clear and the joy would flame.

Gert was present—she was helping Kaes in the station and Gretch a little in the house.

The first part of the meal was eaten in silence. Kaes sat in his armchair near the stove and east window; Toots in her high chair next to him; Gretch, hair ends even more shaggy than in the summer, her teeth lackluster, on the side nearest the stove and the kitchen cabinet; and Elof and Gert together on the west side of the table, with the screen door to the front porch behind them. Snip, the collie pup, sat outside looking in, occasionally whining when the food smells drifted toward him.

At last Kaes looked up from his plate. "Elof, after you get that paint job done, how would you like runnin' my fillin' station?"

Elof, about to lift a fork of gravied potatoes into his mouth, held still. "That I'd have to think over."

"What I want," Kaes continued, waving a fork, "what I want is a steady man there who'll take an interest in the work an', at the same time, won't get took by slickers. Fast ones."

"Don't tell me Gert's been getting rooked."

"No, no. Gert's sharp enough. But it's only that I think gassin' trucks ain't no job for a woman."

Elof lifted the food into his mouth, chewed, swallowed. "What's the pay?"

Kaes leaned over the table, his meaty face excited, his huge hand and arm lifted. "I tell you what I'll do. I'll give you a straight salary of thirty a week, plus a commission on gas sold over a certain figure."

Elof sat still for a moment. Well, now. Such pay was more like it.

Kaes added, winking at Gretch, who didn't respond, "Better still, if you and Gert should finally decide to up an' get yourselves hitched, I'll give you the back rooms for livin' quarters free. Then Gert could use the shanty for a chowhouse."

Gert instantly looked down, her dark brown bob falling around her face and hiding her eyes.

Elof hurriedly loaded his fork again.

Toots broke in, holding out her plate, "I want some more 'tatoes."

"What do you think of the idea, Elof?"

"I want some more 'tatoes."

"Shut up, will you?" Kaes snapped at the child.

Gretch said, her thick lips flattening the words, "Now, now, you don't have to bite the child. She's only hungry."

"I know it, I know it," Kaes said. "But I'm on edge these days." He glanced appealingly at Elof. "I'd sure like to get that station on its feet. I tell you what, Elof, if you should happen to make a go of it, get a lot of business away from that bastard Cooper——"

"Watch the language. Please!" Gretch warned. "All pots have ears."

"Okay, okay. But really, Elof, if you should happen to make a go of it, I'd sell that corner to you, lock, stock, and barrel. The whole kit an' caboodle."

Property? He Elof? And, of all things, a gas station?

He gave it another turn or two through his mind. Well, perhaps here at last was the hero's role he had been looking for: the crossroads glad-hander.

"Well, how does it sound to you?"

"I don't know. I've got to think it over."

"Do that. Think it over," Kaes said, filling his dessert dish with a few canned pears. "Think it over an' let me know." Kaes

slupped a pale yellow half pear into his mouth; swallowed it
almost unchewed. "An' what I said about givin' you two that
back shanty to live in still goes."

Elof helped himself to a dish of pears, too, and ate slowly.
The pears were sweet. He savored each bite and drop of juice.

After supper Elof went out on the front porch with a lesson and
Peregrine Pickle. Snip, the pup, fed leftovers, had curled up for a
sleep on a step.

Elof first tried working at the accounting; but physical exertion
had taken the sharp edge off his critical faculties, and in a moment
or two he was gazing absent-mindedly into the twilight under the
trees.

So he turned to Smollett.

He read a bit—Perry was in the midst of making a treacherous
attack on Emy—all the while vaguely aware of the women washing dishes in the kitchen.

Perry's adventures with Emy reminded him that tonight he
and Gert would be sleeping under the same roof. The idea stirred
him. She would probably sleep in the east room over the kitchen
while he, as usual, would sleep in the south room. On his way to
bed, at the head of the stairs, he would have to pass her door.

He blinked his eyes; forced himself back to the printed page.

But again an idea, this time an outside one, shoved Smollett
from the stage of his mind. He caught himself hating Pa. What
could have gotten into Pa that he should have tried to marry
Gert? Was he crazy? Pa was old enough to be her father. Once
more Elof was reminded that, if one was to believe the stories
old men told one, in a couple of years Pa wouldn't be able to
procreate any more, and then Gert, a healthy young woman,
would find herself hitched to an impotent old buck.

Elof winced. The dirty old fool.

He remembered once having seen Pa's parts. It was just before
he had gone off to college. The old man had been taking a bath
in the kitchen. He was wiping his back and when Elof stepped
in he couldn't get his towel around fast enough to hide himself.
Elof had seen the bull parts of him; had never forgotten them.
Pa had what he didn't have. Size. And just think—if the old
man had his way, those parts would touch Gert.

Elof shivered. And quickly snapped the book shut and got up and went into the house, very much relieved to find Gert still safe in the house and helping Gretch.

The women were almost through with the dishes. Gretch was getting ready to throw out the water and Gert was putting the wiped and shining dishes away into the cupboard.

Elof looked at Kaes. "You like checkers?"

Kaes glanced up. He was helping naked, pea-split Toots into her nightgown. "You betcha. Just as soon as I get this little monkey off to bed."

"Where's the set?"

"Up on the third shelf there."

Gretch offered, "Behind the grape dish there."

Elof opened the glass door; looked in.

Gert came up beside him; brushed against him. "There," she said, "right there."

He set out the red-and-black board on the just-wiped blue-and-white oilclothed table; set up the checkers.

"Say 'Good night' to everybody now," Kaes said, roughly kissing Toots.

"Good night, ev'body."

"Good night."

"Good night."

But saying "Good night" wasn't enough for Toots. She had to give everyone a kiss too, a noisy wet kiss. Even Elof.

Elof laughed; flushed. The impression of her soft moist lips on his lingered. No wonder a few men, just a step off stride, succumbed to the temptation of raping soft child flesh.

"All right, all right," Gretch said, "that's enough." She took Toots hastily away from Elof, steered her for the stair door. She opened it, closed it behind the child. "There. At last. Now for some peace and quiet."

"Yeh," Kaes said, throwing his fat leg over a chair and drawing up to the table.

Dusk was falling outdoors and inside the house it became dark.

"Shall I light the lamp?" Elof offered.

"Please. I've got some sewing to do tonight," Gretch sighed, sinking onto a chair, her child burden suddenly making a lapful.

Gert said, "An' I've got some bookwork to do. My figures didn't come out right at the station today."

"Here, I'll light it," Kaes said, getting up. He took down the gas lamp, pumped in some air, opened the throttle a little. He held a match between the white ash mantles. There was a hissing, a dull orange glow, then blinding white light. Kaes rehooked the lamp to the ceiling directly above the table.

The two men leaned over the board. Since Elof had the black men, he moved first. Four moves into the game, and he discovered Kaes to be a formidable foe. Ten moves later, to the sound of Gretch's whirring sewing machine, Elof found himself cornered.

Kaes slapped his leg. "Wife, get me some lemonade. This is goin' to be fun."

Gert said, "I'll do it. Let Gretch keep sewing."

They played again. Again Kaes beat him. No matter how many traps Elof set up, Kaes was aware of them, had even set up more complicated counter-traps. The last move had been a three-for-six exchange, wiping Elof off the board. Kaes's shrewd peasant scheming, his luring and retreat, surprised Elof.

Elof set his chin. He couldn't show white in front of Gert. The third time he moved more cautiously. But again Kaes won.

"Shucks, this is too easy," Kaes said. "Like rollin' off a greased log. I thought you collech guys learned to use your thinker."

Elof bit a lip; helped set up the checkers again—all the while reviewing the kind of game Kaes was playing. He rolled himself a cigarette, and with the same match lit both his smoke and a cigar Kaes had gotten himself.

Gert set out a glass of lemonade for each; then returned to her gas figures.

Through films of wispy gray smoke it occurred to Elof that, since Kaes was more familiar with the game, Kaes would know how to handle a greater number of checkers than he. The thing to do was to keep trading until the checkers got down to a number he himself could handle.

Elof set to work. He traded one in the middle; one off to the side; two in the middle. Always even exchanges. At last both were down to three checkers.

They maneuvered, smoked, smiled craftily, brooded, sipped from the cooling glass of lemonade.

Outside the open screen door the crickets whirred, frogs bayed, and Snip the pup snored.

Finally Elof got Kaes in a corner. He could trade two for two, and do it in such a way that Kaes's last checker would be cornered by his last.

"I'll be doggoned. That got me," Kaes said ruefully. "Pretty good game, Elof."

"One more?"

Kaes looked at the clock. It was past nine. "Well, all right. One more."

Again Elof set to work cagily. And again, by wearing Kaes down to a few men, cornered him and won.

Kaes finished his lemonade, puffed on his stub of cigar, stood up, stretched. "Awwwaaah."

Gretch got up, too, and closed her sewing machine. "Time to go t'bed."

Kaes turned to Elof. "Take it from here tomorrow night?"

"Sure. But I'll play more now."

"Well—when the old lady says it's time to roost, it's time to roost," Kaes said, smiling. "After all, somebody has to win."

Elof said, shaking a finger at him, "Okay, but remember, tomorrow night I'm taking you."

Gert also got up; put away her papers. "Station should open at six. So . . ."

Silently all began to make moves to retire. The women began to take off their shoes; Kaes and Elof stepped outdoors into the starlight to relieve themselves. Kaes coughed, cleared his throat. There was a hissing sound of water spretting into the dry grass.

Coming inside again, Elof found Gert already gone. Disappointed, he took off his shoes and started for the stair door.

Kaes, standing with his hand on the gas-lamp throttle, asked, "Ready?"

"Yes," Gretchen said, pushing her shoes under her chair and slowly getting up.

"Yep," Elof said.

"Good night."

"Good night."

"Good night."

Kaes turned off the lamp. In a moment the two mantles became dull yellow, flutted, went out. Darkness recaptured lost territory. Elof heard Kaes and Gretchen shuffle across the linoleum floor in their socks; heard them enter the first-floor bedroom.

Elof trudged up the stairs, wondering if Gert were already in bed.

He had one more step to go when he heard the door to Gert's room open and then bare feet come slithering toward him. He stopped stock-still.

She bumped against him. "Oh," she gulked softly.

Elof grabbed her. He didn't know what to say, and blurted, "Hey, I thought you was in bed already."

Weakly she tried to wrestle free. All she had on was a silk slip. "I forgot I had to . . . I forgot."

"Oh."

She wrestled again. "Let me go."

"Aw . . ." Elof tightened his arm. Miraculously one of his hands happened onto her breast. Both because she was tall and because she was a step above him, it was almost into his face. It was the softest flesh he had ever touched, even softer than Toots's.

"Don't," she said.

"Aw now," he murmured.

He wondered what her eyes were saying in the dark. He ran his other hand over her bobbed hair, down her back, pressed her against himself. He felt his pant legs tighten.

Elof raised himself to the last step and, with a strong stubby hand on the back of her head, drew her face down toward him. He kissed her.

She responded lightly.

He kissed her again; tightened his cupping hand.

"We better not," she whispered.

Elof flamed. For her even to think dangerous was angel song.

She drew away from him slowly, at the last moment kissing him full on the lips, wet, as Toots had done. Then she was gone, going down the steps in the dark.

"Gert!" he whispered. "Come back."

She did not answer. In a moment the downstairs door opened; and closed.

Elof stood at the head of the stairs.

A magic moment had come; had gone. And he had failed to take advantage of it.

. . . One thing troubles us. To have survived the numbing discovery that you were a simpleton and not a hero, to have discovered within yourself courage enough to come home to certain abuse and ridicule—could it be that a special quality resides in you after all? That we, pompous and lofty, and warbling with a fancy tongue, are blind to it? That intellect, which we worship just a little more than we fear, and consider our only hope, is as heady a drink as religion? Is as much an opium? To have survived that double strain is perhaps the true hero's toil . . .

The next morning he awoke with a tune on his lips.

And discovered, to his mounting excitement, that things had been happening during the night.

At two in the morning Gretch had felt the first pains. At three, Dr. Mars had come. At four, the baby was born. At five, both mother and boy were doing well.

Kaes was bibbering a wake-up cup of coffee, beaming, waving an arm. "A ten-pounder, too, mind you. What a hired man he'll make."

"Well, now maybe you won't need to rent out the station." Elof grinned, also sipping coffee.

"Oh well . . ." Kaes laughed. "Listen, I'm still serious about that, you know."

Elof nodded.

Gert came in from the first-floor bedroom where Gretch lay recovering. "Mornin'," she said.

"Mornin'."

Kaes asked, "Everything still goin' tip-top?"

"Everything."

"Good." Kaes set down his cup. "I tell you what we'll do today. Gert, you stay home an' help Gretch. Elof, you paint. Toots, she can go over to Gramp and Gramma Hansen. And me, I kin quick hupple the last couple loads a hay into the barn, an' then get me the hell over an' run the station."

"Okay," Gert said, "just so you don't lose any business."

"I probably will. But this is an emergency." Kaes got up. "C'mon, Elof, let's pail them cows."

"Okay. Be right with you."

After breakfast Elof went at the painting as if he couldn't get at a good thing fast enough. He whistled merrily in the September-morning light.

With Gretch in bed, and Kaes at the station, and Toots gone (for her, Elof had suddenly developed a distinct aversion—perhaps the new baby had done it, or perhaps his touching of Gert's softnesses the night previous—in any case, there it was, an unmistakable feeling), it meant that he and Gert were practically home alone.

Elof tackled the north gable. He added another section to the ladder and set it into the peak against the house. He got his pail of white paint, his brush, and his broom. He climbed up.

He noted the dry boards, the cracks, the dirt and dust in the openings.

He saw a fly arching on a rung of the ladder and stopped to watch the harmless creature, the whistling fading from his lips. The six-legged thing was cleaning itself. First it dry-washed its head with forepaws, quite as if it were a human being, scrubbing its neck and digging into its ears. Then the fly cleaned off its forelegs on its middle legs, its middle legs on rear legs, its rear legs again on middle legs. With its rear legs the fly cleaned its blue underbelly, its green rump. And finally the fly cleaned its wings, first on top and then on the bottom. It fluttered, looked around, twisted its head, one way, the other, then, *wissp,* was off.

Elof continued up the ladder, whistling.

He neared the peak. He saw, far in the recess, what looked like a rough diamond ball. He stopped; examined it closely. A hornets' nest—and dreaded yellow jackets t'boot.

Again the tune faded from his lips. Holding pail and brush and broom in one hand, holding onto the ladder with the other, he watched the nest for signs of life.

He studied it quite a while and then decided that, empty or alive, it had to be brushed down. He hung the pail on its hook, laid his brush across it, advanced up another step.

Holding on with one hand, reaching back to get a good swing, he let go. The broom bristles hit.

The nest shook back and forth; hung on.

Again he swung. This time the broom tore off a side of the nest.

Instantly the broken edge became alive with wriggling, buzzing wings. And out of the mass of swarming yellow jackets, two came straight down for his face. One hit; set on his cheek. He brushed it off. The other hit; set on his back. Before he could get at it, it dug in. Yeow!

Elof's instincts threw his muscles into gear, and in a frenzy he whirled, dropped straight down the ladder, sliding as fast as his body would fall, hitting the rungs as he went by, *gung-gung-gung-gung.* Even before he hit ground, his legs were churning and he darted around the corner of the house and jerked open the screen door and shot inside, slamming the door behind him, holding his head, still afraid the yellow jackets were after him.

"Well, for catsake!" Gert cried. She was washing clothes in the sink. "What's ailin' you?"

"Yellow jackets!" he gasped. "Think they got me. Hurry. See if there's one somewheres here in my neck." Elof ran toward her by the sink, head down, his gold hair wild, his stubby hands clawing.

She seized his head, led him to a chair sat down, pushed down his head on her lap, searched his hair.

"See any? See any?"

"Nope. None."

"You sure?" His voice was muffled in her dress.

She searched again. "Nope. Don't see none."

Gretch called weakly from the bedroom. "What's goin' on out there?"

"Nothin'," Gert said.

"Oh. Well, you two, you want to remember we've got a new baby in the house now." Gretch's chiding was gentle, almost merry.

Elof said, "Hey, I just felt something wigglin' there. Right there."

"Must be your imagination," Gert said.

"Imagination, hell. Just take a look there in the small of my back once."

Gert pulled his shirt out of his overall, pushed aside the suspenders. "Huh. One got you there all right."

"Got me? One ran a spear right through me."

She laughed. "Just a minute. I'll pull the stinger out."

Elof felt her nip at something; felt something snap out of his skin.

"Now if you'll wait a minute, I'll get you some soda an' water quick. An' some salve."

She slid her legs from under his head and ran to the medicine cabinet. "You stay right there."

Elof waited.

She came back and took his head in her lap again.

Cold water poured over him. He shivered. She rubbed the soda water gently over the swelling.

After a time she dabbed on the salve. Her strong hands were soothing. She ran them back and forth over his white skin. Soon the pain was almost gone.

Elof leaned heavily on her lap. He put an arm around her.

When he could no longer keep up the pretense, he lifted his flushed face.

It touched him to see how red her cheeks were too. He neared her with his lips and kissed her and then held her hot to his body.

"Think she'll hear us?" he muttered in Gert's ear.

"I don't know," Gert said.

"O God . . ."

"No," she said desperately. "No. Wait till we jump the broomstick. Marry. Please. Please. I want you to like me for a long time."

CHAPTER XX: Token Resistance

. . . You probably won't finish Peregrine Pickle. *Though, of course, if you do, you'll find that you will have picked up a couple of fine stories to tell your sons. They will enjoy the male escapades. They will like the story of Perry showing up his teachers, they will hate his mother, they will love Commodore Trunnion, they will travel to Paris, they will also make the desperate attack on Emy's purity. And the accounting lessons? Those you may forget. Unless, of course, you and Gert decide to build a super-station. In which case you'll have to finish them. Some of the big-time bulls have really sharpened their horns on them . . .*

But marrying Gert didn't quite solve everything. On occasion, living still gave him a cork-dry taste in the mouth.

Not that Gert didn't make a good wife. She did. She made him such a good wife that he considered himself as lucky as any man on that score.

She was neat.

She was an excellent cook—a successful experimenter with new recipes too.

She was decisive—especially in her ideas on how they should run their life. For example, she discarded Kaes's notion about making a chowhouse out of the shanty. Her idea was that a home should be separate from the place of business. After she had cleaned up the oil and grime and had scrubbed and painted the shanty, she moved in a few pieces of furniture, those they had gotten as wedding gifts, and called it home. And out of the two back rooms in the station, which Kaes said they should live in, she made a kitchen and chowhouse.

She was full of uncommon good sense—particularly when it came to touchy situations. On the day of the wedding, when Pa had come grumbling to the ceremony, and without a present, it had been she who had taken the thing by the ears, asking, "Elof, suppose Pa had married me—would you have brought him a present?"

And she was an intimate and tender bed partner. On the night of the wedding, it had been she who had prevented a panic. Blushingly he had crept into bed with her. Tremblingly he had tangled his arms and legs with her. And just as things were about to begin, the first movements, there had been a terrifying bangling and jangling underneath the bed. Elof had leaped out of the sheets, his heart vulsing like an animal wildly trying to escape a sack. But Gert? She had crawled under the bed and had found it—a can of stones tied to the mattress, tied there by Bill Cooper. Gert had laughed; had calmed Elof; and then, because of her fierce notion that they were one and as such were a team against the world, had led them both into a rapturous and dramatic coupling.

All these virtues elicited from Elof grudging admiration; helped him overlook her tendency to be a bit bossy once in a while.

Nor was it the fault of the villagers and the farmers roundabout that he still should feel a little at odds with the world. In them an almost complete change of heart had occurred. They embarrassed him with their amiable proffers of friendship. Gone was the feeling that they considered him an interloper, a no-good college bum. Young Domeny Hillich, Kaes, Wilbur and Cor, the Nelson triplets, many, many others, regarded him a sort of hero for having once hit a mighty home run, for having stayed on his feet while licking a bad infection, for daring to come back to the village to live. Only Cooper and Solen on the other two corners across the road showed him any hostility at all.

There was a lull in the work and Elof, dressed in a green attendant's suit, stood in the doorway of his filling station, looking moodily out to the southwest. It was October and the leaves on the cottonwoods across the road west were dancing flakes of gold. The chokecherry tree beneath them had almost lost all its foliage; what was left was a gray-tinged mauve. The cornfield across the road had been stripped of its ears by a machine, the rows battered and glazed all in one direction. The field looked dazed. In the plowed land beyond, the sun and wind were drying black soil to a toasted brown. Two heavy fall rains had given the grass in the Nelson pasture across the highway to the southeast an unexpected surge of cellulation, and the bright silver-green new growth contrasted oddly with the feeling in the air that chill winds were not far away.

Gert, dressed in a white smock, her brown bobbed hair falling around her face, was out on the drive-in, placing small pineapple-sized stones along the border and painting them. Early in the morning she had expressed the opinion that bright white borders and newly painted buildings gave people who traveled a long way a desire to clean up and get themselves a little quickening in the way of food and drink. And maybe an impulse to get a little gas for the car. Hearing Gert talk that way was like having Ma Lofblom come back to earth.

He couldn't help but marvel at Gert. Of course she was right. But from where did she get the energy? Already the Lofblom Station had attracted such trade as no station on the corner had enjoyed in years. For a quick flashing moment Elof had the vision that their success might be the germ of a new movement: the growth of a town on the crossroads. A town that might even outstrip Hello.

Naturally they were still a long, long way from howling success. Their pile still wasn't big enough to buy the place from Kaes, let alone big enough to buy such necessities as a gas stove, a washing machine, things that Gert had her heart set on—but he and Gert were on the move and they were gaining every day.

He glanced at the miserable place Loren Solen ran. At the moment Loren was sitting on a chair leaning against the station. Behind him bawled a half-dozen kids. His wife was hanging out gray wash. Chicken feathers lay scattered over the yard in back. Elof knew he should feel pity for the poor, should encourage them to live clean if only for their own protection.

Yet he couldn't. In them were concentrated all the worst faults of the insular. They were crudely dressed, they were apathetic in morals, they stooped to bald-faced connivery, and, worse still, they were morbidly curious. Outside of fatty meals, their main fare was sticking their nose into other people's business.

Every time Elof tried some new stunt in the way of attracting trade, like hanging a witty placard in the window, or putting up signs a mile away in every direction, old coughing Solen or his dumpy wife was sure to send over one of the kids to see what it was.

But the Solen sin that offended Elof most, and which Gert didn't quite believe, was that when he and Gert went to bed the Solens turned off their lights to watch them undress. Shades drawn or not.

Yes, the Solens disgusted him.

He glanced over at Bill Cooper's station.

Toward laconic Cooper he should also have felt kindly. Cooper was rapidly losing most of his business to Elof. Especially the trucking trade; the drivers relished Gert's hamburgers.

Cooper really wasn't lazy; he only lacked fire. The little he did have he used playing practical jokes.

Elof tried to forget that it had been Cooper who had first told him about Pa's doings with Gert; tried to forget that Cooper's question, "Gert put on the pants today, chum?" had been asked him a dozen times if it had been asked once. Elof even tried to forget the wedding-night trick.

But one thing Elof couldn't overlook. That was Cooper's fat black-and-white dog, the Hippy who had nipped him on the pant leg when he had first come home.

The tightly packed rat terrier was as wise as a fox. Every morning at ten and every evening at five the dog came over, sniffing, investigating, sometimes barking at customers. It was almost as if Bill Cooper had sent Hippy over as a spy and provocateur.

Worse, Hippy had a habit of lifting his leg and relieving himself against Elof's first red-and-silver gas pump, right in front of everybody, as if showing his, and Cooper's, and Arctic's, and Screech's, opinion of Elof and his Antarctic business. The dog's habit had been so persistent that already the paint was scaling off. Elof swore that someday, when nobody was looking, he would catch the dog in the act and kill him.

A car drove up. Elof snapped his eyes and cuffed himself for his mean thoughts. He forced a happy smile to his lips.

The car stopped. A sunburnt face peered out. "Fill 'er up," the friendly man said in a friendly voice. "Fill 'er up an' look at the oil an' water. Might take a look at the air too."

"Okay," Elof said, quickly pulling rags out of his green station-suit hip pocket and cleaning the windshield. "Be right with you."

The man said, "Grub any good in the chowhouse?"

"Couldn't be better. Best cook in the world runs it. My wife."

"Uh. Think I'll amble over an' get me a burger an' a cup a coffee while you grease up."

"Okay." Elof raised his voice. "Gert. Business. Man wants a burger. Red onion with."

Ten minutes later the man came out wiping his mouth with the back of his hand. "Well, how much'll it set me back?"

"Give me two thirty-eight, and you and I can look each other right in the eye."

That night as they went to bed unease crept up out of his subconscious again. He muttered a little to himself as he sat down to take off his shoes.

Gert was on the other and wall side of the bed, sighing, also wearily getting out of her clothes.

Happening to glance out of the window, past the half-drawn shade, he saw, just at that moment, all the Solen lights go out across the highway.

"There!" he exclaimed, holding his body still to give the illusion he hadn't noticed them, "there. See? Just as I told you. Them Solenses're gonna window-peek us again."

"Oh, come now."

"Dammit. I know they are."

"You're just imagining things."

"The hell I am. By God, in the moonlight, I can even see their faces blurring up behind the screens. Them nosy sonsabitches."

"Oh, don't pay any attention to them. Besides, what've you got to be ashamed of?"

"That ain't the point. It's just that I like the idea of privacy."

Elof's hair hung over his eyes and he glared through the gold blur at the sinners across the way. "By God, I know what I'm gonna do. I'm gonna give them an eyeful they won't forget for a long while." He got up and in pretended nonchalance walked around to the wall side of the bed where Gert was undressing.

"Hey," she exclaimed. She covered up her bosom with a quickly grabbed-up pajama top.

"Take it easy, take it easy. I ain't after you," he said.

Hurriedly he took off his clothes, stripping down to bare skin. Then, suddenly vaulting his stubby body across the bed, and letting the shade up with a snap the rest of the way, he thrust his behind squarely in the window and bent over, brown and all, leaning over so far he could see out between his legs. "There," he growled, "there. I hope you sonsabitchin' Solenses got an eyeful at last."

"Well, for catsake!" Gert gasped.

The next morning he still wasn't square with the world. He cleaned up on the Hippy-sprayed gas pump and tended trade and swept out the station and in his spare moments looked at the diagrams of the motors of the most popular cars, all the while griping and fussing.

At ten o'clock, right on the dot, tubby black-and-white Hippy, the Arctic representative, came over. And, as usual, he sniffed at everything Antarctic and wound up by lifting his leg and letting fly. Except that this time after he had finished spraying the pump he went over and sniffed at Gert's new pearly-white stones and bowed his back and dropped a mess there too. And while doing so, grunted so hard tears came into his eyes.

Elof, jumping with rage, grabbed a can of oil, hurled it at the dog.

The dog hopped up, but not quite in time. On the first bounce the can hit the dog's rear, bowling him over. Hippy scooted across the road, howling and yipping.

Cooper stepped out of his doorway. "Hey," he shouted across the corner, "if I was you I'd watch out what I was doin'."

"Keep that damned purp to home then."

"He ain't hurtin' you none." Even from where he stood, Elof could see Cooper's Adam's apple nervously bobbing up and down. Cooper added, "You throw something at that dog again an' I'll have the law on you."

Elof growled, turned his back to Cooper.

It was after lunch, with the sun glaring down on the drive-in, that Elof's Old Adam tossed up a bright idea. He had recalled an electrical experiment with water that he had performed in high school physics. The idea was so good Elof burst out laughing. And he set out to execute it immediately.

Rummaging through the station, he found two pieces of copper wire. Breaking into one of the light circuits on the first gas pump, he arranged the wiring in such a manner that the bare end of one wire lay exposed on the spot where Hippy usually hit and the bare end of the other in the ground where he usually stood. Then Elof poured water over and around the ground wire.

Sure enough, at five o'clock the dog came out of Cooper's station, stretched lazily, looked across the road to Elof's station.

Elof sat inside, grimly watching through a window.

Hippy started across the highway, waited for a car to zoom past, sniffed at a weed at the edge of the ditch, lifted his leg and jitted it with a few drops, ran on a few more steps, sniffed at one of Gert's white stones, baptized it, and, at last, ran up to the red pumps. The dog instantly sensed something had been changed at the first pump, sniffed it.

Elof's lips tightened slowly.

The dog sniffed again, ran to the other pump, sniffed, ran back, promptly lifted a black leg, let fly. There was a spark, a yowl. The dog jerked; jerked; jerked; couldn't free itself. It cried piteously. And the dog continued to jit and, as long as it did so, stood paralyzed with one hundred and fifteen volts of alternating current running up the stream and through its body.

Cooper came hopping out of his station at the noise; stopped by his pumps; looked across the corner. He stared at the dog, trying to find something wrong he could curse at.

Elof sat unmoved.

Then the dog finished his job. The moment the stream separated into trickling drops, the circuit broke and the dog was free. With a mournful yelp, the dog bounded down the drive-in, yipped across the corner, and hurtled itself into the safety of Cooper's station.

Cooper stood puzzled. He pushed back his cap and scratched his hair.

At last he came over. "What did you do to that dog?"

"As you saw, I was sitting right here doing nothing."

"Huh." Cooper walked around the first pump, looked carefully at it, studied the wiring, jumped back. "Why, you dirty son of a bitch. That's a terrible dirty trick to play on a dog. A poor innocent dog."

"I suppose your letting him come over here and water my pump ain't a dirty trick."

Cooper clamped his mouth shut. His dark lean face became livid with anger. "I'll get you for this someday."

"That'll be okay with me, Bill. But remember, when you do, just keep in mind your dog started this. Or, better still, that you did."

Cooper stalked off, rumbling to himself.

Gert came in from the kitchen in back. "You an' your child's tricks."

Elof laughed. "It just goes to show you that water conducts electricity."

Elof put his foot down. "No. There's going to be no Bible reading at our table. And no praying."

"Still——"

"No!"

Elof and Gert were eating supper, a late one. Elof had finished his eight-to-eight daytime stint and had turned over the filling station for the night to Jack Moss. Jack Moss had become part of their life when, some weeks earlier, Elof decided that if an outsider had to be hired it should be another unfortunate—in this case the one-armed third baseman of the Hello Homebrews.

Elof had taken off his green work clothes and his shoes, and was sitting stubby-legged and barefoot in a pair of white slacks and white jersey. Gert was wearing a flowing white-and-pink housecoat and white open-top sandals.

The window behind him was up a few inches and through the opening came a warm Indian-summer breeze. Outside in the black night, on a siding near Pa's store, a freight train was noisily switching and whistling.

Elof reached for another pork chop, the last one on the meat platter. "No," he continued, "no, not at our table. I want our table to be free and happy. No words of doom." He cut himself a piece with knife and fork; ate it. "Of course, Gert, if you're hungry for doomdom and you want to pray, I won't stop you—as long as you do it by yourself. That's why we got a bedroom and a closet in this place. For privacy. But at our table—nope, there I want it jolly and happy. Free."

Gert picked up the empty platter and went out through the door and into the kitchen in the back of the filling station. In a moment she came back with two more steaming well-browned chops. "All right. You win," she said, "but I only thought it would make it more family-like. When the kids come an' all."

"Praying and Bible reading don't make a family. Our heathen ancestors had families long before God was invented." Elof slid one of the fresh chops onto his plate.

"Well, I don't know about them heathens a yours, but I do know that religion helps keep the family together."

"I wouldn't be too sure about that. I know of one case where it didn't."

"Oh, but you can't count that."

"Why not?"

"Because that was an exception. When the ma dies——"

"Exactly, when the ma dies, the family dies. Religion has little to do with it." Elof pushed back his plate, turned his chair a little, and put his bare feet up on another chair. He picked up his cup of coffee and, holding it in his lap, idly stirred it with a spoon. "And then, look at Kaes. There ain't no godding at his table. And see how free and easy they got it together."

"Pigs," Gert said. "A bunch of pigs. That's what we'll turn out to be."

Elof thumped his bare feet to the floor. He set his cup down carefully on the edge of the table. "That's enough now."

Gert's eyes widened; then subdued. She looked down.

After a while Gert left quietly and went into the kitchen in the other building again. When she came back this time, she was carrying a small jar of jelly. "I forgot to set this on," she said. "I ain't got no dessert tonight, so you better use this on a bun instead."

Elof grunted. "What is it?"

"Taste it," she said, standing before him, with one hand behind her.

He picked up a brown bun, halved it, and buttered it. Then, breaking open the wax seal, he plunged his knife into the jar and came up with a quivering lump of blood-red jelly. He smeared it out neatly. He took a bite. "Hmmm," he said. "Not bad." He rolled the ball of bun and butter and jelly around in his mouth. "Pretty good."

"Like it?"

"Say," he said, forgetting their argument for the moment, "say, this is good. Got a real tang to it. What kind is it?"

"Can't you guess?"

"Gooseberry?"

"No."

"Crab apple?"

"No."

He stared at it. He took a fresh bite of it unencumbered by bread or butter and slid the drop of red jelly over his various taste bulbs. "Cripes, I can't guess."

"Really?"

"Well—one thing I can say. That tang"—he smacked his lips— "that tart tastes mighty familiar."

"It should. It's your favorite."

"My favorite?"

"Sure."

"Oh, by golly."

"Sure," she laughed. "Chokecherry jelly."

He stared at her. "Now where in the world did you get ahold of that?"

"Made it."

"You?"

"Sure. I got the recipe from your ma." Gert put forth her other hand, holding out a sheet of paper. It was burnt brown with age, and covered with flyspecks and oily fingerprints.

An old pain throbbed in Elof. "Where'd you get it?"

"Remember that day at Kaes, when you were shockin' grain? An' you told me about them chokecherries by the railroad track an' how your ma made jelly from 'em? Well, right after, I went over to Pa—to your old house, an' asked if I could have her old recipe for it."

Elof nodded. "Sure enough. Her old recipe. The one she got from Gramma Alfredson." He turned the sheet of paper over. He looked at the writing. The unsteady scrawl was still decipherable. He read:

1872. Chokecherry jelly

Have fruit gathered in fine weather, pick it from stalks, wash, place in preserving kettle (if you use a bell metal kettle for preserves &

jellies, clean thoroly before use. Scour it with sand, then set it over the fire, with a cupful of vinegar and a large handful of salt in it. Let this come to boil, and scour the whole of the inside of the kettle with it. Do not let the preserves or jellies stand in it for one moment after it is drawn from the fire, fill the empty kettle instantly with water, and wash it perfectly clean.) & cover them with water ("sufficient to cook") let them simmer gently till the juice is well drawn from the berries, then strain through fine cloth, do not squeeze them too much, as the skins and the pulp from the fruit will be pressed through the juice, and so make the jelly muddy. Measure the juice, and to each pint allow three quarter pounds of loaf sugar, put these into the preserving pan, set it over the fire, and keep stirring the jelly until it is done, carefully removing every particle of scum as it rises, using a wooden spoon (or silver) for the purpose, as metal or iron ones will spoil the color of the jelly. ("Do not eat test." Also, "do not drink milk after eating raw fruit. Poison. Tragic results. Bad stomach ache." Also, "do not let cattle feed off the leaves in dry years. Pits can be ground to flavor wine any year, though.") When it has boiled from twenty minutes to a half hour, put a little of the jelly on a plate, and if firm, cool, it is done. (When "two drops hang together.") Take it off the fire, pour it into small gallipots, cover each pot with an oiled paper, and then with a piece of tissue paper brushed over on both sides with the white of an egg. Label the pots adding the year when the jelly is made, and store it away in a dry place. This, besides being very tasty and good table jelly, is highly medicinal, good also as a dye, makes beautiful rich shade.

Elof said, hiding his eyes with his hand, "So you made this from her old recipe, huh?"

"Well, not quite." She held out another sheet, this time a fresh white one with her own handwriting on it. "I made this one off of it."

Elof's eyes opened wide. He read:

193– Chokecherry Jelly

Prepare fruit by washing and stemming. Cover with sufficient water to cook. Mash in a porcelain preserving kettle with wooden potato masher. Add one half cup water to each two quarts of fruit. Boil mash slowly for 8 to 10 minutes, stirring often to prevent burning and to break up the meat of the fruit. Put mash into jelly bags and drain off the juice. Be careful not to press the fruit if you want clear jelly. After the juice is drained, measure it. (Reheat.) 4½ cups sugar for 3¾ cups of juice and one package of sure-jell. Follow directions on package.

Silently he handed the new sheet back to Gert. He had trouble seeing. There were too damn many tears.

Gert, who was about to say something, stopped short when she saw his face. She turned instead and began to clean off the table.

When she was finished, she asked, "You want another bun with jelly on?"

"No," he said.

"You can. I got lots more."

"No."

She looked at him again and then, picking up the jar of chokecherry and the bread and butter and his plate and knife, went out to wash the dishes, leaving him with a half-empty cup of coffee.

Elof sipped slowly; and slowly his eyes cleared.

When at last he was sure his face was straight again, he called out through the open door, "Gert, got any more warm coffee?"

"Yip."

"Bring some then."

She came in, carrying the coffeepot. "You're gettin' to be as bad as a baby," she joshed. "Gotta have the tit in the mouth all the time."

"Uh-huh."

She filled his cup and then brought him cream and sugar.

It was after Gert had finished the dishes and had come back into the shanty and had sat down with a reed darning basket that unease began to yeast in him again.

It had been awfully nice of Gert to treat him with the tangy chokecherry jelly, awfully nice, but mightn't there have been a motive behind it other than a goodhearted one? There was just a chance that she had used it to mollify him, had kept the jelly handy for just such a situation.

The more Elof thought of it, the more he was sure of it. And it bothered him; almost angered him.

He lit a cigarette, puffed on it slowly, his lips thinning as he mulled over the thought. There was a taste in his mouth as if he had belched up some gall-bladder trouble.

He had an impulse to get up and get out of the place before he blew up, but for some reason lacked just the extra erg needed to do it. So he sat on, letting the gall bite soak through him.

Gert picked up one of his gray cotton socks and began working on its toe end.

Elof lit another cigarette, using the old one as a lighter.

Gert held up the sock and remarked, "I don't understand it. Most men punch their socks through right at the end. But you, you wear yours out over the second toe."

Elof tightened a little.

Gert glanced over at his bare feet, looked at the sock she was working on, once again glanced at his bare feet, the second time with opening eyes. "Aha. So that's what the trouble is."

"What?" Elof growled, tightening still more.

"No wonder your socks wear out where they do."

Elof took his feet off the chair, hid them under the table. He glared at her.

She laughed a little.

"What're you laughing at?" he snapped.

"At that big toe of yours."

"What about it?"

"Nothin'. Just that for once nature told a lie. You know what they always say: A short big toe means the other one's boss."

"Well?"

"Well, in this case, I'm not the boss."

So. So not even in his own home could he sit around barefooted without somebody commenting on his shortcomings. Not even with his own wife.

For one second Elof was able to contain himself. But the next, he was up and leaping. Could he help it if Pa's, and certain other men's, was bigger? It was the way things were.

He thought first of slugging her but remembered at the last moment that it wasn't civilized to hit a woman. So instead he grabbed her square shoulders, shoulders he resented for their manliness, grabbed them with fierce claws, began to shake her. He rattled her so fiercely, so violently, that the darning basket and the socks fell to the floor. A ball of yarn rolled under the table. "Damn you, woman," he cursed, "damn you, you would have to mention that, wouldn't you? And I thought I had a friend in you. Hell."

Gert didn't fight back, didn't say anything. She only dropped her head so that her hair hid her face. She suffered him to buffet her on the chair.

Her lack of resistance enraged him still more, especially since he couldn't tell if she were laughing at him or what behind that mop of fallen brown hair.

And her stinger continued to dig, going in deeper, going down to where his Old Adam lived. All of his little hatreds, hatreds that conscience had carefully encapsulated with the fibroses of faith and hope and charity, now burst open like trampled-on eggshells spilling yellow insides. What Ma and Old Domeny Hillich had done to him, what Young Domeny Hillich had done to him both in high school and in the Saint Comus Theological Seminary, what State had done to him, what life had done to him, what Pa had done to him, what women had done to him, everything evil, lavaed out.

When Gert still didn't resist his roughhouse shaking, he suddenly let go and bent over her and gripped her mightily around the waist and sat down on her chair and slammed her over his knee. He flipped back her dress, began to paddle her pink-pantied buttocks. He hit with all his might, with the smacking flat of his hand.

"For catsake!" Gert exclaimed. In a bound, she was off his stubby knees and, panting angrily, her gray eyes narrowed, drew back her good-sized fist and, like a man, socked him square on the jaw. She hit so hard Elof was almost rocked from the chair.

Recovering, he dived for her.

Gert dodged. And, as he went by, expertly clipped him with a short jab to the jaw.

Elof staggered into a corner.

Gert was upon him in an instant, slapping home a few more lefts and rights.

"Oho," Elof roared. "Oho. So you want a fist fight, huh? Okay. Okay. That's just what you're gonna get then." He ducked down, got out of the corner she had holed him up in, and, weaving, stepped inside her guard and let go. Since he still didn't feel free to hit her just any place—a man was a sure brute if he hit a woman smack on the breast or in the face—it was as bad as kicking a man in his nuggets—he aimed his balled-up fists at her shoulders and arms.

But Gert stepped back, took advantage of her long arms. Like a ring-wise champion, she held him off and socked him some more. Silent as a she-wolf, she cut at him until blood ran into his left eye.

Half blind, panting, Elof began to tire of the silent and murderous fight. But he hung on, knowing that if he let go now she would have the upper hand for the rest of his natural life.

They swung and ducked, they charged and retreated, they feinted and parried, they hit and they missed. They banged into the table and upset it, they rammed into the wood stove by the window and hit it so hard it ejected its round stove lids with popping sounds. At last they crashed into a flower box under the window, spilling dirt and red geranium petals all over the floor.

The clanging sounds penetrated the flames of anger that had enveloped him; reminded him of the wrestling dance he had once had with Marthea Dix of District Six, she of the broken balance wheel. The moment he thought of the schoolteacher, he realized how ridiculous this fight with his big mare of a wife was.

A particularly jolting right to the eye made Elof decide to end it. And end it on his terms. He went into a clinch, gripping her so close he rendered ineffective her long flailing arms.

"Don't," she said. "Get away. You little devil."

He hugged her tighter.

"Cut it out."

Noting that most of her weight was above him—he had his head beneath her arms and her bosom—he toppled her with a quick snap of his legs and a powerful shove. Both fell to the linoleum floor with a bony thud, Gert below and he on top.

"There," he growled, "there, that'll fix you. Don't ever let me hear you mention my big toe again. Or, by God, if you do, I'll make a one-tit out of you."

She was dazed by the fall. She lay quiet.

"You hear me?" he said, shaking her again. "You hear me?"

Her eyes opened a little. And for the first time he saw that she was hurt.

"Oh," he said, his anger instantly forgot, "oh, honey, I didn't mean—— You hurt bad, kid?"

She blinked.

"Oh, honey," he said, "honey." He became aware of her warm sweating body, felt her full bosom breathing heavily under his chest, and it surprised him to discover—a delightful discovery— how swiftly a man could think a female sweet who only a moment before had meant to hurt him. "Look, honey, I didn't mean——"

A tremendous pounding sounded on the door, interrupting him.

"What . . . ?" Elof looked up.

Again it sounded.

"What in the wide world is that?" Elof ejaculated.

Gert stirred beneath him.

Once more there was a drumming on the door. "Hey there," a voice shouted, "hey there, what's goin' on in there?"

Elof jumped to his feet. "It's Pa," he exclaimed. "Pa!"

Yet again a voice shouted outside the door and a mighty fist thundered. "Hey you in there, what's goin' on?"

"My God! Yup, that's Pa out there all right. What a mess he'll find us in now."

Still a little slow from the blow, Gert got to her feet too. "Better quick straighten up," she said. She held her brow. "Ohh. I feel like I don't belong to this world. Ohhh."

"Wonder what he wants?"

"Never mind. Here, take this washrag and clean up your eye."

Elof grabbed it; cleaned up. He straightened out his clothes. "Such fools. Such fools," he muttered to himself.

Gert brushed back her hair. "Hurry," she said, "hurry. Before he knocks again. I'll put the furniture back."

Elof turned the knob; looked out. "Hello," he greeted. "You don't need to knock down the door to get in, you know."

Before him stood Pa with fist raised, about to pound again. There was an odd look on Pa's face—a question, a laugh. Floodlights from the station out front made all things stand out with blue-edged sharpness.

From behind Pa stepped Jack Moss, Elof's one-armed help, his face ruddy and working.

"You here too?" Elof exclaimed. "My God, two more people and we'll have the whole city of Chokecherry Corner out here."

Moss said, "I'm sorry, Elof. But when I heard all that commotion in there, an' with your pa here wantin' to see you . . . why, I . . ."

Pa said, "Just what the deuce was goin' on in there?"

"Oh, nothing. We was just moving the furniture around a little. Trying to get settled."

Pa guttered a heavy laugh. "From the sound a things, you was sure havin' a swell time makin' up yer minds."

Elof was puzzled by Pa's friendly air. Pa was joshing him like the Pa of old, like the Pa he was before he had beat Ma.

Elof said, "Moss said you wanted to see me."

"Yeh." Pa sobered a little. He turned and pointed to his pickup. He had backed it up against the rear of the filling station. "Where do you want that junk?"

Elof stared. "Junk?"

There on the little truck stood a washing machine and a gas range—just the things Gert had had her heart set on.

"Oh, Pa."

Pa brushed a nervous hand over his face. "You kids got married so fast I didn't have a chance to get you a decent present. Come almost not goin' to the weddin' at all. But the freight came in tonight. And there was the ding-dang stuff." Pa lifted his hat a little, scratched his bald red head. "Well, where do you want the junk?"

"Oh, Pa," Elof said again, and he turned and called into the shanty: "Gert! Gert, come out here."

But she was already beside him.

Pa said, "I was gonna wait till mornin'. But I thought it would be kind a nice for you to get it tonight."

Elof managed to say at last, "But who told you that was what we needed most?"

Pa said, "Boy, I was married once too, you know."

Jack Moss said, "I didn't know where you wanted 'em, Elof, or I'd a had 'em unloaded without botherin' you."

"Bothering me? My God, man, this is one of the most wonderful——"

Pa interrupted. "Must I dump that stuff off on the ground? Or what?"

Elof moved. "Nono. Of course not. Gert, where do you want them things?"

He rose out of sleep, became aware that he was awake and that he was alive and that it was pitch-black dark in the house.

Something had disturbed him. Blinking, he wondered what his Old Adam wanted from him this night.

He noticed that both of his hands, which he still hadn't moved, were lying in rather odd positions. Sleep had thrown the right hand over his chest with its little finger touching his left vestigial nipple, and had protectively dropped his left hand, like a cup over eggs, on his penis and scrotum. Now what in hell could be the meaning of that? It was one for the dream-chasers.

His mind, mooning around, turned to other things: to Pa, to Ma, to Bud, to Hilda, to Gert.

He listened to Gert breathing evenly and regularly beside him. It was with an effort that he kept himself from touching her.

He lay brooding awhile, vaguely hoping he would fall asleep, but knowing he wouldn't.

His feet tingled. They wanted to run, to jump. Or something.

He decided to get up.

He crept quietly from bed, dressed in warm clothes, and slipped outdoors without waking Gert.

At first the floodlights out front hurt his eyes. He stood a moment, closing and unclosing them.

Then, eyes adjusted, he strode west across the road, past the sleeping Solens, toward the cottonwoods and the darkness beneath them, carefully keeping out of sight of Moss in the station.

He looked up. The huge limbs of the trees were sharply silhouetted against the milk-sprettled sky. They were the undulating purple-velvet arms of leviathans.

He stared at the mighty, slow, wrestling limbs awhile, at the whistering treetops, and then, thoughtfully turning, began to pace back and forth beneath them, beside the chokecherry tree.

At the end of one of his turns he happened to bump into one of the outthrust black-knobbed limbs of the little tree, almost stumbling. To steady himself, he put out a freckled hand to it.

We leave you now, Elof, leave you to your life. Whether you become the leader of your little family, or a wife-run male, does not concern us further. You have survived. You are safe. The accident that jarred you out of your path and made you go up a steeping one (would you make it? would you fail?) did not break you. Relieved, we can settle back on our stone. You are safe.

The earth spheres, and the bluff on which we sit is hurled forward into darkness—and into the next day. And so, gone you are. And when this crisp page at last shreds and rots, too, gone will be the knowledge that you were ever gone.

The generations arise, they come and they go, each leapfrogging over the one previous, hopping off into the future.

Elof, the leaf; Lofblom, the flowered leaf . . .